Domestic Life

A Novel in Parts

PAULA WEBB

SIMON & SCHUSTER

New York   London   Toronto   Sydney   Tokyo   Singapore

SIMON & SCHUSTER
Simon & Schuster Building
Rockefeller Center
1230 Avenue of the Americas
New York, New York 10020

SIMON & SCHUSTER and colophon are registered trademarks
of Simon & Schuster Inc.

Designed by Caroline Cunningham

Manufactured in the United States of America

10   9   8   7   6   5   4   3   2

Library of Congress Cataloging-in-Publication Data

Webb, Paula.
Domestic life: a novel in parts/Paula Webb
p.   cm.
I. Title
PS3573.E1984D6   1992
813'.54—dc20   92–11443
CIP

ISBN 0-671-74433-X

FOR LARRY, JIM, AND DONALD

and for
Katie and
John and
Mavena R.,
our new
friends —
"best wishes"
Paula
6·23·93

Part One

Questions You Might
Want to Ask,
If You Were the Sort of
Person Who Believed in
Knowing

Umbrellas

|...

Jenny's mother honks.

The lawyers tell us that honking at the curb for your natural child does not constitute sufficient grounds for a child abuse suit. They do suggest, however, that we make a note of the incident for the file.

"Are you sure about this?" I want to know. "Is it clear we're not talking about a friendly little beep or two here?"

I need the lawyers to understand, and I know it's not easy. For one thing, the term *honk* is too pale for this case. It's more of a blast, like a refinery exploding. Windows rattle, birds abandon their nests.

"There's not a trace of the heraldic here, guys," I tell them from the kitchen phone. "This has got nothing to do with your textbook urban announcement. What this is, is pure vulgarity, in the realm of the grotesque. Plus—are you listening to me?—she's not honking at the curb. She's in my goddamned front yard."

What happens is this: Raylene finally shows up, nearly an hour late. She pulls right into our driveway. She's late, but she doesn't even think about parking her car in the street, coming up to the front door, offering some reasonable explanation, a shred of near-believable excuse. The woman doesn't even turn off her motor. She just idles out there in our driveway, for maybe a full five seconds, and then, when the world doesn't take notice that she's out there and waiting, Raylene falls on her horn with her full body weight, and she doesn't let up until Tenny's scrambling into her booster seat.

"We're talking irrational hostility here, don't you think? There's no modulation whatsoever. It's just loud and long, a single blasting that scares hell out of everything. I think the paint's fallen off the house. Do you get it?"

The lawyers think they get it, although they waffle on the irrational hostility part. Still, they stay firm with their first reading: In Texas, a natural mother can honk anywhere she wants, or feels she needs to, and never risk traditional custodianship or an in-depth examination of her ability to mother. Law is simply too narrow for us. I was thinking years of prison, then extensive rehabilitation, then supervised visitations.

"If Raylene actually drives into the house, day or night, we'd have something to chew on," the lawyers tell me. "Otherwise, Ellen, it's still a cold supper in terms of custody-redirects, the abuse and neglect business. Honking's just not enough, it's too puny, and although we doubt that it will last as a lifelong habit—consistent patterning isn't Raylene's style—do know, Ellen, that we sympathize with you in this current harassment."

Our lawyers sympathize with us regularly, by phone and in person, and we'll be paying for this breach in professional distance at a hundred dollars a month for the next sixteen and a half years. Tenny is nine now. She'll be well out of college by then if she doesn't become a preteen mother, a drug addict, worse. To date, we owe the lawyers nearly twenty grand, and after all these years we're still not, in any party's opinion, finished with this mess.

"We need the overt," the lawyers tell us. "And we need a good number of impartial witnesses to get around the hearsay issue. They'll have to be semiliterate, and they'll have to be stable—permanent addresses, real jobs—and they'll have to still be willing to testify in two or three years when the case comes up."

"You just don't get it," I tell them, and I hang up on them and all their sympathies, real or not.

Dramatic disconnection has no effect: I can still hear them. Way downtown, the lawyers yield to weariness. They sigh heavily with regret and impotence while they fold a new invoice, hot from the printer, 100 percent cotton rag, into a Number 10 ecru envelope which we will use for a shopping list. They lick the stamp, update their accounts receivable, and lament among themselves the intrinsic difficulties of family law. Then they go out for drinks.

I could use a drink myself, a change of scene, but I've got to pick my baby up at day care in twenty minutes, and I didn't get around to lunch. Motherhood, natural or not, forces continual consideration of pending commitments that simply won't wait. Banal but historically pleasant gratifications are delayed, serious responsibilities loom. So, a clean shot of near frozen gin, even a splash of wine, stays in the refrigerator until after six, when day care centers everywhere throw unclaimed children out into the road. Liquor waits, if you take your role as a mother seriously. I do.

I've got these two children, one is not mine. A boy and a girl, a redhead and a blond.

Zack is my son. He believes he is invincible, and I hope he is correct. He is now nearly three, and he is, generally speaking and without any lingering question, the pleasure of my life.

"Isn't this pretty, Mom?" he asked me.

I was putting him to bed, rubbing his back. The story finished, just the night-light on. It was the standard every night stuff, our shadows large on the wall.

"What's that, honey?" I asked him back.

"The shape of you and me in this room together."

This kid knocks me out, always has. I was in deep love for life the moment I saw him, before he took his first breath, before he had a real name.

"Hello, Baby," I said, and he screamed back with everything in him. I got used to that noise, and we locked on the spot like good cement. Even now, way past novelty, the largeness of my feeling for him surprises me nearly every time I see him.

And then there is Tenny, my stepdaughter in a practical manner of speaking. She was conceived in a Motel 6 outside of Knoxville, and her parents took notice of the occasion and named her Tennessee. She is Tennessee Louise Goodson in full, but I don't think she'd answer to it. I tried it once. She kept walking.

Her mother—this Raylene person—calls her Tenny Lou (although Baby Girl is frequently a direct reference), and Kenneth, her father, calls her Tenny, Tenny Penny for fun. They both adore this kid that is theirs, despite the fact that her appearance in the world kept their seedy relationship going far past the reasonable. As for me, the other mother, I call her Tenny, sometimes Tenno, when I can manage to spit her name out.

"What would you like to be called?" I asked her the first time we met formally. She was just three then, but I'd known about her for years. I'd watched her, through any number of chain-link fences, run herself out on city playgrounds.

"Angelfoot," she said. "Call me Angelfoot."

"Your grandmother, your mama's mama, calls you that, right? That's her special name for you, Tenny. I couldn't use it. Now, what would you like to call me?"

"Nothing," she said.

Tenny is my stepdaughter. She fully hates me most of the time. Despite the fact that I've lived with her half her life, we are still nearly strangers, and I've come to expect this will last to the end of it. I believe we will both survive somehow—mostly because I am bigger than she is, and I think I always will be—but in terms of a meaningful relationship, mine with Tenny is a disappointment, a throbbing failure. That is the clear fact of the matter—although I still worry about it—and I've come to think it's not so much the blood issue. It's more like we're aliens, not even of the same species.

"What I think you mean, Ellen," my shrink, Margaret, points out, "is that you are actually jealous of little Tenny, a profoundly sad child with clearly a whole life of trouble ahead of her."

"Hell yes, I'm jealous," I told Margaret. "Did you ever want a pony for Christmas? Raylene's father gave Tenny one. A real, goddamned horse, Margaret. A black and white pony, red ribbons braided in its mane. Could you relate to anyone who actually *got* a pony for Christmas, Margaret? And here it is, just three months later, and Tenny hates it. They're going to have to sell Noel, and she doesn't care, and nobody's even worrying about this. They're working on her birthday stuff already. She wants a trip to Hawaii and French jeans with ankle zippers."

Tenny is blond and blue-eyed, a beautiful child really, although she is extraordinarily tiny for her age. She is nine years old, but until she opened her mouth, you'd swear she was hardly six. She's a good two heads shorter than anyone in her class, and although the doctors think there's no real reason to fret, this is why none of us have retired her old toddler booster seats. She can't see out any car window without one, although she has recently let us all know that she'd prefer something more discreet. We all hope a spurt's coming, but Tenny's got more problems than simply scale.

She's smart, real smart—we think maybe gifted, if you believe the tests. She's certainly got a quick mind, but she's got a quicker mouth, a mouth at ease with meanness. She lies all the time, is what she does. She hardly even blushes when she does it. Her teachers try traditional and not-so-traditional approaches to help her, but by Thanksgiving they all just give up and hate her through the spring.

Tenny is a near-master at working people against each other. She keeps everybody squabbling and off her back. She plays her world—her mother and her mother's family, and her father and me—to her full advantage and is damn successful at it if you count the stuff she gets, the places she gets to go. Stuff is what counts with Tenny. She is swarming in stuff, she is drowning in it, and most of it isn't even paid for.

Tenny is, without any doubt, the most intense child I've ever seen, full to brimming with a caged animal's energy. She can't sit still ever, and it's more than simple restlessness. Tenny is always moving, searching for something every second, and she is desperate for it, whatever *it* is. She breaks everything, nothing is safe; she is always hungry, but nothing fills her up, nothing really satisfies her. She is never content. She is electricity gone unchecked, and I wouldn't be surprised to see her hair spontaneously ignite at any moment. Even when she sleeps, she thrashes all over the bed, sleeps easy only when she's found her thumb.

"You're going to ruin your teeth," I tell her.

"My mother says I can get braces if I want. She'll make Daddy pay for them."

Tenny leaves me speechless most of the time.

"Well, Ellen," Kenneth says, "I wouldn't say *speechless* exactly."

Kenneth and I have her Tuesdays, Thursdays, and alternate weekends. She's supposed to be with her mother the rest of the time, but that doesn't always work out.

They're alike really, the two of them, daughter and mother. They both need to move; they are never at home. They eat drive-thru junk for dinner, shop until the malls close, then drop by and watch somebody else's VCR. Tenny spends most Monday and Wednesday evenings falling asleep on the scratchy couches of her mother's friends. It's a party all the time. Understand: There is *no* bedtime.

But then on Raylene's weekends, Tenny visits alone—her neighbors, her grandparents in Conroe, little girls from school who never ask her back. Her mother's nearly always out of town somewhere. She comes back tan, loaded down with sacks of more new stuff for Baby Girl. She leaves the charge receipts in the bottom of the bags, and the lawyers think we ought to keep them for the file, or at least run a tracer on whose credit cards she's using.

"Tenny is Raylene's lapdog," my friend Grace thinks. "You're the real mother, Ellen. When are you going to get her?"

The lawyers are trying to get her, so far without a lick of success. We have to get Raylene in order to get Tenny, but the lawyers tell us that feeding your child drive-thru junk does not constitute sufficient grounds for child abuse.

"What about bedtime?" I ask them. "What about all this weeknight activity? What's going on do you think, while Tenny's watching 'The Tonight Show'? What about all this stuff she's got? The kid's about ruined, no values. She'll never understand money. Just how many Cabbage Patch dolls does a kid need, anyway? Listen, she doesn't have a normal life."

"Normal is relative, Ellen," the lawyers tell me, "and so is need."

The lawyers are smart—they both went to Rice on full scholarships—and I think, surely, they must realize how ridiculous they sound.

"Just try to remember, Ellen, that your source for most of your information is a kid, Tenny. That's pretty thin, considering everything: her age, her instability, her confusion about allegiances. Besides, if Tenny did testify—which Kenneth still claims he would never permit—you know she'd lie to protect her mother. Then they'd counter by saying we're harassing them, call our suit a frivolous action.

If we go to court today, you could lose what little you have now."

What we have now is Hell, but Tenny gets a balanced meal Tuesdays and Thursdays. Her homework gets checked. She gets a full night's sleep. Kenneth gets the tangles out of her hair, makes her brush her teeth. I'm working on thumb sucking.

"Is this enough?" I want to know.

"It's better than nothing," all the shrinks agree. "We feel it's a good sign that Tenny's bringing her dirty laundry in her book bag to your house. She's figuring out who she can rely on, Ellen. Someday it will all be clear to her. She'll understand and thank you for it."

"I can't wait until she's thirty-five and historically realigned," I tell them.

"Why not?" the shrinks want to know.

"Get something overt and call us," the lawyers tell me. "And be sure to keep notes. And, Ellen, we're sorry."

I believe them. They are genuinely sorry, and they frequently offer us their beach house at Bolivar. They are Bradley and Joan, second cousins from Nacogdoches, in practice together since graduating from law school. They finished in a dead heat for first-place standing, and they could have gone anywhere. They chose to stay in Houston and specialize in family law, an area always pretty sticky. Their reputations, as well as their politics, are flawless. I know. I checked.

"Can you get us results?" is my main concern.

"Anything can happen once we get to court," they tell us, and they think they're being helpful. Lawyers never say anything in the absolute. Clear and certain statements are alien to them. They speak through smoke, waffle continually. It's genetic.

"We're not in the reassurance business, Ellen. The law is continually open to interpretation, and not a thing in law is certain. We can give you opinions, based on historical precedence, and we can outline likely probabilities. We can advise you of your rights, counsel you in terms of procedures, make sure the right forms are filed. We can sympathize with your situation, but we cannot predict what will happen, what some judge will think on the matter. His perspective is crucial; our presentation is everything. Judges hear cases, sign orders, rewrite law. We just discuss it with them."

Law is Performance Art and about as significant. I understand this because I worked in a museum for twelve years. I understand performance. I know presentation. You put your trust only in superior hardware, and then you pray for mild weather.

"So once we get to court, everything's wide open? Anything can happen? You're sure about this?"

"We're pretty sure," they tell us. "We hope we don't get a traditionalist for a judge, and then we hope we do, and then we'll decide on whether to buy new suits all around."

"This is terrorism. Are we ever going to court?"

"When we get something we can present to our favor, we'll go, Ellen. Keep notes and try not to get so discouraged. Do you want the beach house this weekend?"

Bradley and Joan are doing what they can, which is nothing really. We pay for this. While they're quick with an invoice, they're slow on collection. I like them in the main, and I have to believe they know what they're talking about. They believe in our case, they like us, they let us pay over time.

Somebody must be paying them up front though, because as lawyers, they're doing pretty well. Over four years, they've grown from a two-room office with black vinyl couches to half a floor in the upper reaches of the Pennzoil building. They've replaced reproductions of old Texas maps—aged with shoe polish, glued onto masonite—with early Motherwell collages, the Gauloise series, a good blue. The black vinyl couches are gone—at the beach house along with Melville's complete works.

What happened was this: It was a Wednesday, not a Tenny night. I was trying to work, and I had until six to figure out what that was.

It was drizzling all day, magnificent gray and yellow light, a good storm easing up from the Gulf. I was working on some graphite drawings in the studio, feeling pretty good about them and thinking about Vermeer, how I haven't seen nearly enough of that work in the actual flesh, when I heard the downstairs phone ring.

"The machine'll get it," I told myself. "Don't even think about touching that phone. Keep going here. Work. Think." But I was already half way down the stairs, my hand reaching—entirely independent of my brain and will—toward the sound of the ring.

I'm a painter. Since my life took this domestic twist, I work at home mostly, or at least I try to. It's not easy. If the work's going well, any interruption makes me crazy. A phone rings, some stranger knocks at the door, a child turns in his bed—I notice. I think about responding, then kick myself for even considering the notion, but then I've already blown what was looking pretty useful in a matter of seconds. Too quick, my concentration thins, then withers. My brain and generally my feet have already moved away from the work at hand, and I'm checking on sleeping kids, the door, somebody calling and wanting to have lunch.

You'd think I'd learn: It's hardly ever worth the investigation. The check is almost never in the mail, the kids hardly ever vomit in their sleep. But the urgency of the moment is lost, immediacy evaporates, the paint gets thick and goes to mud.

"Somebody better be dead," I said out loud, and then it was clear why I'd jumped at the ring.

Since I've become a mother, I've gone neurotic, although I try to keep it in check. The possibility of tragic accident never leaves me; the world is that frail, fate is that contrary. I am haunted by the image of a phone ringing in a quiet house in the middle of the day. My hand reaches for the phone. I answer, and it is the voice of a stranger with bad news. There has been an accident. I am to come to the hospital immediately, but there is no need to rush.

I shiver in the kitchen, then get furious with myself for being such a fruitcake. I grab the ringing phone and bark, "What?"

"Ellen Agnes McKnighton, please."

"What? Who is this? What do you want?" Nobody but the IRS knows my middle name.

"You are listed on our records as an alternate party of responsibility. Is this still correct?"

My heart pitches right out of my body and onto the floor. "Yes, yes. What is it? What's happened to Tenny?"

Nothing had happened to Tenny. She's at school, and she's sick. Sore throat, threw up her lunch. She's running a little fever, and she wants to come home. The nurse called Raylene and couldn't reach her. Kenneth is out of the office, calling on clients.

"Did you leave messages?" I need to know.

"Yes, of course, we left messages," the nurse says, but her voice is turning on me. She doesn't understand and isn't likely to. I will without question come to get Tenny—it is not possible for me not to—but I've got to figure out how to let Raylene know I've got her daughter.

Understand: Raylene is nuts. She'll go by school, jump to wild conclusions, think I've snatched her baby girl. She'll make a scene there, then come here and make another one. She'll threaten to call the police, and she will certainly call her lawyer, and, any way it goes, I'll have to talk to her directly, pass along a health report, deal with her face-to-face. Seeing Raylene ever is not a prospect I anticipate with any amount of pleasure, and I can just hear her whining about how she's got to go to work tomorrow, and how she can't keep Baby Girl at home, and how we'll have to do it this once, "because anyway, isn't it that asshole Kenny's turn?"

In the school nurse's office Tenny has no color whatsoever. She is absolutely translucent—I could put my hand right through her—and her fever is rocketing.

"God, you're white. How do you feel, honey?" I ask her.

"I feel like shit, Ellen," Tenny says, and for once I don't say anything about her language choices. It seems apt, I believe her, but I see the nurse make a note for her file.

"Let's blow this pit, Ten Pen," and we do.

At home I put her to bed, think about making Jell-O, which is what my mother would do. Jell-O takes too long, plus we don't own any, so I convince Tenny to try some dry toast and a little weak tea. It doesn't stay down, and we spend the greater part of the early afternoon in the bathroom, Tenny retching her guts out, me holding her hair off her face and coaching.

"Get it all out, Tenny. Get all the poison out, honey. You're doing a great job. It's okay."

"I love you, Ellen," Tenny says between heaves.

"I know, honey."

"Promise you won't tell my mother."

Around three o'clock, right when school would be letting out, Tenny starts to perk up. If it hadn't been for all the vomit, I would have been suspicious and discussed it thoroughly with her. Her recovery, however, is not complete: Thermometers don't lie, if you watch them continuously. Still, she's got a little color back, and so I let her come downstairs, rest on the couch under a quilt, watch a little junk TV.

"Now don't fan around," I tell her, my mother's phrase for the circumstance. I don't know what it means, but it seems right. "Eat this Popsicle and don't drip on my quilt."

"When you die," Tenny says, "can I have this quilt?"

It is pink and green, fabulous embroidery, a friendship quilt my grandmother made with her neighbors in 1936. She was my very favorite, and I hate it that she never saw my boy. This quilt and an old kitchen table are all I've got from her.

"That's special, Tenny. My grandmother made it with her friends. I'm going to try and take care of it, and I think it should really be Zack's someday, if he wants it."

I watch Tenny think about this. I worry I'm hurting her. I see her face cloud over, I see her mouth set, and then I see her let her grape Popsicle drip on Hattie May Riley's square.

"It was an *Accident*," Tenny screams, and then she coils up—under her own blanket now—and gives the television her full and serious attention. I know she's sucking her thumb under there because she's not moving too much and because she's not talking, but I don't say anything. My grandmother's quilt's on presoak. I fume, and I don't care about her damn teeth.

Around 4:30, it's a miracle: We are blessed with complete recovery. It's weird, but it happens like that with kids, and I didn't know this until recently. In a flash, they get sick, real sick. You don't see how they're going to live. You take it seriously and hurt with them. You worry. In just as quick a flash, they're well, absolutely fine, jumping around like nothing ever happened. Mothers spend whole days recovering from their kids' twenty-four-hour viruses. Kenneth says it's just attitude.

"Settle down, Tenny. I don't want you to get sick again."

"Where's my mother? When's she going to spring me?"

The phone rings. It's Raylene at Tenny's school; she didn't get any of the messages and is going to sue the nurse.

"Let me talk right now to my baby girl."

Baby Girl's voice thins to the pitiful. She tells her mother how much she threw up, how she nearly died, how much she loves her. Tenny begs her to come and get her immediately.

"I hate it here, Mommy," she says. Then she cries.

I leave the room before I do something I regret, like rip the phone off the wall and hurl it into the nearest planet. I fully hate both of them, but clarity of feeling gets me nothing. My day is shot, my drawings might as well be in Paris, and I can't go back to the studio even now because I've got to watch Tenny, make sure she doesn't ruin everything. I've got to help her wait on her mother who says she'll come right over but is certain to be late. And besides, the light's changed anyway. It still hasn't really rained, but the clouds are building. I punch the television off, thumb through an old *Art in America*, try to get some new ideas.

I fail. I can't even see the pictures. Then Tenny bounces into the room, whirling to high gear. I nearly see lightning flashing out of her.

"My mother's coming right now. We're going to get haircuts."

"Great," I say. Raylene thinks haircuts cure anything, and for all I know, she could be right. "What time's she going to be here, Tenny?"

"Right now. Right after she gets gas," Tenny says, and it begins.

We wait, in a manner of speaking, for forty-five minutes. There's no point in even suggesting that Tenny sit down. She's wild, bouncing at the windows, opening and shutting the front door, pulling at her hair, her clothes, my rag monkey collection on the mantel. She runs to check the clock in the library, runs to double-check the one in the kitchen. Then she's back to the windows, back to the front door, back to the monkeys.

"Can I call time service?" she says.

"No," I say, and I curse the weekend I taught her to read a real clock. She's smart, she had digitals down early, but I never thought flipping numbers presented any of the drama of time moving around itself.

"Come sit down, Tenny. Come sit down, and I'll read you something."

She can't. She can't sit down. She can't listen. Tenny's everywhere, running. She's a blur passing, frenetic. Her face is flushed, her bangs are sweaty.

"Let's get your stuff together, okay? Where's that schoolbag? You want to start on your homework? Let's make sure we get a clean uniform for you to have tomorrow. Check the laundry, will you? Hey, listen, you want me to teach you to iron?"

Nothing works to divert her. She is bent on building herself to hysteria. She meets it full in the face about 5:20.

"She said she'd be here by five o'clock. Where is she? Where's my mother, Ellen?"

"She probably had to run an errand or something, Tenny. She's okay. She'll be here. You know your mother's never on time, Tenny. Remember that log we made? She's probably stuck in traffic again, honey. Hey, did you hear that thunder?"

The storm's broken. It is finally raining, and the first drops on the sidewalk are as big as silver dollars.

"My mother is dead," Tenny says in a flat, even voice, certain of clairvoyance. "My mother is dead in the rain."

"Now hold on, Tenny. Let's think about this. Come on over here and sit down."

She won't, she can't. She's going, she's gone. Her eyes dilate, she flushes to a fever. She's pulling up this vision, clutching at it. She begins with a whimper, but it doesn't last. Inside of ten seconds, it grows to a sob, then a bellow, then a wail. Her furious tears begin.

"My Mother Is *DEAD*," she screams.

It's real to her, absolutely real, this vision of her mother dead in the rain. She roars like someone's pulling her arms off. The veins in her neck stand out angry, against and with her grief. She beats at the window with her fists, then at her own head.

"Come on, Tenny. Get away from the window. Come over here right now, and don't be silly."

My voice is of no use. It sets her off even further, if she can hear me at all. She is raving now, hysterical. There are no bounds. She is completely lost inside herself. I didn't think she could yell any louder, but she can.

"MY MOTHER IS DEAD. *MY MOTHER IS DEAD.*"

Then she just falls in on herself. She collapses in a wet heap on the floor by the front windows. She wraps her arms around her knees and starts rocking back and forth, trying to find some comfort somewhere. She keeps screaming and crying, but she's so far inside her mind, words don't form. They can't get past her mouth.

I pick her up. She's little, especially for nine. She doesn't resist. She would if she were herself. She is a rag, a feather; she has no bones. I rock her in the rocking chair we bought for Zack. Her screams go to white noise. I hum "Waltzing Matilda," a song she likes, but the tears still come, her shoulders still shake. I keep rocking.

Then this refinery explodes outside. Raylene is in the driveway, honking her blasting honk for her baby girl. The sound of her mother's vulgar announcement releases Tenny. Some window in her brain shuts tight again, and she comes back to us, snaps into place, is herself again. What she does is to leap out of my lap in a run and race out the front door at full speed to her mother, who is still sitting on her goddamned honk.

"Wait a minute, Tenny," I yell. "It's *raining.*"

I grab the book bag and a clean school uniform on a good wooden hanger I know we'll never see again. I move fast, but by the time I get to the curb, they're gone, already at the corner, the turn signal not even blinking.

And, Tenny is not strapped into her booster. She is standing up on the front seat, right next to her mother. Her arm is around her mother's shoulders, and their heads are together, and they are laughing about something and turning way too fast onto a slick street getting slicker by the minute.

"We're sorry, Ellen," Bradley and Joan say. "Why don't you come downtown and have a drink with us?"

"I've got to get Zack," I tell them and hang up.

The phone rings again right away. I don't answer, but I listen to the message recording. It's Raylene, at the hairdresser's.

"Kenny, you know I don't think much of that Ellen at all, but I never thought she was the sort of person who'd let a sick child run out in the rain."

She hangs up hard, sounds like she broke the receiver.

I stare at the answering machine until my eyes blur. Then I eject the message tape, write down the time and the date, and throw it in the file, which is really a box we keep on the shelf over the washing machine. Then I write down *umbrellas for Tenny* on the shopping list, *umbrellas* because she'll break one right away, and one she'll take to Raylene's and we'll never see again, and the third we'll keep in the hall closet until the next time it rains. Then I go around and take the C batteries out of all the downstairs clocks.

Kenneth comes in the front door. He is moving fast, in a panic, guilt in his step.

"My beeper's broken, Ellen, and I didn't get the message until I called in from the Shell station. What's happened? How's Tenny? Has Raylene been here?"

"You want the beach house this weekend?"

"I'm sorry, baby. What can I do?"

"Go get Zack," I tell him and head for the gin.

2 ....

Majority Opinion

So, did it help?

Did what help?

The gin, Ellen. Did the gin help?

Jesus, Margaret, it was just a metaphor. Don't you shrinks ever downshift?

You said you headed for the gin, Ellen. You really did, didn't you? You found it, you had a couple of belts, your nose went numb?

Jesus, Margaret.

Well, didn't you?

Yes.

Did it help?

Well, yes. I believe it did. It helped. I felt like I earned those drinks that afternoon, and I did feel better afterwards.

So, you had actually more than the one drink?

Actually, Margaret, I had forty-nine straight shots, and next time I think I won't even use a glass. I'm just going to bite the top off the bottle with my teeth, and then pour it down my throat, slivers and all.

So, you do understand there will be a next time?

.   .   .

Never, never, never, never, never, never, never, never, never, never, never.

Never, never, never what, Tenny?

My daddy is never, never, never going to marry you, Ellen.

I've told you a hundred times, Tenny. We are not going to discuss it.

Mommy told me you're going to rot in hell, Ellen. You're going to fry, and your hair's going to fall out, and you're going to be bald just like Daddy. She told me that this morning.

Forget it, Tenny. I'm not biting. None of this is your business. This is grown-up business. Now get your book bag and let's go.

Don't Touch That. That's my STUFF, Ellen.

What is this, Tenny? What's this old gin bottle doing in your book bag?

It's mine, Ellen. I found it. I'm taking it home for our collection.

What collection?

Mom and I have a collection. We have a whole bunch of these bottles.

How many have you got, Tenny?

Hundreds. We have hundreds of them, Ellen.

How many really?

I don't know. We just started this collection.

And what are you going to do with them, Tenny?

Recycle, of course. That's what you're supposed to do with glass bottles, Ellen. It's on the news all the time.

I see.

First we're going to take pictures of them, soon as we have enough money for film. We're going to get a lot of money for these bottles, Mom said.

Ooops.

You broke it. You Broke It, You're ALWAYS Breaking MY STUFF, Ellen.

It was an accident, Tenny. I'm just glad no one was hurt.

It is my experience, Ellen, that you have a quite limited repertoire of coping techniques. I thought we might address that subject this morning.

I don't much feel like it, Margaret.

Well, what do you feel like, Ellen?

I feel like a wrung-out sponge. I feel like exhausted possibility. I feel old and tired and unappreciated. I feel like leaving, Margaret.

Okay, great, this is good, Ellen, this is very good. This is the right step. I have always believed that Kenneth was a mistake for you, he'll never change, he really is a wimp. My opinion carries no surprise, I'm sure, but I have to tell you, Ellen, that watching you suffer with the lot of them all these years has been a real anguish for me personally. You can't save Tenny, Raylene's always going to be in your driveway, and Kenneth, that Kenneth is simply not worth another minute of your time. So, go on, do it, get out and get out now.

Hold on, Margaret. You don't seem to understand.

I don't? What don't I understand?

I'm not leaving Kenneth, Margaret. I'm leaving you.

I have made some decisions of quite a large scale in the last couple of years. I made some of them with less than complete data, and I do wish things were going a bit smoother now, but nobody can know everything at once. I believe in taking risks, I believe in challenging assumptions, I believe you need to decide what you want and then go get it. I stand with what I decided for myself five years ago.

"I believe they call that blind loyalty, don't they, Ellen? Isn't that impaired commitment? Dysfunctional pairing?"

And while some of those decisions may appear to be quite radical from a rather rigid, conservative point of view, it has been my experience for my whole life that how a thing looks very often has nothing to do with what a thing really is.

"That shrink of yours called your mother this morning, Ellen," my father said long distance. "We don't hold with any of that psychotherapy crap, but she thinks you've flipped. Ellen, have you flipped?"

"I'm fine, Dad, but if I flip, I've got plenty of cause."

"Don't I know it, Sunshine. You just get yourself a real job, and tell them all to fuck off."

Not that it's anybody's damn business, but one reason we're not married is because Kenneth and Raylene aren't divorced. Raylene simply cannot bring herself to sign the final papers, and no one understands this. We've all been living under a joint agreement drawn up in pencil on a paper napkin six-and-a-half-years ago. I helped Kenneth draft it. Tenny was barely three.

"Half a decade and counting. This is perverse, Kenneth," I tell him, but he knows that better than anybody in this hemisphere.

This divorce, supposedly everyone wants, but it's stalled because Kenneth wants formal joint custody of Tenny, and Raylene won't hear of it. Her lawyers tell her joint custody doesn't exist under Texas law. Bradley and Joan—our lawyers and good liberal Democrats—admit Texas courts are conservative on the subject but not entirely against it in specific instances.

"Anything can happen once we get to court," they say. "You're a good man, Kenneth. You're a good father. It's just a shame Raylene doesn't agree."

Raylene thinks Kenneth is scum.

"You'll never get my daughter," she screams to the answering machine. "There's not a judge in the whole country who would listen to a thing you had to say, you asshole. You've never had a real job, and you've never had any money. How could you even think you could provide for a child? You're irresponsible, Kenny, and you're stupid. You're living in sin with that skinny bitch, and you got a child out of wedlock. You're dreaming, Kenny. You haven't got a chance in hell, and besides, *you know* Tenny Lou hates you . . ."

Our answering machine cuts anybody off after two minutes. Sometimes Raylene calls back three or four times to finish her thought. We throw the message tapes in the file box and bless Panasonic.

"Her argument is not without its points," Bradley and Joan warned us at our first meeting. It was early summer, May 1982. "The legitimacy thing we can deal with easily—that's just paperwork—but the work issue is the more difficult here. On the surface, Raylene does look to be the more stable. Her work history, for example."

"It's The Money Thing again, isn't it?"

"Yes, it's The Money Thing."

Raylene works cosmetics at Foley's. She's been behind a counter for sixteen years, and she's hated every day of it. I can understand this. Those pink smocks to begin with, all that time on your feet, not to mention all those mirrors. I'd hate it, too, but what I don't understand is why she doesn't quit and get another job.

"Raylene hates change," Kenneth says. "She'd never think about moving the furniture around."

Raylene got the Foley's job right out of junior college. She majored in marketing, and she's never worked anywhere else. She likes stuff—clothes, jewelry, shoes, anything new—and the employees' discount lets her get more than she might have otherwise, even though she has to put up with some night and weekend shifts.

"All her money's on her back," Kenneth tells the lawyers.

"Can't you get a financial statement out of her?" I want to know. "Let's analyze her debt-to-income ratio. Wouldn't that sink her on this money thing?"

"Yes," Bradley and Joan agree. "If we go to court, we will subpoena that information. This money thing's just Raylene blowing smoke. But still, even holding a time-clock job for sixteen years looks a lot better than playing rock and roll weekend nights in some bar. We'll have to explain all that, and it won't be easy."

I've had to explain this all my life, and it is never easy. The problem with living just outside of mainstream America is Mainstream America, all their damn rules, their narrow notions of what a life should be: the value They put on day jobs with semimonthly paydays, what They think constitutes a healthy profit on a Schedule C.

Kenneth is a musician. Nights he plays rock and roll, days he thinks about it. Music is in his mind all the time. He is always working on it, but he punches no clock. I'm mostly a painter, I understand this. It's one of the reasons we're together.

"Kenneth," Bradley and Joan said, "it would be very helpful if we could present your tax returns for the last three years. How steady are you playing now? Do you have a Keogh set up?"

"I just want a divorce," Kenneth said. "I won't be a stranger in my daughter's life." And he headed for the elevator.

"What do you think, Ellen?" Bradley and Joan said to me.

"I think you ought to get some better art in here," I told them and went after Kenneth.

3 ....

Dancing Shoes

"You know, Ellen," my father tells me. "You never were the sort to pick up strays. Your sister, Ruthie, sure, I could understand, but not you, Ellen. How did you get into this mess of yours?"

My father has been asking me this question since 1982. He got the question in his mind then, and like a dog on a good bone, he can't let go of it. He asks me every time he sees me.

"Do you think your father actually expects an answer to that question, Ellen?"

"No, I don't think he expects an answer, not a real answer anyway, because it's not a real question, at least not in the traditional sense. He's always done that, Margaret. He says exactly what's in his mind, and then he goes on to what's next in his mind. My father has lived his whole life without any response, and he doesn't seem to miss it."

"Just think how lonely he must be, Ellen. How fearful. He's terrified of intimacy, isn't he? He's desperate to control everything. I'm surprised that you are as well off as you are."

"Yeah, well, that's a father for you, isn't it?"

"Kenneth is a father, Ellen. Is he like that?"

"No, he's not, Margaret, and when are you going to get off my back about Kenneth?"

The lawyers tell us that we need to prepare to go to court. I love this idea.

"Great, let's go. Let's get this done and done now. Let's do it this week."

"You must understand," Bradley and Joan tell us, "if we go to court, we're going to have to put you on the stand, Ellen. You are a major party here, you are helping to raise Tenny, you are the third parent. We're going to have to show that you are a capable, mature, responsible person who can handle the job. We have to show your fitness."

"Fitness?"

"Yes, fitness. Can you do it?"

"My fitness? Listen, I don't even know these people."

Kenneth takes me by the wrist and pulls me toward the door.

"This is an insult. This is crap. You don't have to do this, Ellen. We don't have to explain ourselves to anybody. We don't have to put up with any of this shit, Ellen. Come on, we're getting out of here."

"What's the problem here?" Bradley and Joan want to know. They are sensitive people, on our side, and they are alarmed.

"Maybe I could do it, Kenneth. Maybe."

"You could do it, Ellen. I know you could do it, but you don't have to. Come on, let's get out of here."

"What is it? What have we said? Tell us." Bradley and Joan were getting shrill. They'd never heard Kenneth say this many words at once.

"Look, the fitness thing is absurd. I don't like that at all, it's ridiculous, and Kenneth is right: It's an insult. But what's making me crazy is taking the stand. I have performance anxiety. It's sort of acute. I get Nuts is what I get."

"You? You, Ellen? Not you?"

"Yes, me. I can deal with it occasionally if I practice. I'm okay if I've got a technician I trust working the sound system, if I know exactly what's going to happen when, and if I've got ringers in the audience to laugh at the right places. I have to give speeches at the museum all the time. But cold, up there, not knowing what's going to happen. You said yourselves anything could happen. Jesus: *anything.*"

"Okay, okay, let's back up here. This will probably never happen, Ellen. Never. We don't want to go to court anyway. We'll probably settle in chambers or even out of court, but we do need to prepare as if we're going to go to a jury hearing. Prepare, that's all, not necessarily do it. Just prepare. We'd be asking you some questions, real basic stuff, like: Who are you? What do you do for a living? Where do you come from? What was your family like? That sort of thing. Just the existential stuff with a few details. You can do it, Ellen, but you probably won't have to. We might take a deposition instead, but we do want you to start thinking about your answers. We'll work with you, Ellen. Now, how are you on all this, Kenneth?"

"It makes me sick."

"It does not make you sick, Kenneth. You're terrific before an audience. You do it all the time."

"It still makes me sick, Ellen. I'm just used to it. I've got a method."

"You've got a method. What is it?" We all lean forward in our conference chairs. We all want to know.

"Before I start, I take all my fear, and I put in my knee, my left knee. I keep it there. You never noticed it shakes all the time I'm playing?"

"I thought that was rock and roll."

"No, it's fear."

"You are a remarkable individual, Kenneth. You are stunning. I am stunned by you."

"You're pretty good yourself, Red, and you don't have to do this."

"I could practice. I've got body parts I'm not even using, and listen, if I have to speak to my fitness, Raylene has to speak to hers, right?"

"That's right. Can you warm to this idea, Ellen?"

"Sounds better all the time."

"And there's no need to rush, Ellen."

"There's not? Why not? When is this ever going to end? Can't you guys do anything?"

My parents live in Arizona, but they could be moving anytime. That's what they do. They move. I went to twenty-two different schools in six states before graduating from high school, and when I was seventeen, I said, "Drop in anytime," and bought a commercial refrigerator. That was in 1966, late June. I've been in Houston ever since.

"Why are you wasting good money on this piece of crap?" my father said.

It was no ordinary refrigerator. It was a Hussman double four-by-four, a commercial-grade stand-up in beautiful shape. It was white enamel with black lead Art Deco detailing on the cornice and kick-plate. It had interior lights in blue violet neon, and most of them worked. I put all my graduation money down on it. I had to have it.

"The compressor's shot, Ellen," my father said. "We don't have room for this thing."

I found the Hussman in an old storefront grocery near Rice University. The owner, who was also the butcher, had died one of those slow, slow deaths over the winter. His son was dealing with his grief by remodeling the old grocery into one of those restaurants that are everywhere now, the kind that think they invented Hunter ceiling fans, community tables, and Dijon vinaigrette. Zinder Jr. didn't know what he had; he was bleaching the butcher block, trying to get the stains *out*. I got the Hussman cheap, $175, about a fifth of what it cost new in 1937.

"It's crap, Ellen," my father said.

It had double-hung glass doors, fabulous steel hardware that felt good in your hand, and the eight original white wire racks. There wasn't a speck of rust on it anywhere you could see, and it weighed thirty-five hundred pounds. You'd need a forklift to move it properly, if you cared anything about the enamel finish.

"I'm putting it in storage for now, and I'm staying in Houston," I told my parents. "I'll waitress for Zinder Jr. until our deal's paid off, then I'm going to college."

"Waitressing's sure hard on the feet," my father said. "Try and get something better, but for now, you take this twenty and get a good pair of shoes."

Then the three of them—my father and my mother and my sister, Ruthie—crawled into the car, a Pontiac hardtop four-door the color of cream of tomato soup, and took off after the Mayflower van for Midland-Odessa.

"I finally found someone who can fix the compressor," I told my father seventeen years later.

It was summer, 1982, early August. We were all waiting to meet Zack, and my dad and I were sitting in my kitchen in the house Kenneth and I found in the Binz. The coffee was dripping, and I was seven months' pregnant, surrounded finally and on all sides by my stuff. Except for the mess with Raylene, the problems with Tenny, I was happier than I had ever been in my life.

"I told you it was crap, but I'm glad you're not paying that monthly storage. Ellen, you still keeping the milk in the Igloo?"

My father had dropped in. That's what he does now. The two of them, my parents, live sixteen hundred miles away, just outside of Phoenix. They golf. My dad, whose name is Charlie, was in the oil business for over forty years, supply mostly, and a year ago last May when he turned sixty-five, the company sent him a watch in the mail and a stack of annuity bonds.

"Forty-six years, and all they can come up with is a goddamned Seiko," my father told me long distance.

They also came up with a testimonial dinner, which he refused to go to, and a good deal of money, which I thought would make him very happy. My father loves money, the actual stuff itself. He's always got about two grand on him, and given the choice, he won't take anything but new bills.

"I like my money clean," he tells them at the bank. The tellers catch on quick, start reaching for the new hundreds when they see him come in Fridays.

"So now you can finally relax, Dad," I told him when he called about the Seiko. "You can play golf everyday, see a lot of movies, get some gin rummy games going. You know, Dad, I'm thinking about having a baby. You could take your grandchild to afternoon baseball."

"About this baby business, Ellen, I'm sick of hearing about it. You and Kenneth have got to fish or cut bait on this kid thing, 'cause you're getting pretty old. And listen, I don't have any money. The bank's got it."

My father was the ultimate company man. He was born in Oklahoma and grew up through the Depression. He never got over it. The memory of dust and half-filled plates of vegetables cooked to sense-lessness never leaves him.

"It's real misery not having money and your own bed," he says. "I hope you never have to find that out, Ellen. You just better be grateful every day you've got work."

My father was grateful every day he had work. The company was everything to him, and he risked his life for it more than once. I always thought it was for the blasted money. I knew it wasn't for any Japanese watch.

In about '57, maybe '58, we were living on Eighth Street in New Iberia, in southwest Louisiana. The company called on New Year's Day, just before the Cotton Bowl. A skiff delivering a crate of drilling equipment to a Shell rig in the Black Bayou field had capsized. No one was hurt, but the crate was down deep, and could good-old Charlie supervise the recovery?

This was not a real question, but no one mentioned it. Inside of an hour, my father found a diver named Douglas who wasn't entirely hung over, and the two of them drove eighty miles an hour down a two-lane dirt farm road with a police escort, who as it happens were actually Douglas's third cousins. Just before sunset, they got as far as they could go on land, then took a bass boat out to the place where the skiff had turned over. Then the diver, this Douglas, took an intelligent look at the water, the color of ink, and the alligators snoring on the bank, and told my dad to forget it.

"It's a diamond-headed tool bit," my father said. "They need it, we're getting it, you son-of-a-bitch."

The diver still wouldn't jump, so my father did. He was forty-three years old, the father of two; he didn't even think about us. He took a rope in his teeth, kicked off his shoes, and dived blind and without a wet suit into stagnant water no warmer than fifty degrees. Only a lucky miracle let him find the crate quick and avoid a certain heart attack. He tied the rope to the crate with a packer's knot he'd learned in the Merchant Marines, then came up to the surface sputtering.

"You think you and your coon-ass kin could see to pull on that winch now, Douglas?"

By shift-change Shell had their bit, and Douglas and my dad and the rest of them were eating boudin and fried eggs, and mostly getting drunk, at some DewDropInn.

"You could have killed yourself, Dad," I said at the time, and I've said it every time he's told that story since. I'm still furious about it. He was forty-three years old, not in great shape, although forty-three does seem a lot younger to me now than it used to. Still, he could've broken his neck, caught some disease, left us without him in New Iberia.

"You do what you need to do, Ellen," my father says. "I never stopped thinking about you girls. You just remember you never went hungry."

I'm not so sure about that. I'm in this therapy group with Margaret. It's all women in their late twenties and thirties, and a good 60 percent of them have divorced parents. Ten, twenty, thirty years later, they're still grieving about why their parents couldn't stay together, how horrible Christmas always was. They're trying to account for how much they missed of what they think is normal family life, and they're speculating on what manner of hell's going to happen when everyone shows up at their law school graduations.

I can't get into these discussions. I can't relate. My parents never divorced, but I wouldn't say I knew anything about Normal Family Life.

My father was always working. He was gone my whole childhood. I'd see him Monday for breakfast, then Friday for dinner. He was always on the road, the company came first.

"They need us in Hattiesburg," he told us before the meat loaf was even on the table. "We've got to be there by Wednesday. Can we do it?"

We did it, it wasn't a real question. My mother never threw a box away in her life. We called Mayflower and started packing the fragile stuff in newspaper before Huntley-Brinkley signed off. We canceled birthday parties, dentist appointments, the utilities. We collected the library books, had the newspapers stopped, and gave the perishables away to the neighbors. Monday morning, we were out of there, the car packed to the windows, the thermoses full. The library books sat on the front seat, ready to drop in the return box on the way out of town.

"Have we got the shot records and the school transcripts?" my mother said.

"We got them. Let's go," my father said, and he put my sister Ruthie's aquarium half full of water on the front floorboard (my mother had to straddle it), and we were gone.

"I hate this," I told Ruthie, over a stack of bed pillows between us in the backseat.

"You think the fish'll make it this time, Ellen?"

By Wednesday noon we'd found a new house, an apartment. By Wednesday evening, we'd learned the bus routes, unpacked everything, and settled with Mayflower for damages. By Thursday, we were back in school, new kids again, and my father was out on the road somewhere.

"You know, Dad, I hated my childhood," I told my father over coffee.

"Bullshit," he said. "You don't know what misery is," and he went off on one of his stories about what it was like living in Oklahoma when oil dropped to nine cents a barrel.

My father didn't retire well. Not working fifteen hours a day was completely alien to him. Except for the newspaper—oil futures first thing, then the sports, then the editorials—he wasn't a reader. He had no hobbies; yard work had never held any appeal. For six months, he was lost. He aged a good ten years in the shoulders alone.

He slept late, and when he finally did get up, he didn't even look at the paper. He drove my mother crazy, moping around the house all morning in his pajamas—tops and bottoms, striped like a convict's—and then he took the big car to the MultiCinemas for the early shows. He didn't care what movie was playing, but he refused to pay the senior citizen's rate, and one Thursday he about punched out a high school kid working the concessions when she couldn't change his new $100 bill for a bucket of popcorn and a big orange, no ice.

"He's nuts," I told my mother. "He's worked his whole life. Why can't he relax and enjoy his goddamned money?"

"It was never the money, Ellen," my mother said. "He likes new cash, that's true, but our IRAs don't mean anything to him. Nothing counts unless it's fresh and you can feel it in your pocket, he thinks. It wasn't ever the money itself. It was *working for* the money, Ellen. That's all he knows. Your father needs to work to feel alive, and by the way, we're probably getting a divorce."

"Come on, Dad," I said. "Relax. Enjoy yourself. How old do you think you are anyway?"

"I think I'm about forty-two, maybe forty-three tops. Let me ask you something, Ellen. You ever going to quit painting?"

I can't imagine not painting. I've stopped before, when I got pregnant—they think the fumes hurt the fetus—and I haven't worked near
as much as I wanted to since graduate school when I had to get a day
job for money. But, I can't imagine quitting, not doing it ever again.
I make things, that's what I do. I make paintings, and I think about
making them all the time. I see these images, these shapes, and they
stay stuck in my head. Painting's not about money, although it could
be, probably should be. Painting's my work. It's what I do nights, after
the museum's closed, after my check's in the bank. It's what I think
about all the time.

"Dad," I told him, "get a grip. You're driving us all berserk, and
we've got too many other things to worry about here. Infertility, for
example. Do us all a favor, Dad, and get yourself some work."

He did. It was the only thing I ever told him that he heard and did
something about. He lied about his age and cheated on the eye test,
and he got this stupid job delivering cars around the country. He's a
courier, sort of. He gets expenses and a little money, no insurance
coverage. The company's called DriveAway; they contract to deliver
fancy cars across the country, cars some transferred executive can't
live without, cars that cost plenty and still have a year or two to go
before they're fully depreciated. "Trust Your Luxury Automobile to
Us" is their motto, and they've got outlets everywhere. The company
flies my father—coach/no lunch—to the pickup city, and he signs to
deliver in near-showroom shape some big shot's barely broken-in Lin-
coln, Mercedes, Coupe de Ville to Orlando, Cleveland, Hattiesburg.
He has to be bonded—which I thought would insult him but it
didn't—and he has to guarantee delivery within seventy-two hours.
He always has the car washed, the oil changed before he turns it in.
And he has never been late.

"No matter what you do, you do it right," my father says. "You give
them more than they expect, and you just be grateful they ask you
back the next day."

When he's driving east, my father drops in with a crate of
mixed Arizona citrus for an hour or two. He never stays the night,
he's always in a rush. Sometimes my mother comes with him when
she's not playing in a golf tournament or helping the Episcopalians,
but mostly he drives alone and doesn't seem to mind it. I actually
see him now almost more than I ever did, although his actual

arrival is always a surprise. He doesn't believe in making any plans.

Every couple of weeks he calls from a pay phone in Sealy, about an hour out of Houston, and asks if I'm busy, can he drop in? Listen, I'm always busy, but I always say yes. I mostly like him. We sit together for a while, at home, in my office at the museum. We talk politics—he's still missing Adlai—and catch up on stuff we already know.

"How in the hell did you get into this mess of yours, Ellen?"

My father asks these pointed questions, questions that require complicated answers if you want to understand fully. To really know, you've got to have the historical grounding in perspective with the current situational details. You've got a lot of dimensions here, a lot of positions to consider and evaluate. It's more than just how it appears on the surface. None of this is simple. We're talking about layered realities here, domestic complexities, us against them. I need time to present the material fully, illustrate the complete facts, detail all the intrinsic, albeit ironic, nuances. If you want to know, you've got to be open, and you've got to be patient. That is, if this is a real question.

"You're just like your mother, Ellen. You just talk, talk, talk. Listen, hon, I've got to get on the road. Is Kenneth going to get any action on his divorce mess before this kid comes, or what?"

"This kid is your grandson, Dad. You going to be around for the birth?"

"Depends on what the company needs," he said, and I could've guessed that. "Your mother's all packed. We've got the suitcase by the door, film in the camera."

He is pacing, ready to go. He can't sit still. He needs the road. I am filling his thermoses, putting the cream and sugar in the way he likes it, when Kenneth and Tenny come in the front door.

"Grandpa," she screams—she's soft on legal realities—and heads toward him down the hall at a flat-out run. By the time she hits the kitchen, my dad's had time to stand up, turn toward her.

"Hey, Sunshine. I've sure been missing you," he says and swoops her up. He's tall, tallest man I ever knew, well over six feet. Tenny's dangling on the ceiling, delighted and laughing with all she's got in her. I remember this part, only I was running to him out of the house, not into it. I was always glad to see him.

"Stay for dinner," I say.

"Stay the night," Kenneth says.

"Let's make that fudge again," Tenny says. "Let me down, and I'll get the butter."

My father makes fudge about every five years. His mother taught him. He doesn't use a recipe, but he likes an audience, and he insists that you rave. He made it with Tenny last New Year's. It is fabulous fudge.

"I wish just once it would go to sugar," my mother says, but it never has. It's not a real wish.

"I wish I could stay," my father says. "But I've got to get this Seville on to Mobile. Maybe next time," and he's gone, out the door, making no definite promises.

Kenneth and Tenny walk all the way to the curb to wave him away. I stay on the porch. They're still hoping he'll stay for dinner at least, but they'll learn. Once my father backs out of the driveway, he never looks back.

The minute I figure this guy out, he changes. Half way down the street, he brakes, rolls down his window, and calls for Tenny. She races out to the middle of the street—doesn't look *either* way—and I see him slip her something. It is a clean twenty.

"HE WANTS ME TO HAVE *REAL* DANCING SHOES," she yells to us from the street. She kisses him through the window, then cartwheels right past us and into the house to call her mother.

"Well, that's nice," Kenneth says.

"Yeah," I tell him. "That twenty ought to get her about a half a pair."

My father drives on down the street. At the corner, he'll turn east for Mobile. We wave. He doesn't look back, but I think he sees us in his rearview mirror and just doesn't want to let on.

4

Pâté?

Of course, we'll edit this, Ellen, but the judge is going to love it. Your father is certainly a colorful character.

Character is the right word.

Well, you seem genuinely fond of him.

We've had our moments. He's my father: I never knew I had much choice in the matter of fondness. Charlie is actually pretty hard to take. He's a very noisy person, full of opinion, good at keeping everybody jumping. He's exhausting, really. I don't like much jumping. I don't like his fudge either.

We can see that all that moving couldn't have made for a very relaxed childhood. Was money a problem, Ellen?

Well, we never had enough. I'm not sure anybody ever does, and we did spend a lot of time sitting around in bank lobbies in our good clothes, waiting on some Loan Committee to tell us if we were going to eat or not. We always did—eat, I mean—but you should understand that not having enough money is one of Charlie's themes. I think somebody ought to look into the effects of the Depression on the second generation. I think we're all warped by tragic memories that aren't even ours.

And your mother, Ellen? You barely mention her.

I'll get to her. Charlie's easy because of his scale—he does every-thing large—but Frances is the more difficult to pin down. Mostly, she adapts.

Denial is her best friend?

That's good, guys. That's really good. You two ought to become shrinks if this lawyer thing doesn't work out.

Well, we have mothers, plus we've been in analysis for a number of years.

Analysis, huh? My friend Grace is doing that now. It sounds fab-ulous to me to talk for fifty minutes four times a week on a leather couch and not have to argue about every little thing.

Well, a lot of times we're not sure they're really listening.

So you two really think this is going to help Kenneth's case?

Of the three of you, Ellen—you, Kenneth, Raylene—you come from the most traditional background. It's recognizable, pretty stock. Raylene is a divorced child, clearly wounded, territorial; she's crazy but rage is how she survives. She just doesn't know how to let go. Kenneth, on the other hand, is your classic bridge burner: He's cut all ties with his adopted family. Understand, we don't blame him at all. We think he's simply lucky to be alive—we're still reeling about that wooden spoons thing, Ellen—but your parents are still together after nearly forty years. You've maintained contact. Your mother was a brownie leader. By contrast, Ellen, you come from a family right off the TV.

It was just once—that second time in Meridian—and it was for only three months. Nobody wanted to learn how to make pâté in 1956.

Understand, Ellen: Their argument is that you two are living to-gether unmarried with a child about to be born out of wedlock. Ken-neth has very little money and a nontraditional job with no stability. He doesn't know where his next dollar's coming from, Ellen. You claim to be an artist, too, and they're saying you guys are flakes, irresponsible, incapable of caring for one child, much less two. They think you're aberrant, Ellen. We've got to show the court they're wrong.

Kenneth takes care of Tenny. It's not a fucking hobby with him. You ought to see him with her.

We hope to. We hope everyone will, Ellen, but he is living like a kid. He hasn't achieved much professional standing really, and he hasn't been able to resolve much about his past. He doesn't push, he's passive, and frankly, Ellen, we're dealing with the wimp factor here. Just what do you see in him anyway?

I see everything I want to be. He's calm, he's extraordinarily patient. He takes care of his child, and then he takes care of himself. His world is a very small circle. He is not terrifically ambitious, and you need to know that achievement in any art form is relative anyway. Kenneth doesn't expect anything from anybody, and he just wants to play music. He values what he does, and he does what he wants to do. He writes music, he plays music, he takes care of Tenny. He's not interested in impressing anyone. He's smart, he's very funny, but mostly he's quiet, a quality this century doesn't value much in men. Kenneth is very rare. I admire him enormously.

We can see that.

I wish I had his guts. I'd like to quit my job and paint like a real painter for a while.

You've worked in that museum for ten years, Ellen. You draw a salary, contribute to a pension fund. Judges like to hear things like that. Don't quit, Ellen. You look stable.

Imagine that.

Work with us, Ellen. It won't last forever. We think you two are solid, and we've just got to show it. We think you'd be married if Kenneth wasn't still—

You do? I don't know about that.

Please, Ellen.

It's all about lies, isn't it?

Listen, do you want Kenneth to get this divorce, Ellen? Do you want a legal structure to build your future on? Do you want chaos for the rest of your life?

Okay, okay, okay. Is there anything else?

Well, you could start watching your language.

5

Sorry Juniper

Kenneth trusts no one.

This is not to say that he openly distrusts anyone, that he's paranoid, that he believes the world calculates his every move, is at the ready at any moment to pounce on him and lift his wallet. Kenneth doesn't think of himself and his life in global terms at all, and with regard to his wallet, money means hardly a thing to him personally.

"Bradley and Joan said something about a wooden spoons thing, Kenneth. What is that? What did you tell them?"

"I don't remember, Ellen, but are you sure you want to go tonight? You don't have to go, you know."

Simply, Kenneth holds no expectations, counts on no certainties, relies on no one, but after everything, he thinks he will survive.

"I can't believe this," I tell him, and I can't. "All you want to do is survive? How can you think like that? Don't you trust me at least? Don't you just know Raylene would put you in thumbscrews any chance she got? Don't you think Tenny's nuts? Do you really think Gus's check is in the mail?"

Kenneth's playing steady again—well, Friday and Saturday nights anyway—at a hovel Gus calls his own. It's a neighborhood bar that's seen far better times, as has the neighborhood, as has Kenneth's band. The zebra wood paneling, custom backgammon tables, and stained-glass windows were some previou owners' leasehold improvement, installed in the early seventies to court maturing hippies and their recently acquired American Express cards. When the oil crisis hit Houston, the visionary owners got out of the booze business fast and went to law school. Gus picked the place up cheap, put in shuffle-boards, and asked Kenneth and the band to play for tips and 10 percent of the bar, weekends from nine until two.

"Will you pass the jar after 'Don't Be Cruel'?" Kenneth asked me at the second break. "Elaine missed that back table last time, and I think that guy in the blue-jean jacket used to come hear us in the old days."

The guy in the blue-jean jacket, a new one, looks all of fifty and is drunk. He still thinks he's got a chance to get a little tonight, but from what Elaine and I have been watching from the bar, he hasn't got a prayer. The nineteen-year-old he's with is much more interested in checking out her smudge-proof mascara and the guy in the red flannel shirt and nice ass who is currently high-point at shuffleboard. Over the blasting jukebox—Patrick plugs it in during band breaks because he's set up closest to the outlet—we can hear the guy, flushed red from sorry juniper, complaining to Gus about the quality of his drinks and quality in general.

"What kind of a dump is this?" he bellows. "When I order Tan-queray, I mean goddamn Tanqueray."

Gus, who comes in early afternoons to refill brand-labeled bottles with discount booze, tells the guy he wouldn't know Tanqueray from his own asshole, and everyone in the place (except the shuffleboard players, who were all in 'Nam, or wish they had been) turns to see what kind of a fight this is going to be. The guy's date, who has been drinking sweet jug wine out of a plastic glass since 8:30, ducks to the floor to get her purse. She comes up slow, pale as the moon.

"Excuse me, you motherfuckers," she says, clutching for the table edge and turning everything over.

She pushes by the two men, who are puffing up like bantam roosters ready to go at it, and stumbles into the closest bathroom, which—lucky or not—happens to be The Wenches. Even over the jukebox, the Stones and "Satisfaction," we can hear her retch for a long time.

"Jesus, Kenneth," I said. "What are we doing here?"

"It pays the rent sometimes, honey. Will you pass the jar?"

I hate to pass the jar. Kenneth knows this but keeps asking anyway.

"I hate doing that, Kenneth. Can't you get Elaine to pass it again? Where is she anyway?"

Elaine is Patrick's wife and usually my date for part of Friday nights, sometimes Saturdays. We sit together at the end of the bar. She sips liqueurs over chipped ice, I stay with thin orange juice that tastes like cardboard (I used to join her with gin before I was pregnant), and we lead the applause when necessary. We don't know each other very well—talking in any depth isn't generally possible over the noise—and we don't have much in common anyway. She's interested in taking a medical terminology course, for example—I can't imagine anybody ever wanting to do that—and she's been married to Patrick for nine years, watched him play for twelve. Elaine knows all the old fans, keeps the mailing list up on her computer at work, and told Gus if he messed with the Tia Maria, she'd call the Liquor Control Board on him. When she's not there, I miss her. I get tired of fending off men on the hit.

"I'm with the band," I say. "And I'm pregnant."

"I don't mind," they say.

Elaine says, "Tell them you're a lesbian."

"I'm a lesbian," I say.

"I don't mind," they say.

Elaine says not to worry, that they'll go away, and she's right. They go away, and another comes. It's less frequent though when the two of us are there together, and if it ever got really difficult, I think Gus would step in, but I'd hate to count on it.

"He's sleeze," Elaine says, "and so is this joint. You can't count on the toilet being even close to sanitary after ten o'clock. You know, Raylene used to enjoy it, making Kenny crazy in the middle of a set. She'd show up in red leather, all this fringe, looked like a damn tramp. She'd let them buy her drinks, frozen rum things, and then act indignant when they suggested stepping outside to some Cutlass Oldsmobile. Of course, it was a different place then, better, a better crowd, we were all a lot younger. I haven't been able to abide rum since '67. You're all right, you know, even in that, what is that, a tea dress? Honey, have you got any maternity jeans at all? I believe in fidelity myself, and Patrick sure better. Hey, how come Kenny calls you Red, Ellie? Hey, you want to go smoke dope in the truck?"

"Elaine took ten dollars and split before the break," Kenneth said. "Their sitter had a late date, and Patrick'll take it out of his cut. Will you do it, Ellen?"

I do it. I am eight months' pregnant and even drunks at midnight notice and are generous. The problem is, it's a slow night. Gus's gin showdown was the high point, and the thing about bar fights and near bar fights is that they sober people up right away, make them check their watches and think about getting home. Kenneth cuts the break short, but rock and roll won't hold anybody over thirty who's been reminded what time they got up that morning. They drift toward the door in clusters, walk out, right past the band in the middle of the Everly Brothers medley they loved at nine. No one even thinks about skirting the stage, and no one notices the tip jar either, just a third full and mostly silver, on my Thonet kitchen stool by the bass mike.

Kenneth and the band keep playing, loud songs, trying to compete over the noise of late-model cars and light trucks revving their engines just outside the front door, but everyone knows the night's lost. The headlights come on, ten pair, and flood Gus's place for the seedy joint it is. The night is gone, early, a disappointment.

There is, of course, the bare possibility of a late round, late business, couples just out from the ten o'clock show, not hungry for eggs or blatantly urgent for sex. Kenneth will play until one o'clock regardless, unless everybody leaves. Then, he'll judge the room and think about wiping his guitar down. But just after midnight, when it's my turn to pass the goddamn jar, there are only three tables left (talkers, way in the back; they'll leave when the set breaks) and the shuffleboard players, who I don't think ever leave. I collect eight bucks—damp with a day's, maybe two or three days', pocket sweat—and call it a miracle. I charge the haul completely to my quite obvious condition and the fact that Kenneth is singing Otis Redding, which puts most people in a good and generous mood, if they're able at all.

From the back of the bar, Gus announces, "Drinks for the house. Drinks for the best goddamned band in goddamned Houston, Texas."

If you had just stumbled into the place, you might think this was an indication of a generous spirit, respectful patronage, but the fact of the matter is that Gus would rather pull his own legs off than give anything away for nothing. The talkers are drinking coffee anyway and thinking about getting home and maybe/maybe not making love, and the shuffleboard players are beer drinkers as a rule, so Gus isn't going to be out much from his outcry for art.

"Art hasn't got a thing to do with it," Kenneth says over eggs later, and I see he was right.

It's Friday. Gus's wife goes to the beach house with their kids right after school, and Gus drives down Saturday morning with the paper and fresh ice. Friday nights, Gus gets what he can, which I can't think is much, but he hopes and certainly tells, over and over, elaborating in relation to his audience's interest and his own perverted fantasies. The man is sleeze, worse than Rococo.

New business just walked in. A woman, alone, in mouton. She makes for the bar, a little unsteady on her boots but understandable considering the hour. She orders iced Bacardi, white, and Gus says, setting the glass in front of her on a clean white napkin I didn't think he even stocked, "Honey, it's a pleasure to pour a drink for a red-headed woman who knows booze. You got any favorites you'd like my band to play?"

"They know any Les Paul/Mary Ford songs?" she says, and Gus begins to emote about affinity.

I watch him make an ass out of himself over three free drinks and then watch her—Gwen is her name—head for the bathroom and disappear.

About one o'clock, Shawn and Becky show up. They want to know if we'll go for breakfast.

"Couldn't you just kill for pancakes?" Becky says. "The kids are with my mother."

I'm pretty sure I could never kill for pancakes, but I've been thinking about what my life might be like after this baby's born, and how I probably won't have much choice in the matter of late breakfasts out. I won't miss pancakes or Gus, I'm very clear on these subjects, but I do think I'll miss watching Kenneth play. For all the sleeze, it's the one time I'm sure Kenneth is really happy, all on his own, unless of course the crowd's really flat, or too many strings break, or Patrick gets really drunk on his ass.

From the stage, which is really a four-by-eight piece of warped plywood on cinder blocks, Kenneth nods his interest in breakfast, keeps up with "Lady Ryder," but Patrick shakes his head no. We all know he'll change his mind. He and Elaine live nearly to Clear Lake now, and he hates the long drive home alone.

"It makes me crazy," he says. "Just me and the drums rattling in the back of the truck, the moon grinning, no traffic to speak of, and if there is any, you know it's probably drunk teenagers or escaped convicts. Those white markings on the road put me to sleep, and I'm afraid I'll drive off the edge of the fucking earth and make my kids orphans."

"You need coffee," Becky says.

We all go. Bill and Pete, bass and keyboard, never turn down any offer, plus Bill says he can't go home until morning anyway because he's fogging his apartment for roaches, and who knows how long those canisters buzz.

Pete, who's taken off his toupee in the International House of Pancakes men's room, says, "Did we make any money?"

Under the fluorescent lights, too bright, the waitress tired but watching, we count the jar, make stacks around the coffee cups and the sticky plates: fifty-seven dollars, plus the ten Elaine took, and silver.

"I'll take the quarters," Pete says. "I've got laundry. Hey, look. Is that another valentine from Gus?"

On a used napkin, orange lipstick on the corner, Gus prints: You guys are better than the Rolling Stones and you're in Texas. I'm sending you a good check the minute I get to the beach house. Catch me Saturday night for a sweet story about red hair that'll make your teeth ache. Gus.

"So, the check is in the mail," Kenneth says, and everyone laughs, except me.

"I'm tired of that joke, Kenneth."

"Ellen, he's a jerk. That's a bar owner for you. We'll catch up with Gus tomorrow night and get our cut of tonight's booze. He does this all the time, Red."

"I know that, Kenneth," I say, but I didn't. "You're an artist. People ought to pay you right, respect what you do."

"I'm no artist, Red," Kenneth says. "I just play rock and roll."

6

Chairs

This is the life you *want*, Ellen? Sitting in smoky dives half the night? Listening to third-rate, balding musicians play golden oldies? Drinking watered-down booze with people who live in trailers?

I don't know anybody who lives in a trailer, Margaret.

Ellen, I am concerned. You're not a kid anymore. You're almost thirty-five years old, and these people are not of your class.

I hate that word, Margaret. You're a Republican, aren't you?

And you're being argumentative, Ellen. Look at the facts, honey. You have *real* talent. You have a master's degree in painting from one of the finest universities in this country. You work for one of the most prestigious museums in the world. You subscribe to and read *The New York Times*. You drive an old Jaguar, you collect nineteenth-century pottery, you understand Derrida. Ellen, I have seen you walk out of a restaurant simply because they didn't have clean linen on the table. I know you own a cappuccino machine, and I know you know how to use it. Ellen, *please*. You say yourself Kenneth buys canned vegetables. I just can't see you living on generics, Ellen.

What?

Any future with Kenneth Goodson is going to be low-rent. He doesn't even have medical insurance, Ellen. You'll be living on beans and rice and powdered milk. You'll be on welfare in a year, Ellen.

I have medical insurance, Margaret. I don't know what you're talking about. Listen, my life is not going to change. I'm going to live like I always have. I'm going to work, I'm going to work hard, I always have. This is the twentieth century, Margaret. Women can vote now, make their own choices, make their own money. I don't expect Kenneth to support me or this baby.

Well, what do you expect, Ellen?

I expect to be near happy, Margaret. I expect to get some new paintings going. I expect this baby to be wonderful. I expect Mondale to run for president and win and put all of your fascists in prison.

You are going to change, Ellen. Babies change people.

How do you know that, Margaret? You don't even have kids.

I see depressed mothers every day, Ellen. You can't imagine what I hear about squalling kids and cheating husbands. Domesticity kills the female spirit.

I guess all those depressed mothers are the ones who paid for these new Eames chairs, huh, Margaret? These are originals, aren't they? I know how much these cost.

I worry about you, Ellen.

Thank you.

I worry you're getting in over your head. It's not just Kenneth and the money thing, Ellen. It's that crazy Raylene, that nightmare of a child Tenny. It's going to be hell forever. You say you want a different kind of life, Ellen, but I think what you've got is pretty terrific. You have your own money, you have your own stuff, you have a great job. You know, people would kill to have your job.

My job nearly kills me, Margaret. I hate it, I should have quit years ago, they don't pay me enough. And you don't understand: I've got credit, not money.

What I understand, Ellen, is that you know what an Eames chair is. Kenneth is never going to know that.

First, I don't find that to be a globally critical piece of information,

Margaret. And second, Kenneth would never pay fifteen hundred dollars for a thirty-year-old leather chair.

Fifteen hundred? Ellen, I paid twenty-two.

You really got ripped off then, Margaret. That one you're sitting in is a copy.

7

Art and Working for Art

After graduate school, I had to get a job, a Real Job, full time. I went through college and graduate school on full-tuition scholarships—I'm good at filling out applications—and all through school I worked at least twenty hours a week, forty plus during summers and breaks. I punched a clock at art stores and commercial galleries, for the university archives, at the City Museum on Work Study. I managed to eke along, buy paint and a good piece of meat occasionally, but now I had long-term debt and no academic excuse. I had to make Real Money. There was this job opening at the Morris Museum, a small place, elitist, famous for elegant installations, a great surrealism collection. I took the job. Actually, I talked them into it, is what I did. I didn't want to work for any goddamned bank.

I was there forever, nearly twelve years. I was Program Coordinator, which meant I did everything that needed to be done except get credit and enough money to eat. I worked directly with the artists—I loved that, I understood how they worked—but I also opened crates, planned installations, wrote catalog essays, hired and supervised security and front-desk help. I arranged press conferences, ordered coat racks, chilled the wine, and wrote the grants. I picked the artists up from the airport, figured out what they needed to get through their openings, and got them back on the plane for home three days later with real cowboy hats for their kids. Regularly, I worked twelve hours a day, eighteen if there was a problem, which was pretty often, and I didn't ever mind getting my hands dirty. I did a great job, and really, they should have paid me more.

At the beginning I did love working there—getting to be up close to Matisse, Braque, Goya, Cézanne, Magritte, somebody you've never heard of that knocks your head off—but something happens over time to people who work in museums. They quit looking at the art as Art and start looking at the art as Problem. It happened slowly, over eight, nine, ten years. I quit looking, and I almost quit painting, and I think I could have gone on there forever if I hadn't managed to keep my appointment with Sam.

"You know, all I have ever wanted was a permanent address and enough money to buy good paint."

"I don't think so, Ellen," my friend Grace said over lunch. "I think you've wanted every primitive chest of drawers you've ever seen. I've never known you to turn down a good deal on a hand-knit Italian sweater, and with regard to men, Ellen, you've never even glanced at one that didn't have significant attachments."

Grace is probably my best friend, and I've known her for fifteen years. She's a conservator at the City Museum. She fixes things— vandalized paintings, damaged sculpture—and recently she has gone into real psychotherapy with this Freudian named Louis. She stretches out on his leather couch and free-associates four times a week, and I really think he ought to break analytical form and point out her slips.

"Is this museum thing a real job, Ellen?" my father said. "I'd have thought they'd get housewives to do this sort of thing. They actually pay you, Ellen? They pay you real money? They pay you regular? That wallet of yours is going to explode if you try and wedge another credit card in there, sugar."

About me and money, I personally find it vulgar, the stuff itself. Unlike my father, I never have any on me, not even coffee change. I use credit cards mainly—you can get as many as you want if you work six months for any place with a raised letterhead—and I buy things, things that cost plenty.

I like old oriental rugs, kilims and durries, rugs where you can see the hand of the weaver. I like Italian blue faience pottery, red and black Panamanian *molas,* and nearly any piece of nineteenth-century American primitive furniture I see, particularly if it was made in Texas and has the original hardware. I like looking at beautiful things, having them around me. The fact that they cost real money doesn't hit me until the bills come on the fifteenth. I've got a great collection of Mexican milagros, tin and brass, and I can't pass up a piece of unchipped Fiestaware—the real stuff from the thirties, not this recent-release crap—especially if it's that deep cobalt blue.

"Have you bought any paint lately?" my friend Ben wants to know.

Ben's a sculptor, a good one. He can tell the difference between great stuff and crap as well as anybody I know, and it's just about impossible for him to pass up any junk store. He does it though, he passes them up. What he actually does is stay in his studio mostly and plan his traffic routes so he doesn't drive by any. Ben's nearly sixty. He understands how you could blow a whole decade, maybe two, by taking the wrong turn at a corner. He saves his money—I don't think he ever really spent much anyway—and holes up in his studio all week, attending to steel and ideas. It doesn't always go well, but he stays at it. He's stubborn and has a basically despondent nature any-way. I admire him enormously.

"Are you working, Ellen?" Ben wants to know.

Jesus, all I do is work. I'm at the museum fifteen hours a day lately. We're having around a hundred crises. The whole place is on fire, and I'm about the only one with a bucket.

We've got two exhibitions opening practically back-to-back in the next three weeks: Pre-Columbian Textiles on the sixteenth and Con-temporary Japanese Photography on the twenty-ninth. We don't have final installation plans on either one of them, and I'm on the phone all morning trying to get Tokyo to send back the damn loan forms so we can at least have a final checklist. I've been friendly about it so far, but I can't figure out why they're sandbagging. Figuring this out and then fixing it: That's my job.

We've got a hole in the schedule for next spring, and Claudia has agreed to show, but she can't be ready until next fall at the earliest. Claudia's a good painter, maybe a great painter, and she's still hungry. It would be a great show for both of us, but she wants a four-color catalog, and I think she ought to have it. I've got to talk Henry, the museum's director, the big boss, into raising the money to underwrite her book, except I can't get to Henry. He's holed up at home, trying to get his anxiety under control. He won't talk on the phone to anybody for more than ten seconds, so I spend late afternoons sandbagging Claudia long distance from London—I hate lying to friends—and dialing Henry's home number without any real connection.

Judith is my assistant—"and everyone else's in the Western Hemisphere"—but she's been out with the flu, so mornings I'm doing one of her jobs. I'm helping the installation crew hemstitch six-hundred-year-old Aztec textiles onto bamboo dowels with dental floss. I don't sew well, something in the fabric makes me sneeze, and they're not hanging right anyway. They're supposed to look like heraldic banners—it was Henry's idea—but they look like sagging shower curtains in some cheap motel. Judith is much better at this sort of thing than I am, but she's still got fever.

I'm bringing her juice and soup, but what I really need to do is to get over to Rice and grab some new art history students by the ankles. I don't have anybody to work the front desk weekend afternoons. I've got to corner some kids, appeal to their sense of aesthetics, dazzle them with minimum wage plus all the posters they want. I've got to make sure they're largely drug-free, and then I've got to get them on payroll by five. If I don't get to that, it's going to be me on that damn desk this weekend.

"Listen, I'm a wreck, Ben. And I'm broke."

"Yeah, I know," he says. "But are you working?"

Ben means, am I *working*? Am I working on my own work? Have I got anything going in the studio? Is any of it worth looking at twice? Is anything going to cook up?

"I've got a pretty good drawing going," I tell him. We both hear that lie, but Ben doesn't press me about it.

"Make sure that dental floss is unwaxed, Ellen," Ben advises, and he knows about things like this. "You might try steel rods for the textiles, but be sure not to oil them. How's that photography thing going to be?"

"Skip it," I tell him, "it's a dog," but he had already guessed that.

"Ben, I'm dying for that angel hair pasta thing with the garlic shrimp. Let's go to Vincent's next Friday. Come on, Ben: I'll buy."

"If I'm not dead, that would probably be fine, but I think you ought to save your money, Ellen. Call me next Friday morning? I'll try to remember to answer the phone."

I get nervous when Ben won't make definite plans. He's solid, the most organized person I know, despite what he says.

"Hey, how are you? How'd your week go?"

"I went out to get the paper Tuesday morning, and my brain lapsed. I lost two whole days, Ellen. I don't know where they went, I don't know where I was. It was like a blackout, and I'm thinking of canceling all my subscriptions."

Ben's working on a show. The steel isn't cooperating but that's how it goes mostly. I'm not really worried, and neither is his dealer who will make a fortune on his show anyway it goes. Deadlines bring out Ben's best stuff, and Ben's best stuff nearly always raises the heart.

"At the moment I have no future," Ben says.

"You'd be crazy without the *Times.*"

"I'm crazy with the *Times,*" he says and picks up his wheat germ. "Good title, huh?"

"Well, maybe," but I can see his brain's already back at the studio, working on it to make it better. He'll do it, too, or get another idea.

I drop a gallon of cranberry juice by Judith's—she still looks like shit—and go on to Rice to recruit. It's easy, really: I've got scouts on the faculty. Getting over there and finding a decent parking place is the hard part.

"I need two good ones at least," I tell George. We were in graduate school together, and he's acting head of Studio now.

"We got them," he tells me. "Are you working, Ellen?"

I hire a sweetheart named Yolanda right out of a Gothic Art seminar. She's a freshman from Del Rio, going to college on scholarship. She's the oldest of seven—I look for firstborns—and is the very definition of earnest.

"I'll meet you at the side door on Sunday. Be there fifteen minutes before opening. I'll show you how the alarms work and what I need you to do. You can wear jeans, but they've got to be clean. You can study at the desk, but you've got to acknowledge directly everybody who walks in that front door. The guards will tail them, you won't be alone, and you can watch the monitors if anyone makes you nervous. You can always call me at home, or you can call the police. But if you call the police, you be sure and call me. Listen, how are your instincts? Could you tell the difference between a wino and a local artist?"

"I've got an uncle who's a wino," Yolanda says.

She's perfect. I'll keep her for four years if she'll have us, plus I can get her on Work Study and give her a little more money. She needs it. Art history textbooks really cost now. Of course, they always did.

I get another student lined up for Saturdays. He's a local, another freshman. He went to Bellaire High School, he knows the museum, and his name is David, but I don't know. He's so handsome, it grates, and I've had bad luck with pretty boys at the front desk. David thinks he's a printmaker right now, and I'm not sure he'll work out.

"Can you get that ink off your hands by Saturday noon?" I ask him, but it's the fingernails I worry about.

"I won't print after Thursday mornings," he tells me. "I really need this job, and I'm thinking about switching to photography anyway since I can't draw."

I look at his work. He can draw, he just can't draw the way he wants to.

"You've got good sense to like Matisse," I tell him. "Let's try Saturdays for a while, but don't you dare let anybody hit on you while you're on that desk, and I'll shoot you if you're ever late, understand?"

It is a Friday, it is September, it is 1980. I am nearly thirty-two years old, I've held this museum job for eight years, and I barely have an ass left. I mean that literally. I'm skinny anyway, but when I work this hard, run this much, I can't keep my weight up. I'm too thin, I don't feel good, and I don't know where the summer went. I didn't even take off Labor Day, and except for lunch with Ben, I haven't had any real fun in a long time. And I could use a haircut.

I've got a 4:45 appointment with my gynecologist—just the regular annual deal—and I've had to reschedule twice already, but I'm thinking about disappearing just to see if the world really would fall in on itself.

I'd like to drive south to the Bay. I'd like to check into the old Galvez Hotel under an assumed name. I'd like to order room service—a good steak, a pretty good bottle of red wine—and watch pay-for-view movies for two whole days on clean, white, ironed sheets.

"Jesus, Ellen, where are your brains?" my friend Laurel says. "Nobody *irons* sheets anymore. It's not cost-effective in this country. You want Mérida if you want ironed sheets."

Laurel's a banker, about the only nonart person I really know. We spend most of our lunches defining terms and arguing about whose days are more full of crap. Lately, I've been winning.

"I want Caracas, Laurel. I want Buenos Aires. I want out of here. I'd like to try holing up for a while anywhere humid. Somebody else can do everything for a change."

"Do it, Ellen," Judith croaks into the phone.

I can't. I wish I could, but I can't. There's too much to do, it's not possible for me to disappear. I couldn't relax anyway. I'm a hand-maiden to art. I've got responsibilities, duties, standards to uphold, art to hang. And besides, I'm broke.

"Use American Express," Judith whispers in my ear.

This is one solution, a pretty good one until the bill comes. I could do it. No, I can't.

"Shut up, Judith. I can't."

"Then did you remember to order the coat racks?"

I forgot. I forgot to order the damn coat racks. I wrote it down—order racks from Peggy at AtoZ—but I was too busy to even read my list.

We're a small museum: We can't hang coats at any volume. For Thursday night openings, we get metal racks and good wooden hang-ers from AtoZ Rents. We set them up in Publicity behind the wine tubs, then send them back Friday mornings and get on with our correspondence. It's September in Texas, still in the nineties, but it's September, fall, autumn, the Season's begun. Regardless of the real weather, women all over town are getting their furs out of cold storage and stocking up on dress shields. They'll wear them to our openings, want to check their minks as soon as they get through the door.

"I'll order them Monday," I tell Judith.

"It'll be too late," she barely squeaks, and she's probably right. Coat racks are hot with AtoZ in September.

I sign in for my appointment with Sam. He's running late, too—it's why he's my doctor—so I have time to call Antonio at the museum from the waiting-room phone.

There are three women I know sitting there waiting on Sam. They are thumbing through their Weeks-At-A-Glance and making notes on yellow legal pads. They all want to use the phone. They all need to. One's from a gallery, the other two are curators at the City Museum.

We know why we're here—cancer—and we know if we reschedule again we won't see our Pap results until late June when the Season drops off a little.

I like them, these women, but I keep my distance. It's too late in the day, too early in the evening for art gossip—plus I don't know any new dirt—and I particularly don't want them to know how squirrelly our installation's going. I call Antonio and whisper Ben's idea about the steel rods for the textiles. Antonio is the museum's chief preparator; he and the shop crew are in charge of this sort of thing—the physical part, the right nails in the wall—but it's a small museum. During installation, we all do everything. We all worry.

Antonio is as tired as I am, but he's concerned about how they're hanging, too. He'll sew up a model—he's insulted Ben thinks we'd even consider using waxed floss—and I'll meet him back at the museum after my appointment. We'll see how it looks, keep the bamboo for something else.

Doris, Sam's nurse, calls my name. She's pregnant, and it was a surprise to everyone: She's got teenagers.

"Aren't you supposed to know about these things, Doris?"

"It was that weekend at the Galvez over Easter, Ellen. The Margueritas hit me in the hot tub, and I forgot I had sense," she says, but she looks happy.

I'm on the examining table, and while Sam's doing what he does, I'm telling him how much I appreciate the fact that he finally trashed the Renoir prints. He had them everywhere. I hated them.

"First, they were terrible reproductions, and second, they are hideous paintings to begin with. Don't you realize Renoir lost it early and didn't know? He was completely blind at the end. And third, I found them personally insulting. Did you ever really *look* at them, Sam? Renoir never painted any women over fifteen, and they've all got the brains of a Pekinese. What's your market here anyway?"

"They were fully depreciated, Ellen, so we donated them to the Heart Fund rummage. We're thinking about some watercolors. You know this painter Deirdra Burns? She's from Santa Fe. She does these beautiful renderings of fruits and vegetables."

I like it that Sam's considering buying original work, and I like looking at purple onions as much as the next person, but I don't know. Women and cooking. It could be misread.

"Nobody's *from* Santa Fe, Sam. They're *in* Santa Fe. You know, I'd still go with the Panamanian *molas*. I can get you into a great place just outside of Mexico City."

It's just a regular visit, an annual checkup, the necessary yearly Pap. He'll send the smear to the lab; I'll be looking for a plain white postcard with the results. It'll take a week or so, it's routine, no big deal unless you think about it actively.

And, Sam knows what he's doing. He's been my doctor for years. I went to school with his sister-in-law, he brings his kids to Saturday workshops at the museum, and I see him in line at the good movies. I am nearly thirty-two years old. I'm a regular at this sort of thing, experienced. There's nothing to be coy about here. The checkup's important, but we're not going to talk about anything serious unless there's cause.

"Hey, Sam, what do you know about anxiety?"

"I know you've got it, Ellen."

"It's not me. It's Henry's newest thing. He's got his head in a paper bag all the time. He calls these staff meetings, but then he doesn't show up. We phone him at home, and he says his hands are shaking so much he's afraid to drive his car. What's the deal, do you think?"

"Henry is not a well person, Ellen."

"Oh, God, what is it? What's he got, Sam?"

"I saw him at the grocery recently. He's got this theory that fluorescent lights cause impotence. He wanted to know what I thought about it."

"What did you tell him? Jesus, he is so nuts."

"I told him to turn off the lights and avoid convenience stores."

I am laughing, and Sam is laughing, and then Sam is not laughing.

"Hey, Ellen," Sam says in a voice I never heard so serious. The air in the examining room goes hot and white. The charade collapses.

"We've got a problem here."

"I don't think I would have been in this mess," I tell my father and my mother, Bradley and Joan, all the shrinks, my friends, the police, the social workers, "if my ovaries had held up."

I believe it is the complete truth. Before that Friday in September of 1980, I didn't really think about the future, as in not having one.

I know lots of women like me—pretty smart women working their asses off ten, twelve, fourteen hours a day, day after day, for some museum, some bank, some corporation, and not thinking about what they want to do really, what they want their lives to be like. You work that hard, keep your standards this high, you don't have time to think beyond your Week-At-A-Glance. You're busy, running your heels off, attending to a million details, all of which count critically you think. Some of them do, but some of them don't. They can't *all* count. You're so stretched, you can't tell the difference, and you make mistakes you pay for way past the initial oversight in a thousand tiny ways.

You work hard, you know your job, and you're good at it. But you do anything for yourself—like get a haircut during working hours, like have lunch with somebody you really like—you feel like you're cheating on somebody. You work three hours past quitting time to assuage the guilt. You come in Saturday morning for just a few hours to catch up on correspondence, and you're still there at seven.

You're beat, wrung out, spent, you haven't had any time off. So you sneak off for a weekend at a fancy hotel. You stop by pricey antique stores, specialty shops on the way back from lunch and buy yourself things you fall in love with—things you can't really afford and are too big for your apartment anyway—and you get just enough out of those indiscretions to keep the charade going. You forget about your cash-flow problems; you forget that these indiscretions, these lapses in discipline, were just what got you into near-debtor's prison with Mas-terCard in the first place. It's a terrible cycle: You work, you make money. You work hard, you spend money hard. You burn out, you want to quit, but you owe all this money. You can't quit. You work, you make money.

I worked. I worked harder than nearly anybody I knew. I knew how to get things done—that was my job—but so what? I knew how to talk an artist into trusting me, I knew how to pull a difficult exhibition together, I knew how to buy a Sunday review for an overpriced lunch, and I knew how to hang a mediocre painting to make it look good. (You hang it high, is what you do. You light the lower corners and leave the rest dark, and you pray just once somebody out of the field will catch on and ask you why you've got this piece of crap in your place.)

I was good at my work—they should have paid me more—but it was supposed to be just a day job for rent and medical benefits. The problem was, I couldn't ever stop at five o'clock unless everything was done and done right, and that nearly never happened. It wasn't just me; we were all like that. We were hired because we were compulsive and could fake looking animated in most any public circumstance. Museums in the guts—behind that quiet front desk, just beyond that hushed, scholarly, near religious atmosphere—are complete chaos. There's never enough money, and there's never enough time. No matter how much you plan, something always screws up, and it's only by divine grace, and a lot of overtime you don't get paid for, that an exhibition, a catalog, a lecture series comes off on schedule. It's a miracle any painting ever gets up on the wall. It's a miracle they don't all fall off.

My museum job somehow became my whole life. Practically everyone I knew was connected to art—making it or handling it. I did love it in the beginning, the first few years. I worked with people I admired, people who respected art, people who were willing to work all night to make it look right. I do still remember the thrill of helping to coax my first masterpiece out of a crate. It was a real Mondrian and valued at more money than I would ever make in this life or the next.

"Be careful, be careful, be careful. Jesus, it's beautiful. Jesus, go slow, be gentle, watch out, go slow. Goddamn it, be careful. Oh, look, it's alive."

But over time, it just wasn't enough for me—the art or the money or the communal effort. We forgot what we were there for. We forgot art wasn't sacrament to 99 percent of the world. We got pompous and self-important. We lost our balance and forgot our way home. We became precious, we forgot who we were, and largely—those of us who had any to begin with—we lost our sense of humor.

"I think you are particularly well suited to working in an asylum, Ellen," Margaret said. "You were weaned on smoke and mirrors, and you know, Ellen, I think pulling the impossible off at the very last minute is the only way you know how to feel alive."

We did do that. We pulled it off, every time, exhibition after exhibition, eight times a year, year after year. The shows looked fucking fabulous, and when they opened, everybody got to collapse, except me. I had to organize the docent tours, watch the security guards watch the art, clip the press, plan the next show, and work out a deal on catalog distribution. I never got an afternoon nap in Prep-aration. I never got to go down to Kemah in the museum van and eat seafood right off the boat.

"You've got to relax, Ellen," Grace said. "You can't quit your job now. You owe a fortune, and you're having exploratory surgery on Thursday."

"Jesus, Grace, I'm not stupid," I told her. "I'm not going to quit my job, at least not this afternoon. But let me tell you something: If I live through this, I'm going to get my life back. I don't know how I got here. I'm a painter, not a goddamned bureaucrat. I took the wrong turn at the corner, I wasn't paying attention, I'm not doing anything I want. I'm not painting, Grace, and menopause is coming. This is not at all what I had in mind for my life, and I'm telling you, I'm not going to become one of those women who takes it as it comes and dies wondering how it all got away from her. And listen, Grace, I don't think I'm *ever* going to relax."

"Beyond painting a dozen or so masterpieces, Ellen, exactly what do you want?" Margaret asked.

"I want to see Venice. And I want a child."

My first concern, however, was whether I was going to die. Sam thought I'd live, and I had nothing to trust but his instincts. I was terrified.

"My feeling is that it's a large cystic mass that's probably damaged your left ovary, if not destroyed it completely. We're lucky to find it, Ellen. Sometimes they rupture, and then everything is at risk. It would surprise me if it was malignant, but we can't rule that out. We're going to look around, and we need to get in there pretty quick. You want Methodist or St. Luke's Episcopal?"

"St. Luke's," I told him without even thinking, and I could see my mother and every Sunday School teacher I ever had nudge each other in the ribs and beam.

I woke up Thursday night to the sound of Kenneth's voice.

"Hello, Red," he said. "You still mad at me?"

They were all there: Kenneth; Grace; Laurel; Judith; Ben; my sister, Ruthie; Elliot; Joe. Alice was in Europe but sent a wire. Margaret had been by, Henry called—Antonio and the shop crew wanted to know if I needed blood—and Laurel brought me a starched linen pillowcase still warm from the iron. There were flowers everywhere, some balloons, and a jumbo box of Junior Mints. The "MacNeil/Lehrer News-Hour" was on; these people watch the evening news no matter what.

"Am I all right?"

"You're perfect, baby," Kenneth said.

"Yuck," Ruthie said.

She'd been perched on the windowsill since I got out of recovery. She'd been telling her version of family secrets nonstop since one o'clock, trying to get me to come around and argue the significant details. She had them all wrong.

"What's *he* doing here, Ellen?" Ruthie said. "I thought we hated him."

The others thought so, too. Nobody gets it about me and Kenneth. They couldn't understand why he brought me a sack of pumpkins.

"It's not even October. We don't think he's all there, Ellen."

The surgery went well. The left ovary was destroyed—they had to take it—but the right one was all right. Only Sam did find a tumor he wasn't expecting.

"It was attached to your uterus. It was about the size of a Japanese eggplant. It was floating on a stem. I never saw anything like it. We took slides."

The ultrasound hadn't picked the tumor up; the cystic stuff masked everything. It turned out to be benign, and Sam's slides were pretty good.

"What about children?" I asked Sam in front of everybody. "Can I have any? Tell me the truth."

"You're healthier now with one good ovary than you ever were before, Ellen. But I have to tell you, the tumor was a surprise. There might be others later. I'd get after it if I were you. You're not getting any younger."

Every head in the room turned to Kenneth, but he's always had great timing and must have felt it coming. He hates pressure. He's gone. We stare at the door wheezing to a full close, listen to the sound of boots on linoleum fading away down the hall.

"Any bets on Kenneth's final divorce decree?" Ruthie said from the windows.

She didn't get even one taker.

8

Filigree

I heard about the sack of pumpkins, Ellen.
I don't get it.

It's not important, Margaret.

What are you trying to hide?

It was a joke, Margaret.

I like jokes. Tell me.

I like pumpkins. Kenneth knows. That's all there is to it.

And you think that's funny?

Kenneth has a gift for giving me things that please me. I like odd things.

There's more to this, isn't there? What is it?

Look, it's not such a hot story. It's actually sort of stupid. It's a stupid story about me.

So? It's good to know you're not perfect, Ellen.

Okay, okay. The first time I met Tenny, it was almost Halloween. It was the year before my surgery, in 1979, and she was three years old. Kenneth invited me over to his apartment for the formal meeting, and I brought her a pumpkin.

I bet she liked that.

No, she hated it. She hated me, too. She said she already had a pumpkin. She said her daddy had bought her the best pumpkin in Texas, and she didn't need any others.

Well, children can be difficult. It couldn't have been an easy time for her.

I don't think Tenny has ever had an easy time.

So?

So Kenneth said, "Let's carve them up." I took one and the kitchen, he took the other and the porch. Tenny ran back and forth, back and forth, and I got a little crazy.

How's that?

Understand: I was pretty nervous. I hadn't been around kids much, and Tenny was a shock up close. I got a little obsessive about my pumpkin. I was working in a strange kitchen with knives that were not the best, so I started using this Exacto knife I had with me. It got a little out of control.

Did anybody get hurt?

No, but by the time I had finished, I had carved the whole thing away. It didn't even have a face. It was totally abstracted, all light, bizarre. It was like one of those paper snowflakes in the round. You'd really have to think filigree to get the full effect.

That doesn't sound so bad.

Well, it wasn't. I actually thought it pretty terrific until I saw Kenneth's.

What?

Kenneth's pumpkin. He hadn't even used a knife. He took a hammer and knocked out two eyes and a mouth. It took him about a minute, I worked on mine for two hours. His was crude and ugly and leering, positively inspired, incredible. Mine looked like lingerie. His looked like German Expressionism.

A difficult moment for you, Ellen?

Yes, I hate competition. His was better, I had to tell him, and he didn't even know who Edvard Munch was.

You hate competition?

Oh, competition's not so bad. Losing's what's lousy.

So?

So we put them in the window, and I left. Then Tenny ran out to my car and told me she liked mine better but didn't want to hurt her father's feelings.

Well, that sounds like a good beginning.

Well, I was just glad I didn't run over her. It was pitch dark in that parking lot, and she was really little then.

So that's how it all started?

Started? Oh, no, that was just one of the phases. It didn't last. Right after the pumpkin thing, Kenneth and I had a big fight about flat tires, and I hadn't seen him in almost a year when he showed up at the hospital.

How did he know you were there?

I don't know. Kenneth just shows up. He has great timing. He thinks we're destiny.

What do you think?

I think that's funny.

So you enjoyed the sack of pumpkins?

Yes. There were six of them—small and pretty ugly, it was early in the season—and in the bottom of the sack there was a set of jeweler's tools: little hammers, little files, little screwdrivers. I love tools. Kenneth knows.

I see.

The nurses were really glad to see me go home on Sunday. They were beginning to draw bugs.

You could have told me about the pumpkin thing, Ellen. You never told me anything good about Kenneth.

You know, Margaret, I think the pumpkin thing falls right over the edge into sentimentality. It's actually drowning in sentimentality, full-blown and smacking, thick as syrup sentimentality. It makes my teeth ache to talk about it, and listen, I never kept anything important from you.

You kept Kenneth away from everyone you know for years, Ellen. Just what do you make of that? Don't you think your friends knew what you were doing when you disappeared for weeks on end? They knew you weren't painting, Ellen. They knew you weren't catching up on your rest. You were with him, with Kenneth, cutting up pumpkins and screwing in some hot tub in Galveston. How come you kept him in the closet for so long, Ellen? What were you trying to hide?

9

Pancakes

Kenneth's real mother put him up for adoption when he was ten months old. Catholics handled the paperwork. A foster family took him in, changed his name, and beat him with wooden spoons. Kenneth learned early on to keep his mouth shut, his mind closed to most opinion, abusive and otherwise. He developed an interior life based on his own noise—which was music—and he got away. At seventeen, he joined the air force, spent a couple of years in Korea, and then came to Texas with a set of drums, a red Gibson guitar, and a box of yellowing photographs. That was in 1967. He was twenty-one years old.

"Who are these people, Kenneth? Who is this woman in the angora sweater?"

"That's my mother, Ellen. That is my real mother."

"Jesus, she looks just like Tenny, Kenneth. What was her name?"

"Louise."

"And who are all these other people?"

"I don't know. I don't know their names, Ellen. They're my family."

Kenneth's foster mother gave him the photographs on his seventeenth birthday and told him never to come back.

"She said that? She said never come back? Did she mean it?"

"She said I was the worst Catholic boy she'd ever seen or heard about. She said she didn't appreciate me leaving her after all she'd done for me. I can still hear her saying that. I can still see her mouth open and close, saying all of that."

"Well, what about your father, Kenneth? Your real father? Do you know who he was? What about your adopted father? Where was he in all this?"

"I couldn't find out anything about my real father, and Harry went to Vegas when I was about six and never came back."

"He never tried to contact you?"

"No, but the Red Cross got me word in Korea that he had died. I called my mother. She said he was always a sorry son-of-a-bitch and was going to hell anyway."

"So you have talked to your mother since you left?"

"Just that one time."

"She doesn't even know about Tenny?"

"No."

"Does your real mother know about Tenny?"

"She's dead, Ellen. She died a couple of years ago. Cancer. I never got to meet her."

"Jesus Christ, Ellen," Margaret says all the time. "Of all the men out there in the world, why did you have to pick Kenneth Goodson? He has possibly the worst family of origin history I've ever heard. He's completely shut down. There are some things people just can't get over, Ellen. The abandoned, abandon. You ought to know that by now."

"You know, Ellen, I just can't believe your shrink talks to you like that," Elliot said. "Margaret's jargon is nearly understandable, and she's so overt. They're supposed to be subtle and nondirective and at least vague. It always sounds to me like you're in therapy with Adolf Hitler. Honestly, Ellen, I don't know of any shrink in this country who would say what Margaret says to you, a paying customer."

"Well, Jesus, Elliot, you don't think I'd go to just any ordinary shrink, do you? You want her phone number? She's just like every authority figure I've ever known: loud and opinionated and pushy. I'm working this authority stuff out in doses, and I've almost got it knocked. I'm almost cooked, Elliot."

"Well, does Margaret know this?"

"Oh, Elliot. Margaret doesn't know shit."

"Kenneth's not living in the real world, Ellen. After all this time, he can't even get a credit card, much less a divorce. He's arrested in time. Kenneth thinks he's still nineteen years old and is going to live forever on three hundred bucks a week. You're never going to Ireland with that guy, Ellen."

Three hundred dollars is a fat week for Kenneth, but I don't point this out to Margaret. She's against him, always has been. She thinks if I was going to choose to have a baby, I might as well choose a father for my child who could give us a little more than the second verse lyrics to old Beach Boys songs. In the main, really—it's been clear for some time now—Margaret's for money and legitimacy.

"There's not a thing wrong with money, Ellen," my friend Laurel says. "You sure know how to spend it. How much did that black linen suit cost anyway?"

"I got a good eye, Laurel. It was on sale," I tell her, and I decide I'm going to let her buy lunch for her narrow remarks. "You just don't get it about Kenneth, Laurel. Nobody does. And if you think Evan's so hot, you marry him."

It is true I like money. I spend it better than anybody I know—I like good stuff, beautiful things that last, nothing trendy—but I don't form close relationships based on cash availability. This, however, appears to be a minority view.

For one thing, I really like having my own money and not having to account for how I spend it. I've deposited a paycheck at the bank every two weeks since I was seventeen years old. I go in person, during regular banking hours. I wave at the loan officers, I know all the names of the tellers' children and grandchildren, but I keep my deposit slip copies in date order just in case they make a posting error.

"Don't bank by mail ever, and don't use the night deposit box," my father told me all my life. "You never know when you might need to get a loan from one of those bloodsuckers. You're laying groundwork here, honey. You work, you put your money in a good bank, and you let those assholes know you do it regular."

I found this to be good advice on the whole. I do it. I hardly ever use the night deposit box, and I rejected in a flat second the museum's offer for direct deposit of my checks. I work hard, I earn my own money, I spend it as I like. Nobody tells me when to move. Nobody messes with my toaster setting. I change the furniture around when I want, and I don't compromise with anybody on Christmas trees—the kind or the price, or whether to have one at all.

I'd like to have more, of course, more money. Who wouldn't? It's why I keep sending in those sweepstakes coupons, but I'd never be willing to give up my soul for cash liquidity.

You live off somebody else's bucks, you pay for it every day. I'm not talking about just blow jobs here. I'm talking about the dinner parties you've got to yawn through, the charity receptions you've got to pretend to host, the shirts you've got to drop by the laundry. I know a lot of marriages based on economics, and I can't imagine a more miserable life. I watch dinner parties progress; I eavesdrop in powder rooms. I know how it really is.

Evan was rich. He would have married me anytime, and I could have quit my job at the museum. He would have built me a studio with north-light exposure, bought me full-spectrum fluorescents, gotten some graduate student to make me cedar stretchers. I could have painted full time, but I would have paid double for all of it, every day until he died, and he was healthy for fifty-five.

"It's not so bad," Laurel says. "Colin and I are spending Christmas in London this year. Don't you like Dickens, Ellen?"

I don't actually. I'm not crazy about much that's British. But if it was Dublin for Christmas, well, that would be something else entirely. It would hurt to turn down an offer for Ireland, but I'm pretty sure I would do it. I could hold off on black linen suits for a while and take myself there. It's better that way—getting what you really want for yourself and not having to be fucking thankful to anybody.

I would love to be in Ireland with Kenneth. We travel well together, and that's not nothing in the scale of things. He loves looking at junk—he has a great feel for depression glass—and he likes room service in fancy hotels as much as I do. He chokes, of course, on how much this costs. It takes him a minute to recover from reading the room rate sign on the back of the door. But the deal is, he recovers. Kenneth doesn't dwell on the ridiculous.

The thing that nobody seemed to understand was, I didn't need to be married. I started thinking about having a baby, talking about it actively over lunch, and everybody started thinking I wanted to get married. I don't know where they got this idea.

About marriage, I did that already. It was ridiculous. I'm no good at bridge and Thanksgiving turkeys and mingling assets. Mine was short-lived—just two years between undergraduate and graduate school—and I lost a great American Empire settee in the property settlement. I didn't need to do that again, I didn't want to do that again, but what I did want—and I was very clear on this point—was for Kenneth to get his divorce so Raylene would quit calling us in the middle of the night when she couldn't get her car started.

"They've got this great organization called AAA, Kenneth. I'll go in with you on a lifetime membership for Raylene."

"I gave her one for her birthday, Ellen. She lost the card. I've got to go. She's at the Galleria, and Tenny's asleep on the backseat."

He crawls out of my bed and pulls on his jeans. I can't believe this; it's Gothic.

"It's one o'clock in the morning, Kenneth. How did she know you were here? How did she get my phone number? What's still open at the Galleria?"

"Raylene's not stupid. She knows where I want to be. I'll be back. Okay, Red?"

"Take your time, sweetheart honey. The door'll be locked."

I've known Kenneth for years, and it has never been smooth. We've had at least a dozen separate relationships, none of them lasting more than six months, and some of them didn't even make it through a full weekend. From the bar, I've watched him play at dives too seedy to even discuss. I've watched him walk out through any number of doors and was glad to see him go.

Kenneth and I see the world completely differently. We argue about everything, or more specifically, I point out his obvious and not-so-obvious behavioral inconsistencies in a heated tone, and Kenneth walks.

"How come you jump every time Raylene calls, Kenneth? You're Tenny's father, not the goddamned baby-sitter. Isn't this supposed to be Raylene's weekend?"

"I'm not the goddamned baby-sitter, Ellen. I'm Tenny's father. I want to be with her as much as I can, and I don't care what Raylene or anybody else thinks about it."

"She can't take Tenny away from you, Kenneth. You've got to quit believing that. You're a good man; you're a good father. You've got rights. Will you call this Bradley and Joan?"

"I've got to go now, Ellen."

"You don't want a divorce, do you, Kenneth?"

"I'll call you, Ellen," and he does in six weeks or so. I hang up on him. He calls right back.

We have had a number of large-scale public fights. He stood me up one July weekend at a condo on West Beach—he didn't want to go but didn't want to tell me—and I drove back to Houston at ninety miles an hour and smashed up his apartment.

"Why did you do that to all of Daddy's dishes, Ellen?" Tenny asked me. She wasn't there. I don't see any reason why she should have known about this.

"I was mad as hell with your dad," I told her. "That happens sometimes with adults. And I didn't break everything, Tenny. I just smashed up the stuff I'd given him and took my painting back."

"What happened to you when the police came? Did they take you to prison?"

The police didn't come. It was just two coffee mugs—Newport blue, Kenneth's favorite—and a Chemex coffeepot.

"The police didn't come, Tenny. Where did you get that idea?"

"They came when Mom did that at Dad's. I didn't think I'd ever see her again."

I've lived in Houston for nearly fifteen years, and I must know a thousand people on a first-name basis. That's museums for you. You hang around exhibition openings, you can meet hundreds of people you don't care a thing about. It's the cheap wine, which is free or should be; it draws the shallow but well groomed. These people just keep coming in the door, opening after opening. They don't care a thing about the art on the walls; they're just hoping to see their names in bold print in the society columns.

You smile—because that's your job—but you can forget their names because they'll remind you who they are. You have to flip the lights a couple of times to get them to leave, and when they do, they hold on to your elbow, buss you on the cheek, say they'd really like to have lunch sometime soon. Don't lose any sleep here. It doesn't mean anything. They'll never call.

Then there's about fifty people I like, and about fifteen, maybe twenty I really like. I'd give blood for any one of them, and I have when my weight's up. Any one of them would come help me change a tire.

Then there's this eight—Grace and Laurel; my sister, Ruthie; Ben; Joe; Alice; Judith; Elliot. I've got years invested in these people. Most of them work in art somehow, although Laurel's a banker and ought to know better, and Ruthie works at Sunset Animal Clinic but wants to be a singer.

It's not a group thing. I see them separately, alone or in pairs, usually over food. They all know each other, but they don't all like each other—my birthday dinners were difficult for everybody, so we quit doing that—but any one of them could blackmail me easy and might, if I didn't have counterdata.

I depend on these people, they depend on me. They're more my family than my family will ever be. Nobody takes advantage, but nobody minces opinions. We're going to bury each other, if we don't fall out of love over lunch some Friday.

But then there is Kenneth. He fits in no group. We stay inside mostly, my apartment usually, sometimes his if it's a Tenny night. We don't get out in the real world much. We don't go to dinner parties, and we don't go to many movies. I cook, or he does. Nobody knows him—most of the eight had never even met him until the surgery— but they've all got their theories.

"Is it just the sex?" Margaret asks.

"It's got to be the sex," Laurel says. "It's the only thing that makes any sense. I hope it lasts, Ellen. It never did for me. You're sure throwing away easy money in breaking Evan's heart. He'd do anything for you, Ellen."

Evan might have done anything for me. He was basically a kind man, generous, intelligent. He was a biochemist and held an endowed chair at Baylor Med. He was always working on significant projects, and he voted the right way.

"Evan was rich, Ellen," Laurel said. "He gave you great jewelry, and he adored you."

"Well, he didn't know shit about art, Laurel. He thought you could explain it. I told him a hundred times there was only so much words could handle. He never did get it."

Figuring out the unknown was Evan's life's work. He listened, bought dinner, and did give me jewelry. I'm not the jewelry type exactly—nobody ever did that—but it was lovely stuff. Antique bracelets mostly—old silver, Chilean copper, luminous patinas.

"Marry me," he said.

"Let me think about it," I said and went to Venice alone.

Evan would do anything for me except agree to have a child with me. I didn't blame him. He was fifty-five years old, he had three kids already and two-thirds of them hated me. His oldest was four years younger than I was.

"My home is yours," Evan said. "We could build your studio back behind the Jacuzzi. Would you like to meet my children?"

I loved his youngest son the minute I met him. He was a biochemist, too, and building a house outside of San Antonio. He worked on it nights and weekends, did almost all the heavy construction himself.

"Stuart's got a good sense of design, Evan. Why isn't he an architect? This room reminds me of your old house, the pictures you showed me. You know, the house where they all grew up, the house you sold after your divorce. Just look at the pitch on these ceilings, the southeast orientation. Look at those great red violet azaleas he's planted at the windows."

At dinner, we sat at a round table, the best in the restaurant, which was the reported best in San Antonio. I was between Stuart and Evan, the other two—another son I didn't much care for and a daughter I couldn't read—and their spouses took seats to the right of their father. It's how they always sit. I was in the mother's place, and they were watching my table manners.

Evan said, "You know, Stuart, I took Ellen out to your site today. It struck me how much your living room is like our old one on Crescent Drive. Are you doing that on purpose, or are you even aware of it, son?"

Evan's daughter, Tracy, refused any wine and said, "I don't want to steal any of your thunder here, Dad, but I want to tell you that I'm pregnant again. I'm in my second month, and the doctor says it looks like I might be able to carry this one all the way through."

We raised our ice waters to Tracy and her husband, Hank—who never said one word throughout the entire meal—and then we toasted Grandpa, who got up to pay the check. There was never any question who would pay. Evan always pays. Nobody even brought the matter up.

I didn't feel so good about any of this. This is what it could be like. A good round table for eight plus a high chair, my insights continually getting recredited. What would Evan's grandbaby want to call me? When would Evan start expecting me to keep his wallet in my purse?

And then, when Evan's away clearing the bill, but we all know he's in the men's room—he's got a weak bladder—his eldest son, Stephen, leans forward on his chair and asks me what my intentions are.

"He appears to adore you, Eleanor. Isn't that your name? We worry he's going to make another mistake like he did with his second wife. You could talk him into having a baby. He'd do anything for you. Are you going to press him?"

I stand up and slip off the bracelets. I leave them by my salad plate, trust that Stuart will take care of them.

"Get out of Texas, Stuart. Apply to architecture school at Yale. Rice is good, too, but I think you really need to get out of state. And good luck to you, Tracy. I'm going to be thinking of you and Hank next November. And Stephen, you can just fuck yourself, and I think you'd be very good at that."

In the foyer of the restaurant, Evan held me by the elbow, a little too tight. There was a yellow bruise the next day.

"Marry me," he said. "Stephen's always been a jerk."

"He is that, Evan, but he loves you. I don't enough."

"Let me come with you to Venice."

"No."

"Then I'll meet you in Rome. We can get a car and drive north to Florence. I've always wanted to do that."

I've *always* wanted to do that. I love everything about central Italy, and I'd never seen the country part except through a train window. I agreed to meet him in Rome and drive to Florence, a city more than special to me. It was doomed, a mistake. What it was, was the perfect solution.

When Evan gets away from Texas, he gets clingy. He was on me like glue all through the Uffizi. He drove me nuts wanting me to explain Botticelli, Fra Angelico.

"Just *look*, Evan. It's all there in the painting, and can you keep your voice down?"

He couldn't read a map, he couldn't drive a stick shift—understand: I didn't care, he did—and he was in a near tantrum the whole time, suspicious of the food and the prices. He wouldn't discuss letting me pay for dinner, the hotel (where they knew him because he had honeymooned there with his second wife—the concierge told me they fought *all* the time), and he was jealous of every postcard I sent.

"Why do you need all those people if you've got me? Are you afraid of intimacy? I think you've got a sick thing about your father, Ellen."

In an open market outside of Florence he bought a little straw hat for the grandbaby coming. It was a perfect half-sphere, a round bowler with a turned-up brim, a navy blue ribbon hanging down the back. It smelled like new hay. It was a great hat, perfect and worth every bit of the price even before the haggling, which went way beyond the necessary, I thought.

Evan was afraid the hat would get crushed, so he didn't pack it with his real luggage. He carried it and his new leather briefcase with him on the plane. He held that little hat all the way home. He kept admiring it, turning it in his hands.

"Is this a great hat or what?"

It was a great hat. I couldn't keep my eyes off it, and it was a very long flight.

"Marry me," Evan said outside of Customs. "We'll have a baby if you want."

"No," I said and took a cab home. I was never more certain of anything in my life. It was the last time I was that certain of anything.

Evan called a couple of times, sent white tulips to the museum, wrote me letters. I had a drink with him at the Warwick Hotel bar to explain it again. He's not stupid. He finally bought what I had to say—which was, "Not on your life would I ever marry you"—and I let him take care of the tab. I wished him good luck, and I meant it, and within the year I heard he had married a dancer from the Dallas City Ballet.

"I saw them at the Science Museum ball," Laurel told me. "She's gorgeous, but I don't think she's even twenty-five. They're remodeling that house and planning on July in Spain. Any regrets, Ellen?"

"Not even one, Laurel. I never liked Spain much."

"Okay, Ellen," Margaret said. "I understand Evan would smother you. He would try to control your life, and you don't want to be an orna-ment on anybody's arm. I get it, Ellen. I support your decision to dump him, but was he your only other real choice?"

Look, it was 1982, I was nearly thirty-four years old then, and while that sounds a lot younger now than it used to, I just didn't figure I had the time to research any new men. It takes too long to find out how they really are.

First, you've got to find a fairly good one, and that's never easy. Then, you've got to study them and their habits. With a smooth one, it could take months before you're clear that a life with them would mean raking their dirty socks off the table every day before you sat down to eat. You understand after watching for a while that you'd be listening to them bitch about their tax brackets every single April. You'll be wincing on a regular basis when they call you by their first (sometimes second) wife's name in their sleep, this after you've been witness to them drink too much single-malted scotch while they watch "Wall $treet Week" every blasted Friday night. You'll be spending every holiday with their friends and family, people who are always going to outweigh you in history and anecdote, people who largely would just as soon see you die as live.

"Not everybody with money's a Republican, Ellen," Laurel says.

"No? Well, how come they all act like it then?"

Artificial insemination was my other choice. I was going to be thirty-four years old in November, and I couldn't wait any longer for any man I knew or might meet suddenly to get over it—whatever *it* was—and come around.

"Ellen, you do whatever you want," Alice said. "I know you will anyway, but I've got to tell you I think you're overreacting a little here. You're only thirty-four years old. You've got a lot of time left, honey."

Alice has been married twice and has three grown children herself. I like Alice, I listen when she talks, then I do what I want and pay for it for a long time.

"Look, Alice, I know I could skate along for another five years or so with getting hysterical. I really think that danger business about having children once you're past thirty-five is a lot of hype. But see, I've only got *one* ovary now. What if something happens to that one? I've just got to move on this baby thing."

"Okay, but are you sure it's over with Evan?"

"Absolutely, Alice. Why are you asking?"

"I thought I'd call him for lunch. Would you mind?"

Understand: There was not a thing frivolous about this baby business for me. It was no notion of the moment, a quirky reaction to Sam's diagnosis, the aftershock from that surgery. I always wanted a child, I just hadn't had the energy to consider when and how I was going to do it. The surgery stuff pushed me off the fence. I quit talking about it over lunch, and I started looking into the matter. And I was damn thorough.

I spent two years reading everything written on the subject of children—conceiving, birthing, raising, the works. I talked to parents, day care centers, pediatricians, pharmacists, lawyers. I read everything Marie Montessori had to say (in translation and in the original Italian), and I also read Piaget, Bettelheim, Brazelton, Spock, and Leach. I made a will, named Ruthie and Grace as custodians of any offspring or extra money. I bought serious life insurance, and I rented a safe-deposit box for the birth certificate and the shot records. I collected data, I had boxes of the stuff everywhere—I'm good on research. I was going to have a child somehow, providing my body (which I took swimming every day) would cooperate. I hate regular exercise—all that jock junk, particularly swimming—but I did twelve laps anyway in the Rice gym pool. I wasn't going to miss it if there was a thing I could do about it.

"Do it anyway you want, Ellen," my father said. "I wish your mother and I had had a hundred kids. Just know that I'll love the little bastard however he gets here, but just do it and quit talking about it. And listen, I can't tell you how relieved your mother is that you're finished with that old fart."

Too many women I know wanted children and missed it. They let their lives get away from them, they stayed too busy. They got too old, they didn't take care of themselves. They stayed too rigid about how it had to be, they married the wrong man, they didn't want children enough in the first place and didn't know how to admit it. I'm no traditionalist anyway, I don't care what anybody thinks about me, and while I'd prefer a good man in my life, the absence of one didn't mean I couldn't have what I wanted, did it?

"Does it? Is there only one way to do this?" I asked everybody I knew.

"It wouldn't work if you were a banker," Laurel told me, "but you're so odd anyway, Ellen. Do it, sweetie. I wish I could, but I'm from Mississippi, and I just can't work traditional methodology out of my system. You'll be a great mother, Ellen. Do it."

Judith and Elliot particularly thought artificial insemination was the way to go. Without a known father, you don't have to deal with their rights, and I appreciated this position. I watched Kenneth too many years have to share Tenny with Raylene on Christmas Day.

"You know this means jelly on the kitchen table for fifteen or so years?" Ben said.

"Jelly? Jesus, Ben, I'd never feed my child jelly. What kind of person do you think I am anyway?"

Sam was arranging for the artificial insemination business. He explained the genetic risks—you don't really know what you're getting, some medical student's done this for cash—and had me keep temperature charts for three months to track my ovulation cycle.

"Let's try it the Monday after Thanksgiving weekend, Ellen. Are you still sure this is the way you want to go?"

"What are my chances for conception on Monday, Sam?"

"Pretty good for your age: sixty-five percent, maybe seventy. We can't be completely sure, Ellen. Some of it's still magic, you know. Monday? Are you sure this is what you want?"

"Monday," I said. "I'm positive about this, Sam, but thanks for asking."

I was ready. I didn't want to talk about it anymore. I had cleared up half of my debt, and I even had a little savings. I paid my car note off early, and I doubled up on the last of my graduate school loan payments. The way I figured it, I had eight weeks of vacation coming, another four weeks of maternity leave, another three of sick time. If the baby was born in late July or early August, I could be back at work by the middle of October easy and never miss a check.

"Don't worry about any of it, Ellen," Henry said. "I've got nephews; I like kids. I'll tell the board something, but I don't think they'll care really. You'll answer your phone, won't you? Judith knows what you do, doesn't she? What is it that you actually do anyway, Ellen?"

I changed my life. I got ready. I didn't buy anything for myself for eighteen months, and I was looking in to rent houses. A child needs a yard and a dog and a playhouse. Moving was the only thing I wasn't looking forward to, but I was saving boxes.

I left Sam's office late on Wednesday afternoon, and in the car I decided to buy veal for Thanksgiving dinner. I was going to paint through the four-day weekend and then get pregnant on Monday. I was prepared, and I felt lucky, and it would have gone that way, too, if I hadn't run into Kenneth at the grocery store.

"You can't do it like this, Ellen. It's not right."

"What is this, Kenneth? Some Catholic flashback? I'm ready, I want this, I'm tired of waiting on romance. Good-bye, and I mean it this time," and I left him standing there with a loaf of white bread and a jar of grape jelly he was buying for Tenny's lunches.

I've been in love with Kenneth Goodson for years and years, and I've tried to fall out a hundred times. He's not good for me from any practical point of view. He's screwed up, he's married, he's got this kid who's nuts. He doesn't have any money, and he's not worried about it. Kenneth doesn't worry about anything. We don't have a thing in common except red hair, and he doesn't have hardly any left, and mine's not even red and actually never has been.

"How did you meet him anyway, Ellen?" everybody wanted to know. "You've never told us. You never tell us anything anymore, Ellen."

I met Kenneth Joseph Goodson in an elevator in 1976. I'd just had a root canal and wasn't feeling too hot. I wanted to get home and sleep for about six years; I was still buzzy from the drugs.

I got on the elevator, and Muzak was playing—the Beatles' "You

Say It's Your Birthday"—except it wasn't the Beatles playing. It was 101 Strings, that violin band.

There was this guy with long red hair in the elevator already. He was whistling along with the Strings and didn't even stop when I got on. He did nod at me, smiled my way. He had on jeans and an Astros cap, and he was carrying a black briefcase. I took my hand off my jaw and listened. I thought he was cute.

I recognized that tune in five notes and said, "Can you believe They are playing our music now?"

And he said, "I think real success would be to get on some elevator in Portugal and hear a song you wrote come crackling out of bad speakers."

I found this to be a remarkable retort, if somewhat wrong-headed.

"But it's 101 Strings. You want some pap band playing your songs? Where are your standards?"

"I'd like anybody to play my songs," he said. "Imagine anybody actually remembering your lyric and humming along."

Then the elevator lurched or stumbled or whatever elevators do when they're trying to kill you.

"Just think of this," I said. "Whoever installed this thing got the job because they were low bid."

And then I blacked out, fainted dead away, the first and only time I've ever done that in my life. I figured later it was the drugs from the root canal, the lurch of the elevator, not eating breakfast, something. I passed out; I actually saw stars. I fell forward, right into this stranger who I thought might or might not be a moron.

When I came to, I was still in the elevator, but flat on the floor, my head propped up against what I thought was a briefcase but was actually Kenneth's guitar case. He was still there, sitting on the floor with me, still whistling.

"So," he said, "you come here often?"

I've been very successful at keeping Kenneth out of my daily life for whole periods of time, years even. I've dated a fair number of men. I've lived with a few. I've traveled a lot, and I've sat in the mother seat at any number of dinner parties. I'm a monogamous person really. My adult sexual involvements have been sequential usually, not concurrent. I've been happy, unhappy with men—the basic female stuff—but on the whole, while holidays can be tough, I'd rather be alone than sleep alongside an asshole with an American Express Gold who holds me by the elbow.

"You sure know how to make your life hard for yourself, Ellen," Margaret says. "You live on extremes, and they are going to kill you."

"Couldn't you have done it the easy way just once?" Laurel said. "Evan would have been so easy, Ellen, and I just can't understand why you didn't keep those bracelets."

"She can't do it," Grace said. "She can't do anything the easy way. It's got to be close to impossible for Ellen to even consider it. She thrives on complication, don't you know that? It's got to be the sex, at least that's what I think. And Laurel, she never liked those brace-lets anyway."

Listen, I don't have stupid friends. Of course it was the sex. Ken-neth is a wonderful lover. When we make love, that's all that's going on. When Kenneth is there, there in my house, there in my white iron bed, he's there, really there, 100 percent. His mind's on nothing else but what we're doing, which is all about pleasure and just forgetting about the time and everything else. We're talking about full-strength pleasure here. Nothing is diluted with a thing of the mundane.

Making love with Kenneth is full and complete, fast and slow, as close as our bodies and imaginations can take us. It is us. It is all about us, us together. We are in a houseboat floating untethered in the middle of a smooth, cool lake. We have everything we need, we don't need anything else. It is quiet, extraordinarily quiet, the mer-est hint of a cooling breeze, but it is also exciting, and known, and still brand new and often pretty hot. We can get out and dance on that lake. We do that quite often. It is that safe, our lake. We are that graceful.

When Kenneth is there—which was more than anybody ever real-ized—he is there. We've made love a thousand times, probably more, but it is still a surprise what a pleasure it is. It is not just the sex. It is the before and the after and the again. I love Kenneth, I always have. He is fresh air running through my heart. He is the yes everyone is looking for, and I myself have always been glad to see him.

· · ·

"So, we have to know, Ellen: After your little nineteenth-century number in the elevator—a swoon, for Christ's sake, *really*, Ellen—what happened? You check into a motel? What sort of motel did you check into? How sleezy a motel was it? We've got to know, Ellen."

"We went for pancakes."

"Just who in the hell do you think you're talking to, Ellen? Come on. Jesus Christ, *pancakes?*"

I needed to eat something. I was still light-headed, and I didn't think I should drive.

"I'll drive you home," Kenneth said.

Despite what we'd been through—Kenneth, a total stranger, catching my head so it didn't splinter—I wasn't too sure I wanted this guy to know where I lived. We rode up and down half a dozen times and discussed it.

"I'm a married man, if that makes you feel any better."

"That doesn't make me feel any better."

"I'm not a happily married man."

"That doesn't make me feel any better."

"Look, I'm practically bald. I am actually completely bald on the top where it actually counts. I am a bald man. I am impotent. I am a bald, impotent man with a sad past. You don't have to worry about a thing."

"I could just call a cab."

"Okay. I'm a bald, impotent man with amnesia."

We were both still on the floor of the elevator. It stopped to let somebody on, and Kenneth said, "We're having an emergency here. You can't ride now," and then he pressed Close. We left people with their mouths open.

"I think I just need to eat something."

"Have you got your legs back? Can you stand up?"

"I never had legs. I have sticks for legs. I always wanted Legs."

"They look pretty good to me. Do you think you can eat with your mouth like that?"

We went to this coffee shop across the street and got a table for three: me, Kenneth, and his Gibson. We drank a lot of coffee and several milk shakes. We pushed pancakes around on our plates, and we talked. We talked about his crazy and surprisingly pregnant wife and my crazy and not surprisingly stupid ex-husband. We talked about

abstract expressionism and rock and roll, medieval manuscript illumi-
nation and why Bruce Springsteen should simply be locked up. We
found out a lot of things about each other—we're more alike than
anybody knows: We have the same clock, for example; we both prefer
working nights—but we didn't make love for four years. We didn't
take the obvious road. We became unlikely friends, running into each
other accidentally and on purpose for years. It was hard on both of us,
but nobody is ever going to believe it.

"We don't believe a word of that abstinence crap, Ellen. You've
never abstained from anything you've ever wanted in your life, and
despite what you say, you two don't have a thing in common really.
You must spend all your time defining terms and explaining yourself."

I don't have to explain anything important to Kenneth. He understands as much as anybody can about needing to work, wanting to
make art, and having to make money. He doesn't know much about
painting, but he's got a good eye basically. He understands that a lot
more goes on than what you finally see. But he's not interested in *how*
I do it. He's interested in *if* I do it. He knows what a jackass I can be
when I haven't painted in a while, when I'm working too hard on
something else, some show at the museum.

"You're not working, are you, Ellen? You're getting sharp with
waiters again."

He's always right about this. I'm a first-class bitch if I don't get into
the studio—which is my other bedroom—every couple of days or so.
But other than this reminder, Kenneth doesn't comment on my behavior. I can do anything I want. I don't have to take care of him. He
does his own laundry. I don't have to sit at the bar and watch him play
unless I want to, and I don't need to be jealous of anything or anybody, except maybe Tenny.

"I want to be the father of your child," Kenneth told me through my
car window that Wednesday before Thanksgiving. "I want to be with
you, Ellen. I want to raise a child with you."

He left his groceries—his Thanksgiving turkey in the child's seat of
his shopping cart—and followed me out of the store and into the
parking lot of the Dunlavy Safeway.

"You're just being dramatic, Kenneth," I told him. "You know I hate grandstanding. Get away from my car. I can't believe you were buying white bread."

"I love you, Ellen," he said. "I've always loved you. You're all I want."

"I know that, Kenneth, but so what? We don't have a thing in common really, and I'm finished with waiting."

We don't have a thing in common really. Kenneth could live forever in an efficiency apartment and eat lunch meat over the sink. He's short on ambition—being the opening act for Randy Newman at the Summit is the biggest gig he can imagine—and he can watch junk TV for hours and just skip the news without a trace of shame. All he cares about is taking care of Tenny, but he does that very well.

His is a one-bedroom apartment actually. The bedroom is Tenny's. Kenneth sleeps in pajama bottoms on this hide-a-bed in the living room when she's there. It's a wonder his back hasn't given up on him. That mattress is not America's best.

Tenny has a good bed. It's shoved up longways against the wall so she's got a fifty-fifty chance of not rolling out and breaking her arm some Tuesday or Thursday night. She's got a dressing table and an easel, a big mirror, an extra bed for a friend to stay over. There are toys everywhere, dolls and stuffed animals, a lot of pink things. There are books, a desk, cigar boxes of crayons and paste and construction paper, a tape recorder so she can listen to music (Mozart, Gershwin, Bert and Ernie, no Springsteen) when she's going to sleep. There is a night-light in the shape of a lamb, and there are photographs everywhere of Kenneth and Tenny, and a framed one of her mother near her bed. Her school activity schedule is taped to the refrigerator; inside, half-filled bottles of prescription medicines stand just behind the milk and the low-fat yogurt.

Kenneth says the best way to pick up women is to take a kid with you to the beach. I think that's probably true. My eye's followed a good many Sunday fathers horsing around in the surf with their daughters. I'm a guppy for father/daughter stuff. It's good to see anytime. I remember all of that.

The thing is, Kenneth is much more than a Sunday father. He is there every day for Tenny. I've watched him wash and fold her clothes for years now. He hems her school uniforms. He's made a thousand grape-jelly sandwiches for her lunches. He buys, then wraps birthday presents for her crummy little friends, and he takes her to the parties and picks her up. He brings paper napkins to her school barbecues, and none of this is extraordinary, in the realm of public performance. It's a dailiness. It is all about taking care of Tenny. Kenneth is there every day for his daughter; he'll always take her call.

Understand: From his point of view, he's not rescuing Raylene at the Galleria in the middle of the night. He's going for Tenny. He'll get that car going—he'll call AAA is what he'll do, Kenneth is not at all mechanical. He'll follow them home, and he'll carry Tenny—a dead weight at forty pounds—into the house and put her to bed. If she wakes up during any of it, he'll be there—"Hello, Daddy"—and then she'll go right back to sleep. Then, Kenneth will leave and come back to me. I almost always let him back in. I like him. I like it that he hangs prisms at Tenny's bedroom windows so she'll wake up in rainbows.

"You're a good father, Kenneth, but your life is a mess. Get out of my way before I run over your feet."

I go home and pour myself a glass of wine while I cook my veal. I'm not waiting on any Thanksgiving parade, and I haven't had veal in a long time. I made myself a salad, fresh butter lettuce and snipped herbs I grew myself in my grandmother's memory. (She was a farmer, southwest Arkansas. Corn and snap beans were her specialty, and she wouldn't know basil from Italian parsley. I loved her anyway.) I put anchovies in the salad (I am the only person I have ever known who really likes them; I alone support their market in Texas), and I listen to Art Tatum while I eat. (Kenneth hates jazz, he says it goes nowhere; we don't have a thing in common really.) I am looking forward to not seeing anyone I know for four whole days. On Monday, I'll be pregnant.

I work in the studio until about two, breaking only to watch the ten o'clock news and make some more coffee. Painting's exhausting, aging; like nothing else, it demands a fully alert brain and nearly total physical health. There's the actual painting and then there's the looking at the painting. It goes together, more looking than doing usually. You've got to see what you've done, before you can do more; you've got to make rational choices about what to do next.

I sit across the room from this painting that was yellow at nine and brimming with possibility, red at midnight and just shit. I was tired, but I kept wrestling. It's 2:30 in the morning, it's blue now, and I can't tell what I think, which means it's time to go to bed. I lived in the real world today: I was out of bed at seven, on the phone at the museum by eight.

I unplug the coffeepot; I am washing out my brushes in the bathroom sink. Over my shoulder, I can see part of my painting reflected in the medicine cabinet mirror. I can just see the corner of it—it is a good corner—and I like the way my face is floating on top of it in the reflection. This mirror is the only one I have, I realize. I don't own it. It's rented.

"This might go somewhere," I say out loud, and then I hear this knock on the door.

It's Kenneth. It can be no one else. It's nearly three o'clock in the morning. He's been working. It's been a good night, they've played through to bar closing, and I really should have figured he'd come. I can't tell you how many times I've opened my door to him after midnight over the years.

"Forget it, Kenneth," I tell him through the door.

"I love you, Ellen. I want to have a child with you. I mean it."

"Look, Kenneth, you're nuts. You're married. You've got that crazy kid, and she hates me. You don't have any money, and you don't have any hair. There's nothing you've got that I want."

"Ellen," he whispers, because some lights are going on in windows all around. "I brought you pancakes."

Aw, shit. I can't believe this. This is not going to be simple at all. This is not going to be easy. I'm going to let him in. I can't believe I'm going to do this. I'm going to fall into a life of pure hell for cold pancakes. I can't believe this. Everything was arranged, and I'm probably infertile anyway, and I sure am too old for this crap.

"Just a minute," I tell him. I'm stupid, but I'm not that stupid. I unplug the phone.

Then, against all reason, against everything I know, everything I can explain, I open the door and let him in.

Part

Two

We All Take the Leap of Faith

and Consequently Learn

Some Hard, Hard Lessons

We Never Could Have Gotten

Ready for

Anyway

10

A Good Lavender Might Keep
Us All Calm

Understand: Raylene didn't always honk. Sometimes she just walked right in. She'd just open the door and walk right in, right into our house.

I couldn't believe it. It was like she thought she lived there, like she thought she was someone we wanted to see. It was as if she believed she was simply entitled to come on in anytime, and an icy reception, sharp words didn't seem to even register with her.

"An attitude of entitlement is one of the classic features of the arrested narcissist," Margaret said. "I, however, believe it is a complete waste of time to try and figure out how Raylene's brain works. She's nuts, Ellen. How much more do you want to know?"

"First I want to know how you get a moat built in the late twentieth century. Then I want to know if *nuts* is your professional opinion and if you'd be willing to testify to that in court."

What Raylene did again and again was to simply appear uninvited in the middle of our lives. She never parked in the street. She parked in our driveway like a relative. She'd block both our cars in, and it made me crazy. On alternate Sundays I'd start getting close to actual claustrophobia a good hour before she was even due to come get Tenny. I hated it that she got to me, plus I knew she'd be late and that made me even crazier. Raylene's never been on time in her life. I don't know why she wears all those cheap watches.

"Why does she have to come here at all, Kenneth? Can't we just take Tenny by Raylene's at six o'clock on Sundays?"

"You want to camp in her driveway until she shows up? She's never there, Ellen, and I don't want to leave Tenny with those neighbors. It could be hours until Raylene showed. Listen, you don't have to do any of this, Ellen."

"Well, why does she have to go to Raylene's on Sunday nights anyway? She could stay here, get a good night's sleep, get to school on time Monday morning. Raylene could pick up Tenny from school Monday afternoon, and we'd never even have to see her."

"It's The Tuna Fish Rule," Bradley and Joan told us. "Every single mother since creation argues that they need their kid back home on Sunday night to eat tuna fish sandwiches at the kitchen table and get the tangles out of their hair. They always win that point."

"But Raylene doesn't even cook, Tenny would rather eat dirt than tuna fish, and I don't think Tenny's ever had a comb pulled all the way through her hair. How come we have to put up with this bullshit?"

"You just do, Ellen. Sunday night tuna fish at Mom's is an institution."

My new domestic world turned on Raylene's insensitivity—unless I thought she was doing it on purpose, which made me really nuts—but still, in any case, I was goddamned if I was going to move my car out onto the street, which is where Raylene should've parked if she had any sense.

The lawyers told us that a lack of sense does not constitute sufficient grounds for a child abuse suit, or any other kind of suit, generally speaking. They're sorry about this, but the law is the law.

"She's blocking our cars in," I told Bradley and Joan. "She's ruining the lawn. She's in my house, goddamn it, I think she'd go through my mail if she got a chance."

"You ought to get that door fixed anyway, Ellen," Bradley and Joan told me. "It could get a lot worse."

They were absolutely right. It got a lot worse, but I was new to all that then. It was late April, May. I was four months' pregnant and looking forward to an easy natural childbirth. At the time, I couldn't have imagined a thing worse than Raylene in my bedroom.

"The problem with the joint custody approach," Bradley and Joan told Kenneth, "is that it's still pretty controversial for most family law judges, particularly those in Texas. Most courts operate from the traditional assumption that the best place for a child is with the natural mother. It's the standard sexist approach to parenthood, and while judges are hearing cases every day now of fathers wanting equal rights, duties, powers, and privileges in their children's lives, most courts remain skeptical about awarding joint custody in even the most benign divorce proceedings. They won't do it if they expect any trouble at all between the parents. With respect to your case, Kenneth, we honestly don't know of a court in the entire universe who would even consider ruling for joint custody. That wife of yours, Kenneth, is—as they say in Nacogdoches—loose between the ears."

When Kenneth and I decided to have a child together, Tenny was nearly seven years old. She'd been shuttled between addresses Tuesday, Thursday, and alternate weekends for almost five years. Her shrink didn't think this was such a problem.

"The Tuesday/Thursday schedule is Normal Family Life for Tenny," Gretchen told us.

"But is that healthy?" we wanted to know.

"Well, health is really so relative, isn't it?"

I couldn't believe flipping between houses every day could have any benefit. I still don't, unless I consider the fact that possibly it was keeping Tenny alive. What I really thought was that Tenny should be in one house through the week anyway, and that that house should be ours. To do this, the lawyers said, we'd have to prove that Raylene was grossly unfit to get any judge to even consider ruling for Kenneth as Managing Conservator.

I started keeping a record, but Raylene is not as dumb as she looks. Hardly anybody ever saw or heard her do what she did. It was our word against hers. The hearsay problem haunted us continually.

Raylene claimed that she wanted a divorce, but after five years, she

94   PAULA WEBB

hadn't done a thing about it. She worked hard at staying pissed off at Kenneth but that didn't keep her from calling or dropping by unannounced whenever she felt like it. I drove around the block of Kenneth's apartment any number of times when I saw her car pulled up behind his truck, or even next to it, in his neighbor's space. Raylene wouldn't ever think about using the visitors' parking section. Understand: She doesn't think of anyone except herself. She is the sort of person who regularly abandons her shopping basket in the middle of grocery store parking lots.

"You're leaving me HERE *ALONE?*" Tenny screamed through the car window.

"Lock the doors and relax," I told her. "I'm just taking the cart back to the store, Tenny."

"IT'S AGAINST THE LAW TO LEAVE CHILDREN IN CARS. I COULD COOK IN THIS HEAT," she bellowed, and people started to look our way. It was February. We had on sweaters.

"Hey, Tenny, I'll be right back. I'm going to take this cart and put it just inside the store. That's what you're supposed to do."

"My mother says that's stupid, Ellen. That's what they pay the Mexicans to do."

"I don't like that kind of talk, Tenny. Find yourself that yogurt and shut your mouth."

I wheeled off, feeling glorious. This kid needs a proper role model. I accept the job, I can do this, I can save her. I got back to the car in time to see Tenny ripping the top off the last of six cartons of low-sugar yogurt. It was all over my leather upholstery.

"What in the hell are you doing, Tenny?"

"You just bought plain, Ellen? I HATE PLAIN."

"At least it wasn't the fruit kind, Ellen," my sister, Ruthie, said later. "That stuff really stains, and you know, Ellen, I really don't think you can save Tenny or her teeth."

About avoiding Raylene, look: I was invited, I was expected, dinner was waiting, we were going to the movies. But I circled every time I spotted Raylene's car. I didn't ever feel up to dealing with Raylene face-to-face. I wasn't sure I could keep my tongue under control, and I didn't want to make a scene in front of Tenny.

"You're afraid of Raylene, aren't you, Ellen?" Margaret said.

"Damn right," I told her. "Crazy people scare me. Don't they scare you? I don't understand a thing about that woman. I don't understand why she doesn't want this over after all this time. Why doesn't she just sign the papers, get on with her life? She *hates* Kenneth, Margaret. We're together openly now, I'm pregnant, we've leased a whole house, put up utility deposits. Would *you* want to stay legally connected to a situation like that?"

"Well, no, but frankly, Ellen, I've never understood what anybody sees in Kenneth. I just hope he's telling you the truth about pushing for the divorce."

Kenneth got a divorce lawyer's name out of the Yellow Pages. The guy told him he could get him a decree in sixty days, but when Kenneth explained about Tenny, about the Tuesday/Thursday deal, this lawyer backed off.

"I can't help you, son. A child's place is with the mother, particularly a girl child. That'll be fifty bucks now. Cash is appreciated, I don't take credit cards, and to tell you the truth, I'm queasy about checks."

Tenny's shrink, Gretchen, recommended a woman lawyer who had sympathies for the paternal position.

"I understand the problem here," she said, this Deborah Sullivan. "Now *you* understand, Mr. Goodson. As far as the law goes, these last five years or so have meant absolutely zero. When we go to court, the judge is going to deal with the case like you've moved out the day before. They're going to argue abandonment. That paper napkin won't hold up anywhere. You notice that she never signed it? Your best bet is to snatch Tenny the next time you have her. Possession is what counts; don't forget it. I'll file for a show-cause hearing, and we'll get temporary orders to keep the mother away from her. This will take about ten days to two weeks, and then we'll go to a final hearing, and we'll get your daughter for you."

"Huh?" we said.

"Getting your daughter's what you want, isn't it? Listen, I'll need a thousand as retainer this afternoon, and then we'll begin. Have you thought about how much money you want in child support from the mother?"

"I can't do it this way," Kenneth said and headed for the parking lot. I was right behind him.

Raylene threatened to take Tenny away from Houston nearly every day. It was just hot air, everyone thought, but it still kept us from sleeping deeply. Raylene doesn't have any integrity, Kenneth always said, but he didn't think she would really snatch Tenny and take her out of state if it got down to packing suitcases.

"Yeah," I told Kenneth. "Who would she call to change her tires in Florida?"

I found Bradley and Joan through Laurel, and I went with Kenneth to see them the first couple of times. I liked them. They understood right away they weren't dealing with a textbook case.

"Let's try some different strategies," they suggested. "Let's draw up an agreement based on the paper napkin. Let's see if she'll sign it."

Raylene threw the papers in Kenneth's face. He put them in her mailbox, then went to get Tenny at school. It was a Tuesday, he could've had her served at work, but he has never been into humiliation. She drove wild—she was in her bathrobe, but her hair was combed—over to Tenny's school and threw the papers at him in the cubby room. Everybody saw her do it, everyone heard her yelling, everyone, including her daughter.

"You must think I'm nuts," Raylene screamed. "I'd never sign a piece of crap like this. You're not fit to be in the same room with my child, you jackass."

The argument has always been, of course, that if Raylene thought Kenneth was so horrible, how had she allowed Baby Girl to "visit" Tuesday, Thursday, and alternate weekends for nearly five years? Why was it irresponsible Kenneth whom she called first every time she got a shift change at work, every time she got a once-in-a-lifetime opportunity to go out of town for the weekend? What about all those flat tires? Those cars that wouldn't start?

"Divorce is not rational, Ellen, so forget about logic for now," Bradley and Joan said. "We will lead the judge to ask those questions when we get to court, but for now, let's try it again with the papers, this time via a registered letter. And Kenneth, you have got to toughen up. Divorce isn't friendly either. You tell Raylene to get somebody else to fix her flats."

I was at Kenneth's apartment alone with Tenny. He'd gone for milk and laundry soap, was gone only about twenty minutes. I was trying to get these barrettes in her hair. I'm no good with those things, and

Tenny let me know. The phone rang and rang. I answered, someone hung up. Then it rang again. I answered again, someone hung up. This happened maybe five times. I took it off the hook, Kenneth put it back on when he came in from the grocery store, and it rang again right away. It was Raylene.

"How dare you unplug your phone, you bastard? You're trying to keep me from my baby girl. You're not the only one with a lawyer, you asshole. You'll be hearing from mine."

"It's lawyers, Raylene," Kenneth said. "The whole firm is involved, and they'd be happy to speak with you or your attorney at any time, day or night. This is their phone number . . ." but Raylene had already slammed her receiver down.

Bradley and Joan tried a dozen approaches, a dozen sets of papers bound in blue. All Raylene had to do was to sign them. Kenneth gave her the house, which was their only real asset; they bought it on his GI bill, but he didn't want it, and I sure didn't want it. It was a ranch thing, seven-foot ceilings and knotty pine kitchen cabinets. I'd rather die than live in a house like that. He gave her the tax exemption, and he would have given her Christmas morning with Tenny forever if Bradley and Joan hadn't refused to type that clause in. If Raylene would just sign her full name, Kenneth would pay all the legal fees, go to court, take care of everything. It should have been simple. It wasn't. It went on for years and years and years.

"There's no way we can convince a judge to award joint custody in a hostile case like this, Kenneth. Everything would have to be done— agreements made and signed, the appearance of pleasantries—before we went to court. We can't even get Raylene off the mark here, so what we'd like to do now is to file for sole custody of Tenny for you. That's difficult to achieve in Texas, but we don't think we'll ever really have to go that far. See, we'll never really go to court, but we'll prepare like we intend to. We'll set a deposition hearing up, and we figure she'll hang herself in about forty-five minutes with a court reporter. If her lawyer has any snap, he'll strongly advise her to sign the original agreement, and that will be that."

"What can I do?" I asked Bradley and Joan.

"You can help keep the records, Ellen, if you have the time. We want a list of every call she makes to Tenny, every threat to you or Kenneth. Raylene made a mistake flying off like that at Tenny's school. Get the names of everybody who saw that incident. Keep notes. Take photographs of Kenneth's apartment before you move; we can use them to some extent to establish what kind of life Kenneth made for Tenny before you were in the picture. Take photographs of the new house. Write down every birthday party you take Tenny to, every activity you do with her. Keep accurate records on every dime you spend on her—clothes, haircuts, Astroworld tickets, multiple vitamins. Keep records on Tenny's emotional swings. We'll be talking to her shrink, her teachers, her grandparents, her mother's neighbors. We'll get this settled, and then you'll have some structure to build a life on. That other attorney was right. The last five years don't mean a thing in terms of legal legs."

I was born to be a painter, but I'd earned a living as an archivist. I knew what they wanted, and they'd take my call anytime I had questions or news.

"I don't like any of this," Kenneth said.

"Nobody does," Bradley and Joan told him. "It's just a set of tricks to get you what you want, and what you want is for the good of everyone. Don't you agree?"

Kenneth agreed. He hocked his drums and gave Bradley and Joan their retainer.

"I want this divorce," he told us all, including Tenny, who in the middle of Ninfa's slipped her cheese enchilada into my purse.

"It was an *accident*," she said.

"Be sure to keep good notes," Bradley and Joan told me, and I took this dead seriously. The first thing I unpacked at the Binz house was a yellow legal pad to keep by the phone. By Christmas, I was into three-ring binders and considering fireproof file cabinets.

What Raylene did, over and over, was to arrive a good hour, hour and a half late. Then she'd park in the exact middle of our two-car drive and never explain herself. You couldn't make any plans for an early dinner on an alternate Sunday evening, and you couldn't have gotten out of the driveway if there had been an emergency. But Raylene wouldn't have thought of any of that unless her brain was on, or unless she was a lot smarter than she looked, unless she was doing it on purpose. I stayed up a lot of nights thinking about Raylene's brains and

purposes, but Kenneth said he was tired of losing sleep over the ridiculous.

Raylene would park, then cut across the yard—she wouldn't even
look at the sidewalk—and come up on the porch. Then she'd try the
door. Raylene wouldn't even knock. She'd just reach right out and
touch the knob, turn it, and if the lock was off, damned if she wouldn't
come right in, right into our house.

The first time she did it, I met her by pure accident on the second-
floor landing. My arms were full of dirty clothes, mostly Tenny's—she
goes through three or four outfits a day, it's one of her activities—and
there on the landing I ran smack into Raylene, Tenny's mother,
Kenneth's wife, her face to my face, her child's dirty school uniforms
between us. I couldn't believe it, I about had a heart attack. SHE was
here. SHE had walked right into my house, right up my stairs. I
couldn't believe it.

Raylene offered no explanation. She didn't even say hello. She said
in this ordinary voice, "Where is my Tenny Lou? Where is my Baby
Girl? Where is her little room?"

What was I, the goddamned tour guide?

Before I could recover enough to tell her where she needed to go,
Tenny appeared out of nowhere—drawn, I believe, by the current of
her mother's rather overpowering perfume, or more probably some
mysterious genetic pull (which I couldn't hope to understand myself
until early October), or possibly even prearrangement. The longer I
know the two of them, the more I believe that the third possibility is
not, as paranoid as it sounds, unlikely.

"Mommy, Mommy! You're here, you're here!" Tenny yelped, like
she hadn't seen her mother over a candy bar breakfast the day before.
She bounced up and down, up and down, almost her full height,
although, as I told you, she is extraordinarily small for her age.

Immediately after greeting her mother and making the windows
shake in their putty, Tenny abandoned formal and recognizable language altogether and began to simply screech. I couldn't help but
think right away of the unsettling cries of Rhesus monkeys just before
feeding time at the zoo, except I knew Tenny couldn't possibly be
hungry. She'd just finished two servings of meat loaf with fresh green
beans and yellow corn that I myself had fixed for her not a half hour
before.

The primal greeting complete—my mouth still open and unable to form expressive enough words—Tenny then flung herself onto her mother. The stairs and I trembled. I was afraid she was going to break her legs or her mother's back. I was afraid she wasn't.

Then there was more screeching and more jumping, this time from both of them. They began to do their funny face thing where they screw up their faces and kiss each other with their chins. They always do this when they meet by chance in public, mostly in Mexican restaurants or at community fireworks exhibitions.

"I love you, I love you, I love you, Mommy! Come see my new room! It's blue and white."

"Oh, poor Baby Girl. And you hate blue so. It makes you so listless. Now look here, darling, I brought you a surprise from Atlanta. I knew you'd need cheering up."

We are all still on the landing—Raylene and Tenny, me and the laundry. They are jumping with each other now, the stairs are going to collapse, and they don't even see me.

Is this not my house? Am I invisible or what? Do I want to die with these people? Is that not the biggest box of peanut brittle ever made, and is it not going to rot Tenny's teeth on the spot?

"Her room is actually not blue and white," I said directly to Raylene. "I like blue and white myself, but Tenny's room is lavender and cream. Lavender Dawn actually. We used it last spring for this French print show at the museum—it's good paint, Pratt & Lambert—the color really holds up over time, but it's a soft color, meditative. Dr. Peters thought it might help keep Tenny calm."

I don't know what I'm talking about. It doesn't matter. No one is listening to me anyway. They are jumping.

"Tenny said she loved the color. She said lavender was her favorite."

I should have saved my breath. They're not listening. They're gone, the two of them, Tenny and Raylene, daughter and mother, on up my stairs, both talking fast and loud, completely enveloped in one another. I am talking to a Chinese white wicker laundry basket spilling over with dirty socks, and they are stuffing themselves with Georgia red peanuts and corn sugars. They are gone, they are upstairs, they are off on a full tour, bathrooms and everything, of my bridal cottage.

.   .   .

Well, okay, it wasn't exactly a cottage either. It was a three-story house designed sixty years ago by some architect who loved Romanesque architecture but didn't understand much about it in the round. It was an odd house, brick and stone, set on a triple lot. It was huge is what it was.

It had flagstone sidewalks, a formal entry hall, thick English ivy everywhere, enormous trees on all sides. It was built in the twenties in the old Binz area of Houston (just east of Main, west of Almeda), and it had twelve-foot ceilings and plaster walls. I loved it immediately, I had to have it. Kenneth got used to it—he appreciates a wall cool to the touch—but it was falling apart more than we knew or could ever have imagined.

"Isn't it a great house?" the rental agent said. "Sure, it needs a little work, but we're talking character here. Would you like a little drink?"

It was ten o'clock on a Thursday morning. This Maxwell was drinking straight Seagram's out of an iced-tea glass and pushing us to sign a two-year lease.

"Let's do it," Tenny said. "It's a fairy-tale house."

"Do you spray for bugs regularly?" I asked.

"We don't do anything," Maxwell said. "Look, you can have the house. You can do whatever you want to it. Just don't burn it down unless you call first. You want this place or not?"

We wanted it. It was the scale of house I dreamed of living in when I was growing up in two-bedroom garden-style apartments with antique brick facades and wrought-iron gates, the kind constructed around some builder's notion of old New Orleanian charm. You can find that kind of place anywhere now between Midland and Mobile, and while my parents found that comforting, I hated the sameness of those places. It wasn't the kind of continuity I would have looked for or needed, but nobody asked me.

"It's sort of a short castle," I explained to my parents.

"That's kudzu, not ivy, Ellen," my father said. "It'll grow right through the windows and strangle you all in your sleep."

Kenneth and I rented the Binz house for the walnut-paneled library, for the laundry chute to the only cellar in Houston, for the Art Deco hardware on the doors and heating grates, and for eight hundred bucks a month plus a security deposit. The rent was a lot more than we really wanted to pay, but the place was so big, so fabulous.

"You're going to fix that leak in the kitchen ceiling, aren't you?" I asked Maxwell. "I just don't think two air conditioners can cool four thousand square feet in August."

"Just feel these cool plaster walls," Maxwell said between sips. "They're still holding February's cold snap."

We decided to sign the lease (we got three extra air conditioners on our own in July—plaster walls hold humidity, too; they sweat like crazy is what they do). It was, from all appearances, a great house, and I wanted to get on with serious nesting. The baby was due in early October—the sixth, actually—and I had two exhibitions coming in over the summer.

"Let's do it, Kenneth," I said. I had Clifford at Bekins standing by for my call.

We took the house, we signed the lease, we were tired of looking anyway. Finding a place to live was one of the first things Kenneth and I had ever done together in the outside world. The prospect of moving made both of us squirrelly. It brought out all our differences. We wanted it to be a consensus decision—everybody happy—but over the past six weeks there had been a number of nasty disagreements about address.

Kenneth wouldn't have a thing to do with West University. Republicans live openly there; we were in total agreement against West U. I liked Southampton, the Rice University area—my neighborhood for nearly fifteen years—but the house rents were too high, and Kenneth thought the Rice area was still West U. Kenneth wanted Montrose—his old neighborhood—but I was afraid of the porno shops and the drug traffic. The Heights area was completely out of the question: Raylene lived there. Outside the 610 Loop was simply unthinkable.

We were driving around—that's how you find a place to live in Houston, nobody reads the want ads—and Kenneth spotted this great old house with a sign up. We called, we liked what we could see, we did it. We abandoned our old neighborhoods, although if the wind was right, you could still hear the bells chime the quarter hour at Rice University; hookers, men and women, sipped coffee outside the UToTeM three blocks up. We took a chance on somewhere different

and signed up for twenty-four months with Maxwell and his notary
seal on a Thursday morning in late April. Then we went for a late
breakfast, and Tenny spilled blueberry syrup on my best Italian
sweater. We believed we were being sensible and sensitive: The size of
the place would offer each of us—the three of us now, and the fourth
one coming—enough room to maintain our own private interests
while we got used to being a family.

"It was an ACCIDENT," Tenny screamed, and the waitress came
over to check.

Kenneth took the whole third floor for his music room and office.
There were window seats on either end of the room, a room as long as
the whole house was wide. Shutters opened out onto the tops of trees.

"You've got kids, right?" Maxwell said. "You better shut those
windows up. Get bars or something. They used to raise carrier pigeons
up here. We cleaned everything up, but anybody could fall out those
windows, and I have to tell you honestly it does still stink up here a
little after a heavy rain."

It was a huge room, wood floors, a lot of storage. Kenneth could
practice with the whole band up there and still be close. In his old
apartment, he couldn't keep his drums set up and get into the broom
closet. For a big job—horns and extra amps—they had to practice in
Patrick's garage, and Clear Lake was a good hour's drive, back and
forth.

I took the upper-front bedroom with the northeast light for my
drawing studio—I could use the garage apartment for painting big floor
things—and we gave Tenny the back bedroom. It was a great room,
too—windows on two sides and French doors on a third that opened
out onto a wrap-around sleeping porch. The place was fabulous, except for the kitchen ceiling, which needed some serious repair: The
upstair's shower leaked.

"We'll get the plumber over here before you get really settled, but
don't ask me for anything else," Maxwell said. "Do you want it or not?
I've got plans for lunch."

There was our bedroom and the fourth little bedroom that connected to ours—the baby's room. I had wallpaper in mind, a ceiling
fan. My friend Joe was going to paint everything during the day—I
couldn't be around the fumes—and he needed the money.

Joe is a fine abstract painter, but he'd worked for years with Antonio's crew on installations. He's good, he's got a steady wrist, and when it comes to painting interiors, he doesn't need to use tape when he trims out a window. Joe hates all this—"casual painting" he calls it—and he quits the museum in a fit about every three months to work on his own stuff. Antonio hires him back in a second when his money runs out.

"Best drywall man I've ever seen," Antonio says.

There were three full baths, an enormous living room with a fireplace, a huge dining room with copper wall sconces. There was a pantry, a serving window between the kitchen and the dining room that Tenny wanted to use for puppet shows (once I explained what one was). There were built-in bookshelves in the living room and the library, floor-to-ceiling casement windows a good four feet wide, wood floors everywhere, and a three-inch-thick, solid oak front door with a bad lock.

"I've got to live here, Kenneth."

We signed the lease that Thursday, started moving in the following weekend. Kenneth brought all his stuff over in one load in the back of his truck. Three Bekins men picked up all of mine from my apartment, then made two more trips to get everything else out of storage.

"Where did you get all this stuff, Ellen?"

"Everywhere. Don't you love it? Did you see my Chambers stove? Did you see my other one?"

Kenneth loved it, I loved it. I was home, finally—an address without an apartment number. We were together, and this baby was coming. The Hussman was in the kitchen, and the compressor man was due Monday. I bought a new washing machine, Kenneth bought a used dryer. We had two of everything else of practical value, although most of Kenneth's stuff was crap, except for this fabulous ElectroLux vacuum cleaner he'd gotten at an estate sale for three bucks.

"They didn't know what they had," he told me.

"Say, how do you feel about shelf paper, Kenneth?"

I needed to know. Grace was bringing over samples.

I left the laundry basket on the stairs and went to find Kenneth, who was in the cellar with an old mop handle trying to fish out the dirty clothes we had put down the laundry chute earlier.

"They're lost forever," he said.

"Get that bitch out of my house," I said.

"*Our* house," he said and passed me the mop handle. I felt his tone was a little sharp for a new co-habiter, but I was relieved to see him climb the stairs two, then three at a time.

I stayed in the basement—"you *hid* in the basement is what you did," Margaret said—and I did notice that my hands were shaking. This surprised me. Until recently I had never thought of myself as the type to let a social unpleasantness get to me.

Kenneth found Raylene and Tenny on the second floor touring my studio with great interest. Raylene was browsing through my photographs and unpaid bills while Tenny thumbed my software and crumbled a fresh box of Nupastels to dust.

"Exactly how do you know Ellen doesn't wear panties under her nightgown, baby?" Raylene said.

"Because," Kenneth said from the door, "Tenny hasn't figured out what a closed door means, Raylene. It must be genetic. Tenny, this is Ellen's studio, her office, where she works. We don't come in here without her inviting us, and we don't touch her stuff."

"Then what are you doing in here, Kenny?" Raylene said.

"Yeah, Dad, what are you doing in here?"

"It's way past time for you to go to your mother's house, Tenny. Run get your schoolbag and a clean uniform, and meet us at the front door."

Tenny ran off to her room (she thrives on clear assignments, structure keeps her even), while Kenneth took his legal wife by the elbow and talked her downstairs to the door.

"Don't do this again, Raylene. When you come to get Tenny, wait downstairs, or better yet, wait outside. This is not your house. This is our house, Ellen's and mine. This is not your house."

Listening from the basement, I found Kenneth's voice surprisingly even under the circumstances, and I fell in love with him all over again. Unfortunately, however, his words and tone were wasted on Raylene, who had revved herself up to a shrill and bitter scream.

"I am Tenny Lou's mother, and don't you forget it, you son-of-a-bitch. I have every right to know exactly what's going on in her life, and from what I see and hear you're living as irresponsibly as you ever did. You're an asshole, Kenny. She's supporting you, isn't she? I never remember you're being that good."

"Your memory was never your strongest asset, Raylene," Kenneth said at the front door. "I'll write this down for you if you need to refer to it. *This is not your house.* Wait downstairs in the future, or I'll get a writ to keep you outside by the garbage cans."

"How dare you threaten me, you fucking bastard. I'll see you in court for keeping my daughter from me, and from what I see around here, I think we might be talking about unsuitable environment for a baby girl."

Baby Girl, seven and smelling blood, ran down the stairs, her McPhearson plaid school jumper waving behind her on a pink plastic Barbie hanger. Kenneth had just ironed it, I bought the hanger; we'd never see either one of them again.

"It's *my* house, it's *my* house, too, Dad!" she screamed. "Mommy, Mommy, Mommy!"

"Just look how you upset her, Kenny. If you were any kind of father at all, but of course you're not, you'd watch what you say in front of your daughter. Now, now, Baby Girl, calm down. We're going straight home this very minute. I've got a really special surprise for you there. Come on, Dumplings."

And then she picked her suddenly very quiet seven-year-old daughter up in her arms (although I did notice she was on her own feet again at the car—I could see everything through the old coal grate in the basement), and they left, finally, disappearing into a whole other zip code, out of my life until the next day at six.

"Want to eat out?" Kenneth said and retrieved the mop handle.

"*Dumplings?*" I said.

"Raylene's grandmother called her that. She was fat as a kid. Probably be fat again."

"Tell me again why you married her, Kenneth."

"Drugs," he said.

"Really? I thought it was the microphones."

"Microphones?"

"Yeah, you know, she helped carry the equipment out to the truck after closing. The microphones? It was her considerate and generally helpful nature that drew you to her?"

"You okay, Ellen?"

"Oh, sure," I said. "I'm great. I just hate her, that's all."

"Which one?"

Kenneth's voice had dropped to serious. It was low in his chest, close to his heart. I'm not deaf: I knew that the rest of the evening, if not our whole life together, hinged on my response.

"Both of them, Kenneth," I said. "I hate both of them when they're together, particularly when they're together in my house. *Our* house."

Kenneth abandoned the mop handle and turned to me.

"Listen, Ellen, I know Tenny's difficult. You don't ever have to shore me up. This move's been hard on everybody, but we'll settle down soon. Raylene will get it eventually—well, maybe she'll get it—and Tenny certainly will. She does love you, Ellen. This is going to be good for her and all of us. We're going to be very happy."

"How long is *eventually* exactly?"

Kenneth grabbed me around what was once my waist. "I'm starving," he said. "How about dinner?"

"How about more conception, Kenneth? How about Basement Love?"

"How about Mexican food, then much more conception, anywhere you want?"

"Pretty short honeymoon, Kenneth. Your priorities seem to be shifting here, honey."

"That happens when you start signing leases for life in West University. Listen, Ellen, I mean it: I'll fix that damned lock."

He said he'd fix it, but I knew he wouldn't. Kenneth is just a flat fool with anything the least bit mechanical, but I did appreciate his new domestic attitude.

II ....

Mexican Beer

I spent all summer watching the Yellow Pages fall open to Plumbing, Emergency at the slightest touch. I was making lists and waiting on the plumber, any plumber, and this baby boy we saw swimming during the ultrasound in June. I was nesting, getting ready. I was dealing with window coverings and crazy people with varying success.

"Are you still upset that it wasn't a girl?" Elliot asked me recently. I ran into him over eggs at Colin and Laurel's brunch. I don't see much of Elliot anymore since Zack came, since Elliot quit art history and went to law school, since I spotted him on the television news wearing a Reagan button.

"What are you talking about? I think torts have turned your brain funny, you know? You're out of touch, Elliot, and I think you always were."

"I remember you wanted a daughter, Ellen. I remember you were shocked it was going to be a boy. You called me, we talked about it, don't you remember? You brought the ultrasound pictures to lunch."

"That *it* you're referring to is my son, Elliot. And have you forgotten he has a sister? Get out of my way, you jerk. I can't get to the waffles."

I thought my baby would be a girl. I thought I'd be alone, without anyone, and then I'd have a daughter. I was going to name her for my grandmother. Her name would be Georgia, her eyes would be brown, and I would understand her because we were female, alike, the same kind. We would be happy together, if a little odd. I thought all this, and I believed it.

Well, Tenny is a girl. Ovaries, as it happens—one or two, maturing or developing—don't count for much commonality. I sure don't understand Tenny, and, as certain as I've always been that I love my son, Zack, a lot of times I don't understand him either. He cut the top of his hair off at school last week. He's been banned from scissor work.

"Why did you do this, Zack? You're one of the big boys now. You're almost four years old."

"In my way, Mom. I got more."

A lot of times I don't get it about Zack, but I can't imagine him being anyone but who he is. He told me in the car he knows why streets curve: "So they can fit around our world." I love this boy.

"Hey, Laurel. Do you remember when I thought I was going to have a girl? Before the ultrasound that June?"

"This is an important party, Ellen," Laurel hissed. "We're recruiting for Colin's law firm here. You're not going to talk about childbirth, are you? You're not going to go graphic, are you, Ellen?"

Laurel's lost it since she married Colin, and I'm pretty sure she's got permanent damage from clenching her teeth like that. I hate Colin, and I don't know about Laurel most of the time lately.

"You've got to relax, Laurel," and I had to pull her into the kitchen. "You might remember who helped you shove that tacky sectional couch of yours into the garage this morning. Christ, I hadn't even gotten the paper open when you called for help, and I told you not to buy that couch in the first place. You were nuts this morning, Laurel, and you might remember, I didn't point that fact out at the time."

"I'm sorry, Ellen, but they didn't deliver it until this morning, and I knew right away it was all wrong. I don't even think it's real leather, do you?"

"It's rubber, Laurel. Have you ever seen a teal cow?"

"These brunches make me crazy, Ellen. Colin gets so intense, and he would have killed me if he knew we even owned that thing. I'm sorry I called so early, but I didn't know what else to do. Ellen, my life is a torment."

"Fuck Colin, Laurel."

"I'm trying to, Ellen."

We sit together for a moment on her washer/dryer and share a drink out of an everyday juice glass. Laurel's good champagne flutes are all in use or getting rinsed, and the caterers are starting on the dessert crepes and need all the counter space. The party is on its own now anyway, and nobody will miss us, except Colin, who—tieless from the start—is working hard to appear dazzlingly casual. It's a monumental job for him.

"Okay, just one more, Ellen, and then I've got to get back in there before Colin comes looking for me. He's probably already had a stroke. You know there are three federal judges out there?"

We have two more mimosas, just to test her theory—I venture Colin doesn't even know they have a laundry room—and Laurel says, "Listen, Ellen, I really don't remember you ever wanting anybody but Zack, but that was so long ago. Five years, a lifetime, huh? You were beautiful that summer and, I do remember, nuts yourself."

I was beautiful that summer and nuts myself. I had shopping lists for the house and shopping lists for the museum. I had To Do lists for home and To Do lists for work. I was keeping the Raylene List for Kenneth and the lawyers, the Tenny List for her shrink, and I was working on a list of everything I knew about museums for Judith. She was going to cover for me when I went into labor, but she was young, only twenty-three. She didn't know any of the finer points. I was in my twenty-fifth week, and I didn't have time to oversee a paced development. There wasn't time for any subtleties.

MEMORANDUM #16

June 14, 1982

RE: *Calling an Artist*

Judith,

It is never a simple business knowing when to call an artist on the phone. Timing's everything, is my experience in the matter, and content doesn't have a thing to do with it.

For example, you might want to let a painter know you heard over lunch they're under consideration for the next Venice Biennale. Ordinarily, anybody'd think this was happy news. It's not. Letting on about a gossipy thing like that at the wrong time could kill a painter, drive them to total dysfunction. On the other hand, slipped into a conversation at just the right time, that kind of news could turn everything around, get them moving ahead, working fast and strong, doing their best work in years. You just never know, but you better think about it a while before you dial.

Nothing's casual in art, Judith, particularly gossip. Even if the rumor turns out to be true, even if they do get in the Biennale, it's got to be a pretty unusual character whose work—after the first rush from the news—doesn't go completely to hell for the next six months, maybe longer. Most artists really prefer a good cold Mexican beer to champagne anyway, so I advise you to just let somebody else drop the Biennale news. Then, stand by.

But, say a sculptor's having an exhibition in your museum. Say it's an exhibition of their work of the last three years, and nobody's seen it outside the foundry. Say it's really good, breakthrough stuff. You're proud to know the work, are completely behind it. *Newsweek* and *ArtForum* both bite on your publicity bait. They plan to attend the press preview—they bait you back with color-photo spreads—but they want invitations to the black-tie dinner after the opening. They hint that you could pay their hotel bill. You hint back that you'll consider it, but you don't write that down anywhere.

But then the truck arrives, and it's all wrong, or some of it anyway. You see immediately that the new floor pieces, which looked so good, so very good in the New York studio, look, in Texas, like no less than five round piles of green crap. The show opens in six days. You've got to have a long, diplomatic discussion about this with the sculptor, and you've got to have it now.

You've got to consider that if the pieces stay in the show, that's all anybody'll see. They'll hate it, local critics anyway, and particularly the viewing public. They'll turn mean and dismissive, hurt your artist's career and your museum's reputation far deeper and much longer that five tons of green cowshit ever could. You've got to finish up the phone call with this Yankee sculptor agreeing together to pull the floor pieces from the show, and you've got to be gracious about redesigning overnight the installation it took you five weeks to do.

This is tricky business at any time, Judith, but call too early, and you're just asking for a possible psychotic episode. Call late in the week, is my advice. Call late Friday afternoon, when they're closing the studio up for the weekend, packing for the country, have other plans. Tell them straight, don't baby them. Then talk about philistines. Do it and get it over with, and convince them you have their best interests at heart, which is the real truth, or it had better be.

"But what is the ideal time to call, Ellen?"

"It's in the memo, Judith."

"It is not. I read it twice, and it is not."

"Okay, okay. I still can't believe it's a boy, Judith. Two-forty."

"What?"

"Two-forty, their time. That is the ideal time to call an artist."

"Why two-forty?"

"Lunch and naps are over. You don't ever want to wake them up, Judith. If they've got school-aged kids, they've got to go get them by three, so they're winding down anyway. Or, if they don't have kids, they're about to leave to get their hair cut, get to the gym, get to the grocery, meet friends for drinks. And if they're rich, they're waiting on the masseuse to show."

"They have masseuses who come to their houses every day? How do they do that?"

"They bring their tables with them, Judith. But see, any way it goes, nobody's working at three o'clock in the afternoon. They're doing their domestic things then. Call at two-forty. That way, you catch them before they get in the shower. It's going to be a short call, which is what you want."

"You're sure about this?"

"I've got years of research on this, Judith. If they've had a good day, they're taking a break until after dinner. If it's been a bad day, they're going to be thrilled to pick up the phone and talk to anybody. In that case, however, you will have to cut them off after ten minutes, Judith. You don't want to help them not work. Lie, is my advice. Tell them the building's on fire, and you have to get off the phone."

"How do you get a masseuse exactly? How do you interview them?"

"Ask Claudia, Judith. She has one come over every day she's not teaching."

"Well, what about photographers? You didn't say anything about them, Ellen."

"Just call them anytime. Particularly if they're over thirty, those chemicals have already rotted their brains, and they, as a group, have never known the difference between day and night anyway."

.   .   .

After working for art for a hundred years, I did know when to call and when not to. It was a gift I didn't much value, but I think it was why I had a job. I wasn't afraid of calling, but I understood the possible consequences, so I took my time. I didn't call without a good reason.

It's one thing to call an accountant working in an office at 9:15 in the morning, but most artists I know sleep pretty close to their paint. You're calling their house usually, where they really live. You're risking interrupting their privacy, horning in on a late breakfast, disturbing their sex lives. If it's a good day and they're early risers, you chance disrupting their work, getting them off track early, and helping them blow their whole day. It's hard knowing when to call, or even if you should. You've got to be sensitive here, and from the larger view, a pithy postcard is really just as effective without the complications.

I like artists. In the main, I am a painter, and I worked with artists all the time at the museum. There are two kinds of good ones: those who have sold enough to do it and keep doing it, and those who are holding down day jobs and hoping to quit and join the others. Dealing with the first kind was my job at the museum. More often than not, they became my friends. I knew how and when they worked, when to call and when not to, and how to break bad news. It was part of my job.

"It's broken. It's lost. It's been defaced. We hate it. Where's Ellen?"

The first time this happened I was still in graduate school, working mornings at a commercial gallery, taking classes afternoons, and wrestling with my own stuff most of the night. The truck arrived from New York, and while most of the consignment work was there, the eight paintings for the next exhibition hadn't made it.

"How could you forget the Sackners?" Gillian screamed at the driver, a young sculptor from New Haven fighting for custody of his daughters and picking up extra money trucking art cheap and uninsured from New York to the south and southwest in a rented van.

"The mailer's already out. I'm going to have your ass. Where's that letter, Ellen?"

I had written the letter. It was chatty, too chatty. I worried, was it my fault completely? I liked Stefano. In the letter I'd listed which studio, which gallery he needed to go to, what to pick up, who to contact, when to call first, what to expect in the way of scale and weight, where the freight elevators were.

There it was, big as life, the fourth item: Get eight Sackners from Emmerich warehouse on West 7th, see Milo.

It wasn't my fault Stefano missed the pickup. He'd gotten the Motherwell drawing (Item #3), the new Garver piece (Item #5). He just skipped the Sackners. He was overworked, he was spinning on speed. He was dyslexic, stupid, lazy, depressed. Whatever Stefano was, still I felt responsible, which was what I was hired to do.

"Take care of everything," Gillian told me at the beginning.

Had I overwritten? I hated being witness to Gillian's initial screaming, then not screaming. Gillian was a brooder, could make her mouth stay tight and focused on a big or little mistake for days. She would begin an ordinary enough conversation later in the day, then remember the error, the oversight, and her face would cloud over, her mouth would go tight. She'd turn on her Ferragamos and walk away, disgusted, furious, leaving my stomach to rumble and fret. It could go on like that for days until something else got her attention.

Gillian was your basic dealer, running an art gallery on a trust fund and two art history courses she'd taken fifteen years ago at Smith. She had an eye for masterpieces and accelerating profit, and she buddied up only to established, big-time artists. Gillian tried her awkward best with museum directors and second-generation collectors. She met frequent enough success to keep the doors open and her furs in cold storage. Anyone else in the world was an irritation. She was particularly mean to young artists—the unrepresented—and she hated beer, any kind. She distrusted the experimental, anything new, particularly if it had words on it.

I cringed watching Stefano take Gillian's rage, however justified it was from her point of view. I watched him begin to fray, then lose his Greek temper, and call her a fucking bitch, which anyone could see was the truth from almost anywhere you wanted to stand in the area. Then he stormed out of the gallery without his check.

"Pissant," Gillian spit at the slamming door, a heavy one that closed like a coffin. It was the darkest gallery in Houston, no natural light, cold as a rented meat locker.

What to do here? The show opened Saturday week, Sackner's first exhibition in fourteen years, her first ever in Texas.

"Fix this," Gillian said and left for her shrink's, then her hairdresser's.

I set the alarms, I closed the gallery, I found Stefano at a beer joint up the street. It was eleven in the morning, but the place still reeked of last night's smoke, and the doors were standing wide open. Stefano was at the Texas table, sitting at the panhandle and staring at Amarillo. He was working on his third Corona.

"I'm sorry," I said. "Here's your check. Cash it quick before she thinks to stop payment."

"My life is in pieces, Ellen," Stefano said, and it was the clear truth. "At the deposition, my wife's lawyer asked me whether I thought it was right for a man to buy lingerie for little girls. I said, you mean underwear? Yeah, I told them, I think a father ought to make sure his kids have underwear. Then they wanted to know if I bathed them, if I think that's right. Appropriate, is what they said. Jesus, Ellen, they're my babies, four and six years old. I make sure they're shampooed, I told them. I think that's appropriate, I comb their tangles out. Then they wanted to know if I dry them off and how I do it. I got so crazy at what they were insinuating that I lost it. I hit the lawyer in the mouth and broke two of her teeth. I'm never going to get to see my girls. We're never going to finish the myths."

"The myths?"

"We were reading them out loud. We did all the Greeks over spring break. We were just starting on the Norse."

Forgetting to pick up eight paintings in New York City seemed pretty minor under the circumstances. I had half a beer, Stefano cleaned up another three. Over salted pistachios we chewed over the overt and covert biases of child custody laws, father's rights, what to send the girls for Christmas. Stefano hadn't had much sleep, the beer hit him quick, and I talked the bartender into letting Stefano sleep in the stock room.

"This is the worst it's ever going to be," I told Stefano, who was trying to get comfortable and stretch out on six dusty cases of Lone Star.

"You think?" he said and passed out.

"You think?" said the bartender, whose name was and still is Bernard. "You really think this is the worst it's ever going to be, Ellen?"

"Nah," I said.

Gillian had gotten back from getting her roots fixed and was wild about me closing up in the middle of the day.

"You're ruining me," she bellowed. "We could have lost a sale, Ellen."

The fact that nothing had sold in two and half months seemed to have deserted Gillian's mind. Plus, it was the middle of August. Nobody buys art in August, in Texas or anywhere else.

"Call Sackner, Ellen. I've got a headache," but she doesn't go lie down on the old sofa in storage, she doesn't get her ice mask out of the freezer. She goes into her office, keeps the door open. She paces, listens.

I dial. It's just after two in New York. Sackner's had her lunch—she eats pasta early—and is just getting up from her nap. What to say? How to say it?

"Ms. Sackner, it's Ellen in Houston. I have horrible news."

Gillian flings herself out of her office, is ready to vault right over the desk and grab the phone.

"Who's dead now?" Sackner says.

"It's not that bad," I tell her, and I felt her heart and mine turn over. Sackner's nearly eighty, and horrible news means death, suddenly or finally. Sometimes Sackner doesn't even pick up the phone, lets it ring and ring, just doesn't want to know right then. Death is news that keeps.

"Our guy forgot to get your paintings. I'm sick about it, and I really was looking forward to seeing them today."

"Oh, art stuff. How are we going to fix this, Ellen?"

We fix it. Sackner's nephew works for Eastern Airlines; he'll help wire the deal, gives us the flight schedule. Stefano's brother Mitchell picks up the paintings at the warehouse, Milo helps wrap them in bubble paper, clean cardboard; they get them to Kennedy. Over the course of the next day, eight paintings fly—alone or in pairs—to Texas. They rest safe in the first-class coat closet. They've got a lot of room; who with any sense brings a coat to Houston in August?

I borrowed a pickup, and Elliot and Joe came with me for company and lifting. We waited in the bar at Houston Intercontinental over the course of a long hot August afternoon and evening. We sipped weak gin and tonics, and watched an Astros double header with Atlanta. We claimed the paintings one by one on the even hours, we saw that they had all traveled well, and we dropped them at the gallery. Then we went out for Mexican food.

"It's fixed, Gillian," I told her Thursday morning, but her mouth stayed tight. At noon it did crack open just wide enough to tell me to put a stop payment on Stefano's check. That's when I walked.

12 ....

Dope

Look, I know difficult people. I've spent my whole life dealing with them, and I've had fair success with any number of assholes. I've got fifteen years of tax returns in a box somewhere: I work. I know how to get things done. I know how to fix things that screw up at the last minute, and I can fix them so well that hardly anybody would ever notice or even remember how bad the situation was just hours before. I'm experienced, I've got a great Rolodex, and I thought that at thirty-four years old I could draw easily and at any time on prior experience to get me through anything.

I was dead wrong. I was a dope. Nothing I had ever seen or done prepared me to deal with Tennessee Louise Goodson and her crazy mother. I wasn't doing too well on setting up a real house either.

In June I called my mother long distance in the middle of the day.

"How do you do this? I've still got boxes everywhere, the place is a mess, I can't even get to the kitchen, and I've lost the good scissors. We're getting these notices from the library about Tenny's overdue books, and we're going to have to get a signature loan to pay the fines.

How do you do this, Mom? How did you get us all settled by Thursday night after moving in Thursday morning?"

"I never thought you even noticed," my mother said, and she was thrilled to hear from me on the subject. "You always had your head in some book, Ellen, and you told me a hundred times you were simply above domestic drudgery."

We moved at least twice a year when I was growing up. It was a mess Thursday morning, boxes everywhere. We had doughnuts for breakfast, little cartons of skim milk with red and white straws. My father was already gone, spot-checking the warehouse inventory, firing the old staff at the office.

My mother took Ruthie and me to the new school, got us registered, and then left us with strangers and a map of how to get home at 3:30. When we got home, the boxes were gone, and there were pictures on the walls. There was a pot roast in the oven and clean towels in the bathroom, and my mother was sitting on the couch reading the local paper and asking us questions about our homework and whether we wanted to do scouts this town.

"What you do," my mother told me in the middle of June, "is cheat, but don't ever admit it. I'd get back from taking you two to school and shove the big furniture around until I got tired of it. You can't get it right the first time anyway, Ellen, so just put the couch some place logical and adjust everything later when you do heavy cleaning. Then I'd make the beds and take the tape off the front of the chests of drawers—we never boxed clothes; I think it's a waste—and then I'd clean the bathrooms, put some new towels out, and leave. I'd find the closest decent grocery, meet the head butcher and talk meat. Then I'd come home, put the roast in the oven, hang a few pictures, and shove the boxes under the beds, back in the garage, anywhere out of sight. Lots of times I didn't even unpack that stuff, Ellen. We never missed it, plus I got a jump on the next move."

"I'm never moving again, Mom. We're going to stay in this house forever. I've just got to figure out a way to buy it."

My mother cheated. I never would have believed it. She's very rigid about how a thing should be—the right linens, the proper forks, how a good Episcopalian ought to live. We always had balanced dinners—moving-day doughnuts for breakfast twice a year was the closest we ever got to junk food. My mother believed in doing everything right.

She joined the PTA that first day, met all our teachers and had them over for lunch at the end of the semester.

"It was the only way we could get Ruthie out of the fourth grade," my mother said. "And then there was that year you almost flunked geometry, Ellen. My trout almondine saved that *F* and your college career."

I never knew my mother was so calculating. She was against lying always, adamantly for early Sunday school until we were teenagers. I had to wear a petticoat under my dresses, she never paid a single fine on any library book, and she thought Kotex napkins were just fine.

"I think you could get a disease from those tam-poon things, Ellen."

I quizzed my mother for a good half hour at midday rates on how she did it. She cheated on any and all household matters but took full credit anyway. Appearances outweighed ethics every time for her, and it was just "your problem if you didn't ask more probing questions about the matter at the time or even later."

At a Christmas party we had once—we always had a Christmas party, a hundred people came, my father made Tom and Jerrys in the fifties, Bacardis in the sixties—my mother put Johnson's Paste Wax on the heating registers and then turned up the temperature. The house smelled great: evergreens and paste wax and rum. It was like a magazine: stockings at the mantel, a six-foot pine tree twinkling, everybody happy.

"I don't know how you do it, Frances," my mother's friend Nell said. "Your house looks wonderful with all these candles, and I can't believe you've had the time to wax these floors."

"Well, Christmas is so very special to all of us," my mother said. "I don't mind the extra work if it makes everything a little nicer."

My mother said this. I was standing right next to her. She had on a new red dress, I had on yellow. I had forgotten all this. She lied: There was dust everywhere.

"You couldn't see a speck of dust in that light, Ellen, and you wouldn't have noticed then anyway because you were just a kid. Listen, honey, you just can't do everything."

I wanted to do everything. I wanted everything to be perfect. We'd been in the house for seven weeks, and you could hardly see any progress. I called in every marker I had and agreed to do simple tax returns for everyone I knew for the next decade. I know how to put a

Schedule C together; it's another one of those things I can do that I
don't much value.

"I need help," I said on the phone. "I'll do your taxes for the next
three Aprils for nothing, and we can negotiate for after that."

There were people in the house all the time. Ruthie just moved in
for six weeks. She slept in the baby's room and organized the kitchen.
She planted the summer basil, put the barbecue pit together, and
worked on leveling the patio. Judith was making curtains for Tenny's
bedroom—six big windows plus the French doors. She ran her laundry
through our machines while she sewed in the dining room and sipped
cold gin. Antonio hung the new ceiling fans and fixed the front door
lock—Kenneth would never have gotten to it—and Laurel found a
place to get my rugs washed and blocked, undermats cut so no one
would slip. She took Kenneth's truck to pick up the kilims.

"Jesus, it was just like Mississippi in that truck. Has it *ever* had a
muffler?"

Grace, Joe, and I sat at the dining room table—I needed a new one,
the scale of my old one was all wrong for this house—and watched the
light shift in and out one Sunday afternoon. We were trying to decide
on paint colors, and it was hard. The light was amazing in that house,
cool all the time and changing because of the trees. Paint chips at the
hardware store couldn't tell you a thing. We painted big squares of
sample colors everywhere, watched them dry, watched the shadows
play on them. I wanted it to be perfect.

"It's got to be that browned gray in here, the living room, too," I
said. We all knew gray was right, but the one that looked so good at
three looked like mud at six. Too much blue, not enough raw umber.

The doorbell rang. It was Raylene coming to get Tenny for Sunday
night tuna fish, and she was nearly on time. Kenneth got the door—he
was practicing with the band on the third floor but had been looking
for Tenny's ride—and he left Raylene in the living room while he
went to find Baby Girl, who was painting some pretty nice pictures on
her sleeping porch and had lost track of the time herself for once.

Raylene walked all around the living room, fingering stuff on the
mantel, turning her neck at book titles. She didn't see us in the dining
room, and we didn't let her know we were there. She picked up some
pictures we'd taken of Tenny at Easter, and she was just slipping a

Polaroid into her pocket when she caught us all watching her from the dining room table with our mouths open.

"Grace, Joe, this is Tenny's mother, Raylene," I said, and we all got up and walked over to her. We surrounded her actually.

Raylene flushed, mumbled hello, but didn't shake any hands. Tenny galloped up right then, and they were gone, out the door without the book bag, moving quite a bit faster than usual.

"I got her. Did you see her take that picture? Let me get my notes. What are your full names and addresses? What is the exact time? Can you believe this woman?"

We were mean.

"So what?" Grace said. "She's a bitch and a common thief. Worse than that, Ellen, she's a common bitch."

We were really mean. We should have told her we were there watching her, but we didn't. We caught her red-handed being herself; there was no need to frisk her. We knew what she was, and we saw what she did, and I couldn't wait to tell Bradley and Joan on Monday morning. There were actual witnesses this time, and one of them— Grace—had a real job. Joe was still off from the museum and thinking about moving to New York City, going to look it over anyway. He was house painting for the airfare, but Joe would have shown up for any hearing. He's a good person and a fine colorist.

Kenneth and I went out for Mexican food that Sunday night. I couldn't get enough flour tortillas and green sauce the whole time I was pregnant.

"Your mother was the same way," my father told me on his way through to Baton Rouge, "and good Mexican food was hard to come by in Oklahoma."

"Where'd you go for it, Dad?"

"Dallas."

When we got home around ten, there were police all around, parked in the driveway and even on the lawn. Neighbors we didn't know— we'd never met any of them, not a one of them ever brought us a pie—stood in the street in their house shoes and watched the cops search our house for drugs.

"We got an anonymous tip about an hour ago," the police told us. "Your neighbors say they don't know you, but since you moved in, they say there are people in and out of here at all times of the day and night. What can you tell us about this? What's going on here? What do you do for a living?"

"You know," I told them, "I never would have been in this mess if my ovaries had held up."

I'm about to tell them the whole story—they're more than a little interested—when I see a car I know as well as my own edge around the neighbors still gawking in the street. I can't see clearly who's driving, but the face in the passenger window is Tenny's, and she's yelling at her dad to bring out her book bag.

About drugs, I don't know anybody born after 1945 who didn't mess around with drugs regularly in the sixties and early seventies. They might not admit it—you pay for history now—but in art or music at least, drugs were just around, they still are. Everybody did something, and they didn't worry about it, at least until they had kids and started thinking about their three-year-olds puffing on joints.

"We knew it wouldn't be simple," Bradley and Joan told us the Monday morning after the dope search. "But we didn't think it would go to the actual grotesque."

"You didn't?" I said, and I was amazed.

With her lawyer's full blessing and clear direction, Raylene and Tenny had recently joined the First United Methodists in Christian fellowship. Their membership was to be put on the evidence table as an example of the kind of moral environment Raylene provided for her daughter. The whole scam made me nuts, particularly since Raylene had given them our address as Tenny's. We got Methodist mail all the time—announcements of Bible study classes, invitations to Wednesday potluck suppers, notices of forthcoming garage and cake sales for the poor and/or unfortunate. (Listen, I didn't open any of these envelopes; these were just the postcards. I don't read other people's mail.) Raylene had also given them our phone number, and the Methodists called once a week at dinnertime to remind Tenny about her pledge.

"This is sick, Kenneth. This is perverse. This is that moral majority stuff."

"It's just tactics, Ellen," Kenneth said, and I was amazed at how flip he'd become since he'd engaged attorneys. He really thought the law was going to take the time to understand our position and then expose Raylene for the bitch she is.

"You need to know, Kenneth, that I'll leave you if you decide to go to law school."

"Ellen, if it comes to it, I could out Bible-verse Raylene on the stand. I went to Catholic school, and she freezes in front of an audience unless she's drunk."

"Raylene's lawyer called this morning," Bradley and Joan told us. "He wants a breakfast meeting tomorrow, and he sounds smug. You sure the police didn't find anything, Kenneth?"

"What will happen now? What will we do? This is hell on earth, guys. Plus, we're broke."

"Relax, Ellen, this isn't going to cost a thing because we're going to let Raylene's lawyer pick up the check. He will, too, when we insist on drug testing for both Kenneth and Raylene. Listen, don't worry. We went to school with Raymond: He's a bully, all mouth, and he always chokes before the bench. But as a counterstrategy, you two might think about joining up with the Lutherans. And Kenneth, you better trash your stash."

I don't smoke dope myself. I was pregnant at the time, and I believed the reports about alcohol and drugs, their effects on developing fetuses. But even if I hadn't been pregnant, drugs are not what I do. I like booze myself, if I'm going to dissipate. Drugs scare me, marijuana makes me sleepy, although I've certainly had the opportunity to get over that reaction.

Kenneth, on the other hand, loves marijuana. He smoked it all the time then; pot was his gin. The police didn't find anything that night. It was still in some box somewhere, or Kenneth was out. I didn't keep up with the dope inventory. The cops thought we were selling cocaine, making something in the basement. They made apologies for the disruption and introduced themselves.

The police traced the tip call to a pay phone at a Heights UToTeM; it was a woman's voice, but that's all we could get on the subject. I couldn't believe it. But I did begin to believe that Sunday night that I was dealing with the devil herself.

The thing was, Raylene used drugs all the time. She and Kenneth smoked marijuana every day of their life together—serious smokers, never not stoned, that early morning scratching in the shoe box lid while the coffee drips. I don't know how they got anything done, how they worked without falling on their faces. I can't do it, I don't even like it recreationally. They also did a lot of hallucinogens, usually weekends, at least before Tenny was born. Kenneth didn't smoke around his daughter after she was three or so, but I didn't think Raylene had ever let up. Of course, I don't really know, although I did see Tenny snort white sugar through a straw at an airport coffee bar. My mother was there. We were waiting on my dad's plane.

"What in the hell are you doing, Tenny?" I said. My mother couldn't speak.

"Officer Friendly showed us at school. This is bad for you, and so are those cigarettes, Ellen."

Raylene and Kenneth's relationship was all about dope, a lot of first marriages were, but I couldn't believe Raylene of all people could find the nerve to finger Kenneth on drugs.

"I don't think Raylene thinks like that, Ellen," Grace said. "I think she made that call to get to you."

Well, she had, she got to me, and from that Sunday night on, I lost all faith in the ultimate triumph of good over meanness. I began to believe she and Tenny would actually disappear out of state some Friday afternoon. I believed Raylene would drive her car through the front of our house anytime, day or night.

"She's all noise," Kenneth told me. "And we don't know for certain it was Raylene who tipped the police, Ellen. Any of these neighbors could've called the cops."

I didn't believe a word of this. We were under siege, and I seemed to be the only one who understood this. I ordered burglar bars, installed an electronic security system.

"It's just like a prison in here," Tenny said to her mother on the kitchen phone. "That Ellen just pushed me down the stairs, Mommy. I think both my legs are broken. I'm bleeding from both ears."

Understand: Tenny was no ordinary child adjusting to domestic change. She'd been in psychotherapy since she was two and a half, before Kenneth and Raylene even separated. The director of her Montessori school said she either had to go to Dr. Peters or leave the school permanently.

"It was a biting problem," Kenneth said. "She had her teeth into everybody."

It was more than biting. It was much more than the grim result of spoiling a firstborn child senseless. Tenny was uncontrollable. She was just fine with one other person, provided that one other person was giving her full and undivided attention. But if another person's shadow even crossed the two of them, Tenny lost it. She'd bite anybody, anything. Then overnight she quit biting and became a choker. She'd try to strangle any intruder; she had Lorna Wilkes so fast around the neck one afternoon that the kid passed out right there under our geodesic dome before we could get to either one of them.

Groups were Tenny's problem; they still are. Any number larger than two presents real anxiety for her. She's arrested emotionally at about three years old. She's a total narcissist. She views the world as hers alone. Baby-sitters exist solely for her entertainment.

Early on I called Gretchen Peters, Tenny's shrink for four and a half years. As it happens, I knew her. That wasn't so unusual really because, remember, I knew hundreds of people in Houston. I'd been here for nearly twenty years, and Gretchen's husband, Roy, who is also a shrink for kids, did a study with a man I used to know. Daniel was also a shrink, but he didn't know shit about kids, and actually I almost lived with him. The two of them—Daniel and Roy—and some other shrinks and shrink-types were studying transitional effects on couples who were becoming parents for the first time. The twosome to the threesome approach, couple to family, what remains, what dies, can anything be done, does anyone care?

Daniel's interest was in the couples—he was never having kids (believe me: I knew) and was collecting data to support this position and his academic advancement. Roy's concern was with the babies, how fast they got screwed up listening to their parents scream about the cost of diapers. Daniel and Roy got actual government money for this study, and eight years later I could've told them plenty, but I don't speak to shrinks socially anymore unless I have to exchange auto insurance coverage with them in some parking lot.

"The best thing that could happen to Tenny is to have you in her life, Ellen," Gretchen told me face-to-face. "She's arrested at pre-Oedipal. Her parents split so early, and they hate each other so much,

that Tenny's never had to deal with the necessary developmental step
to triangulation. She's always got one parent or the other. Frankly,
she's pretty unstable, Ellen. You can help her there. Don't let her walk
all over you, and stay on her about consequences. Be clear about
limits, yours and hers. She's a sad little kid, Ellen, but a lot tougher
than anybody knows."

I let Tenny walk all over me. I spoiled her along with her parents.
I thought she needed more, not less. I thought I could figure out what
that was, the thing she didn't have that would complete her, make her
feel safe, and relax, for Christ's sake. It was all ego: mine. I thought
I could save her.

Our first night together in the Binz house I gave her a pair of ballet
slippers—pink leather with roses hand-painted on them. I gave them
to her after dinner. They were house shoes actually, not real dancing
shoes, but Tenny loved them. She wanted to sleep with them on.

"Shoes in the bed? What will the neighbors say? You'll have dancing dreams, Tenny."

"GREAT," she said.

She took the shoes in her book bag the next day to show her friends
at school and her mother that night, and I never saw them again.
When I asked about them, told her I missed seeing her wear them,
Tenny didn't seem to remember the shoes at all. I think Raylene
burned them, but that was just a dream I dreamed—I was paranoid
about her even before the dope search—but I did find out, after years
and years of watching, that Tenny is a sieve. You can give her something every five minutes; it goes right through her. She is always
starving. She never has enough to fill her up.

"So then why do you keep buying her stuff, Ellen? You know yourself she doesn't need any more crap."

"I don't really buy much for her anymore, but I guess I do still think
the right thing might work."

"That's a little pathetic, don't you think, Ellen?"

"Yes, it's one of the saddest things I know."

If it was just the two of us, Tenny and I got along fine. She could
be a painter: She's got a wonderful imagination, a good sense of color,
and can be very amusing. I cook for fun; she likes kitchens and kitchen
costumes, and she was easy to con into helping. I honestly don't think
I could've made all those cheesecakes without Tenny: She's good at

the creaming, monotonous physical activity doesn't make her feet itch, and she won't allow any lumps. No lumps in cake batter and fixing her hair right are the only two things I know that fill Tenny with any pride. I do keep looking for something else to put on that list.

But if Kenneth was there with us, there was a real problem. He never touched me when Tenny didn't pounce over and get between us. He'd hug me, there she'd be, crowding in, and I mean physically pushing us apart to get in the middle. Kenneth started hugging her hello first, trying to fill her up—that was a good plan that didn't work—but then when it was my turn, there she was, pushing in between us, elbowing and shoving at my ballooning belly. I didn't know whether she wanted me or her father. I don't think she knew either.

"This is my hug, Tenny. Get your own and butt out of mine, and you just look out there for your baby brother."

She'd get furious and try to strangle me. She'd lunge at my neck, claw at me, punch, kick. She bruised me a hundred times that first year, the next. We had to keep her nails trimmed so she wouldn't rip the skin. We had to watch her every second, know where her hands were, be ready to grab her, contain her. We could never relax. We had to be ready to catch her hands and spin her around, hold her from the back. We had to keep her in a tight hug, fight to keep her fists pinned under her arms, wait for her screaming to stop.

"I HATE YOU, I HATE YOU," and it was pretty clear then who she was talking to.

We'd have to send her to her room. She had to learn: Time Out for breaking the rules, for yelling in the house, for being rude, for attempted murder. She never went easily and sometimes we had to carry her. She'd kick at our faces all the way down the hall, up the stairs; she'd scream as if someone was ripping at her, a wild thing. She'd calm down after a while—twenty to thirty minutes, most of it at the screaming level—then sneak out of her room and find a phone.

"They're beating me up, Mommy. They smashed my head against the fireplace, and I don't see so good now, and I think I'm going blind. They're making me sleep in a closet with rats again. Please come get me, Mommy. I hate it here, I hate it here."

It took me too long to realize that eight times out of ten she was talking to a phone way across town ringing unanswered.

13

Memo

"Ellen, what do you want me to do with all these goddamned memos?"

"First, I want you to laminate them, Judith, and then I want you to memorize them. There's going to be a test."

"Ellen, you're going to have a baby. You're not going to goddamned Mars. I could call you if I had a problem, Ellen. I could leave a message on your machine."

"Judith, there's just so much to know."

"Ellen, there's just so much you can know. We wind up winging most of it around here anyway."

"You look at those graduate school catalogs I ordered for you, Judith? As soon as this baby's born, I want to see you out of this pit and into a good MFA program."

"Don't you have enough on your plate, Ellen? I've worked here two years already. I know most of this stuff anyway. I don't want any more of these fucking memos, Ellen."

"I'm pretty busy here, Judith. I've got a thousand things to do today, and I've got another thousand to do tomorrow. Just read

them, Judith. I'm going to fire you the minute I get back from having this baby."

"Hey, Tenny Penny. How was your day, sweetie?"

"Judith called you."

"What did she call me?"

"Huh?"

"You're really not supposed to answer the phone, Tenny. I've told
you that many times. You're supposed to let the machine get it,
Tenny. Where's your dad?"

"Upstairs. He's playing. He's always playing, Ellen."

"What did Judith want, Tenny? Do you remember? This is why I
don't want you answering my phone."

"Yeah, I remember. She said she hated you and something about
ashes. Are we ever going to eat, Ellen?"

"Look, I brought you something for your costume box, Tenny.
What do you think? They're gloves we use to handle paintings at the
museum."

"Yuck, they're gross. What slobbered on them?"

I pitch them right in the trash and start on the alfredo sauce.

"Best macaroni and cheese on this earth," Kenneth and Tenny
think.

14 ....

Bok Choy

 I didn't get pregnant right away. For me, it was not like my mother said.

"Mess around just once at the drive-in movies, and your life is over, Ellen."

It didn't happen that Thanksgiving weekend, and we certainly worked on the matter. In the middle of December I called Sam.

"I'm infertile, aren't I? It's too late for me. I've missed it. I'll never be a mother."

"Shut up, Ellen. We're not even going to discuss that question until the summer. Relax, enjoy the holidays, and keep your feet up."

It was Christmas, we think. Zack was born nine months to the minute counting from Boxing Day, but we can't be sure. No switch clicked on, no sign lit up. We heard no NASA-like voice: We have conception; we have conception. It happened, we wanted it to happen, but it was just an ordinary sexual experience with Kenneth.

"I think it was that time in the car," Kenneth always says, but we can't be sure. There wasn't anything ordinary about that. There was a big storm that night, lightning everywhere.

We were sure on Valentine's Day when we did the at-home test.

"I can't look, Kenneth. You look. Is there a circle in the fluid? Tell me the truth."

"Hello, Mom," he said and sent white azaleas that afternoon to the museum.

I panicked some. There is the Idea, and then there is the Reality of the Idea. Reality hit me hard, and this was a surprise after all my research. I looked in the test bottle, I saw that ring, I saw my Arkansas grandmother's brown eyes winking at me.

"Am I doing the right thing?" I said to Grace over an early lunch.

"It wasn't lunch. It was breakfast," Grace remembers. "It was barely eight o'clock in the morning, and you didn't even touch your eggs, Ellen."

"Listen, Grace: I'm a wreck. I've lied to you and everyone I know. I'm really not off cigarettes completely."

"You're always a wreck, Ellen, but I want to be there when you go into labor. Promise you'll call."

I worked all summer, at the museum, at the house, getting everything ready and shrugging off what I couldn't. I was never sick one single day, although I did get a little weird toward the end. I'd be standing in a long line at the grocery, presenting some new exhibition idea at a curatorial meeting, washing my hair alone in the shower—my eyes would fill up for no reason, tears would fall down my face and catch on my belly. It happened all the time, all through August, for nothing specific you could track. I didn't feel any different, I'd just start to leak. Everybody at the museum got used to it, but I did get my groceries paid for quicker than I should have. People with full carts just stood to the side and pushed me forward.

"I'm all right, really," I told them.

"No, it's okay. Please go ahead. We remember, we were pregnant once, we saw a documentary about this on TV."

I was eight months' pregnant for about five years. No one should be pregnant in Texas in late August, early September. It lasted forever, I was enormous—the baby sitting on my knees—and I was getting pretty tired of this red Guatemalan cotton dress. Still, I kept going, doing everything I always did, getting things done and done pretty well at the very last minute.

We opened our fall exhibition—a good one—Thursday night. I handled the press Friday morning, then had lunch with Ben.

"Are you working, Ellen?"

"Shut up, Ben."

I hadn't painted anything since Christmas, and I was setting up a whole household from May on. The baby was due in two weeks, and I hadn't finished his room—the wallpaper had been late coming; only two walls were done, and I was going to get to that—but I also hadn't bought any diapers or bed linens.

Friday afternoon I went by Sakowitz and bought three sets of baby sheets and down-filled comforters; it ran right at six hundred dollars. Then I went to Target for my first box of newborn diapers, the first box of the four thousand or so I would buy over the next three and a half years.

Ralph, our pediatrician and a near Marxist, told Kenneth and me at the prenatal interview to save our money on baby beds and sheets.

"Just get him a box to sleep in," Ralph said. "Use a drawer, anything. It doesn't matter to them, they just want you."

Well, I like Ralph. I trust him, and he could say things like that. He's got five kids of his own, he is in the business of babies. Kenneth accepted Ralph's advice—Raylene was still forwarding him bills for Tenny's layette—but I wouldn't hear of it. Jesus, it was my baby, my first and probably my last. I had to go with the antique French wicker.

I got the diapers, a jumbo box, and I was proud to buy them—I didn't think or know about the ecological issue at the time—and then I stopped by Mr. Woo's in Chinatown and bought stuff to do in the wok for dinner.

"You will have a happy life," Mr. Woo predicted, his hand on my belly. "But you better take this fresh bok choy for insurance and better luck."

Home, on the back porch, I was trying to keep my balance and hold on to everything, but I couldn't get the goddamned back door open.

Is a little grace too much to ask for? A little luck? I couldn't get the key in the lock. I couldn't get the lock to turn. It was ninety-five degrees, and I'd been pregnant for thirty years. I was exhausted. The baby rolled all night, and Kenneth woke me up every thirty minutes to ask me, "How can you sleep?"

"I will not leak. I will not leak. I will not."

I leak. I didn't want to, it just happened, and Jesus Christ, I couldn't even open the goddamned door.

Gracefulness and late pregnancy are not comfortable partners; they're not even familiar with each other. I was warned of this by mothers who still remembered and told, and it was all over the pre-natal literature, which is still in stacks everywhere. Corroboration didn't help at all. I was unprepared, despite what I knew, and in that last trimester especially when I was just so big, bigger by the day, and hot all the time, so hot I couldn't rest, what was left of my patience— never my strongest quality anyway—disintegrated in the most ordinary of situations. For the first time in my life I was unable to maintain any emotional control, and over nothing in particular I cried fat, furious, and embarrassing tears.

I was clearly crazy out there on the porch, but I would not yield to the obvious. I dismissed completely the logical solution of putting the groceries and the diapers down on the steps, resting a minute, check-ing to see if it was the right key, trying it again calm and unencum-bered.

My father told Kenneth, "Well, it'll be interesting for you, son. She's got style, always liked drama, but you might as well give up reasoning with her when she gets pissed off. I think she'll be a good cook if she ever slows down long enough to take the feathers off the chickens."

I wedged most of myself and the groceries against the door jamb. I kept at it, still crying but pressing on, and it wasn't easy, particularly since the door had also swelled in the heat, and the lock itself needed considerable tickling to work ever. With unpredictable and completely surprising luck, the key caught, and the door fell open abruptly on the third try. Prepared as I was, stubbornly determined to last out a five-minute siege, I lost my composure and balance momentarily, and practically fell on my face into my own kitchen. I cursed Jesus and architectural hardware, and I barely caught myself and the groceries on my Arkansas grandmother's domestic legacy, which is a drop-leaf, spindle-legged oak table with original blue milk paint detailing. I found it years before in the back of the smokehouse before the farm was leased out for Christmas tree futures. On wet days, it smells of decades of curing bacon.

"Kenneth," I nearly screamed, to announce myself and declare my near prenatal accident, but I didn't quite get the word out. His name caught at the hard *K,* truncated in my throat, and I thought I might be having a real heart attack because my whole body went stiff, simply shut down all at once, except for the increasing pounding in my chest and ears. Unbelieving, I blinked to adjust my eyes more thoroughly to the light inside, focused again to be absolutely certain, and realized that no, it was not a dream, not even a nightmare, but that yes, there in my kitchen in actual three-dimensional lime green form was Kenneth's wife, Raylene, her head in my Hussman stand-up.

"Raylene, may I help you?" I said, and I was instantly furious with myself. I sounded like a fast-food attendant.

"I'll let you know," Raylene said from the refrigerator and continued to root.

"Where is Kenneth, Raylene? Where is Tenny?"

"Where Kenny Goodson might be is your primary trouble now, not mine, honey. Frankly, I couldn't care less where that bastard might be," Raylene said, and she backed out of the Hussman with an open bottle of $20 beaujolais leaking from the cork—it was my sister Ruthie's—and the last apple.

"Christ," she said, turning to look me full in the face, "you really have put on the pounds. Haven't you cooked that kid enough yet? You are some kind of huge, Ellen."

I rightened the grocery sacks on the table, pocketed my keys from the lock, and wiped my face, hoping Raylene was as blind as she was stupid. I thanked God I had left the diaper box outside in the geraniums.

Then what I did was to position myself on the sink side of my grandmother's table, the kitchen window behind me, the west light pouring in. I hoped I looked pontifical, and I asked in a reasonable enough voice, "Where is Kenneth, Raylene?"

"Laundry," Raylene said through my apple. "He was with the laundry. I came for Tenny Lou, and just like always, she wasn't ready. Kenny really can't do anything right, you know? She needs school uniforms, her red bathing suit. We're going to the beach for the weekend."

"I packed Tenny's blue bag this morning, Raylene. It's by the front door. Let me show you where it is."

"You are a help, aren't you, Ellen? Hey, have you been crying again? You get that red rash all over your eyes, don't you? I had an aunt like that. She married wrong and cried all the time."

"Kenneth. Where is Kenneth, Raylene?"

"Well, he's been all over this filthy house for an hour at least, trying to find that red striped suit. Tenny's been looking, too. She's frantic. Do you know it's her favorite?"

"Kenneth," I called to the basement in my projected voice, the voice I use to begin docent lectures in museum auditoriums with unreliable sound systems, my strong, authoritative, professional voice. "Kenneth, could you come up here now, please?"

"Oh, wait, Ellen, there's no need to bellow. They're not here. They went out to get a new bathing suit, said they'd be back soon as they can, but you know Kenny, it could be days. I just hope we miss the traffic going south. I just hope Kenny doesn't wreck my car. He was out of gas. He always is, isn't he?"

"They're gone? You are here alone?"

"That's right, Ellen, and I am just starved. You know, you haven't got a thing to eat except bran?"

Margaret told me this was going to happen. Sooner or later, I was going to have to deal with this bitch face-to-face, read her the rules. I wouldn't always be able to circle the block until she disappeared. I couldn't hide in the basement forever.

"Okay, Raylene. I'd like you to leave now. That would be immediately, Raylene. Right now."

"Aw, come on, Ellen. They'll be right back. I've got passes to Seaworld, and it will just kill Tenny if she misses it. Have a glass of wine and relax," and she set the leaking beaujolais, sure to make a ring, on my grandmother's table.

"Raylene, try to understand this. It is inappropriate for you to be here. You shouldn't even be in this house, much less here alone."

"My daughter stays here, Ellen. I come here to get my daughter and take her home."

"I want you out of this house, Raylene. Right now. Please think for once about what you're doing. Dr. Peters believes that Tenny's condition is exacerbated by all this chaos, and what we've got to do is . . ."

"There is nothing wrong with my daughter, Ellen. Nothing. Tenny is just fine. She's a normal, healthy, beautiful, five-year-old baby girl."

"No, Raylene, she's not. For one thing, she's *seven* years old. She causes trouble at school, she has no friends, she has all these accidents. We think she hurts herself on purpose. Tenny is a very sad, confused child. And we all have to work here . . ."

"Don't lecture me, bitch. What would you know about it? You're no mother. All you know how to do is talk down to people. Tenny is just fine, Ellen. Everything was just fine before you came around, you know? Tenny was perfect and happy, very, very happy. I told Kenneth that shrink was full of shit, and I'll get a court order to keep you from taking my baby daughter to him."

"Dr. Peters is a woman, Raylene, and you know it. Gretchen's an authority on children with problems like these."

"There is No Problem, Ellen. When are you going to catch on here? If anybody's got a problem around here, it's you. I'm thinking I just might have to see my lawyer about a change in the visitation."

"There is No Visitation, Raylene. There is nothing because you won't sign the goddamned divorce papers. But you know, you are right about one thing. I do have a problem: I don't like you. You're not welcome here, and if you come in this house again, I swear I'll call the goddamned police. And by the way, get your fucking face out of my refrigerator."

"DON'T YOU TALK TO MY MOTHER LIKE THAT."

She was screaming from the kitchen doorway. I couldn't believe it. How long was she there? What had she heard? Apparently, she was there long enough to hear what she wanted or needed to. Tenny hurled a white Penney's sack across the kitchen at me. It missed its mark and hit the canisters.

"Sweetie, you're finally back," chirped Raylene, and I thought there she goes: white sugar. How does she do that? Why don't her teeth just fall out of her mouth one by one and hit her shoes? "It's okay, Baby Girl. Ellen's just hot."

Tenny ran, tripping over her shoelaces, the full three feet to her mother, who stooped down and picked her up like a baby just born. Over Raylene's shoulder, Tenny mouthed "bitch whore" to me, and then she stuck her thumb in her mouth, closed her eyes, and nestled against her mother's neck. It was yet another clear triumph for blood.

"Now who really loves you, darling?" Raylene said, first adjusting her forty-five-pound daughter to her hip, then setting her down on the floor. "Did Daddy even think to get you lunch? I bet my Baby Girl's just starved, huh?"

And then the two of them left, hand in hand and probably skipping—I couldn't watch—out of my kitchen.

"Sweet Jesus, let them keep going," I whispered, and I felt sick.

I turned away from where they had been and found myself staring out the kitchen window at a yard that needed serious mowing. My mind was suddenly full and racing with mundane, domestic thoughts. I looked down at a sink that needed a good scrubbing.

"I can't do this," I said. "I can't breathe. I've got to get out of here," but I didn't. I started scrubbing.

The physical world does offer some tangible comfort. Dirt is something you can do something about and feel a kind of satisfaction, even a mild pleasure.

"Too mild," Judith said later. "You should've stabbed them both in the throats."

My own mother, a champion wall washer, did The Dirt Thing for years, until she realized even hack golf was infinitely more satisfying. Dirt was easy, she found out. Of course, by then she had the money for domestic help.

The baby, silent since Mr. Woo's, kicked hello.

"Hello, baby boy," I whispered. "Everything's all right, except that your sister's in trouble and your mother's nuts."

There was no need to whisper since Tenny and Raylene were already gone, out of my sight, out the front door with Tenny's blue bag (a Sunday dress packed in white tissue paper, the original red striped bathing suit in a dry plastic food bag). They were off for a weekend of junk food at the beach.

"That Ellen sure has a vulgar mouth on her, Kenny," I heard Raylene say as they left. "She talk like that around my daughter all the time?"

"Have you got sunscreen?" Kenneth wanted to know.

I don't know why he even bothered to ask this question. We both knew if they had it, they wouldn't use it. Tenny will be back here Monday with a storming fever and a second-degree burn like the last time, the time before that. One of us will be bringing her lunch on a tray.

"We tan," Raylene said, and Tenny laughed, a real laugh. She sounded just like a normal, healthy child who was very, very happy.

Then they were really gone. The front door closed, the sure, solid, substantial sound of the closing of a fifty-pound solid oak door built by carpenters who cared. Kenneth locked the new double locks and put on the night chain, even though it was just late afternoon.

I, however, was no longer comforted by false securities, thoughtful attention to detail. Kenneth, whistling "She Was Just Seventeen," walked back through the house toward the kitchen. He was coming slow, scuffing the wood floors, but he was coming.

I heard him, his footsteps amplified in old boots, getting louder, closer. He made it to the kitchen door just in time to catch the fresh bok choy with his face.

15

Blame

You know, Ellen, Raylene would never have been in your kitchen eating your last apple if you hadn't gone into overfunction.

I really don't need this today, Margaret.

You were the one who had to get in the middle of things. Kenneth and Tenny and Raylene really were doing just fine until you got in the pie.

What?

You just had to control things, didn't you? You see where control gets a person, Ellen?

Huh?

If you hadn't decided to pack up Tenny's things, none of that would have happened, Ellen. Raylene would have come by, put Tenny and a grocery sack full of clothes in her car, and been gone. You never would have seen either one of them, Ellen.

I guess that's right. I was trying to help.

You were trying to mess up an old pattern, Ellen. You wanted it to be all your way.

Their way is a mess. They never plan anything. They just react.

That's their way, Ellen. But see, even having to do what you have to do—control everything, make it your style, make it handsome—you could have told Kenneth what you had done. You could have told him the suitcase was ready, where the swimming suit was, you could have told him it was all there by the door. You could have left him a note. You didn't, Ellen. I'm worried you're getting self-destructive, and listen, nobody packs anything with tissue paper any more.

My mother does, Margaret. I do. It was acid-free tissue paper. I stole it from the museum.

And now pilferage. How low are you going to get, Ellen? What's the chorus think of all this?

The chorus?

All those opinionated friends of yours. Your support group? What do they think of this mess you're in, Ellen?

Well, they hate Raylene, but they like Kenneth. They feel sorry for Tenny, but they won't baby-sit. And they also hate you, Margaret.

That really hurts my feelings, Ellen.

Really?

Yes, really. I'm not your friend, I'm your shrink, but I do have feelings. We have a professional arrangement. You don't pay me to be your friend, Ellen. You pay me to help you. I tell you what I think. I think you're drowning here, Ellen.

So what do you think I ought to do, Margaret?

I think you two ought to start seeing Nathan. He's a psychiatrist who specializes in families on the brink—you are on the brink, Ellen—and I also believe you ought to let Kenneth take care of his daughter. He has for a long time, and by your account, he appears to enjoy it. Butt out, Ellen. Call Nathan. Let Kenneth do the cooking.

I hate Kenneth's cooking, Margaret.

I'm not going to say I told you so, Ellen.

You're not?

16

Dogs and Cats

"Are we ever going to get to see that kid of yours?" my father said long distance one Sunday night in late September.

"Jesus, Dad, I've got another two weeks. Don't you have any other questions in you?"

I had things to do, and I needed every minute of those fourteen days. The wallpaper wasn't up, Joe wasn't finished with the painting, and I had another hundred things to tell Judith. I needed another month is what I needed.

"I just talked to Judith, Ellen. I called the museum 'cause I thought you might still be working. Judith told me the honeymoon's over— something about cabbage?—And she also said she's going to quit if you give her another one of those memos. Judith says she knows all that stuff, Ellen."

"Well, you didn't believe her, did you, Dad? Judith is just a punk, a kid, a kid with a big mouth, although it is true I am still not talking to my son's father."

Judith would never have quit like that. We had an agreement. She was going to cover the museum for me while I had this baby, and then I was going to fire her when I got back. Judith was born to be a figure painter, and I wanted her to get into a good MFA program and make some new friends.

"This country's going to hell, Ellen, and I can't hear a thing you're saying on this cheap phone. I'm on the interstate right out of Tampa, and I've got to get this Chrysler on to Birmingham. I'll call you Wednesday, and I'll be thinking about you on the road. I just got this feeling, Ellen."

I needed another month, maybe two to finish everything, and if that wasn't work, I didn't know what work was. My father called from a pay phone on I-10 Sunday evening around ten o'clock—it was right before the news—and I went into labor just after midnight.

"Damn that dog," I said.

Sunday afternoon Tenny's dog Felicity had gotten off her chain, and I'd had to chase it to Almeda Road. We should never have had a dog. That was one of my dumbest ideas ever, but I couldn't let it get hit by some bus.

"You really don't see any link between your father's call and your going into early labor?" Margaret said. She was dead serious.

"Jesus, Margaret, that's pretty abstract, especially for you."

Margaret didn't understand. My father had one of his feelings nearly every week of my life. It was one of his hobbies, but it did get a little out of hand the summer we were waiting on Zack. Four or five times a week my father pulled off some highway in a flash of insight. He called me at all hours from the emergency pay phone on the feeder, and I could barely hear him over the roar of the trucks.

"I like metaphor as much as the next person, Margaret, but I think it was running after the damn dog, not my father calling, if it was anything. It was probably just time, you know? Two weeks isn't early anyway, and it just means I'm going to be two weeks late for the rest of my goddamned life."

The pain came two weeks early because of a dumb idea I had to pay for a number of times. I lay there next to Kenneth who was sleeping, and I felt the sharpness. It wasn't so bad, I could do this. I woke him up at two.

"I can't do this, Kenneth."

Somebody ought to tell expectant women how bad the pain really is. I couldn't believe it at two o'clock, and it got a lot worse over the next seventeen hours.

"Why didn't you tell me?" I asked everybody I knew. I could have prepared better, it went on and on, why didn't anybody tell me?

"I was on drugs," my mother said.

"It was a long time ago," Alice said.

"You can't prepare for everything, Ellen," Margaret said. "In time you'll forget."

Listen, I'll never forget, that pain. I can't, I don't see how anybody could. It was brutal and unyielding and violent. It changed me forever.

Understand: I'd spent years in research. I'd read all these books. I'd learned to breathe deeply, relax, and focus. Kenneth and I took the good down pillows to Lamaze classes Thursday nights all through August, and we saw a number of films on the subject. We prepared, we got ready, and none of it helped. Childbirth, natural or not, is a mutilation of the body and spirit. I have never believed anything I have ever read again, and I have never believed a thing any doctor has told me since. Every defense mechanism I had exploded like a bamboo hut. Certainty left me, all confidence, all faith. I wasn't tough anymore, and there wasn't a thing I could do about it.

My son, Zack, now nearly three, was born at the end of a seventeen-hour nightmare I foolishly thought I could prepare for. The pain ended abruptly, like a stage curtain crashing, quite suddenly and without cue, and Sam said, "It's a boy. Finally," and handed him to us.

He was all blood and screaming, which didn't bother us because there had been a lot of blood all day, not to mention the screaming, although most of the time I didn't recognize that screaming as mine. It was like someone else raving from the other side of the moon, and occasionally, between contractions, I would ask who was that screaming and couldn't something be done about it.

The attending nurse said, "This isn't a hotel, white girl honey. Now push, push, push."

And I said, "Look, bitch, I can do anything, but you've got to tell me how much longer this is going to be, or else I'm going home."

But then another contraction would begin, and my resolve would be lost. The room would simply collapse, and the only thing that was certain was Kenneth, very near, breathing with and for me, big tears running down his face and catching in his beard.

Sam warned me near the end that it was going to feel like someone was ripping my guts out—and he was right, the guts, all gone—and then suddenly and unexpectedly after hours and hours, the pain was over, and there was this baby, mine, ours, a real person and no longer a dreamy idea. He was looking to us for answers as to what in hell had happened to him, his mouth was wide open, and I remember thinking it was as big as his whole face and how was I ever going to figure out what he was telling me and what he needed. Less than a minute old, he looked as if he had considerable need, and I felt as humble as I ever have, but held on.

Kenneth said, "Good job, Mom," and wiped my face and the baby's.

And I said, "Don't forget yours," because he was still crying, and then I said, "Call Tenny."

Tenny was seven when Zack was born that Monday. It was not a Tenny day, she was with Raylene, and we did not have to use any of the backup plans.

Say I go into labor Tuesday/Thursday/alternate weekend:

Plan #1:   Judith picks Tenny up from school and explains she's going to be a sister. They are to wait by Judith's phone.

Plan #2:   Ruthie comes over in the middle of the night to stay with Tenny and be ready to explain that she's going to be a sister. They are to wait by our phone.

Plan #3:   We drop Tenny by Grace's on the way to the hospital and promise to call her there whenever anything happens.

All three have call waiting, so there shouldn't be any problem there, and Grace and Judith each have a suitcase in their hall closets with a change of clothes for Tenny and a new toothbrush. In any case, Tenny can have whatever she wants to eat. Judith, Ruthie, and Grace each hold a new twenty for this purpose, and Tenny is leaning toward delivered pizza or cashew chicken. Further, Tenny does not have to go to school unless she wants to (an unlikely choice, given her feelings on formal education), and she is invited to come to the hospital as soon as the baby is born.

I explained all this in the note to Raylene—I thought she might be wondering—and she left a message on the machine.

"I don't know what you could be thinking about, Kenny Goodson. You can't believe I'd allow some stranger to pick up my baby girl and take her home with them? What's the matter with you, you jackass? I've had my lawyers call the school, and they now have orders not to release Tenny Lou to anyone. You might have tried for once, Kenny, to be a little sensitive to your own daughter's feelings. That baby thing of Ellen's is killing Tenny Lou. She has nightmares about it all the time, and she says she doesn't want to be there for the damn birth, and I think it's just plain sick you would even suggest this to her. Haven't you got any sense of modesty at all? She's just a baby, Kenny, or have you already forgotten that? And you can just tell that Ellen never to send me another one of her fucking memos. Who does she think she is anyway?"

"I want to see my brother being born," Tenny told us.

"Forget it," I said. "You can come as soon as he's here. You wait for our call and draw him some pictures."

We switched hospitals at the last minute because Methodist couldn't make up their minds whether children under ten should be allowed in Maternity. We reregistered at St. Luke's, Tenny came with us for that tour, too, and Sam wasn't happy about it.

"Would you reconsider, Ellen? Methodist is so much closer to my office. I'm going to wear out a pair of shoes."

"Hey, whose baby is this anyway?" Tenny said. "Don't you know my brother needs his sister as soon as possible?"

Sometimes I just loved that child.

Kenneth called Raylene Monday night about seven and asked to speak to Tenny. Raylene said over the television noise that Kenneth must be in flashback because didn't he, "Asshole, know it was Monday" and that was her night to be with her daughter, "alone and unharassed."

Kenneth told Raylene the baby had come, two weeks early. He told her that Tenny had a brother.

This news shut Raylene up momentarily, which allowed Kenneth the opportunity to ask if he could come and pick Tenny up, despite it being a Monday evening, and bring her to the hospital so she could meet him. Raylene started sobbing then and apparently handed the phone to her daughter without any preparation.

"What's wrong?" said Tenny, and she was scared. "Dad, is that you? What's wrong? What's wrong with Mom? What have you done to her now?"

"Nothing's wrong," Kenneth said in this solid voice I've heard a hundred times. It was a voice that until Tenny was about twelve (when everything failed to work) nearly always reassured her, calmed her down, and made her listen.

"Ten Pen, your baby brother's here, a little early, but he's terrific. Want to come over and sing him 'Happy Birthday'? We need you here, Tenny."

Tenny started to whoop—I could hear her because Kenneth held the phone out—and then she stopped and said, "What's his name? What's my baby brother's name? What did Ellen decide?"

"We both need your help with that, Tenny. Put your mother back on the phone."

Raylene was still crying but had recovered enough to say that we had left her with no choice but to say yes. Tenny could go to the hospital, but she had to be back by 9:30 at the latest to get "some sleep at least, since you might remember it is a school night, but I guess it isn't every day you get a brother, but just don't think me letting you take her just when you want to is going to become a habit."

Kenneth said, "Thank you, Raylene," and I think he meant it. He hung up and turned back to me.

"I don't want to leave you alone, Ellen."

"Help me fix this blanket around him, Kenneth, and then let everybody in. And can you call my mother before you leave?"

All day long women—my friends, most without children at all, and others with kids grown up and away—collected outside the door of the birthing suite. At first they sat in reception and thumbed magazines, but when it went on and on—we checked in at eight in the morning thinking, fools that we were, that the birth was minutes away—some of them had to leave. They sent in little letters and jokes, even a few prayers (from the ex-Catholics and the Easter Baptists), and they pleaded with the obstetrics nurse to be called if and when it was ever over.

Grace and my sister, Ruthie, never budged, but agreed around five o'clock that they couldn't stand it any longer. They found folding chairs in the cafeteria, and claiming that they didn't speak any English, they dragged them down the hall to just outside the room where we were working so hard. Sam, my doctor—coming in and out, in and out—heard their questions and kept them informed, complaining all the while that birth by committee didn't come into his fee. When Kenneth left to get Tenny, he told Grace and Ruthie that I was fine, but they didn't believe him and scrubbed. Just behind the cleaning crew (three aides who looked like Curly, Larry, and Moe), in they came, Grace and Ruthie in yellow gowns and masks, expecting the worst and looking about as exhausted as I was supposed to.

The fact was, I wasn't at all tired, and Jesus, I had reason. Instead, I was elated and starving and wondering whether I could and should sneak a cigarette. Curly smuggled in two dinner trays—hamburgers, cold and hours beyond well done—and told me that the Push-Push-Push was, from all inside reports, not only a bitch but also a moron. Grace and Ruthie asked if they could hold the baby, and I said sure, my pleasure, and decided against smoking forever. Then Kenneth came back with Tenny in a kid-sized scrub, all big blue eyes and speechless for a change.

"Hi, Tenno," I said, like nothing unusual had happened since I'd last seen her, nothing like seventeen hours of torture, hospital hamburgers worse than any known drive-thru junk, my radical initiation into motherhood in a birthing suite decorated in white wicker and looking like a Hyatt Regency, only way more expensive.

Tenny sat down in the rocker—her feet didn't even reach the floor—and Grace put the baby in her lap, and then I did get a little nervous because Tenny was holding him, and there wasn't much I had ever seen Tenny hold that she didn't drop, by accident (she said) or on purpose (I nearly always thought).

Kenneth read my mind, or his own, and sat down right next to her to anticipate and be ready, and we watched Tenny, stunned, look at her brother, and rock him a little. Then all of a sudden she burst into convulsive sobbing, real tears and not one of her acts, and Kenneth took the baby and gave him to me, and then he took Tenny on his lap, held her, rocked her.

"What is it? What is it, sweetheart?"

"Mom says you won't love me anymore because you have another family. She says you don't need me anymore."

In the middle of the proudest and sweetest moment of my life to date, Raylene's mean-spirited mouth came in uninvited and spewing sulphur. I don't see how she could have said that to Tenny, and I wanted to kill her for hurting her daughter and for making me mad on my son's birthday.

Kenneth said, "Tenny, you will always be my daughter. Always, always. Tenny, do you hear me? I love you, and I always will, and so does Ellen."

What I thought right then was, well, that's almost true. I do love Tenny, Tennessee Louise, but I couldn't make a promise about the always. I wasn't asked at the moment, of course, which was all Kenneth and Tenny's, so I didn't need to admit to any reservations.

Still, it was pretty clear. Here I held my son, an hour old, there sat my stepdaughter for all practical purposes. I have two children, one is not mine.

When Zack was born, I got him completely, all at once. I fell totally in love and could pledge to anyone at the moment of his birth and at any moment since that without any hesitation, any reservation, I adored him and always would. It was a promise I could keep, no hedging a possible factor at all. I understand mothers of mass murderers sitting for months in courtrooms. I would die for this child, unquestionably, and if I lost this boy, I can't imagine any future.

But with Tenny, there are clear limits to my affections, bounds I had never realized or even knew before the comparison. I care for her, this wild girl. I care for her more than she knows, but I never held her as a baby, fed her smashed green beans, helped her learn to walk, talk, kiss. I met her when she was just three, and she will never be mine.

Raylene is a liar and a cheat and a bully, and I think really crazy, but Tenny adores her. She adores the mother that is hers. I feel sad for Tenny, and then I feel a good deal of guilt. They have three years on me and blood. I think the years will even up somehow, but the blood never will. I know, watching Zack, I can never love Tenny like this, and I can't save her either, so I offer her what I can and hope that will hold her until she can figure it all out herself when she's thirty-five or so.

"Want to hold him again, Tenny?" I said.

She took him, my boy, and he raised a fist in greeting.

"He likes me. Did you see him wave?" she said. "Let's call him Michael. Doesn't he look like a Michael, that angel one?"

No one said anything. Michael was Kenneth's name before he was adopted, and while I had thought early on about that name for the baby, Kenneth said he thought that would hurt too much. Tenny didn't know anything about any of this, we were pretty sure, so when she said the name, we all felt this chill.

"That was my first name, Tenny," Kenneth told his daughter, and I found it almost unbearable to listen to him tell her about his first mother and then his second.

"I think everyone should have their own name," Kenneth said finally. "Does he look like a Zack to you, Tenny? We've been talking about a Zack all day. What do you think?"

"Zackery Michael Goodson?"

"Zackery Michael McKnighton-Goodson. He's my boy, too, Tenny," I said, and it was the first time I'd said that.

"You're going to be an M, and you're sure going to have to learn a lot of letters, Zack-o," Tenny said. "I've got those down, you can ask me anytime. I'm home Tuesday and Thursday nights, and you can always call me at Mom's."

We all agreed on his name. Tenny spit for emphasis, a riskier and somewhat more spontaneous baptism than I would have wished, but I let it go. I had to.

"She's had her shots, hasn't she?" whispered Ruthie.

"I'm breaking her hands if she goes for his throat," Grace said.

And then we began to sing, Kenneth leading all of us together, very softly, "Happy Birthday," Tenny and I both quite a bit off-key—it's the one thing we do have in common—and after that, we went right into "Good Night, Irene."

We stayed in the birthing suite for another day, another four hundred dollars, another set of yellow sheets with American beauty roses. I couldn't sleep and didn't want to. I was still reeling from the pleasure of having the pain over, seeing my boy. Zack stayed with us in a Plexiglas box. Kenneth took the hide-a-bed.

"I dreamed about you in Venice that time," I whispered to Zack. "I didn't take a gondola ride. I was waiting to go with you."

I watched son and father sleep, made a hundred photographs, talked on the phone, and received flowers from men. Women came to see and stayed all day. My mother arrived from Arizona and climbed in bed with me.

"How's my baby girl?" she said. "I hurt with you long distance all day yesterday, Ellen. If your father had known how much it hurt, we never would have had Ruthie. You know I have sheets just like these? Now where is our baby boy?"

Sam said, "Could I see you alone for just a minute? I'd like to check your stitches."

They all got their purses and waited in the hall, and Sam said, "You're fine, and your baby's terrific, but your friends and family are driving me nuts. Get out of here."

A nursing crew came by, three mean ones in spiked caps.

"This is how you feed him, this is how you bath him, this is how you change him. Don't use powder, don't use oil, sing if you really want to, but he doesn't need much more than maintenance. Try not to kill him. Good luck and get out of here."

Tenny, flat on the linoleum, finished her math homework on her belly and told Zack, "You know, I'm real good at arithmetic. Listen, don't you want to bust out of that box and go for a couple of elevator rides?"

We left, charging the birth on my American Express and stealing a good many nightshirts and flannel blankets.

"Take as much as you can," Ralph, our pediatrician, said. "You're paying for it anyway, and this is about the last time you'll have any tangible return on your money. Kids are all greed. This boy is going to soak you for thousands."

Kenneth brought the truck so we could haul all the flowers home, but he forgot the infant seat.

"You are going to kill that child," the aide said and took the wheelchair away.

I thought about getting in the back with the baby, it might be safer, but I couldn't stand the image: too Oakie.

"We ought to be in a limo," I said. "I hate this truck, Kenneth."

We climbed in the front, Kenneth driving, me holding the baby and wondering how exactly I'd shield his head if we hit anything. Tenny sat in the middle advising her father on his driving and asking when she could bathe Zack.

"Never," I said.

Six blocks later, thankfully without incident, we were home. My mother was there at the door in an industrial apron she must have brought with her, and my friend Joe was there, too, hurrying around, trying to finish up the trim painting in the breakfast room. Tenny's dog Felicity was off her leash and inside the house, jumping around and urinating on the dropcloths.

"You didn't tell me about the dog," my mother said. "What's the matter with it? And Tenny's mother just called and said she's bringing over some cat."

For Tenny's seventh birthday, Kenneth and I went to the SPCA and bought her a puppy. It was my idea. I figured she could practice taking care of a small thing, learn how delicate they were, how much attention they needed, how much they'd love her. I wanted her to learn about loyalty, and I wanted her to have a friend, and I wanted all this to happen before the baby came. It was a great idea that was doomed early.

For one thing, Tenny hated the dog. At her birthday dinner we wrapped a bag of food up as a present, led her through a trail of written clues, had a lot of fun that night. She found the puppy finally in the front bathroom and was thrilled, although to be frank, thrilling Tenny anytime isn't too hard. She loves getting anything, is always dramatically grateful, a little too loud. She milks the moment, then forgets.

Tenny didn't know how to handle a dog who turned into a pony overnight, and it was just about impossible to help her learn Tuesdays, Thursdays, and alternate weekends how you had to take care of it every day. The dog was all legs, nervous, a jumper, and even more nervous when Tenny was around. Tenny said she was scared of it. Raylene said the dog was crazed and would probably chew Tenny's nose off if given the chance. She had read about something similar in the paper, and Tenny wouldn't go near it after that bedtime story.

Plus, there was something wrong with it, we were sure. Besides being a nervous sort, poor Felicity couldn't control her bladder, and I spent most of my time at home mopping up urine and sorting through regret. When she chewed the fringe off my best kilim, I decided Kenneth was right about dogs as outside animals, and we put her out on the screened porch off the living room. She jumped right through the screens, and we had to go to chain.

When Tenny got home from school, she was required to say hello to Felicity, which she did pretty regularly if you reminded her, but she wouldn't touch the dog. She wouldn't even go out on the porch.

"Doesn't that make you sick, Ellen, that slobber all over the windows? It stinks in here."

I felt sad for the dog's miserable life, but couldn't decide what to do about it. If we gave the dog back to the SPCA, what would we be telling Tenny about responsibility? On the other hand, if we kept it chained on the porch and jumping in its own crap, the SPCA might come by on its own.

"Joe, please take this dog."

"Not me," Joe said. "I like my nose where it is."

My mother was pretty good with dogs, we had black and tan dachshunds once, and she couldn't believe we kept poor old Felicity chained up outside.

"She slept with me last night and urinated all over the bed. I bought Clorox and a new mop. What do you want for lunch?"

Raylene was always buying Tenny animals. To buy Tenny anything, to take her with you especially, is to ensure a happy, loving child for a full eight to ten minutes. Raylene and Tenny shopped, and after clothes and shoes, animals were a big favorite. They went through birds, hamsters, and fish like crazy. They all died.

I could understand this. Really, who knows what you're getting in those pet stores? How do you tell how old a goldfish really is? What diseases has a hamster got? When I was eight—we were in Shreveport, then Waco—I bought a goldfish every Saturday at the downtown Woolworth's, came home with it on the bus in one of those Chinese take-out containers. It was always dead by midweek.

Maybe with a similar idea in mind (helping Tenny get ready for the baby—Kenneth says this notion is *much* too generous), just after her birthday Raylene bought Tenny a kitten, also from the SPCA. They don't stay home much, so after the initial cuddling, the cat was pretty much on its own in their house. It did cat things: scratched at the upholstery, turned things over, took to using Raylene's bed for a litter box. Raylene called Kenneth and said she couldn't take living with the cat anymore, but that Tenny loved it, cried when she talked about giving it away, and, "for Tenny, wouldn't we take it?"

Now I like cats. A cat would have been a much better idea for us than a dog. They're cleaner, they're more ornamental, and they have infinitely more character. I told Kenneth that was probably all right if Tenny would take care of it, but couldn't we wait until after the baby was born?

Home ten minutes from the hospital—I was just showing the baby Kenneth's studio—Raylene drove up and parked in the middle of our driveway. She had the kitten beside her on the front seat in a shopping bag.

"Zack," I said. "That bleached blonde down there is Tenny's mother. She thinks she lives here, but she doesn't. You let me know what you think about her."

What she wanted, of course, was to see the baby, our Zack, her daughter's brother. I guess that's not so weird, but it's the woman's methods I can't stand. I stayed up on the third floor, and my mother told Raylene in her best Episcopalian voice that we were both asleep and waking either one of us up, after all we'd been through, was just not possible.

Raylene left, talking about her own pain in childbirth, which Kenneth found funny since Raylene got knocked out on drugs early, and Tenny was delivered by emergency C-section.

My mother said over lunch, "Kenneth, it's hell anyway it goes," and I found myself thinking she was right. With or without drugs, it's worse than any hell, and I hold real respect for women I don't even like who are mothers.

Of course, this new attitude didn't last.

17 ....

Bone Dead Tired

My mother stayed for ten days. She did all the cleaning and all the shopping, all the cooking and all the laundry. Other than that, she wasn't much help.

"So, how do you do this, Mom?" I asked her. "I need to do this right. Show me everything you know. How do you take care of a baby?"

"You know, I'd really forgotten how little they are here at the first. You know, I didn't have boys so I really don't know about this circumcision stuff. You know, I bet somebody's put all of this on one of those videotape things. Hey, is that the roast burning?"

She ran off. She left me and her only grandchild wailing in his first tub bath. I heard her feet, her bare, sixty-five-year-old feet, pounding fast and dangerous down the stairs to the oven. I grabbed my son, wrapped him in a towel, and went after her. The stairs slowed me up—I had to take them one at a time, I was afraid I'd fall and kill us both—and when I got to her, the roast was already cooling in its own juice on the cutting board, and my mother was folding her latest load of whites.

"What's the matter?" I yelled to her over the roar of the washer, which was churning on final spin and shaking the tomato paste off the shelves. "And what in the hell are you washing now?"

"Sheets," she said, and I heard her voice crack. "Tenny's sheets and all the towels from this morning. We'll need more detergent before tomorrow."

"Look at me."

Tears were running down her face faster than she could wipe away. My mother is a crier by inclination, but I never saw much more than two or three tears, a couple of sniffles. Her face was a river.

"What's the matter, Mom?"

"I'm really sorry, Ellen. The truth of the matter is, I can't help you with Zack."

"Come on," I said. "What is this? I'm your daughter, this is your grandson."

"He's beautiful, you know? You did a great job, and I'm so proud of you. I'm sure you're going to be a great mother, sweetie."

"I already am a mother, Mother. What are you talking about?"

"Babies scare me, Ellen."

"What do you mean babies scare you? You're my mother. You had two younger brothers, you took care of them some. You had Ruthie and me, you took care of us. What is this?"

"I can't help you. That's it. I love you, and I love him. I'd walk through fire for either one of you, but I can't help you now. He's too little. I can't help you bathe him. I can't help you feed him. I can't hold him because I really think I'll drop him. I'm no good at this, Ellen. I'm better when they can read."

"You're nuts," I told her.

"Yes, I think so. I'm sorry."

I needed my mother. I needed her to show me how to really take care of my son.

"I need the mechanics, Mom. How do you do this?"

"The mechanics are easy, honey. You're smart. Read up on it, or call those nurses again. But what I think you really want is the other stuff: where you get that blind strength to hold on to your own, care for them, and not be afraid. I never could do that, Ellen. I was terrified the minute I saw you, and I think I still am. I'm afraid I'll be witness or worse, the cause, of something horrible, a freak accident. I'm afraid I'll kill him."

Frances is nuts. I never knew any of this about her, my own mother.
"Who took care of me?"

"Your father did nights. He's fearless on the subject of helplessness.
And my mother came. She came on the bus from Arkansas, rode all
night, got sick on the smell of chicken bones rotting under the seats.
She was wonderful, knew just what to do. She had this confidence
about being able to really care for people. My mother knew what she
was doing, and babies felt it immediately. You notice how Zack cries
every time I touch him? I miss her so much, I can't tell you. You're
alive because of her, Ellen."

My mother and I knock back a couple of glasses of iced tea to my
grandmother's memory. The tea is still warm from the brewing, strong
as ink and sweetened to near obscenity; it is the way my grandmother
made it every morning of her life. Ice hasn't got much chance of
effectiveness this early; it melts, then rises to a foam at the top of the
glasses. We add new ice. We drink. We hold the tea in our mouths
until the ice slivers melt. They cut the heat and the thick bitterness
and the awful sweetness.

"You really like this stuff?" I asked my mother.

"You know, Ellen," my mother said, "it's a wonder any of my family
kept their teeth after drinking this syrup crap. Do you think mint
would help?"

My mother and I give up on the whole iced-tea thing and go to a
nice Chardonney Alice gave me when Zack was born. We have a
glass, and then another, and we toast my grandmother and her great-
grandson at eleven o'clock on a ordinary weekday morning. Zack
watched the two of us from his automatic swing thing. He has my
grandmother's eyes, and my mother's, and mine, but other than that,
he's all Kenneth.

"He's a nice-looking young man, that Kenneth. I've always liked
him, Ellen, if you're counting up votes. You think he'd mind if I took
his truck again?"

My mother wouldn't drive my car. It was a 1974 Jaguar sedan—
black with tan leather upholstery—I'd paid for about seven times. It
was always in the shop, and my father thought I should buy a good
station wagon made in Detroit. He's union basically and thinks you
should buy American. The fact that he owns two white Volkswagen

convertibles in mint condition and a brand new Mercedes-Benz doesn't strike him as inconsistent.

"They're investments," he says.

My mother wouldn't drive my car because it was English. She wanted Kenneth's truck to take to the grocery.

"It's a Toyota, Mom. It's Japanese."

"Oh, don't tell me that, Ellen. We need Clorox."

My mother wasn't much help. She cooked all the time, day and night. She loaded up the freezer with casseroles and when that was full, she called all over town about renting a cold storage locker.

"I don't think they have those anymore, Mom."

"This is the biggest city in Texas, Ellen. You can get anything you want here if you know where to call."

She did take Zack for a walk in his stroller every afternoon, and she met all the neighbors. I was supposed to nap while they were gone, but I couldn't. The house was too quiet, I missed Zack's noise, and I kept thinking about what would happen if the wheels fell off the stroller and both of them became unnerved out there in the road.

"This is a tough street to crack, Ellen," my mother said. "These people don't even know you live here, although I think you could count on that Mrs. Florita Reynolds in the white house if it was a real emergency. She's had the flu lately, wouldn't touch the baby, but she'll come up sometime soon."

My mother finished hanging the wallpaper in Zack's room, but she hung the border pieces upside down.

"Elephants lie on their backs sometimes, don't they? Where'd you get this stuff? I'll redo it."

"I got it in Italy, Mom. It's nineteenth-century remainders."

She met the meter readers and newspaper carriers. She spent all one morning visiting with the college kid who cut the grass, and she greeted the mailman every day with a cup of fresh coffee.

"His name's Alexander, been on this route since the late forties. He's from Little Rock, and he's got five granddaughters who'd love to baby sit for you anytime."

She surveyed all of Tenny's clothes and bought her new underwear—days of the week embroidered on the panties, she refused to believe Tenny wasn't here everyday—and she beat Kenneth downstairs every morning to make Tenny's sack lunch. She did all the mending, and she ironed all the bathrobes, even the terry-cloths.

"Tenny's a pretty little thing, but don't you think we could talk her into cutting some of that hair, Ellen?"

At the time, Tenny's hair had never been cut. Kenneth and Raylene loved it long, but it was a mess to get a comb through it. Ruthie and I always had pixies, much more efficient in the mornings—you could sleep another twenty minutes.

"I ask her all the time about a haircut, Mom. She says short hair is too butch, and her parents would kill her if she cut it. We could try."

My mother left after ten days. She cried all the way to the airport.

"I'm sorry I wasn't any help, Ellen. I have ordered you another deep freeze. It should be arriving Friday. Call Windell at the Sears on South Main if there's any problem at all, and as for mothering, you're smart and you're also odd. I think you might just wing it, sweetie."

"Mom, please take this dog."

"Okay," she said.

Frances Ellen McKnighton told Delta Airlines she was blind and took Felicity home with her in economy. Collusion or dramatic altitude seemed to help the mutt, who had no urinary accidents on the flight or since. I called to find out how Felicity was doing, and my mother told me she had changed her name.

"Felicity is no name for a dog, Ellen."

"Well, what are you calling her?"

"Her name is Mrs. Dwight D. Eisenhower. I'm calling her Mamie, and your father is not speaking to either one of us currently."

"He hates Republicans, Mom. I do, too."

"We are what we are, Ellen. You keep working on your winging and send me a Polaroid every day of that angel boy."

I tried. It was the hardest job I ever had, and I'd had plenty. Home from the hospital fifteen days, I had a dinner party—I thawed my mother's wrapped veal thing, is what I did—and all these women came: Grace, Laurel, Judith, Alice, Ruthie. I'd been missing them, and I wanted to do something normal.

In his bassinet in the dining room, Zack slept like the angel he was and still is, but just as we were getting ready for coffee, he woke up and started screaming. Six women formed a circle around his bed. They leaned forward on their toes and peered in. He screamed, he turned red, then blue, and not a one of them moved to pick him up. They stood with their hands behind their backs, their mouths slack. He didn't stop, he got louder, and five of these women looked at me. I had to pick him up: He was my son. He still screamed.

They hung their purses over their shoulders, put their fingers in their ears and headed for their cars. I held him, my boy. He screamed, and I couldn't even wave good-bye. It was the last time I ever saw them all together as a group.

Kenneth was working in his studio, but the noise was hard to miss. He came downstairs and took our son. He put Zack in his little feeding chair, put them both on top of the dishwasher, and then turned it on. It began to fill with water, then shake on wash. Zack quit screaming.

"How do you do that, Kenneth? How'd you know to do that?"

"It used to work sometimes with Tenny."

"I can't do this, Kenneth. I can't."

"You are already doing it, Ellen. It's going to get easier, and then he'll be in the Cub Scouts."

"That Kenneth is such a good father, Ellen," my mother said long distance. "You tell that boy I'm sending him a pie tomorrow by Federal Express. You think a meringue would make it?"

We were exhausted, we were dead to the bone, we didn't sleep more than two hours at a time for weeks and weeks. Then Kenneth hocked his drums to make the rent, took a weekend job in Beaumont to make some money, and left me alone with this baby.

Zack was five weeks old, doing fine and screaming continually. I never got out of my nightgown. I'd wake up in the morning, then it was night again. Zack screamed all the time.

I was trying to get some sleep, but I was hungry. I was thinking about poached eggs, a thin hollandaise with a touch of Tabasco. It was three o'clock in the afternoon, and I hadn't eaten all day. Then Zack woke up again. He was screaming.

I put my head under all the pillows and screamed with him. I imagined going in there, getting him by the feet, beating him against the wall—his body a bat—until his head exploded and his screaming stopped. I couldn't believe this image, I couldn't believe I could think something so horrible. I screamed even louder. The image went away.

"You would never have done it," Kenneth said later. "You couldn't do that, Ellen."

I came up from the pillows. Zack was still screaming. The kid was tough. He outlasted me every time. I went to the door of his room, stood there. He saw me and toned down a notch.

"What is it, baby? Diapers or dinner? You want me to read you some more from the Grimm boys, or would you like a little Flaubert?"

Zack put his head down and howled. He hates Flaubert.

Then Zack was nearly four months old. He was just beautiful and doing all right, but I'd put on about ten years, and I don't have a history of overt concerns with vanity.

"It's just temporary fatigue," everyone said. "It gets better. Really, all new mothers are exhausted and look like shit."

We'd barely caught up with all the sleep we missed the last two months of the pregnancy when all he did was roll, and the first three months of his life, when all he did was scream. Kenneth and I sat up out of habit, then incredulousness the first time he slept all night through. Early into it, one of us checked him every hour or so to make sure he wasn't dead, and then we realized after midnight that this might be the night. I wasn't about to miss it, and Kenneth went along. We pulled both rockers into Zack's room, watched him turn in his sleep, and guessed at his dreams. At six we drank a whole quart of frozen orange juice laced with flat Sprite and promised ourselves a more balanced life, a happier future, vacations at the beach, regular sex. Zack slept all the way through the "Today Show," and I called my mother long distance to tell her.

"It's over," I said. "He's ready for college."

"I'm so happy for you both," she said. "You know, hearing your voice long distance in the middle of the day about gives me a heart attack."

For a few weeks we were happy, days and most nights, except for the crap with Tenny and Raylene, which is always there, and the fact that we didn't have enough money, which never is. I wanted to wean the baby, do it slowly. Zack didn't seem to mind, and breastfeeding on a regular basis wasn't hard to give up since, for me anyway, it never did come even close to transcendence.

Everything was fine, no catastrophes for once. Raylene was in remission, Tenny seemed steadier, the plumbing held. We got cocky, thought the worst was over, all wrapped up, everything under control. We relaxed and thought about getting back to some real work.

We put the baby in a Mother's Day Out program at the neighborhood Methodist church for one trial morning, just three hours. Zack seemed to love it, the Methodists were big on rocking, and Kenneth and I knew we loved it. Three whole hours off, a lifetime. It was like a gift you never thought you'd get, and boy, did we need it and sure as hell did we deserve it. Kenneth had a late breakfast meeting with the band, worked on a new song list.

"Let's do 'Woolly Bully,' " I heard Kenneth say, and I could actually remember how that one went.

I concentrated on getting my studio back in shape, made a list of supplies I wanted, and threw out all the oil paint that had calcified in tubes I'd left open when I went into labor. I really thought I'd be getting back to them in just a couple of hours, but I didn't know shit then. I felt nearly happy that morning, functioning on all cylinders for the first time in months. I was thinking about stretching some canvas, playing with a new scale, looking at Ingres again, and replacing all the cadmiums. I stuck a Polaroid of Zack (we'd made it that morning on the front porch, Zack propped up against his diaper bag: "His first day at school") in a blue enamel frame I'd bought in Belgium years ago. I put it on the corner of my drawing table and knew I had initiated myself as a working mother. I barely thought about my boy after the first hour or so.

We tried it a second morning, and then a third. It was heaven. We caught up with the laundry for half a minute and made fresh pesto before all the basil went to seed. We actually read a newspaper printed sometime in this decade. I was working on some watercolors, trying to shake the rust loose, when they called from the church just before noon. Zack was running a fever, 101. Could we come get him as soon as possible?

I kept the accelerator on Kenneth's old truck flat on the floorboard and ran every stop sign between our house and the Methodists. It was only five blocks, but it took a lifetime. My heart was pounding so hard

I thought my chest might crack wide open before I even got there, and when I caught sight of the building, its pompous little steeple and the boxwood hedges, I jumped out and ran. I just left the truck wheezing in the middle of the road, and I didn't even take the keys. My whole life was in my throat. I was terrified, and if I had taken the time to think about it, I'm sure I could have vomited all over the new carpeting in the formal vestibule.

They had Zack in an old crib in a darkened room in the back part of the community building. He was dead-out asleep, all chalky looking and burning up. He'd kicked his blankets off and was surrounded on all sides by bright plastic early development toys. By contrast, they made him look all the paler, all the tinier, and why the hell hadn't anybody covered him up?

"Oh, honey. Oh, honey" was all I could get out, and that was just a whisper. It took about an hour to get from the door of the room to his crib.

"Oh, honey," and I picked him up, held him to me. He was on fire.

"We don't believe in taking any chances here at St. Paul's," they told me in these ordinary, everyday voices. "Their eyes start glazing over, we isolate them back here right away, and call the mothers."

"What do you think it is?" I asked. "What's he eaten? Is he going to be all right?"

"He's just got a little something. Bring him back anytime, after he's free a full twenty-four hours of all fever, and of course, any rashes. He's a sweetie, your Anthony."

I waited an hour and three-quarters in the pediatrician's office to find out what's happening to my baby. Zack woke up in the truck on the way over, it was a pretty wild ride, and he wouldn't stop crying. I walked with him, up and down, up and down the long orange and blue reception area, about four hundred trips, bounced him in my arms a little, which sometimes works but not this time. He still screamed, I wanted to, but kept pacing.

The waiting room was jammed, hardly a place to sit down anyway, full of three dozen sick kids, all wrapped in dirty-looking quilts and nestling against briefcases. They all had wild eyes, the kids and the parents, and there wasn't any coffee. I couldn't find Kenneth by phone, he'd gone out early on errands in my car, and I thought my arms would fall off just any minute, but I didn't care and kept bouncing my boy with no noticeable success.

The nurses decided Zack was the loudest, so they pushed him ahead of about a dozen other feverish kids, and I didn't even apologize or say thanks. A Vietnamese lab technician named Stephanie stuck his toe with a needle on a board and drew a whole lot of blood out into a glass tube.

"Hey, Mom," she said. "Relax. It's his toe, not yours," but I would never swear to that.

"Ralph, what is it?" I was finally able to ask. "What's wrong with my baby?"

"You know, we've been real lucky so far with this guy. Some little urchin at the day-care place gave this little urchin a nice little virus. It happens. It's just a little something. He'll get everything for about six months until his immunities are settled in."

"But he's so hot, Ralph. His fever's a hundred and three right now."

"He's strong. He can fight it. Just listen to those lungs. Take him home, Ellen. Soak him in a warm bath, give him another squirt of this baby aspirin, and put him to bed. He'll sleep it out probably. Call me if he's running fever tomorrow, or call me anyway and bring him back if you want. He's going to be fine, Ellen. Babies do this, get sick, run real high fevers. Now, have you got any gin in the house?"

"Gin?"

"Put him to bed, and then pour yourself a good strong drink. Straight up, no ice. You need one."

I never *needed* a drink in my life.

It was just a little something. Zack's fever was down the next day, gone completely in two. He was fine, all pink, you would never have known he was sick, but it took me a good week to get back to being my just-exhausted self.

"This is hell," I told my father over the phone. He was home for a few weeks; Charlie takes most of the fourth quarter off to plan his year-end tax scams. He sneaked off to call us from the pay phone at the Shell station every morning until Zack's fever broke. My mother sneaked off and called from the grocery store around noon, and then they called together from home at night just after the rates changed.

"I've got to go back to work at the museum soon. I don't know what I'm going to do, Dad."

"You know, Methodists never have any sympathy for anyone but their own," my father said. "You put that little fucker in that snowsuit we sent and fly him out here. I'm wiring you money for tickets right now. We'll take care of him, fix him up. You know, it's probably his tonsils. You were sick all the time until they ripped yours out."

"If you really love me, Dad, send a case of Bombay," but he didn't hear me because he was out of quarters and the operator cut him off.

We tried the Methodists one more time, and Zack got sick again. Ralph wasn't surprised to see us.

"You'll work this out," he said. "Everyone does."

The museum said I could bring him with me afternoons if I'd just hurry up and decide when I was coming back.

"Benefits don't last forever," they told me. "We need you or some-body else. Don't you need the money?"

Kenneth got a part-time job afternoons at a caterer's. It paid less but was steadier than lunch gigs. He liked the chef hats, I liked the leftovers, and Kenneth could keep Zack mornings. For lunch I ran home, or Kenneth brought him to me at the museum. We fed him together, still some breastmilk but mostly formula in bottles and rice cereal from my own silver baby spoon, which my parents remembered suddenly and sent via UPS. Zack slept pretty well most afternoons in a sculpture crate on my credenza. He cried only when I was on the phone long distance to Europe.

Then Tenny got the flu, and Raylene said it was Kenneth's turn to keep her. I didn't think Raylene was right—didn't we keep her the last time?—but I hadn't been keeping the log up, so I had to start a new one. Zack didn't get the flu from Tenny, but Kenneth did, a bad case that lasted six days, high fever, a lot of vomiting. He couldn't work. Then Zack got a pretty serious ear infection, the left one, and then his teeth started coming in, one tooth, then another, and it was like starting all over again. He couldn't sleep, and he couldn't eat, and all he did was scream all the time and run a fever.

"I can't take this, Ralph. I can't. I can't take this."

"Don't goddamned tell me what you can't take, Ellen," Ralph said. "You've got to wait until this kid calls you from Mexico at three o'clock in the morning and needs bail money before you can say that. You've got to wait until he steals your new car when you're out of town, and then wrecks it in Lake Charles, and you hear about it long distance collect from your insurance agent. This boy hasn't even had a serious head wound yet, Ellen, not one broken bone. Don't tell me what you can't take. You need a good eighteen years on you before you can even begin to think like that, so you better get ready. Do you hear me, Ellen? *Get ready.* He's just having some trouble with his first teeth, for Christ's sake, but I am a little worried that he's not gaining weight."

I shut up right then because I really like Ralph, and I really care what he thinks about me. He's a great pediatrician, I knew him before I needed one, and Zack likes him and all his stupid engineer's hats. I like him because he looks right at children and talks to them directly; they're crazy about him. They draw crayola pictures for him while they're waiting. They send him their grammar school photographs, high school graduation announcements, wedding invitations. Then they bring him their kids.

Ralph sticks everything he gets up on the walls of the examination rooms. The first time I was there, I thought it was tacky until I heard him in the next room. He was cutting the cast off a little girl's arm and commenting on how pleased he was to get her Halloween picture of the cat with the broken legs.

"You know, your mother liked to draw when she was your age. She did a real good job with birds, but I think you've got it all over her with your cats. You want to keep this stinky cast or pitch it?"

He's got warm hands he rubs together to make a little warmer before he touches any baby, and he nearly always asks you what you've been reading. He likes the Latin Americans, is down on the French, open to the Italians. He subscribes to *Art in America* for the waiting room, which is a nice complement to *Hi-Lites*, and he follows the Astros. Zack gave Ralph one of his first real smiles, and Ralph said he would honor that gift forever. We believe him, and we like him a lot, not to mention need him, so I was pretty ashamed of myself for threatening to go belly up over a new tooth, particularly when I thought about his daughter.

Ralph had six children, now he has five. His oldest daughter died all at once two years ago in the cross fire of a neighborhood UToTeM holdup. Ralph didn't tell me, I read about it in the paper. She was twenty-two years old. You'd think you'd be done by then, not have to worry anymore. When Ralph was raving at me, listing what was coming for me and any new parent, he didn't mention that late night phone call from the police, but it was all I could hear, that phone ringing in the middle of the night. Motherhood's made me neurotic, real neurotic. I don't know anything about scale anymore, and I don't like myself so much.

"I'm a jerk, Ralph. I'm sorry."

"You know you really are, Ellen. Take this and get it filled, and bring this kid back next week."

The prescription had my name on it: "Buy a very good pair of Italian shoes. Consider cerulean blue."

The pink billing form said "No charge, reschedule for followup," which was a surprise and a relief. We'd seen Ralph nearly a dozen times in two and a half months. At fifty-five bucks a pop, despite insurance coverage, we'll owe MasterCard for decades at this rate. The diagnosis was "F.T.T."

"What's this F.T.T. mean?" I asked the appointment nurse. "How come you medicos never talk plain?"

"F.T.T.?" she said. "Why, that's Failure To Thrive."

18

Working Drawings

It all went to hell after that. All of us failed to thrive. That had been going on for a while actually, but now we had a diagnosis.

#1

Ralph gave us a scale. He actually carried it out to the car and put it in my trunk. We had to weigh Zack every four hours, before and after he ate. We had to weigh his food. We had to keep a record, detailed charts and line graphs, and we had to bring Zack to Ralph's office every three days for professional weighing. Ralph worried there was something wrong with him inside, something that failed to process his food properly. Zack ate all the time—every three hours—but he wasn't gaining weight as expected. He wasn't growing.

We started him on strained fruits and vegetables. He liked beets, an actual fact no one could believe. He gained three-quarters of an ounce in five days; Ralph was pleased, but we still had to keep the scales, the graphs, the worry.

My mother sent Zack his own silver spoon after I dropped mine down the garbage disposal. When it happened, I bent over the sink and cried.

"It's an *objet* now, Ellen," Kenneth said.

"It was an *accident*, Ellen," Tenny said. "You didn't mean to do it, and do you know you're getting that rash on your eyes again? It's yuck, Ellen."

#2

Tenny asked me every day I saw her if her father was shit.

"I don't like your talking like that, Tenny. Your father loves you. You better respect him, or I'll kill you."

"Mom says he's shit. Is she shit?"

"Your mother loves you, Tenny. You better respect her."

"Do you love me?"

"Not all the time."

"Well, how about now?"

"Let me think about it for a while, Tenny. I'll give you a call."

#3

The cat died. Tenny came into our bedroom about seven o'clock one Sunday morning. It was barely light. I'd had about two hours of sleep—Zack had this colic—and Kenneth had played late. He'd gotten home just after four.

"THE KITTY IS SICK," she said, and everybody woke up except the dead and the near-dead.

I got up to see about it. The kitten was out on Tenny's sleeping porch living on newspapers. We were trying to protect the bedspreads, keep the water bill down. I touched it, this little gray thing. It was a rock. I'm no good with dead things.

"Kenneth, the kitty is DEAD."

He got up, and Tenny started crying. Then Zack started. I was feeding Zack, Kenneth was looking for the shovel, and Tenny was hysterical. There wasn't any coffee in the house.

I watched the funeral ceremonies from the window of the second-floor landing. Kenneth was comforting Tenny, putting the kitten in a cigar box, talking about death with his daughter. She was crying hard. She put the box in the hole, shoved a little dirt in, then got bored with the whole thing and snapped back to her old self. She was running around the backyard, her hair flying in a tangle behind her; she was trying to catch a butterfly for Zack. Kenneth shoved the rest of the dirt over the box with his house shoe and was about to come back inside when I said from the window, and I didn't intend to sound like such a bitch, "Don't leave those tools in the yard. We don't do that, Kenneth."

#4

Joe left for New York City. Zack was sick, sick with some fever, some tooth. We didn't even get to have a last lunch together, and the house wasn't near finished.

"It is never going to be finished," Joe told me on the phone. "The painting's done, the new house numbers are up, but I really think, Ellen, that refinishing the floors would be a waste of time and money until your kids are gone."

"They're going?"

"They're just visitors in your life, Ellen. You've got a few years of hell left, then good-bye."

Joe's gone. He's working at the Whitney, and he'll never write. I just hope he paints.

#5

Laurel actually said she'd baby sit one Sunday afternoon. She came over in starched jeans and flat shoes, soft Italian leather the color of new plums. She looked like an alien, but Laurel has always been the sort of woman who looks all out of scale in anything but high heels and silk dress suits. I had actually forgotten how short she really is.

Laurel crawled into our bed with the Sunday papers, both locals and New York's. We put the baby with her—Tenny was going to assist—and we left. It felt like a break out, an escape from hell.

My car was in the shop, and Kenneth had two flat tires on his truck, so we walked the five blocks to the Contemporary Art Museum. I was thinking about Joe in New York, walking, walking everywhere, and I walked right into this writer I barely know, this Donald.

"I hate domestic life," I told him.

"It gets better," he said. "Believe me."

"Tell me that sixty times."

He began, and he got to a full three count before he had to run off and save his own child's life. His two-year-old in pink corduroy Oshkosh coveralls was climbing all over a rusty John Chamberlain floor piece. He got to her just before she fell on her face and had to have plastic surgery at weekend rates.

"When do they get those tetanus shots?" I asked Kenneth, and we headed for home.

Laurel was still in our bed with Zack when we got there. She was pale and looked considerably older.

"I was afraid he'd roll off the bed and bust his head open. He didn't ever move, and I thought he was dead, and I didn't know how I was going to tell you. I love you—I love you, too, Kenneth—but I can't do this, and Tenny's outside digging up some cat."

#6

Kenneth and I took Zack to Arizona for Christmas. Ruthie came, too, but Raylene wouldn't hear of Tenny being away from her, not even for her brother's first Christmas.

"Okay, we'll stay in Houston," I told Kenneth. "My parents will get over it. They're not sulkers, Kenneth. They'll just reinvent what happened."

"No, Ellen, I want us to go. We can have an early Christmas with Tenny here, and I think she'll like the doubling up on holidays once the benefits occur to her."

We got a tree—a skinny fir that spoke to me at the Safeway. Kenneth and Tenny wanted to use an artificial one.

"Think of the forests," Tenny said in the checkout line. "You're a murderer of wood, Ellen. How can you sleep?"

I buy the tree out of my own checking account, I order a hundred things from catalogs, and I get Judith to knit up stockings for the mantel.

Tenny gets twenty presents—clothes, toys, a birthstone ring, a new winter coat, a good reading lamp, a crate of navel oranges from my parents. She rips through all of them like a rabid dog.

"Is that *all?*" she says.

She's mad she didn't get Tub Town, some bathtub thing that'll mildew in minutes.

"We told you we weren't getting you Tub Town, Tenny. You've got enough mildewed stuff."

"Everybody got presents but me," she tells her mother from the kitchen phone. "We're not even going to have a turkey, Mom. It's that goat junk again—*baby* goats, Mom—and Ellen just told me there wasn't any such thing as Santa Claus."

"Hey, Tenny," I whispered in her free ear on my way to the dining room. "How'd you get that phone to work?"

She was sprawled all over the kitchen floor, and I had to step around her. My arms were full of hot pies.

"That phone hasn't worked for me, Tenny, since last Monday when lightning hit this very room."

Understand: My parents taught me to adapt or die. Charlie and Frances get actively and immediately involved wherever they are. In three months, they know a place better than any native ever could, but then they've had a lot of practice setting up new community relationships.

It is mostly my mother. She pounds the streets until she finds people she wants to eat with, and once she's let them in on a few recipes, she keeps up with them for years. Charlie and Frances must get a thousand Christmas cards. The phone rings all the time over any holiday, people calling from everywhere, old neighbors who knew me when I was eight.

"So, you're an unwed mother now, Ellen. Well, that's just wonderful. Frances sent us pictures, that boy is a beauty, he's a god to your parents."

They haven't had a real Christmas tree in years. They hang lights on a five-foot barrel cactus, the desert approach to Nativity.

"We're going to get busted this time for sure," Ruthie told Kenneth. "You know, cactus is considered endangered in Arizona."

Kenneth took it all in pretty well. He didn't say much is what he did—which is one way to survive—although he did confide to me over the Bacardis that he thought holidays brought out the truly bizarre in all families of his experience.

"Listen, you just better be glad they're not still in Corsicana," I told Kenneth.

That's a little hole of a town in central Texas, just southeast of Dallas; it's the fruitcake capital of the world. The half year we lived there my mother had candied pineapple and cherries strung up all over the place.

Christmas morning Kenneth gave me five perfect walnuts. We were broke. We spent it all on Tenny and airfare. I gave him a prism of his own, and my parents gave us a TV. We had four already, but that's what they give you: Zeniths. It's my father. He bought the first RCA available in Oklahoma. Then he bought the second one.

My parents gave Zack a bicycle and a set of brass knuckles.

"He's only three months old."

"It's a tough world out there, Ellen. You've got to be prepared and know how to cheat when necessary."

"You never bought me a bike. I still hate you for that."

"Jesus Christ, Ellen, you couldn't ever see shit," my father said. "You always had those glasses."

"I think really," Kenneth said later—we were in the real guest room with a door that closed; Ruthie, who they still think is twelve, got a sleeping bag on the sofa—"they were afraid they'd lose you to traffic, Ellen, and just couldn't bear it."

Kenneth and I left Zack for whole hours with Ruthie and my parents. We actually saw four first-run movies. We slept, we ate, we cleaned no bathtubs, we did no laundry.

All Christmas Day we tried to call Tenny. She was not at her mother's, not at her grandparents', not at any of Raylene's sisters' or brothers'. They were in Houston, they hadn't left, they'd been everywhere, they had just walked out, they were expected any minute. We left messages. We asked for her to call us collect.

Tenny never called, but Raylene did. She wanted to make sure we were coming back to Houston for New Year's Eve, which was our weekend. She wanted to remind Kenneth that Tenny Lou was his responsibility, his baby girl, and no, he couldn't speak to Tenny right now because she was gone. She was outside with her uncle Gary; they were taking a ride on the Eastex Freeway on his new motorcycle.

#7

It was in the twenties for four days in January. This doesn't happen in Texas much. Two water pipes broke. When we turned on the heat, we got headaches inside of fifteen minutes.

We camped for two nights by the fireplace under antique quilts I paid a fortune for. The fireplace smoked. The third night we checked into the Warwick Hotel, ordered room service and watched pay-for-view movies. The fourth day the heating man came and fixed the gas leaks; it cost a fortune, and the landlords are never going to reimburse us.

We roasted through January—I loved it at eighty, I had a new baby in the house—and Entex sent us a bill in February for $450 in prior month usage.

"What is this? This can't be right?"

"You're burning straight gas in a fifty-year-old floor furnace. Most of those caught fire years ago, Ellen."

They let us pay the January usage out over time. We were current by mid-June.

#8

I am back at work, which is to say I am going to the museum and sitting there. I am not painting. I don't have any time, I don't have any energy, I don't have any ideas.

I do take a lot of photographs, mostly of Zack, mostly Polaroids, and it is Grace who points out that I am cropping the pictures in the camera so that no one has any hands.

"Well, Ellen, you know what Louis would say about this?"

Louis is Grace's analyst, this is not a real question, and I don't care what he would say anyway.

#9

Raylene calls and wants us to keep Tenny for the night, for the weekend, for ten days. She's going to San Francisco for the hell of it; Park City, Utah, for the winter festivals; Maui for a once-in-a-lifetime opportunity. Kenneth says yes, yes, yes.

We have Tenny undiluted for days on end. She breaks the last of my Italian pottery and is exposed to chicken pox. She's apparently immune, but Zack and I come down with them and are in bed for a week, ugly for two.

"You look like shit, Ellen," Tenny says from the door.

"Write this down, Tenny: *Get out of this room.*"

#10

Alice is in Europe for the museum all spring. She sends postcards of places she knows I love: Orvietto, Venice, Prague, Seville, Dresden. I stick them on the refrigerator. I always hated those trendy magnets—and I still do—but I've had to concede to utility in many areas of my life since natural childbirth. The postcards get covered up with grocery lists, Tenny's school announcements, Zack's weight charts, Kenneth's gig schedules. They peek out from the bottom of things, remind me where I might have been, which some days, lately, tires the heart.

In February, Laurel marries this excuse for a human being, this Colin. He is a lawyer with money and five kids, three of them in college, another two in prep school; his ex-wife wants to be a dentist. Laurel is happy, she says. I can't stand the man, or Laurel currently, and I drink too much at the wedding and let them both know.

Grace is working fifteen hours a day. I never see her, although she reminds me by phone that Laurel always gets married in February. Grace wants to know if we can have lunch, and she says she'll buy. I book a table at Vincent's for September of 1992, but Grace doesn't get the joke and writes it down in her ten-year Week-At-A-Glance.

Judith is getting weirder.

Henry is in the hospital most of the time.

Eight times out of ten when I pick up the phone, someone hangs up.

#11

Kenneth comes home early one Saturday night in April, sits on the end of the bed, and says he's giving up music.

"Come on, Kenneth. It was just a bad night."

"We don't have any money, Ellen. I had to hock the drums for the rent twice this spring."

He's hocked those drums a hundred times. It's what Kenneth does.

"Look, Ellen, I'm thirty-eight years old, I'm bald, and I don't want to do this crap anymore. They hated us. They fired us in front of everybody. They didn't pay us a dime, and we played four goddamned hours."

"Well, let's sue them," I say. "Let's call Bradley and Joan right now."

"I hate lawyers, Ellen. I'm going to work days."

For years Kenneth has hocked his drums. He gets the cash, pays his bills, earns some money, goes and gets his drums back. I even got them out of pawn a couple of times, his birthday, that time my tax refund came early. Monday, I got them out of pawn. Tuesday, he put an ad in the Greensheet and sold them Saturday to a fourteen-year-old kid just learning to play.

"Can I pay these out over time?" this Ricky asked Kenneth.

"Sure," Kenneth said and threw in the high hat for nothing.

Kenneth worked harder at finding a job than anyone I ever saw. He was on the street in a suit and polished shoes, his beard trimmed, by eight o'clock every morning. He read the want ads, stood in lines at employment commissions and alumni offices, and stayed optimistic.

"Nobody gets a job out of the want ads, Kenneth. Don't you know anybody?"

"No," he said, "but this beard's going if I don't get something in two weeks."

"I'll leave you if you do that," I told him, and I meant it.

It was destiny, a miracle: He got a great job and kept his beard. He sells videotaped educational programs to school districts in Harris County. He works for the local PBS station, gets a car allowance and wears a beeper. He's home by 5:30 weekdays, and in a year he was making 60 percent more than I was making at the museum after a decade.

"Don't you hate it? Don't you miss playing, Kenneth?"

"No," he says, but I know he's lying. He wants to take me to Ireland, but I don't see how we can do that until Tenny's eighteen. Her mother would never keep her for us.

He did need a good car for his new job. Neither one in our driveway was reliable on the road and traveling county-wide was his new life. Kenneth couldn't actually buy a new car—we didn't have any cash, plus there were community property issues, Bradley and Joan told us—so he leased a new Mazda sedan. He dropped Tenny at her mother's one Sunday night. Monday morning early, somebody egged it and ruined the finish.

#12

Bradley and Joan kept working on the divorce thing. They met regularly with Raylene's lawyer, and every time we were about to get some action—all we needed was a goddamned signature—Raylene got crazy and switched attorneys.

Every one of them started off hostile—their reading of the situation colored by Raylene's mouth—but over time, a few months, they mellowed with more complete data, an understanding of the fuller picture here. They advised Raylene to sign the papers, get on with her life, make some arrangement to get her bill current. She fired them and got another asshole.

"I can't stand this," I told Bradley and Joan.

"We're not happy about it either. Would you consider the Unitarians?"

#13

At seven months, Zack gurgled his first word. It was "Idea." I wrote it down and called Arizona. He didn't say another thing for a month. Then it was "Da-Da."

#14

Through it all, every week or so, Ben called.

"Are you working, Ellen?"

"Shut up, Ben," I told him.

He always called back.

Damage

$\bigcup$udith calls from the museum at the crack of dawn. It was actually just after ten o'clock in the morning, but I had in childbirth lost all sense of the scale of time.

"Ellen, I'm sorry to bother you at home. Are you coming in? Is Zack okay?"

"God, Judith, I'm trying to get there. I'm still waiting on Lydia to show up. What's wrong?"

"It's Claudia's big diptych, the red one from eighty-two. It came in early this morning. We've got damage, Ellen."

It happens more than anyone realizes—damage to art—but no one ever gets used to the news. Just hearing the word sinks the spirit.

"How bad, Judith?"

"Not bad, but bad enough. The left panel's got a scratch at the far top. It's thin but deep, clear to the gesso. It may have cut the canvas, and it's nearly three inches long. It's pretty bad, Ellen."

"Jesus, what happened? What's the crate look like?"

"The crate looks okay. It's dry. The corners are clean, doesn't look like it was dropped. But Claudia didn't use any spacers between the painting and the shipping frame, and it must have shifted around a lot inside. The top two butterfly hinges are broken on the diptych, the screw's exposed. That's what did the damage. Are you coming in? Should I call Claudia? What time is it in London?"

Painters should never be allowed to crate their own work. They think their work's invincible and is going to live forever.

"No, don't call her. I'll do it. Judith, make sure you get a full set of Polaroids, okay? Do call Huntington Block right now, but don't take it out of the crate until I get there. I'm on my way this minute. Is Henry there yet? Does he know about this?"

"Where are your brains, Ellen? That asshole hasn't even called, but maybe it's in the water, huh? Listen, have you got Claudia's slides with you? The ones you took the last time you were in London? I looked everywhere in your office, and I can't find them. This painting looks a little different than I remember from the transparency. I think she's worked on it some since you were there."

"I've got the slides here at home. I'll bring them with me. Hey, how's the painting look otherwise?"

"I hate it. It's fabulous," Judith says, and the two of us pass quite effortlessly from the real but pedestrian concerns of handmaidens to art—fretting about shipping damage and complicated insurance claims while we build up our retirement annuities—to the broader, juicier, and far more engaging perspective of two painters admiring another's new one. We find it necessary to own up to our jealousy along with our pleasure, although it wouldn't be safe to do this in just any company. In this case, as long as it's not ours, we're glad it's Claudia's.

"Not me," Judith says, but she's young, just twenty-three. "I want it to be mine."

"Can't you fix it, Ellen?" Henry wants to know.

Sometimes I can do restorations, if the damage isn't too severe. I'm pretty good at mixing paint to match, plus I know how Claudia works—she buys Windsor & Newton cadmiums exclusively, uses some cigarette ash to flesh out the paint. But this time the canvas is ripped, reweaving's necessary. It's beyond what I can do.

"You better call Grace, Henry. I'll tell Claudia."

Grace doesn't work for us. She's on the City Museum's payroll, but she's a first-class conservator. As a group, they're like the Red Cross, the Salvation Army: They'll go anywhere in a minute when they hear about trouble. They don't do it for the money, although they make piles of it comparatively. They do it for love.

Grace has already heard what's happened. She's got an ear to the ground all the time for this sort of tragedy, a second sense about damage. She's packing her kit already. She'll be here in ten minutes.

You have to move quick with fiber damage. The weave begins to fray with the split, the tension of the canvas works against the rip. The warp and woof actually begin to shrink, and the tear continues to grow every second.

"It's not too bad," I tell Claudia. "Grace is here, we can get to it right away, don't worry. It's a fabulous painting, Claudia. One of your best."

"You mixing the color, Ellen? I was smoking Players in eighty-two."

"I was just about to ask you that. I'd forgotten," I tell her, although this is a lie. Judith has already gone to the Warwick Hotel to buy two packs. We'll get headaches making that ash, and we really could use any brand, except that we want to do it right.

"I'll send you photographs this afternoon of the restoration, Claudia. Don't worry. We can fix it. I'll call you."

We fix it. Grace is fantastic, the steadiest hands in the business, the strongest wrists.

I was mixing the paint for her when I got a call from Lydia. She's this illegal alien—Guatemalan—we found to keep Zack. Kenneth is working real days now, and I can't have the baby at the museum anymore. He's awake almost as much as he sleeps now, and he needs developmental experiences, rides in his stroller, walks under trees.

Lydia and her husband came up through El Paso, got to Houston somehow. They're not political particularly. They came to make money and are hoping to go back with some and get their kid. It's a boy, their four-year-old son, and they left him with her parents. I don't know how they could do that, but I've got no idea what a life in a Guatemalan jungle might be like. Her husband, Guillermo, carries a bone-handled knife in his right boot. That knife is unsheathed.

My Spanish is pretty good, and Zack likes Lydia, who is maybe twenty and can whistle like a bird. I run home for lunch every day to give him his beets, and Lydia meets me at the door with a sheet wrapped sarape-style around her waist. She carries Zack on her back, my boy her papoose. She bounces him, slides around on the wood floors in her socks, dances with him on her back. He laughs; she sings, then whistles. I teach her to dial my number at the museum and explain about the double locks on all the doors.

Lydia is hysterical on the phone. I can't understand her, she's talking too fast, something's happened to my boy.

I yell for Antonio. Antonio's mother is from Mexico, and Spanish is his first language. Antonio is talking to Lydia, he is talking fast. I'm getting my keys out, I'm leaving. I'm at the door, and Claudia's red paint mix is going to mud.

"What's she saying, Antonio? Is he still breathing?"

Antonio hangs up.

"You're out of orange juice, Ellen, and you need a better house-keeper."

Then this drunk rear-ended my car two blocks from home. I had both kids with me. It was late afternoon, a Friday, a little drizzly. We were all in the front seat; groceries, dry cleaning, and schoolbooks in the back. We were in the turning lane, turning for home, cars coming toward us. I could see in the rearview mirror this big white Pontiac swerve into our lane and not slow up. I knew it was going to hit us, but I couldn't do anything, so I said, "Get ready," and then this tank crashed into us.

My car shoved forward about half a block and stopped. My chin bounced twice on the steering wheel, and Tenny's knee slammed hard against the gear shift.

"My knee, my knee," she cried. She was screaming her head off in her own behalf—there was blood everywhere—until she glanced over at her brother in his car seat. His eyes were closed. He was completely silent.

"OUR BABY, ELLEN."

Zack didn't move. I really thought his neck had snapped. I watched my hand reach over Tenny's bleeding knee and touch my son's chest. He was breathing.

I threw open my door, screamed at two black kids watching on the corner to call an ambulance, the police, and punched the Pontiac woman—reeking of beer and crying at the side of my car—full in the face with everything in me. She fell forward in the street and started heaving. I jumped over her—I should have kicked her face in—and ran to the other side of my car. I opened the door and felt Zack's chest again. He was alive, but still not moving.

"Come on, baby," I whispered. "Come on." He didn't budge, and I was afraid to pick him up. Spinal injuries.

Tenny was hysterical, holding her hand against her knee to try and stop the blood. She was rocking.

"HE'S DEAD," she screamed.

Out of nowhere came this calm voice, mine.

"He's just sleeping, honey," I said, and as it turned out, I was right. I put her hand on his chest. "See. He's okay. Let's not wake him up, all right?"

She shut up, didn't say another word, but she kept rocking, her body trembling. Tears kept running out of her, and I didn't think they'd ever stop. She took her hand away from Zack's chest. The blood on her hand marked his white flannel blanket.

"Oh," she said, looking first at the blood on her hand and then at the red print of it on the white blanket. "Oh. Oh. Oh."

"Come around here, baby," I said, and I remembered all at once where this was coming from. It was my mother's voice, her understated approaches to bloody emergencies.

"Now let me see that little cut on your knee."

It wasn't such a little cut really. Fourteen stitches in Texas Children's Emergency. I had to call Raylene because I couldn't remember where Kenneth was playing that evening—he was still playing some weekends, happy hours here and there: acoustic guitar, no drums—and the hospital needed parental permission, not to mention proof of insurance coverage, before they would sew her up.

"Will it leave a scar?" Raylene wanted to know.

"Oh, I hope so," Tenny told her mother on the pay phone.

To be safe, they did an EKG on Zack.

"No problem," Ralph said. "Don't you wish you could sleep that well? Next time, Ellen, just lie and tell them you're the mother."

We went home in a yellow cab. The police had taken my car, had it towed somewhere. It looked totaled to me, but you never know until they call. In the cab, Tenny and I balanced ourselves on the edge of the passenger seat. We wedged Zack between us and the seat back—my boy, her brother, a bolster pillow. We were afraid of another arbitrary accident, another cold kiss from fate. His infant seat was in tow somewhere.

Tenny was nodding, all washed out, exhausted. She nearly went to sleep in the taxi, but Zack, who was hungry and wet, was crying himself sick. He kept us both as alert as we could be under the circumstances.

"It's good to hear him scream, isn't it, Tenny? Does your knee still hurt?"

"I don't know," Tenny said and fell asleep with her chin on the front passenger's head rest.

The cabdriver carried her in for me, took her upstairs to her room, put her on her bed. I took Zack to the kitchen, got him a bottle, met the cabdriver on the stairs.

"Lady girl, you got your hands full here."

"Yeah, and I don't have any money."

I didn't even have a checkbook, a credit card. Everything was in my purse, and that was in my car, and I couldn't even remember where the police said they'd have it towed.

"I'm sorry," I said, and I guess he could have knifed me there on the landing for $4.25 and at the moment I wouldn't have even resisted much.

"No problem," he said. "My name's Willie. Here's my card. I'm independent. Pay me when you can, call me when you need me," and he left, closing that heavy front door quietly behind him. He double-checked from the outside to make sure the lock had caught.

I changed Zack, put him to bed with a bottle, which you're not supposed to do. It sets a bad precedent, they say, not to mention the fact that it can rot his teeth, promote thumbsucking.

"Please go to sleep and don't tell anybody," I said. My baby boy complied.

I threw a blanket over Tenny, propped pillows around her knee to hold the ice bag, pushed her hair off her face, and took her thumb out of her mouth. Then I went downstairs to get ready for Raylene, who

I was sure would come roaring through the door any minute, tearing at her hair and reaching for her baby girl.

I got ready. She didn't come. She didn't even call. It was just like her—unreliable, unpredictable—but she still surprises me. I just don't get it about her. What kind of mother is she? Fourteen stitches, ambulances, all those tears that wouldn't stop, that pale face. When Kenneth got home finally at two, I was furious.

"Well, it was just a little cut, wasn't it?" he said, and I had to explain all over again about the drunk and the stitches and my genuine concerns about his attitude lately.

"We could've all been killed, Kenneth."

"But you weren't, Ellen, and I don't see getting crazy about what didn't happen. I'd have thought you'd be happy to have Raylene *not* in this house for once."

"I can't do this, Kenneth. I can't do this anymore."

"You're doing it, Ellen. Come on, let's go check on our kids."

20

Float

Tenny will be eight. She expects a party.

"What kind of party?"

"Big," Tenny says.

Tenny expects a party, a big party, full scale, one hundred presents wrapped in—

"What colors, Tenny?"

"Huh?"

"You know, the colors. What's the theme here? What's the glue for this party, sweetie?"

"Huh?"

"What colors do you like this week, Tenny?"

"Yellow and pink."

Tenny expects a party, a big party, one hundred presents wrapped in yellow and pink. She wants a tiered cake, balloons, magicians, and everyone she's ever met in her life in attendance. Her history insists on this.

"She's always had a party, Ellen."

• • •

Last year Kenneth rented this skating rink. The year before, Shobiz Pizza. All the kids in her class come, the girls anyway. They bring these junky presents, get dizzy on white sugar, giggle until they're sick. Someone always gets hurt and cries.

"Was it Tenny who got hurt last year, Kenneth?"

"No. Last year it was Raylene."

Raylene fell trying to roller skate backwards and bruised her tailbone. Her stepfather had to take her to Methodist Emergency for X-rays, and Tenny thought her mother was going to die. Kenneth wrote a hot check for the whole party thing because Raylene took all the cash for the emergency room. She never did pay Kenneth back. The party was a disaster. I was glad to have missed it.

"The most fun anybody had was the ride home in the back of the truck," Kenneth said.

I have avoided Tenny's birthday parties for years. I don't like birthday parties, particularly kid parties. All that greed, those junky presents, the fostering of thin sentiments. None of those kids care a thing about each other, and last year when Tenny was seven, I was pregnant and we were just moving into the house. I stayed home and considered my options for window coverings. Nobody missed me. I didn't know Kenneth wrote a hot check. I didn't remember anything about Raylene falling on her ass.

"Did Raylene ever actually sue that skating rink, Kenneth? Listen, how much does a party like that cost anyway? Exactly how much does Raylene owe you, Kenneth?"

"Those parties are pricey, Ellen. You pay for convenience. They supply everything for five bucks a kid, and afterwards they just hose the room out and bring in the next group."

"I hate birthday parties, Kenneth. Couldn't we just have a nice dinner together? I'll make that shrimp thing she likes. We could get her a new bike. A good bedspread. Gloves."

"Gloves? Ellen, it's July."

• • •

I took Tenny to Courtney Anderson's birthday party in April. We were right on time, two o'clock straight up. No one answered the bell, so we nudged the door open and peeked in.

"I told you we were late," Tenny screamed, and then disappeared into a swarm of two dozen hysterical eight-year-olds already wild on white sugar. In lavender organdy party dresses and black patent leather shoes, they churned like tornadoes all over the house, hurling confetti and broken noise makers at each other. I picked my way through them to find Courtney's mother, who looked like she'd been up for three nights in considerable pain.

"Here's a little something for Courtney," I said. "Are we late? Are you all right?"

"Just put it in the den," she said over the squealing. "We're just getting started."

There was a stack of boxes on the coffee table two feet high, all wrapped in cheap paper and used ribbon. They were all big.

Courtney, the stinkiest kid I ever met, began ripping into them like someone starved. I was pleased to see Courtney's mother make her pause a second at least between dives. It was hard work for both mother and daughter—this developing of social graces—and more than painful to watch. On cue (a nudge on the shoulder, an elbow in the back, a slap on the side of the head), the birthday girl mumbled a general thanks in the appropriate direction, then fell on the stack again like a buzzard picking fresh meat.

The crowd's attention actually held for three or four openings, then began to waffle and turn mean at the fringe.

"Tenny, does Courtney need earrings? Are you sure her ears are pierced? These are pretty expensive, honey."

"She's my best friend, Ellen. My very, very best friend. Everyone's giving her silver earrings."

While I was watching, Courtney got one pair of silver earrings and about two hundred beauty kits from the dime store. The nail polish— the real stuff, the color of raw bacon—was by and large an enormous hit. They cracked the bottle seals open on the edge of the coffee table. The banana smell of new polish drew them together for the moment, and they got down to it.

"Watch your dress, Tenny," I said. "Watch Courtney's mother's table. Jesus, get a paper towel at least."

"Are you staying?" Tenny said. "None of the mothers stay, Ellen."

"You're sure you don't need any help?" I said at the door. "It's okay if I go?"

The woman, Courtney's mother, looked a little vague. Her eyes just glazed over trying to form a response to my question. You could see she was down to nothing, and it was very early in the event. I thought she might be on drugs, or should be, but I couldn't remember her name, first or last.

"Oh, no," Courtney's mother said. "You must go. Everything's under control, considering. We'll do cake at three-thirty. You've got to come get her by four. Hey, who are you anyway? None of the mothers ever stay. Don't you know that?"

I didn't know that—nobody tells me anything—but it was a relief to be out of there, away with just the touch of a headache from all the rabble and the fumes of vanity.

Why do they make nail polish smell like ripe bananas, and why do people name their children Courtney? Don't these people care about their furniture, and why does anybody give birthday parties for un-grateful children anyway?

"Guilt," Kenneth says, and he knows a lot about the subject, generally and specifically.

I only had one birthday party in my life; it was horrible. I was nine. My mother had a sit-down dinner for the girls in my class. She made her veal schnitzel thing with fresh ground Hungarian paprika, sour cream on the side in dark green bowls. Martha Spencer, who was getting breasts early and talking about it, kicked the finish off a leg of the dining room table. She told Irene Lewis the borscht was blood, and Irene vomited in the laundry room and went home early.

"I never had a birthday party," Kenneth told me.

"Do you want one?"

"Nah, I don't want one. A nice dinner and new underwear is fine with me."

"Do you need new underwear, Kenneth? What kind of underwear would you like? Jesus, Kenneth, all you want is underwear?"

"What I want, Ellen, is to have a birthday party for Tenny in this house."

I bought the bait. A party at home, not in a rented hall. Tenny's first party in a real home. Tenny's first party at home in our home. I know how to do parties, big parties, hundreds of people. I can do this. I can do this right.

"You are such a sucker," my friend Grace told me over lunch.

"You think so? Listen, Grace, how many round cake pans have you got? How many springforms?"

I'd just gotten home from picking up the helium and the last of the stuff for the treasure hunt when Kenneth told me over tuna fish in the kitchen what nature of hell we were going to be living in on Saturday afternoon.

"This is a joke, right, Kenneth? This is one of your horrible, wicked, terrible, terrible jokes. I'm dead tired. Please don't do this to me now."

"It's no joke, Ellen. I wish it were. Tenny's mother will be here tomorrow for the party."

"What are you talking about, Kenneth? What's happened?"

"We don't have to make a big deal out of this, Ellen. Tenny has invited her mother to her birthday party. That's it. Her mother will be here sometime Saturday afternoon. You want to bet the rent money she'll be late and overdressed?"

"You can't mean this. Are you completely nuts? You actually invited that bitch to be a guest in my house?"

"Wait a minute, Ellen. I didn't invite her. Tenny invited her. It's Tenny's birthday party, and we told her she could invite whoever she wanted. She wants her mother at her party."

"That's ridiculous, Kenneth. That's really nuts. And awfully sudden, don't you think? When did this come up exactly? This sounds like Raylene's idea, Kenneth."

"You're probably right there. Tenny did just call, and the timing does have that special Raylene taint."

"So, you explained to Tenny, right? How inappropriate that would be? How that's simply not possible? How sick this is?"

"No, I didn't."

"You didn't?"

"I didn't."

"Well, what did you say to her?"

"I told Tenny it was her party. I told her she could have anyone she wanted here. Raylene said she wouldn't miss it."

"Jesus Christ, Kenneth, where are your brains? That bitch. In *my* house."

"Hold on, Ellen. I don't want us to get crazy here. It doesn't have to be a big deal unless we let it. And, Ellen, what is this *my* house stuff?"

I am up at 5:30 on Saturday morning ironing my Battenberg lace tablecloth. It takes a good hour to do it right. Kids may not care, but I do. This party's going to be fabulous.

I talk Kenneth into rolling out of bed at seven and starting on the balloons.

"Ellen, we're not blowing all these up? There must be five hundred balloons here."

Kenneth doesn't get it. You've got to blow some up early so they'll begin to drop. You don't want all the balloons stuck on the ceiling.

"Kenneth, let me explain about float."

"Who else has Tenny invited, Kenneth?"

I have the nerve to ask this question about eleven o'clock on Saturday morning; it occurred to me at 10:55. The party starts at two.

"Just Raylene's parents—her mother and her stepfather—and her sister and her husband, and their four kids."

"We're out of gin, Kenneth."

"Are we having gin? I thought you bought champagne for the adults."

"Champagne's not going to get me through this, Kenneth. Go get the gin."

I am thinking about the devil when I start on the crepe paper. I'm using just a little; crepe paper can get tacky quick. I'm hanging it on the door jambs. I want it to flutter with the late afternoon breeze. I want it to look like heraldic banners, a medieval joust.

Suddenly, everyone I know is there. They are taking their seats in the grandstands. Flags of two colors—white and near-white—wave on bamboo poles.

I enter the field, which is my living room. The crowd is partisan: It roars. It is my crowd. I wear jeans and a T-shirt—Magritte's green apple silkscreened on the front but underneath it reads: *This is NOT a poisoned apple.*

The crowd roars and continues to roar. They are on their feet, jumping, they are jumping for me. They adore me. Trumpets herald my pending but certain victory. We are ready to begin. At last: the fight.

The air grows dark and still. Thunder claps, then lightning strikes. The scent of sulphur is everywhere. THEY have arrived.

Grace, in blue sateen, hands me my weapon: a gleaming French boning knife still smoking from the grinding stone.

"Where are they?" I ask her.

"They've never been on time in their lives," she reminds me.

Out of the stench, out of the smoke, a creature comes. I take my stance at the fireplace. My crowd roars approval at my brilliant strategic maneuver. I grow arrogant and do not apologize.

We watch the shadow creature in aubergine net come toward us from the powder room.

"Now, now," the crowd roars.

"Prepare," I call to the shadow. "Face now the consequences of all your evil deeds. Come into the light, Narcissistic One, and smell justified vengeance."

She steps into the light. The crowd gasps. It is Tenny, not Raylene.

"Where's your mother, kid?"

"She's getting her legs waxed. She sent me in her place. Let's do it."

I can't. I can't do it.

In my ear Grace whispers. "Just one toe, Ellen. Just one fat little toe."

I move toward Tenny. I take aim. I throw. I let the knife tumble in the air. It rolls over and over on itself, gleaming in the gray-brown light, hunting for its mark.

"Get that thumb out of your mouth, Tenny," I tell her.

The knife stops in midair, turns back to me, and plunges in a straight and certain course right through my heart. I stagger. I collapse on the floor in front of the windows. Tenny grins, puts her thumb in her mouth, then breaks all my tureens—first the lids, then the ladles, then the things themselves.

· · ·

The house was beautiful. I never saw it so lovely. There were daffodils and white tulips in crystal vases everywhere. Pale yellow and white balloons, just a few pink, floated about in the living room and the dining room, in the hall, on the screened-in side porch. The table was against the windows; the Battenberg lace looked exquisite. Crystal and silver bowls held party favors, noisemakers, pastel butter mints. A six-tiered lemon Italian cream cake—iced in palest yellow, pink Old Gothic lettering with barely green leaves—sat like a crown on a glass-footed cake plate I rented at the last minute from AtoZ Rents, where I also got little glass plates and punch cups. Paper was all wrong: You just don't know until the last minute sometimes.

A basket smelling of lavender holds three dozen white linen napkins starched to paperlike stiffness. There is a sprinkling of confetti every-where. The west light is coming through the windows, illuminating the glass and silver; they sparkle and reflect in one another. There isn't a speck of dust in the entire house.

"Jesus," Grace says. "It's Bonnard."

She's right. It's lovely. It is a moment I treasure. It didn't last but ten minutes, and I must have known. I took two rolls of photographs.

"Listen, Ellen, I can't stay," Grace tells me. "What are you putting the punch in?"

"The Italian thing. The footbath. The one with the yellow and pink on the rim."

This is no ordinary footbath. I found it in Milan on my first trip to Italy. I carried it back on the plane in my lap. It's late nineteenth century, a white ceramic oval with hand-painted garlands on the rim. I've used it for punch before. It's fantastic, as near to perfect as any-thing I have.

We put the lemon sherbet punch with fresh (which means they float) southeast Louisiana strawberries in the foot bath, which has been cooling in the Hussman, which is my commercial refrigerator, which is no ordinary refrigerator.

"When you die," Grace says, "can I have the Hussman?"

"No, Grace," I tell her again because she keeps asking. "You know the Hussman is Ruthie's. I've got you down for the little Chambers stove and your choice of armoirs."

I've got five minutes before they all arrive. Kenneth has gone to get the birthday girl. Raylene's coming when she gets to it. The house looks beautiful. It's going to be a great party. I know: my stomach's jittery.

"Where's Zack?" Grace wants to know.

"Sleeping," I tell her. "I'm going to have to go up and take care of him when he wakes up in about thirty minutes."

"Aw, you're not going to hide upstairs, are you, Ellen?"

"Are you nuts? Of course, I am. God, don't you love this house?"

Grace can stay until I change. I don't have time for a shower; those napkins took forever to iron. I throw on some bath powder, a little mascara. I don't stink. I'm just not a primper by nature.

The doorbell is ringing, and ringing again. A din is building. They're here, Tenny's crummy little friends, all two dozen of the little tornadoes. For the noise, they could be two thousand. Kenneth and Tenny are receiving the presents—I didn't want presents, it's all crap, but I was overruled—and the magician is beginning her act.

"I've got to go," Grace says. "Good luck, and be sure and call me. I want to hear all the gore. By the way, HER parents are here. They don't drink, and they're in the kitchen looking through your cookbooks."

I want to get in the car with Grace. This party's over for me. I open the door to let her go and run smack into Raylene, who had her hand out, was just about to try the knob and come on in.

"Welcome to our home, Raylene," I say.

I can do this. I can talk to anybody disgusting for three minutes, and I am sure I am going to hell for this.

"I think I just ran over some cat," she says to me and swoops into my house, looking for her baby girl who spots her in all of one second. In two, they are jumping in the middle of my living room. Every crystal vase in the house trembles.

I go right out the front door. I'm looking for a dead cat. Raylene's parked in our driveway again. I don't see anything under her car, but it could have crawled off somewhere to die.

The treasure hunt's begun. The birthday girl's very best friends are all outside, running with their party skirts up, their good panties showing. Not a one of them had on a petticoat, and they are shoving at each other, snatching at dime-store junk hidden everywhere in the yard. I had baskets ready at the side door for the hunt. Kenneth must have forgotten to pass them out. They are filling up their skirts with plastic crap, squabbling over penny whistles that cost a buck, and coin purses with blurry photographs of Dale Evans and Buttermilk on them.

"Who's this cowgirl?" Courtney asks me.

"Stay out of that ivy, kid. We keep rats in there."

What I am, really, is a little drunk, perhaps very drunk. I'm drunk, and I'm outside my own house, looking for a dying cat and supervising hoodlums.

I see Raylene's parents leave. (Her sister never came, never even called; I could have saved that extra trip to the dime store for more favors.) They leave, and I don't even wave. They don't either. They've got their fingers in their ears. They climb into their Buick, which is parked right next to Raylene's in our driveway, and head south. I would have gone with them if they'd asked.

From outside, through the windows, I can see Raylene in my house actually sitting on my grandmother's smokehouse table in my kitchen. Kenneth is pouring her some wine. He is using my last Baccarat glass, and it is a water goblet. I can't look; I know she'll break it. She does. He pours her another glass. It's rented.

I walk all around the house. I look in the windows. The place is a mess. We'll have to get the hose out. Tenny is in the dining room pouring punch for anyone who flies by. Her parents sit in the living room on either end of my sofa, talking about what I cannot imagine. I see them framed in a gazebo, linked for life, forever on either end of my couch.

Tenny, the birthday girl, looks feverish. She is spilling the punch on the tablecloth, and she doesn't appear to even care. I rap on the window, startle her.

"Watch the tablecloth, Tenny."

She glares at me like a wild animal, then smiles and pushes the footbath over with both hands. It falls to the floor, breaks into pieces as big as your hand. Melting sherbet punch oozes toward my best kilim, which I did have sense enough earlier to roll up and shove against the south windows.

"Goddamn it, Tenny. I saw you do that, you little bitch."

Her parents are turning their necks toward the new noise, which is me. Tenny's eyes go flat and gray as cardboard. She stoops to the floor, comes back up with a piece of the footbath, and with her eyes on my face, she slashes blind at her own wrist.

21

Nuts

There is nuts, and then there is Nuts. Monday at eleven I go in and finish up ten years with Margaret and my self-indulgent exploration of white, middle-class neuroses.

I know too much. That's my problem. I rely on knowing, I believe in knowing, but watching Tenny through that dining room window, I saw that nothing I know and nothing I can ever learn is going to put that image in any tolerable perspective. I can't get her face out of my mind, the blood everywhere.

"I don't think this is a good time for us to terminate, Ellen," Margaret said. "You're as depressed as I've ever seen you, and you look terrible."

"It's been interesting talking to you all these years, Margaret. I've learned a great deal arguing with you, and I appreciate your time, all your questions. I've never known an almost total Apollonian before, Margaret, and it's been fascinating, but I'm too old for this now."

"You're just a kid, Ellen. You've just gotten started. You don't have any perspective right now. You need more data."

"I am drowning in data, Margaret. I am choking on it. Data doesn't mean anything at the finish. It doesn't protect me or anybody else from being blindsided by fate, circumstance, evil, drunks on the freeway, the shock of a child. I couldn't have prepared for any of this, and I think you can investigate only so much, and then you've just got to wing it and try to save some money."

"Don't worry about your bill. I'll speak to my business manager and explain."

"I'm sick of explanations, Margaret. I'm concerned about effects now, not causes. Diagnosis doesn't interest me. After ten years of this psychotherapy crap, I've still got my mouth open eight days out of ten, unbelieving what I see, amazed at what I hear. I'm never going to be cooked, Margaret. I'm not healed. I don't feel normal, I still feel stupid, I still ache."

"Kenneth is no good for you, Ellen, and Tenny is a lost child. He can't see that and never will. They're both lost and you can't save either one. You're a painter, Ellen, but you're not doing it. Nobody could under these conditions."

"You just don't get it, Margaret. It's messy, that's clear, and this has been the worst year of my life to date, but I love Kenneth. We need a vacation in Mexico, not a separation. We have a child together. I'm hooked to him forever, no matter what my address is. I'd never be able to split Zack in two, like Raylene does Tenny. I hooked to them for life, too. It was a package deal, Margaret, and I resent your talking about Kenneth like this."

"You're having some problem with prioritizing your own needs, Ellen. You're not differentiating well, and I really think you should stay in the Tuesday night group at least. You need support now. You can't give up."

"I'm not giving up. Who said I was giving up? I like the group, Margaret, but not a one of those women has a thing to say to me that means anything of consequence to my present life. You don't have an unwed mother or an artist in the bunch. I'm tired of entertaining them, and I'm sick of exploring neuroses. I'm sick of sorting through data, shuffling information, trying to know. Knowing's nothing, and I don't need any more people in my life, Margaret. I've got good friends I haven't called in months. I don't give up, and you ought to know that by now."

"I think this is a mistake, Ellen, but I'll be here if you need me," Margaret said. She held out her hand.

"Fuck professionalism, Margaret."

I hugged her until her back cracked.

There is hurting yourself, and then there is Hurting Yourself. Tenny's shrink, Gretchen, believes Tenny is nuts, but not a self-mutilator. She believes Tenny got caught up in a drama of the moment and that it backfired on her.

"She doesn't understand anything about real consequences," Gretchen tells me. "That blood surprised her as much as it did everyone else. She's an angry child, Ellen. She's furious all the time. We're working on that Tuesdays, trying to get her to express her feelings more appropriately."

Gretchen has seen Tenny every Tuesday night from 5:00 to 5:50 for four and a half years. Kenneth takes her. He plays with Zack in Gretchen's reception area, I go to Margaret's group, and then we all meet at Ninfa's for fajitas and green sauce.

"I don't think this approach is working," I tell Gretchen. "She had to have six stitches, for Christ's sake."

"Think about it, Ellen. She didn't cut the inside of her wrist. She didn't sever any major arteries. She cut the *top* of her wrist. It was surface stuff. Tenny doesn't want to kill herself."

"Jesus, Gretchen. I think your differentiation is a little too subtle for an eight-year-old. Slicing at your wrist anywhere at your own birthday party is not normal behavior."

"Oh, Ellen, you don't understand. We're not ever going to be dealing with normal where Tenny is concerned. You're expecting too much from her. You want her to walk, and this kid's got no legs."

"What are you talking about? What is her exact diagnosis, Gretchen? What's wrong with her?"

"Anxiety dysfunction, moderate to severe depending on what's going on in her life. Holidays are horrible for her. Any disruption in her routine confounds her to near break point."

"What?"

"Ellen. Tenny is not normal and is never going to be. She is, in your language, Nuts, Ellen."

"Do her parents know this, Gretchen? Kenneth thinks her problem's related to the divorce going on forever. He's drowning in guilt, and Raylene thinks there's not a thing wrong with Baby Girl."

"Nearly everything is wrong with Tenny, Ellen. It's on the bill."

There are diagnosis numbers on the top of Gretchen's statements. There are no words. She reads me what the numbers mean—Anxiety Dysfunction—from the diagnostic manual that insurance companies also keep on their credenzas.

Inability to maintain peer relationships; overt interest in sexual activity; age-inappropriate coping mechanisms (thumbsucking, for example); inability to control anger, express affection appropriately; intense emotional swings; restlessness; repeated questioning, constant need for attention or reassurance-seeking behavior; small motor activity, body tremors, flushing, dry mouth, dilated pupils, appetite swings, nausea and vomiting, blood pressure leaps, fever spikes; difficulty concentrating causing unawareness of surroundings; orientation to past, not present or future; frequent urination (bed-wetting common); fatigue, worry about possible misfortunes.

I listen to the words. Then I read them myself, and then I read them again. I stare diagnosis in the face, and I think, well, this could be any of us on a given Monday. We're all nuts sometimes, and I think being a parent especially allows, requires, even justifies a certain level of continuous anxiety. A good many of these catchy phrases certainly fit me in recent months, but who it is—day and night, any hour of the week, any time of the year—is Tennessee Louise Goodson.

"Why is she like this, Gretchen? Is it the divorce crap? Is it Raylene?"

"It's just how she is, Ellen. She was born like this. The chaos in her life doesn't help, but Tenny would be like this in any family."

"You've got to tell her parents all this, Gretchen. I swear they don't know."

"They know, Ellen, or they know on some level. You have to be careful dealing with disturbed children. You scare the parents off, and you can't treat the child. See, I'm the only stability in Tenny's life. I'm the only one who understands her."

"I don't think you know Tenny much better than I do, Gretchen.

Five and a half years of playing with Barbie dolls is not my idea of anything. You've got to tell Kenneth and Raylene. I know they don't know."

Gretchen's child was in the same Montessori school as Tenny. The director referred Tenny to Gretchen, and I always wondered if Gretchen and Roy got a discount on tuition. Tenny spends Raylene nights with Gretchen's kid, and Gretchen's kid comes to Tenny's birthday parties. Gretchen takes the two of them to the zoo, shopping at the Galleria, roller skating. We kept Gretchen and Roy's kid when they went to the Caymen Islands. On Tuesday nights, Kenneth pays $100 an hour for professional assessment: "Clearer boundaries are what she needs." Gretchen thinks she and I are old friends, and she bills Kenneth for my session with her.

"It's not you, Kenneth. It's not Raylene, it's not me, it's not the goddamned divorce papers. It's Tenny. You've got to do something about this, Kenneth. You've got to go see Gretchen, let her read you this thing. You've got to call Bradley and Joan. You've got to get her. You've got to save your child's life, Kenneth. You've got to hear the diagnosis, and then you've got to get her away from Raylene and that Gretchen who is really Nuts."

Kenneth is listening while I scream at him. The image of Tenny through the dining room window, the memory of Gretchen reading the diagnosis never leaves me, even when I sleep. I've gone over it three, maybe four hundred times with him. We've been all over the house. I'm going over it all again for him, when Kenneth stops walking from room to room, turns to face me, reaches his hand out, and slaps me full in the face. It was the first and last time he ever hit me. He never hit anyone before.

Kenneth's legs buckled. He collapsed to the floor. He held his head in his hands and cried for all of us.

"She's still my baby, Ellen, no matter what anybody says, no matter that's wrong with her. I can't stand to hear this again, and I can't believe I hit you."

There was blood everywhere. I was sober immediately, but I couldn't move. I held onto the window ledge, watched Tenny's mouth open and close. I couldn't hear a sound.

Kenneth was right to her. He grabbed a handful of white linen napkins, held them to Tenny's wrist, picked her up, and yelled at Raylene who already had her keys out. They were gone, out the front door in no less than fifteen seconds. They took Raylene's car—there wasn't another choice available—and Kenneth held Tenny on his lap in the passenger seat. He rocked her, held the napkins tight to her wrist. Raylene drove nonstop to Texas Children's Emergency, honking steady through any light, red or not.

I know a good many single parents, men and women, raising children on their own. I was considering it myself. In some ways, it could have been a lot simpler—actually, quite a lot simpler—if it weren't for The Injury Thing. I believe the reason it takes two people to have a child is so one can drive like hell to the emergency room and the other can hold the kid, try and stop the blood.

In the backyard, I snapped back to real life when the front door slammed behind Kenneth and Raylene. I had to, I had no choice. There were twenty-three little girls screaming hysterically all around me. The news of the blood spread like a virus. They all had their noses to the window. They were all screaming their heads off.

"Okay, ladies. Let's calm down. It was just an accident."

I sound steady. I actually sound steady. They buy it and quit squealing temporarily.

Zack's bedroom window is open, and I can hear him from outside beginning to wake up. When the front door slammed, it locked. We can't get into the house.

Some things are worth knowing: I was a great tree climber as a kid. I shinny up the fig tree, push through the screen on Tenny's sleeping porch—it was old, it gave with just a few kicks—and I broke a windowpane in the French doors. I reached through and opened the door from the inside like any common urban thief.

"HURRAH," the girls shouted from below.

I waved a length of pink crepe paper in the spirit of victory, then dropped it to them, but my heart was not in so shallow a gesture. It floated like a feather in a slow dream, then caught in the ivy. They all scrambled for it, and they're never going to be able to wear those party dresses again.

It was just three o'clock. The parents and the parent-types weren't due to pick their girls up for another ninety minutes. I found Tenny's school telephone book in Kenneth's studio. I had done the invitations and knew they all lived close by, in 05 or 06 zips. I grabbed Zack and a bottle of formula.

"Okay, girls. How about a nice ride in the truck?"

"Aren't we even going to cut the cake?" Courtney Anderson said. "We're starving here."

Kenneth and I went to see Gretchen. She read the diagnosis to him twice. He cried both times. He didn't know.

"What's her prognosis? What kind of treatment are we talking about here?"

"More therapy. We could try some drugs. It won't go away, and your job is to learn to deal with a dysfunctional child in your family."

"You've got to tell Raylene, Gretchen," Kenneth says. "If you don't, we're finished with all of this talking bullshit."

Gretchen did call Raylene on the phone, suggested an appointment, referenced the birthday party incident.

"Tenny's fine," Raylene told her. "There's not a thing wrong with her, and when she wears her new Swatch watch, you can't even see the bandage."

Gretchen swore she tried. Raylene did bring Tenny in one afternoon late in the month—I don't know what shrink trick got her there, it had to be a good one—but the session must have been too subtle.

Tenny called us that night, the night of that last appointment with Gretchen. It was during the ten o'clock news, late, way past her bedtime.

"Gretchen told Mom I'm a liar, Dad. We hate her."

There are any number of ways to learn about loyalty, figure out your allegiances, find out what you'll tolerate and what you won't. Diagnosis doesn't mean shit, except to insurance companies. We try to stay calm, do what we can, attend to each other, wing it, and hope somebody keeps the drunks off the road.

"We hate her, too, Tenny," and that's no lie. I wanted to sue her, for incompetence, for mismanagement, for gross arrogance at the very least, but Kenneth was finished with all of that.

. . .

We finished up with Margaret and Gretchen, but stayed with Nathan for a while, the reason being that he thought Gretchen's reading of the situation was all wrong. Grotesque, is what he actually said, particularly about the no legs part.

"Even a child with problems like Tenny's has to learn to deal with the world. Expecting appropriate behavior from anyone is not extraordinary."

"You don't know Raylene," Kenneth and I say as one voice.

"Her mother's influence is certainly a difficulty here, but listen, Tenny isn't institutional," Nathan said. "You underestimate very much your role in her life. Her mother treats her like an infant, spoils her, keeps her dependent. You two give her a great gift by treating her like an ordinary eight-year-old. She's not ordinary, but she's not Nuts either. She's watching you two work your lives out together. Any child of divorce wants that second relationship to fail, but if you split up, she's won, but really lost again. Plus, you just look at the power Zack already has with her."

It is true about Tenny and Zack. I expected problems between them—like Tenny's hands tight around his neck—but there was never any of that. She adores him, and he's crazy about her. After Idea and Da-Da, it was Ta-Ta. When he learned to speak in whole sentences, one of his first full questions was: "Is this a Tenny-day?"

"Look at these lucky X's on the bottom of his feet," Tenny said. Zack, maybe three weeks old, was having a ride on the dishwasher, and Tenny was playing with his toes. "My baby brother's safe from *everything*."

I like Nathan. I like his thinking. It's practical, balancing. Kenneth barely tolerates it.

"She's just a kid," Kenneth said. "She's not nearly as powerful as some of us seem to think here."

"I couldn't agree more, Kenneth," Nathan said, and he wants to work with Kenneth and his family origins, find out who his male role models are.

"Elvis Presley and John Lennon," Kenneth tells him, and Nathan's mouth drops open, amazed.

Still, Nathan is practical. We're dying for the practical, sick of the abstract. We work on new house rules. Kenneth is going to keep Raylene from the house as much as possible, take Tenny home himself on Sunday nights, figure out a way to keep her mother off our street and out of our neighborhood. I'm going to shut up about the divorce papers, call Bradley and Joan only in emergencies, and refrain from asking Kenneth if he's missing music.

"What are we going to do about all of this, Kenneth?"

"We are going to survive, Ellen."

"What I think you guys need to do," Nathan said, "is to get some reliable baby-sitters. It's important that both your children see you as independent from them. Don't you miss going out?"

We never went out. We never needed to. We try it.

I have on a new dress, navy rayon crepe and white pearl buttons. Judith found it for me at the Salvation Army during one of her lunch shops; it's from the forties, cost eight bucks, and is fabulous. Kenneth wears one of his new Office Man costumes—gray stripes, a vest, wing tip shoes.

We wave good-bye to our children, who wail at the door and clutch at our ankles. We drive around the block, park down the street. We stand in mud and peek in our own front windows.

Our kids aren't even whimpering. We're gone, and they've forgotten us. They're already into the second bowl of popcorn, and Tenny's coaching Zack on his forward rolls.

"Don't forget to tuck your chin, Zack-o," we hear her say. "You could break your neck, and then we'd never make the Olympics."

"My shoes are ruined, Kenneth."

"You still got great legs, Ellen."

Kenneth and I sit at the bar, turn on our stools and listen to jazz. I am drinking champagne cocktails, Kenneth orders iced tea, no ice. It's a nice place, a good American restaurant, none of the sleeze of Kenneth's old Friday night gigs. There are fresh flowers everywhere, starched white tablecloths, pleasant and witty enough waiters. Candles in clear, crystal votives sparkle like a party, throw shadows on the wall. Everyone looks elegant and quite well fed.

Arnett Cobb is playing. He has only one lung now, but it's a hell of a lung. He stands propped up between two crutches, and plays the saxophone from his whole heart, which is also considerable. He must be eighty-five. I love jazz, particularly live jazz. Kenneth hates it.

"It doesn't go anywhere, Ellen."

Jazz goes everywhere, I think. Of course, I don't know much about music. I quit listening to it in 1968. It wasn't an active choice: The radio on my old Volkswagen just stopped, broke, disconnected, and I didn't get around to fixing it before that car blew up. I lost the habit of having a radio on. Play me anything past The Vanilla Fudge, and I don't know what it is. I think Kenneth wrote everything.

"It's just Vanilla Fudge, Ellen. It's not *The* Vanilla Fudge," Kenneth tells me.

"Well, I never liked them much anyway."

I do love listening to jazz, live jazz, hearing it circle on itself. I love watching a master teach good students. It's alive. It's inventing itself on itself, and you get to watch. It's like baseball—anything can happen—and I am listening, and my brain is following the music way past places I can even articulate with words or near-words.

Cobb begins "Tenderly." He lets his band—the mean age of which is maybe forty, less than half his age, and a lot paler in majority—take the melody. They mess with it. They're good, damn good. Cobb nods his approval, they take his nod and barely blush. Then he takes the song back, "Tenderly," shows us all how it really is, how it could really be, what it might mean on the very best of nights.

"None of this is spontaneous, Ellen," Kenneth says. "It's all on their charts."

"Do you know that for sure, Kenneth? Are you that certain? Don't you have any faith at all? Let's dance."

We dance. We never had before, in the literal sense: cheek to cheek, our feet shoving salt around on a parquet floor. Kenneth, as it turns out, is a lousy dancer. Experience was his problem: too many years on the bandstand and not enough on the floor.

"Let me lead, Kenneth."

"Later," he says. We get better with practice.

I am watching and listening and dancing. I am thinking and not thinking. I am drinking excellent champagne (Kenneth had thrown away all his dope and his dope stuff, I'd sworn off gin except in emergencies), and the memory of walking through Paris my first night there—late April, ten years ago—comes back to my mind.

There wasn't music that night but there should have been. I was twenty-six years old. I checked my bags at the hotel and began walking. I walked everywhere that first night. It was muggy, and I got lost, but I always felt right, safe, at home somehow.

I waited forever to get to Paris. I went alone. I found the Louvre by miracle and luck and necessity. I waited all night on the steps until it opened the next morning. I couldn't wait to see the real stuff, and I didn't know European museums don't open until eleven at least, more likely noon.

But if there had been music that night, this would have been it, this jazz, this saxophone stuff, this "Tenderly," this feeling high in the heart. Maybe it was the champagne, and the music, and the dancing, and the new dress. Maybe it was getting out of the house for the first time in months and months, behaving like a fully functioning adult for once, safe knowing my sister, Ruthie, wouldn't let either one of my kids die without risking her own life first. Maybe it was just luck, but whatever it was, whatever combination, I started thinking about color, then shapes, then whole paintings I wanted to make and knew I could.

Painting came back to me right there at the bar, Arnett Cobb and Kenneth Joseph Goodson as witnesses. It had been gone a while, and I hadn't realized how much I'd missed it. I was thinking about paintings and making paintings for the first time in, God, years really. I was sketching on bar napkins, knowing this is exactly what I should be doing.

"Jesus, Kenneth, is this a great night, or what?"

"Can you see that red guitar, Ellen? The Gibson? The lead guitarist's? The one on Arnett's right?"

"Yeah, I see it."

I do know which one's lead. Kenneth can be a real elitist sometimes for a rock and roller.

"Ellen, I think that's my guitar. My old Gibson acoustical. The one that got stolen out of the truck in sixty-seven when I first came to Texas."

Kenneth loved that guitar. I'm going to try and find him one just like it if I ever have money.

Part Three

This Ain't No Fairy Tale

22 ....

The Window in the Door

I started working again. I worked on draw-
ings evenings after dinner. They weren't very good, but they were
better than nothing. Over time, they got a little better.

Since Zack became the anchor of our lives, I was not what you'd call
100 percent at the museum. I took stuff home, I still worked hard, but
I didn't have as much to give to the place as I once did. I had to stop
at six o'clock and go get Zack—I wanted to stop, I wanted to go get
him—and it was hard to get there mornings before ten.

Amazingly, the place didn't blow up. Shows still went up, and
shows still came down. We got good press. I did a lot of work at home,
Judith covered for me, and I returned my calls every day between noon
and one when nearly everybody's out for lunch. I was efficient, I left
messages, and I would have given anything not to do any of it. I was
doing it solely for the money, unless it was an exhibition I liked, and
that happened less and less. I was sick of nursing art. I was sick of
looking at it.

But, working on my own stuff at night from 8:00, 8:30 to maybe
11:00 was all I could do. I paid for this anyway: It meant not seeing

Kenneth and Zack much, Tenny when she was there. You work on your own stuff, you feel like you're cheating on your family.

"Cheat, Ellen," Kenneth said. "We can't stand you when you're not working."

I did it. It was going all right. I was working on a drawing series from this idea of dead life. *Nature morte* is still life in French. I was drawing objects that are dead but still have emotional meaning to us. It worked better in the mind that on paper. I was drawing a lot of dead cats.

I did learn to save energy through the day, so I'd have something in reserve at night. I did learn to say no, and when I couldn't say no, I said maybe. I wished I could be one of those people who gets up smart at 5:30 in the morning, paints until noon, and then goes out for pasta. I missed working with and under natural light, like I could in graduate school. I'm not so smart, but I am better early, an hour or so after I get up. I kept sending in sweepstakes coupons, and if it weren't for the money, I would have quit the museum in a flat minute.

"You've got such a great job, Ellen," people told me all the time at openings.

"Yes, I can clean a toilet with the best of them. Just have a look at that urinal in the men's room. It's spotless."

At the Morris, we did everything. I didn't clean the bathrooms on a regular basis, but I had, we all had. You just do what has to be done. You get the mop buckets out the back door just as the press walks in the front for the preview. You learn to bring your good clothes with you the morning of a Thursday night opening; moderate to moderately expensive evening clothes dangle on wire hangers from the handles of your file cabinets. You throw the last bag of ice on cheap wine cooling in a #2 washtub, then change into your silk dress, and go open the front door. You wear a lot of body powder—nobody knows the difference—you flush with hard, physical work, not makeup, and you talk for two, three minutes at a stretch to people standing in front of art you, more and more often, don't care a thing about and they wouldn't ever understand anyway.

I was sick of all of it, is what I was. But I was luckier than most: I knew what I really wanted to do.

I am thinking about dead cats as metaphor on the way to work one Tuesday morning, how Judith and I will discuss this over coffee, what Joe would have had to say on this topic.

Monday was payday. Our spirits buoyed along with our bank balances for a moment. Now we're flat again. I park where I always do, and notice that Judith's car is not in the lot. I get this gnawing feeling that grows to a heart-sinking certainty when I hit my office door.

In the middle of my desk, on top of stacks of papers—unopened mail, art magazines, the rough art boards for Claudia's catalog, correspondence I've got to get to, pink telephone messages I've really got to return—is a flat of just blooming pansy plants, deep yellow and red violet, a few blues. Underneath is a note from Judith, a little damp, dirty on the edge.

I hope these aren't drooping too badly by the time you see them, Ellen. I'm sorry to do this to you now, but I'm busting out of here, and this should come as no surprise. I'm catching the midnight flight for London, I'm using the last of my MasterCard credit limit for the ticket, and Claudia says I can build stretchers for her until I figure out what I'm doing. I'm not sure that will ever happen, but I've been in Houston seven years now, working with you for four, and I haven't got very far down the road I want to be on. How long does it take for a painter to turn into a geek, Ellen? I wish you'd think about that and get out of this pit. I'll call when I get some money, I'll write. You know I won't do either, but I'll be thinking of you, hoping your sweepstakes check comes through soon, and your kids stay well. Love to everyone, even the assholes.

Judith

Next to the pansy flat is a white paper portfolio. It is completely dry, no coffee rings, pristine. Inside are drawings of Tenny and Zack. They are graphite drawings of my children, sleeping.

Jesus, can Judith draw. Judith is really good. She made the drawings on New Year's Eve when she kept the kids for us. They are beautiful, neoclassic drawings of sleeping children dreaming their dreams. Judith can modulate pencil line on butter paper better than anyone I've ever seen still breathing. Her drawings are beautiful.

"You're biased," Henry said. "They're just pictures of your damn kids, Ellen. I knew that punk Judith would walk out on you some day. What do you expect from someone who wears paper clips in their ears? We don't have any money in the budget to replace her now, Ellen. You'll have to take care of your own ass. Claudia's show is killing us in expenses, and nobody seems to give a damn about that except me."

With Judith gone—I miss her every minute—I had to abandon my evening sessions in the studio. I was determined to get back to them after Claudia's show opened in late September. I wasn't going to let another year, two, three, ten flash by me. But, I had to do my job and Judith's, plus oversee the design and printing of Claudia's catalog, work on Henry's essay for him, and try to meet deadlines no more than two weeks late.

"Have you got that essay yet?" Henry said. "That book's going to still be wet at the opening if you don't get on it, Ellen."

"I'm on it, Henry. Relax. We're printing the color plates tonight."

I call Kenneth about ten o'clock, just before the news. I'm still at the printers, and it's not going well. The gray they want to use is way too blue. Middle management and I have been arguing about it since seven, and we're not going to get any real work done until shift change at eleven.

"It's a *greened* gray," I tell them. "It's got to be right. Where's your ink man?"

The bosses at the printers hate me. They don't want me to be there, but my museum is paying for this book. Claudia is my friend and a good painter, a fine colorist; it's her mid-life retrospective, and the separations have got to be correct. I'm here. I'm staying until it's done and done right.

"How's everything going, Kenneth? How far did you get with the famous mouse? I miss you guys," I whisper from the print shop wall phone (it's white, a poor design choice; it's covered with inky fingerprints).

Kenneth has a great reading voice. We've always taken turns reading to the kids at night, but when it's his turn, I like to listen. I do the back rubbings, Kenneth reads. They both fall asleep easy when you can get them to relax, and we read all of Chekhov's short stuff and most of the Grimm Brothers slow over the summer. We had to do *Snow White* three or four times. It was Tenny's favorite.

"Then the wicked queen, the stepmother, cursed and got so very frightened that she didn't know what to do. At first she didn't want to go to the wedding at all, but that gave her no peace; she had to go and see the young queen. When she came in, she recognized Snow White and stood motionless from terror and fear. However, iron slippers had already been put over a charcoal fire and were now brought in with tongs and placed before her. Then she had to put the red-hot slippers on and dance until she dropped to the ground dead."

"I really like that one," Tenny said.

We're taking a breather from the grotesque now and are working through *Stuart Little* a chapter at a time. It is every bit as wonderful, and Kenneth and I keep reading aloud even after the kids nod off.

"Home is holding steady," Kenneth tells me. "The kids are currently dreaming well, and Stuart is driving north in a tiny car. How late are you going to be, Red? You want me to stay up for you?"

I work all night at the printers. The graveyard shift understands what I want. We've done this before. They relax on union restrictions and let me mix the ink. We do three color forms between midnight and seven. They're as close to the actual paintings as technology will allow. They're beautiful. They glow on the page. I thank everybody, sign off on the proofs, and get home in time to retrieve the newspapers before they go soggy. I get to have breakfast with Kenneth and my kids.

"You want pancakes or French toast?" Kenneth wants to know. He is dressed for work, a white baker's apron over his dress shirt and pants. He is beating eggs in the big metal mixing bowl with a salad fork.

"I just want coffee. I don't want to even talk about food now," I tell him. I don't know why he keeps asking me this. He knows I can't eat early in the morning.

"Hey, Kenneth, how come you're using that fork to beat those eggs, honey? Where's the good whisk? How come you're not using one of the wooden spoons at least?"

"That whisk is all affect, Ellen, and none of us want splinters in our eggs. Listen: Can you name this tune?"

I listen to Kenneth beating a half a dozen eggs, metal fork against metal bowl.

" 'Woolly Bully'?"

"Good ear, Ellen. Excellent ears, both of them. Now what's this one?"

We both cook, Kenneth and I, but we've got entirely different approaches. Weekdays, Kenneth does the morning stuff, distributes the vitamins, packs the lunch kits. Zack is nearly three, in Montessori school now, learning to pour water out of one side of a cup. Tenny's in the fourth grade, improving her social skills but blowing her conduct grades to hell.

Kenneth makes real breakfast every day for himself and the kids: eggs, bacon, wheat toast, sometimes oatmeal. I buy the supplies but don't participate. On weekends, I give the kids yogurt while they watch cartoons, let Kenneth sleep, and make a big brunch. I start with a good cream soup and finish with a green salad I dress at the table.

Kenneth does most of the laundry and the vacuuming. Tenny dusts—she pushes it around anyway—and I do weekday dinners usually and most of the grocery shopping, although lately we've been dicing with delivered junk: vegetable pizzas and Chinese cashew chicken spiked with pounds of MSG. Claudia's show is taking too much of my time, and I've succumbed to anything close to lukewarm that comes to the door in twenty minutes. It is, however, not a habit that will last. I promise everyone.

"This place is a mess. Look at the dust on those spatulas, the actual grease on everything else. When this show gets up, we're going to review the chore list around here, guys."

"Uh oh," Zack says and puts his hands over his ears.

"Where were you last night?" Tenny wants to know. "Are you cheating around on my daddy, Ellen?"

"They wanted to use this textbook blue ink for the gray. I had to actually get up on the press and mix it to green myself. I guess I could've been killed, but it had to be right."

They're finished with breakfast. The dishes soak in the sink, the spoons and forks stand handles up in the juice glasses. They are ready to go. Suddenly, they're running late. Kenneth herds Tenny and Zack into the car, checks to make sure all the book bags, lunch kits, nap blankets, Show and Tell *objets* have made it into the backseat. I wave from the porch, they wave back. They're a handsome group, my family, although Kenneth looks like a Mormon missionary these days—dark pants, white shirt, plain tie, jacket over his arm, briefcase. It's hard to remember he ever had a pigtail down to his waist, and he really needs better ties.

I'm beat. The coffee has no effect. I want to lie down on the floor of the shower.

"Five minutes. I'm taking five minutes," I tell myself.

I've been up all night, but I've got to get into the museum and wrestle with Henry's essay. We've got to go to blue lines tonight.

The fact is, I'm not as young as I used to be. I'm almost thirty-six, and I can't hold on to time anymore. I'm going to have to break down and buy a watch. I'm going to have to look at it occasionally, although I know time can get away whether you're watching or not.

I stretch out across the bed for five minutes and wake up four hours later in a chill. My bathrobe's still damp, my hair's in a matted mess, the doorbell is ringing and ringing. It is Henry. His face is near black with rage; his blood pressure going to tilt.

"I've been calling you all day. You're fired, Ellen," he screams, and I see my neighbors peek out their front blinds.

"Come on, Henry. I just laid down for five minutes. I'm dead tired, I've been up all night, and you're going to have a heart attack on this porch."

"You're FIRED, Ellen."

Henry's fired me about every two months for the last twelve years. Firing me is what he does.

"What's the problem, Henry? You want some coffee?"

"I told you we were budget broke on this show, Ellen. You pushed that printing crew into double time without approval last night. They're charging us $10,000 over base bid for last night's overruns. You should have called me, Ellen. You should have been at the budget meeting Monday."

"I did call you, Henry. I got your machine. That first set of separations was crap. They had to be done over. They had to be right."

"Look, it's not goddamned Leonardo, Ellen. It's your third-rate buddy Claudia Ferguson. This level of compulsiveness was unnecessary, Ellen. We can't pay the printers' bill. We're overdrawn, it was just payday, and the bank will cover only so much in overdrafts. Jackson says he's not going to release one page to us until he's got cash in hand. We've still got the text to do, goddammit. We've still got the black-and-whites to print."

There are printers, and then there are printing companies. I can work with printers. They know how to make things; they understand what Right looks like and means.

Management doesn't know shit. Jackson doesn't care about anything but getting the work through the press and out of the shop as quickly as possible. Profit is his game. Quality doesn't mean a thing.

"Jackson was trying to get the evening shift to change the paper weight, Henry. He's an asshole, and so are you. That's a cheap shot about Claudia, Henry, and what did you do with all that NEA money?"

"It's long gone, Ellen. You would have known that if you had shown up at work every day or so for the last three years. We're broke. Grant money's drying up. We got cut by thirty percent last year. We've got to bring our standards down or close up."

"We don't do it that way, Henry. We're a museum, not a goddamned corporation. Jesus, we do it right. We don't cheat on quality. We don't fake it, Henry."

"You're *fired*, Ellen. We're going to save a fortune in insurance premiums alone with you off the payroll."

I can take a lot, but I'm tired. Henry's always right on the edge of hysteria before a show opens, but his shot about insurance was cheaper than most. He was in the hospital four times last year—"exhaustion," his doctors said. I could tell him something about exhaustion, but I don't have time. I'm doing half of his work anyway, covering for him totally when he's in St. Luke's. I bring him a potted plant every time he checks in, a fruit basket every time he checks out. He forgets all this when he goes crazy. All Henry does is go to lunch and take roll during his stupid Monday curatorial meetings. If anyone's been responsible for raising our insurance rates, it's Henry, although I am probably a close second.

"Get out of my house, Henry, before I say something I mean."

"You're FIRED, Ellen. I got enough already to drown you on insubordination alone."

I slammed the door on him. I prayed I broke his nose, caught his foot or some significant body part. Then I headed for the kitchen phone, dialed and stooged on Henry in a loud voice to three board members. They couldn't believe it. I had years of stuff on him. Barbara Sands said she would call the others, get a quorum together, convene an emergency meeting to deal with all this.

"Could you run the museum for us, Ellen?"

"I have for years, Barbara."

I was tired, I'd been tired forever. I was mad, and I had cause. I was always underpaid, but that didn't stop me from working my ass off for twelve years. I had to blackmail Henry into putting Judith on full time in the first place, getting her any real money, any benefits. I was going to have to go through hell to get him to approve a replacement.

Ten thousand dollars is a lot of money, but we could have raised it with a few phone calls to Claudia's collectors. She was up for the Biennale this year; her prices are rising every day. She's no Leonardo, but she's no shot in the dark either: Her dealer valued her damaged red diptych at $8,500. We owe her a good catalog—we put her show off for three years because Henry booked his cronies' friends onto our walls—and her book would be good for us, too. Henry doesn't know shit. That printer Jackson will do anything if you bring him a good bottle of scotch or a little dope.

All of this was true, and Henry would admit to every bit of it when he chilled out. We could fix all of this. The problem was, I was tired. I wasn't thinking any clearer than Henry. I made a mistake calling the board right away, not letting my own blood pressure drop down to rational.

I showered again, got dressed, and made myself a good lunch. It was about four o'clock. I drove to the museum, parked where I always did, punched my pass number into the alarm system. There was no buzz back. The staff door didn't leap open, so I walked around the building and came through the front door like a regular public visitor. Yolanda was on the front desk. She looked scared.

"What is it, sweetie?"

"Henry told us all he fired you. I'm supposed to call the police if I see you."

"Let me tell you about Henry, Yolanda. In short, he's Nuts."

I used my pass key to go through the front staff door on the other side of book storage. I walked into my office and found Antonio there. He was dumping my desk drawers into Bekins boxes.

"I'm sorry, Ellen," he told me, "but you've got to give me your keys. I'm putting your personal stuff in a separate box—the pictures of Zack and Tenny, these diapers, all these sweepstakes coupons, these little jars of beets. I'll bring it all by your house later, but Henry wants everything else to go to Lou Beth. He's giving her your desk, Ellen, and I'm going to miss you more than I can say in English."

My mistake was in calling the board. Museum board members are of two kinds: rich and very rich. Sometimes they let energetic types sit on museum boards, but they've got to have gone to the right school, have a good address book, own a tuxedo. They work the energetic ones to the breaking point, accept their resignations with regret, and then find another Ivy League graduate to handle the membership drive.

You can lunch with a board member, drop some hints about how things really are, let them start asking questions. I've got friends on the board who know exactly how crazy Henry is. The problem was, I told them clearly how it was; I wasn't subtle. I didn't lead them to ask any questions. I gave it to them straight, and they didn't like that. They felt incompetent and out of touch, which is what they are. They checked right away with the insurance carrier to make sure the premium for the board's liability insurance was paid up.

The other real problem was the ten thousand dollars. People with money understand bottom line numbers, and that's about all they understand. When Henry told them what happened at the printers—leaving out a few hundred salient details—they couldn't believe it. Board members care that shows go up, shows come down; they care about reviews in national publications, and largely about pictures of themselves in the Tuesday society pages.

I never took direct credit for any exhibition, any catalog essay, any press coverage. Henry was in charge of taking credit, and he paid for it by having to go to all those tree trimming parties at the board members' houses on Christmas Eve. Henry owns two tuxedos, one always at the ready. He keeps three pairs of dancing slippers polished and holding their shape in cedar shoe trees in the front of his closet. He has to eat with the rich and near-rich all the time, and I didn't. I never wanted any part of that. Henry loved the fluffy social stuff, and I got the real work done. We had a nice little understanding about all of this until Claudia's catalog needed to be done right.

What I really did was to break the one rule you can never break in a museum: I went over the director's head. I stooged directly to the board on him. They listened, they gasped, but they had no choice but to back him up and let me go. It was him or me, and with them—considering my mouth and the fact that I didn't own a tuxedo—they were all with Henry.

"I had no idea you were out so much these last months, Ellen,"

Barbara told me on the phone. "Henry's been covering for you for years. He's such an elegant man."

"He looks nice in a dress, too," I told her and slammed the receiver of the grocery store pay phone down as hard as I could. I hoped it broke Barbara's ear off.

The irony was that they're going to give me twenty-four thousand dollars in severance pay—

"Twelve years is a long time," Barbara said. "Henry fought for you hard on this point, Ellen."

—and they'd carry medical insurance on me and Zack for the next twelve months. Keep me, they save at least fourteen thousand dollars. They don't see it this way. Logic means nothing to the socially prominent.

"You think you sabotaged yourself, Ellen?" Grace wanted to know. "Were those first separations really that bad? I couldn't believe you called Barbara, Ellen. You know, she's a Republican."

The news of my firing spread like a virus through the whole art community. I got calls as early as the six o'clock news from people I never want to see again, and they knew that before they even dialed.

"I don't care to think about it anymore, Grace. It's over, and I'm not getting any of that money for three months anyway—cash flow. I'll believe it when the check clears. You want to come for dinner? I'm doing that veal thing."

"Is it a Tenny-night?"

Grace needed to know. Tenny upsets all my friends' appetites. They all know firsthand how you can't hold an extended conversation on any subject if she's in the same block. They all feel guilty about this and buy her Christmas presents way too expensive.

"It's Wednesday, Grace. Where are your brains?"

"I'll bring them with me," she said.

Three months went by in a flash. I did all the cleaning, all the shopping, all the cooking, and all the laundry. Kenneth gained six pounds, and I lost twelve. I beat him to the kitchen four mornings out of five. I cut the crusts off Tenny and Zack's sandwiches. I had the lunch kits ready and waiting before he even got out of the shower.

"When are you going to paint, Ellen?" Kenneth asked me.

"I'm thinking about it. It's always in my mind. As soon as I get this house under control, I'm going to get right to it."

I didn't get right to it. I couldn't paint. I became a domestic geek: unmade beds drew me like magnets, dust seduced me with false promises. I scrubbed baseboards with toothbrushes; they gleamed, then turned chalky within forty-eight hours. I scrubbed them again. I washed all the spice jars to get the grease off; the labels came off in the sink, and I had to make new ones. Then I took all the scissors to be resharpened.

I was cleaning the top of the hot water heater when Kenneth came home in the middle of the day.

"You want lunch?"

"I want to give you two things, Ellen. This is called a Watch; this is also called Time Passing. This is called a Mirror; this is also called Time Passing. You cleaned that thing last week, Ellen. Nobody cared then either. Paint, Ellen. And by the way, I miss making their lunches."

Then he left for some afternoon appointment and didn't even kiss me or wave good-bye.

I thought right away about dropping the watch down the garbage disposal, hurling the mirror against the big Chambers stove. I would have done it, too, except I knew I'd have to be the one to fix the disposal, sweep up the glass. The kids could cut their feet open on the splinters and bleed to death.

I went upstairs and opened the door to the studio. Here we've got real dirt: ashtrays brimming with cigarette butts, newspapers and oily rags, every brush I own soaking in rusting coffee cans everywhere. I want to back right out, go get a box of garbage bags, go get the ElectroLux. I felt this way the last time I opened this door, weeks and weeks ago.

I backed right out, I found the garbage bags—the box was in my hand—but I got lost coming back up the stairs. The window on the landing was catching the light just right; the stairs were filthy, and so was that window. I fell to my knees and scrubbed until it was time to go get Zack.

Finally, I had to put a gun to my back—Kenneth helped hold it—and I picked my way through the clutter to my drawing table.

"Twenty minutes," I said out loud. "Give yourself twenty minutes here."

I worked for forty-five. It was crap, the drawing. For the first time in my life I had a little money and some time. Both kids were well, and there were no more excuses. I missed them, those excuses. This was hard. I didn't know anything, and I had to admit it to myself. My hair was turning gray around my face, veins on my legs were popping. I was getting older, and I hadn't even started yet.

"Jesus, I hate being new."

"Get over it, Ellen," everyone I knew whispered, but it was a firm whisper.

I threw the drawing in the trash, got another piece of Arches triple-weight. I began again. It was crap.

Claudia's show opened on time in September. The catalog was beautiful and dry. Lou Beth is a better writer than I thought, although she missed the Baudelaire references in Claudia's blue series from '84. Lou Beth didn't even see them.

The local press was good. *Newsweek* came through with two color reproductions, only one of which they printed backwards. Crowds were moderate, and every artist in Houston went back to see the show two or three times. In short, we're talking successful exhibition. Minneapolis and Boston finally signed to take the show after Houston, and Henry was working on a European booking over a pricey lunch. I didn't have a thing to do with any of it.

"That's not true," Claudia said in front of my bathroom mirror. She was on her way to her opening. She looked fabulous in a chartreuse crepe dress beaded in black, a new permanent. She flew in from London for the festivities, but planned to stay only three days. Claudia was born in Amarillo but will deny being from Texas even if you ask her directly.

"I can't take much more of this interview shit, these dinner parties with Republicans. Plus I hate Texas. If I stay more than two and a half days my face breaks out, my voice goes to twang, and I'm fifteen all over again."

Claudia is fifty. She looks it. She moved to London thirty years ago and hardly ever comes back. She taught art until two years ago when her paintings started to sell and sell well. Now she just paints. And she is getting better all the time.

"Can I use your mascara, Ellen? How do I look? Christ, I feel like a hooker. I'm a mess. I hate the viewing public. I look fine, don't I? You know, Ellen, your hairdresser Jerry is the only one in the world who could ever do anything with my cowlicks. I always wanted those straight bangs. Jerry told me to get over it."

"Straight bangs like Tenny's?"

"Yeah, just like Tenny's. This show wouldn't be out of my studio if it wasn't for you, Ellen. The book is fantastic, a valentine; the color gradations in those plates are damn miracles. Come with me to the opening at least, you can be my date at the dinner later if you want."

"Forget it, Claudia. You're on your own with those jackasses, and besides I'm going for your dry ice."

Claudia loves London but misses Texas cooking. She's taking a big Igloo full of flour tortillas and Antonio's mother's homemade tamales back with her on the plane. She wants red-eye gravy, too, but it'll clabber by the time her plane's over Washington. We tried it last time, the time before that. Dry ice is her last hope.

The show opened in late September and ran ten weeks. The Wednesday after Thanksgiving Claudia came back to Houston to do her lecture. The NEA put up a chunk of money for the exhibition, and an artist lecture was part of the grant package. This is all the rage now.

The NEA wants to fund art exhibitions that reach deeply into the community. They have to justify every penny they grant to Republican bureaucrats, suspicious of art in the first place. Outreach is the buzz-word, and of course, the NEA is all Republicans now, too.

Museums agree with whatever they say, deposit the checks, and schedule artists' lectures late in the show's run to boost attendance figures, a factor the NEA finds more than a little significant on the final grant reports, both the financial and narrative.

The thing is, artists aren't always the best people to talk about their own work. They're the most informed about making it, but talking about it is something else entirely. A public lecture would kill Ben, for example. Claudia can do it—talk and make sense to an audience who is partisan to begin with and wants her autograph, a thread from her hem—but she doesn't like it.

"I hate this," she tells me. "I just agreed to do it so I could get more tamales. Judith sends her love, Ellen. I don't know what I'd do without her. She wants to know, and so do I, are you working?"

I'm containing my genetic inclination for domestic geekness and trying to work in the studio every day. I've got a million real reasons not to—Zack's sick, Tenny's sick, we're out of milk, Christmas is coming, Grace/Ben/my sister Ruthie/total strangers call and want to have lunch. Every day I've got to shut all that out of my mind, and get in the studio before I'm fully awake, and do it. Just do it.

"I've brought you a new answering machine, Ellen," Claudia tells me on the phone. "It won't even ring if you don't want to hear it. How's Kenneth's divorce thing going anyway?"

"Raylene is thrilled about my firing, Claudia, and Bradley and Joan are still frowning on the whole subject. Raylene says it never was a real job anyway, and what kind of mother could I be to raise a child on welfare."

"You're on welfare, Ellen?"

"No, I've got cash until June. But she has also suggested that I am a pornographer."

"What?"

"I've been doing these drawings of Zack, Claudia. He's a great model. He still naps, and you know he's always been beautiful. Tenny told her mother about my drawings of him. Nudies dudies, she calls them. Raylene's lawyer loved hearing about that; they couldn't wait to call Bradley and Joan. I had to take a portfolio downtown and justify myself and the whole history of Western art. They're not even nudes, Claudia, and now Raylene makes Tenny carry a roll of quarters with her everywhere."

"Quarters? Why?"

"So Tenny can call her from the Shell station if I ever suggest doing any drawings of her."

"Raylene is Nuts, Ellen. I hate her, but I want to see those drawings. I want to see all your work, Ellen."

"They're just studies, Claudia. I'll show you when there's something to see."

We are talking on the phone like teens. She's in Houston for her lecture and called to get my hairdresser's phone number. Her late September perm's falling out, and she wants to talk to him about value for money.

"I'm leaving right after my talk tomorrow, Ellen. It could be years before I get back to this hellhole. I'm coming over right now, right after I check my slide carousels. I'm bringing Henry and Reynolds, and we'll be on your porch at four-thirty."

You might as well forget about talking Claudia out of anything when she's made up her mind. She's stubborn and nearly six feet tall. You cross her, you watch out. I once saw her tie an eighteen-year-old punk thief into a virtual knot in New York City. He was trying to lift her wallet out of her bag. We were on the subway, and it was getting dark.

"Jesus, Claudia, you could've been killed. I could've been killed. He could have had a gun," I told her when I finally found my voice again. We were leaving the police station.

"I work hard for my money, Ellen. I'd rather take lead than let some pissant kid get away with lifting a penny out of my purse. I hate this country."

"They don't have punks in England?"

"Sure they do, but they put their cigarettes out before they get on the subway, Ellen."

I had twenty-six drawings of dead things, mostly cats. I threw away ten after Claudia called. I knew they were crap, but I just hadn't gotten around to maintenance in the studio area. I hauled them all the way out to the curb, to the big cans. I shoved them in. I fastened the lids. I felt I had done the right thing, or at least gotten away with it.

I heard the garbage truck coming. I stayed on the curb and watched big, burly men in yard gloves dump bad art in with the blue remains of somebody else's Thanksgiving dinner. I should have cleaned out the Hussman, thrown our turkey carcass out, too. The last time I looked it was green and beginning to fuzz.

"Good-bye," I say to my drawings. They crumble in the masher.

"Good-bye, Ellen," the garbage men say, waving their nasty gloves. "Are you working?"

I've got two hours until Claudia comes. She's a prompt sort, and I'm a wreck. I pick up the studio a little, dump the ashtrays anyway, and hang twelve of the new drawings on the east wall with silver pushpins. I step back, rip down two. Ten drawings in four months. I don't know how to do this anymore. I don't know if I ever did. They're too precious, too neoclassic, but I am learning to draw. I don't rely on color alone anymore.

I'm watching the time, working at the easel. I'm drawing what I remember—dead cats snuggling against blue turkey bones. It's so bizarre, I like it. It surprises me, and I really like that. I'm working in a deadline fever, drawing in a frenzy. I don't have time to think about what I'm doing, I'm just doing it: putting marks down, stepping back, making adjustments, erasing, stepping back, putting marks down. I'm working. The drawing has energy. It is the dead that is alive that is dead. The image of the dead cat fades in the ground, then sinks. The rib bones come to the fore, then rot on the spot, picked clean of any clinging flesh by the sharp young teeth of Courtney Anderson whose blue-white eyeteeth have just come in. She grabs the tail of the dead cat, pulls it into a rope, lassos it around the edge of the paper to make a frame, more than just a nod to Picasso's caned seat. Two big hands in dirty white cotton gloves come out of nowhere, hold the rope frame, and pull it into a noose. The gloved hands are missing some fingers.

"What in the hell are you doing drawing dead cats, Ellen?" Henry wants to know.

I can't believe I've let him in my house. Claudia insisted he come right in, come right up the stairs to my studio.

"He's got a good eye when he's not drunk, Ellen," Claudia says in front of all of us on the porch. "Besides, you don't need any more enemies."

"Welcome to my home, you jackass," I tell him.

"Hello, sweetie. I miss you every day, but I have to deny it publicly."

Henry used to have a good eye, and really he still does for a certain kind of art. Henry's not so bad once you get him out of a tuxedo, but don't expect him ever to buy your lunch.

They look at the drawings on the wall. They don't say anything. They all smoke. They look, they smoke, they don't say anything.

"You found facility, didn't you?" Claudia says finally. "You're drawing like a champion. These are beautiful, Ellen."

"They're all right," Reynolds said, "but they're too cold for my taste, Ellen. They're not dead enough."

Reynolds is a British art critic, a friend of Claudia's. I respect his writing, and I caught myself just as I began to apologize for the condition of my house when I shook his hand at the door.

"That's the point," I tell him. "See, I'm working with this idea of dead nature/natural death, from the French . . ."

"Yes, I understand," Reynolds says. "I see the idea, and it's an interesting one, but those on the wall are too precious, too perfect, too beautiful, nearly neoclassic really. They could be medical illustrations in another setting; they look laid out by undertakers. Don't get me wrong. I like them. Just not very much. I need more than clean decay. I need meat on my bones."

"How much meat do you need?" I want to know.

I show them the new one, the one not two hours old. It's head and shoulders above the whole ten dangling on the wall. It's a leap I didn't know I had in me.

"Now that is vulgarity," Henry says.

"This could work. This is the right road, I think, Ellen," Reynolds says. "I'm pleased to see you do away with that dead cat. It's too domestic an image."

The cat's in there, but Reynolds can't see it. It's buried in layers and layers of other images—the turkey ribs, the three-fingered gloved hands, Courtney Anderson's new eyeteeth. I started with graphite and an eraser, but moved to Craypas oil sticks pretty soon into it. I used lighter fluid to dissolve the wax crayon, a little coffee when I couldn't find the raw umber. What the drawing is now is masked images layered in deep space. It's not finished, but it is mostly blue, and you'd still have to call it abstract if you were pressed. I've actually written on the surface *The Kitty Is Dead*, but all you can read clearly is the *K* and the last *d*.

"I'm glad to see you using color again, Ellen," Claudia says. "If I have any problem with those on the wall, it's that they're too apparent, too dry. This one's got juice, Ellen. You're beginning, finally. When are you going to canvas?"

We talk. We look. I forgot all about serving coffee, offering booze. It didn't even cross my mind.

"And listen, Reynolds, I don't see how you can say dead cats are a domestic image," Claudia says. "I think there's sexist undertones to that conclusion. Everybody's got a domestic life, some more articulated than others. Just because you don't do your own laundry doesn't mean you're free of domesticity. You don't live in the woods, you know? You've got sheets, don't you? Indoor plumbing?"

We talk. We talk about women making art, and men making art. We talk about women looking at art, and men looking at art. We reach no plateaus of understanding, but there aren't any fistfights either, and I leave them all rooting through the Hussman when I went to get Zack.

"Jesus, all she's got in here is bran," I hear Henry say as I close the front door and head for the car.

The problem with Henry is that he never did know where to look.

In the middle of January I got this call from George at Rice. He wants me to take a teaching job at the community college.

"I just got this call, and they need somebody to take their second-year painting class in January. I told them you'd do it, Ellen."

I can't teach. I haven't done it since graduate school, and I didn't like it then. I don't know anything. I've got my own kids, one's Nuts, one's a Toddler. I don't need any more kids to take care of. My house is a mess. I've got a number of tax returns to do and dirty laundry everywhere all the time. I'm working on these paintings all day now, and I don't have any energy left by seven o'clock. And, I think forcing art classes on the masses is a mistake. I think art ought to be available, that you ought to do it if you want to. I don't endorse the promotion of false hopes.

"So you'll do it?" George says.

"Didn't you hear *anything* I said, George? No, I can't do it. No."

"Listen, they'll pay you. Two thousand dollars; you got something against money, Ellen?"

"Two thousand a month? I can't live on that, George."

"No, two thousand for the whole semester, Ellen. Look, it's just six hours a week, no preparation time. You don't have to grade any papers, and you only have to appear at two faculty meetings for the whole fifteen weeks."

This is why I never taught: no money. I don't see how people live on teaching jobs. It's an obscenity.

"Listen carefully, George: No."

"What are you going to do when the Morris money runs out, Ellen? Work in some bank, get some more of those Italian shoes you like that'll take six months to pay for? Just try this teaching job, Ellen. The money gets better, sort of. I never knew you were such an elitist."

It's a second-year painting class, portfolio review for admittance. It meets from seven to ten on Tuesday and Thursday nights. Kenneth doesn't need me to get the tangles out of Tenny's hair. They'll all be fine, and seeing Tenny a little less can't hurt since she hates me anyway. I don't have any income anymore, and my bankers are concerned.

I do it, I take the job, but I don't commit to much. I'll see how this teaching is before I type up a résumé and shop for good Italian shoes on sale later in the spring.

The kids were stupid, their portfolios were horrible, and I loved it from the minute I walked in the door. It was the smell of rotting paint and new canvas, the scale of the room.

"I like Gauguin, too, and I think copying paintings you admire is one way to really understand their structure. Art students have done this for centuries, but come on, you can't do this forever. If I let you in my class, are you going to keep this copy work up?"

"Yes," he said, this stubborn nineteen-year-old with a James Dean haircut.

"Are you prepared to fail this course?"

"Yes, I am."

"Okay, but I'm going to work your tail off," I tell him and approve his application to my class. He reminds me of me. I was just this stubborn about Matisse's line drawings being the only way to do it.

Most of the applicants I reroute to Basic Drawing.

"I already took that course," more than one tell me.

"This time, take it and learn something."

About four have some actual potential, for beginners anyway, but every one of them's caught up with color, using it to mask what's not there to begin with: ideas, structure, commitment to staying with what's going on until it's finished no matter how it comes out. They never get to the moment of decision: where you declare something finished and decide to keep it, or change your mind and work it some more, or simply get it out of the studio quick—pitch it—and start over.

"You know this is a black-and-white course? No color allowed."

"Since when?"

"Since right now."

They think I'm mean; they haven't even thought about what you could do with gray. I ban brushes, make them paint with sticks and mud on newsprint.

"What textbook are we using?" they all wanted to know. There are bureaucrats even in community colleges. It's a college course, you've got to have a textbook.

"*Madame Bovary*," I told them. "Read it by the first class meeting and bring a list of five images you think might make a painting. That's F-L-O-W-B-E-A-R."

They write it on their shirt cuffs.

I remembered all the tricks I know, those that got played on me, those I heard about. I got the facile ones to use their left hands exclusively for the whole semester. I made some of them work on just one painting all term, and I made others finish one painting every class session. I imposed restrictions on support—only paper, only wood, only homosote—I explained what working against and within restrictions means. I showed them how to stretch canvas properly, once with brass-headed nails, once with canvas pliers; I explained what good canvas is. I showed them a million slides. I got to look at Ingres and Giotto again.

The last portfolio is the worst I have ever seen. The line is timid, the colors are out of magazines and so is the subject matter: all *Saturday Evening Post* sentimentality. The student is a woman in her late fifties. She wants to paint.

"Why?" I ask her.

"I can't explain it. I can't get my hands to make what I see. I see these images all the time, these shapes. They stay in my head, and I can't get them out."

"What are the images that you see?"

"All kinds of things," she says, and her hands are trembling. "The cast from my son's broken leg, my mother's grave in the snow, a box full of watches all set to different times. Am I nuts?"

"Yeah," I say and sign her up.

I teach the basic stuff, about materials, about the approaches—traditional and not so traditional—to making art and looking at it. I have to explain what I haven't thought about in years, and I come home Tuesday and Thursday nights beat, dead tired, spent. I hit the bed by eleven, but find myself sitting straight up almost every night around four in the morning. I am dreaming. I am startled awake by some dream that is more recollection than invention.

I am in the fourth grade, and we are living in Mobile. I am walking home with Lorna Simpson and Connie Hanes, who are cousins; their hair is braided in tight French braids, red ribbons at the ends. Edmund Gleason is pitching rocks and pieces of new bricks at us. We ignore him, which is what our mothers advised, and keep walking. But then I turn around to see if he's finally stopped, and I catch half a red brick with my forehead.

There is blood everywhere. I am running down an alley, watching my feet, my new white patent leather shoes turn to crimson. Edmund is running along beside me, screaming, "I'm sorry, I'm sorry, I'm sorry, I'm sorry, I'm sorry." We run.

I reach my house. The back door is orange, and it has a little square window in it, high up. Only my parents are tall enough to look out or in. I am banging on the door, kicking at it, yelling for my mother. There is blood everywhere. I am jumping and trying to see through the window.

Ruthie and my mother are playing jacks on the pink and gray kitchen floor. My mother sees me, my bloody head bobbing in the window, and I see her. Her eyes dilate in terror, but her mouth goes to this smile. She gets up from the jacks, comes to the door, opens it.

"Let's have a look at that little scratch, Ellen."

I slide out of bed. Kenneth is sleeping heavily. I grab a sweatshirt, pull it on over my nightgown, and go into the studio. I take a new stretched canvas, four feet tall by six feet long. I turn it on its end to make it a vertical. With a half piece of crumbling charcoal, I reach high, draw a square way in the top of the canvas. I begin. The painting turns out to be a good one, not—I hope—the best I'll ever do, but it's a good one, a beginning for something, and at the finish it's green.

"I can't have lunch, Ben. I'm working."

"You're always working, Ellen. How's it going?"

"Glass in the gut, Ben."

"That good, huh?"

23 ....

Losing

There has been an accident.

The two of them, Tenny and Zack, have fallen out of some boat. They are thrashing face down in the water, their arms flailing. They are drowning. My hand stretches out to grab Zack, but I can't reach him. My hand stops just short of him. He keeps kicking.

Tenny is a little closer to the boat, but she is also drowning. I reach for her. She's gulping for air. I can't reach her, she's too far away. I stop, turn, reach for Zack again. I can't get to him, I can't get to either of them. I stop. I freeze completely. I can't move.

They both begin to sink. They're both giving up. I jump in the water, reaching for either one of them. I grab at the dark. I can't feel them. I can't find either one. I come up empty-handed, and I dive again, I dive deep. I am searching for anything, an arm, a leg, a cuff of either one's pajamas, Tenny's long hair. I grab at shadows in the water. I clutch but find nothing.

They are gone. They are both dead. They are sleeping way below on the floor of the ocean, curled up the way they do, covers kicked off, sleeping deeply, dreamless, dead.

I wake up in a sweat.

"You don't understand, Kenneth: They're both yours. If they were both in danger, which one would you save? I want to save Zack, but I have to save Tenny, but I can't save Tenny, and they both die anyway because I can't move. I can't decide. There isn't time to save them both, Kenneth."

"You'd save them both, Ellen. I'd save them both. You'd make the time, you'd do it, and Ellen, you've got to quit having that stupid dream."

Sometimes it's not water. Sometimes it's fire. I can hear them both screaming and then, not screaming.

I screwed up with Tenny again. I do this all the time. I misread reality, got invested in a lost cause and tricky agendas. I wound up feeling stupid and disappointed, and I paid for a lunch I didn't want. I didn't do too well at electing a president either.

I was seriously watching the last Mondale/Reagan debate. Kenneth was upstairs bathing Zack and discussing pending toilet training with him, and Tenny—fascinated with any penis—was excused from the lesson. She stomped downstairs in a snit and flung herself on me and the couch.

"Don't suck your thumb, Tenny. Come watch this with me. It's important."

Mondale's been brilliant. How could anybody see anything in that Reagan jerk? I tuck my grandmother's green and pink quilt around us and draw Tenny close enough to hold her sucking hand.

The moderator says, "Mr. Reagan, your rebuttal," and Tenny's mouth drops open. Her eyes get real big.

"Can they say that on TV?"

"Huh? What?"

"He said, 'Mr. Reagan, you're a butt hole.' That's what he said, Ellen."

This kid knocks me out sometimes.

The debate concludes. Everyone stands up and applauds, gets ready for on-the-spot analysis, and Tenny says, "Okay, so who won? Which one is president now, Ellen?"

The kid is nine years old and in the fourth grade. I don't know what they're teaching them at that stupid school. I explain it all to her: politics, history, fascism, why we need unions, why we can't call the homeless hobos anymore. Tenny nods and appears to actually listen to most of what I have to say.

"Haven't you ever gone to vote before, Tenny? You want to go with me on Tuesday?"

She's wild for the idea.

Politics are important to me. My grandfather organized Oklahoma for the A F of L. He didn't do such a great job, but he felt passionately about it. My father still grieves for Adlai, and one of my earliest memories—me in the middle, child witness to a pretty serious domestic unpleasantness between Charlie and Frances—had to do with my mother's working door-to-door for Ike in '52.

"Your mother doesn't know shit, Ellen. Let's get out of here and go get us a working man's drink."

It's ironic that my parents wound up finally in Arizona—Goldwater country—but of course, they could be moving any time. My mother still campaigns, but on the sly when Charlie's on the road, and she won't discuss politics over dinner.

"Individual preference is guaranteed in this country, and so is the secret ballot. It's your right to decide for yourself, Ellen."

"See what I mean?" my father said. "Your mother doesn't know shit, Ellen."

"I'll come at noon," I tell Tenny. "Don't bring a lunch from your mother's on Tuesday, and we can eat at that Milano place after."

"Who are you voting for?" Tenny wants to know.

I explain how you have to look at all sides and decide for yourself. I explain how voting is a right and a responsibility. I explain about the secret ballot.

"Yeah, yeah, yeah, okay, but who are you voting for, Ellen?"

"Well, Mondale, of course. He's the one up with any vision, and he's got a good wife who knows art."

"He's my man, too," Tenny says. "You won't forget me?"

Election Day I go get her. I keep promises, but I don't get any credit for it. I promised to buy Tenny a dozen pair of barrettes for Christmas last year. Her mother could have told us she was getting her hair cut on Christmas Eve. Kenneth was furious, but I was secretly relieved because Tenny's hair was always a nightmare for me. I dreamed a thousand dreams about combing that hair. I combed, I combed. It got longer and longer and longer, like taffy. I had to go outside and all the way around the block to get to the end of it. Then I had to come back inside and start all over again from the crown.

I'd been looking forward to all this, taking Tenny to vote, having lunch with her, electing a president with a full brain. I park at her school. There are red, white, and blue crepe paper banners everywhere. They've had a straw vote.

Tenny says, "I was going to vote for Mondale, Ellen, but Hillary and Stephie were voting for Reagan, so I did, too. Are you mad? When are we going to eat?"

"Well, no, I'm not mad, Tenny, but I am confused. Where did you get that Reagan button?"

"Mom gave it to me. Isn't it great? I'm starving, Ellen."

I took her in with me to vote, but made her take off the button. I told her that was electioneering and that was against the law, which of course is a nearly bald lie—nobody's going to take a button off a kid—but I had to do something. I had to.

"Take it off or you're going to prison," I told her.

Our precinct votes at the fire station but has gone this year to punch ballots. I miss the old voting machines, the swish of the cheap black curtain, all those levers, the seriousness. I miss the drama and the secrecy.

"You would have made a great Catholic, Ellen," Kenneth says.

I begin, and I can almost smell my father's after-shave two states away. Tenny watches me punch for a while, then gets bored and starts her gymnastic routine.

"Don't yell at me, Ellen. You're embarrassing me. Nobody can see my panties. Aren't you finished yet? Aren't you ever going to feed me?"

We go to the restaurant. It's crowded, and we have to wait.

"This is a terrible idea," I say, and I'm willing to leave right now and find a drive-thru for junk.

"I don't mind," Tenny says. "I've already missed my math test."

We take their next offer on two seats at the bar. I order fresh pesto and a Cinzano; Tenny wants a hamburger, which is not on the menu, but the kitchen thinks they can throw something together. The food takes forever to arrive, and I make Tenny do long division on bar napkins. I see she's pretty much on top of it, and I order another Cinzano, and then I pay the check. Her hamburger cost eight bucks.

"It was great, Ellen," Tenny tells me in a voice I thought was louder than necessary.

We are at the door of her classroom. All the kids turn toward us and away from the teacher who is pointing at big maps with a stick and talking about where Iran is. She's pointing at Egypt. They all watch Tenny swagger in and find her desk. She's learned how to use her knees to make her butt move in her clothes.

"I'm practicing for later when I've got a good one," she says.

Tenny looks smug and full for the moment. I wave good-bye to her and her friends and mouth an apology to her teacher for getting her back late. Her teacher looks annoyed—but don't they always?—and I hurry out before someone asks me who I am, and I have to tell them.

"I'm the stepmother, more or less, and I'm a little drunk, although I have cause, which you might understand if we could talk for a few hours, maybe days."

The next morning—Wednesday, a Tenny morning—she's got the TV on real loud. It's Tenny's way of waking us all up to get her yogurt, which I think she really could do herself now, but Kenneth says he likes to. She hears the election results and bounces into my bed. I've been sick about all of it since midnight—when I finally believed that the nine o'clock predictions were true—and Tenny says to me, "Some of us really know how to pick winners, huh?"

I ignore her. I pretend she doesn't exist. I erase her completely and pull the covers up over my head. She leaves the bedroom, stomps downstairs and sniffles to Kenneth that I hate her. I stay upstairs until she's out the door with Kenneth and Zack. Then I smoke.

"I hate my life," I tell Grace on the phone. "I can't believe I keep doing the same old crap with that kid. I think I can give her something I've got that she can use, something that she needs, something of value. I get all excited about it, and then it goes to hell, just like this, every single goddamned time. What do you think?"

"I think that kid suckers you every time, Ellen," Grace says. "Kids don't know anything anyway—that's why they can't vote—and I think next time, Ellen, you ought to make Tenny buy lunch."

This is easy enough for Grace to say now. She hasn't had to deal with her stepdaughter in months. That kid of Jack's—LouAnne—is the devil, and Thanksgiving's coming. Grace will be completely un-raveled by the time the turkey's out of the oven, if she can remember to turn it on this year.

24 ....

Us & Them

We hate them.

We hate them, our stepdaughters.

We hate them because they are rude and because they are materialistic and because they are without any character.

We also hate them because they are, the lot of them, bald manipulators, prick-teasers, completely self-interested, and, in the main, really dumb, we think.

We think all this, and we think a good deal more, and regularly over food, Laurel, Grace, and I consider all aspects while we flesh out details.

"We hate them."

There are three of us, and three of them. We are Grace, Laurel, and Ellen, and we have known each other for fifteen years. They are LouAnne, Stephanie, and Tennessee Louise, currently twenty-two, sixteen, and nine, coldly calculating and horrible young women, who as it happens, are now linked to us for life no matter what.

The three of us had enough in common to eat together for another fifteen or twenty years. We didn't need and we weren't looking for any new topics to discuss over soup. However, due to a series of unrelated but quite large events, we find ourselves regularly choking on a new, unwelcome, and increasingly bitter commonality.

Overnight, in a matter of speaking, we became archetypes. It is still a shock: We are the Wicked Stepmothers. We did not lobby for this job, we were virtually drafted into the position, and we are not happy about it.

"Hey, listen, you think they might feel the same way? You know, not happy?"

"They don't feel anything, Laurel. They're sharks, all teeth and jawbone. They have no blood."

It is not at all fair. We have no audience, no supporters except our own kind (and we are frankly wary about a number of them). There is not a spring chicken among us: Each of us took a gamble on a second or even third chance on bliss or near-bliss. We actually have much more to lose in the way of face and equity, except no one but us even empathizes. They, in purely political terms, clearly have and have always had the better p.r.

Nevertheless, the truth is plain: We hate them, and they hate us.

"Do we really hate them?"

"This is a manifesto, Laurel. We have to be succinct. No waffling, okay?"

"Okay, okay. Man, oh man. I hate her."

We believe they are all at the very least generic Republicans, if not fascists, and we are only thankful that none of them can vote.

"LouAnne can vote. She's twenty-two now."

"Does LouAnne know she can vote, Grace?"

"Nah, she's stupid."

We hate them because they would not vote even if they knew they were old enough to vote. They are simply too stupid even to know they could vote.

We also hate them because they do not read or think anything of substance, and we hate them because what few books they do read (largely loans from our own personal libraries) they dog-ear and lose at the beach.

"She took my Pollock catalog to Galveston, Ellen. I loved that book, I hand carried it back from Paris in eighty-two, and now it's landfill."

They borrow, without asking, our best sweaters, the last tampon in the house, and their fathers' full attention. They come to our doors, bringing their nasty animals and their seedy friends. They tie up our phones and empty our refrigerators, and they leave their stuff in heaps around our houses—book bags on the stairs, dirty socks on the coffee table, apple cores rotting away at the wicker in the upstairs trash. They let their birds shit in our guest rooms, and they don't even mention it.

We find these things, the evidences of Them, and we voice concern, amazement, shock. We construct, then deliver at the dining room table, poignant lectures on the value of communal consideration. Our presentations are of no use: They are already gone. Our objections carry no weight at all. They have the substance of smoke.

Should, by slim chance, our complaints reach their ears and by overt miracle their consciousnesses (of which they have nearly none), dinnertime phone calls from their mothers—and then their mothers' lawyers—are likely to occur, not to mention a string of quick and hot exchanges with their blind, but loyal daddies, our husbands, literally or in a manner of speaking.

"So I told him, goddammit Jack, you can just clean up her bird's shit then."

Hours, days, even weeks of harsh arguments and dark brooding follow. Eventually, over time, the incident grows pale, is put away, gets lost, forgotten, blown off. And then, the doorbell rings (you couldn't trust a one of them with a key), and there they are, voracious and looking smug, tracking in God knows what, acting like they owned the place.

Well, we have to hate them, these girls, these daughters of our husbands. They are the tangible evidence of previous and quite large marital mistakes we had, generally speaking, nothing to do with. Nevertheless, we have to live with them, regularly or occasionally. They are the holiday children, witness to all our intimacies and exempt from any household chores, and we have little or no choice in the matter because our marriages were package deals.

We find ourselves dusting their baby pictures.

"Hey, listen, Ellen, I don't dust," Laurel says. "Who has time? I arrange for dusting. Do you dust, Ellen? You're not dusting again, are you, Ellen?"

We find ourselves dusting or arranging for the dusting of their baby pictures, those few their fathers managed to sneak out of the maternal archives. They are framed in new silver or silver plate, prominently displayed in our houses alongside our best stuff, and we wonder who are these fat and grinning babies, round as globes, all chins, and what are they grinning about?

They do not grin at us. They sneer and spit, appear cordial only if anyone's looking. They are sneaky and often nasty. They can lie, steal, cheat, and are of continuing difficulty for us. Even after they're gone, their ghosts linger, fingering our cosmetics, interrupting our sex lives, and costing us money.

So, we hate them, and we do often feel bad about it, but we hate them, and we hate their mothers, and sometimes their fathers. We hate them because they are not ours, but they are, and we hate them because they are blond.

"No, wait, that's not true, Ellen. I'm blond."

"We mean *really* blond, Laurel. All three of them are *really* blond. We are not. We hate them."

"I can't say that. I can't say I really hate Stephanie, Ellen. A lot of the time I actually like her."

"Yeah, and what about the rest of the time, Laurel?" Grace says. "Did you get your diaphragm back yet?"

Margaret, my former shrink, said all this was normal.

"Society expects the worst possible of the stepmother/stepdaughter relationship. You and you chorus friends are right on track here. You're supposed to hate each other, and it might help to consider this from a historical perspective."

"Who cares about history, Margaret? These are our lives we're talking about here. These are our days and nights. These are our vacations. We don't care about history. We are tired of trying to understand and exercise patience. We don't need them anymore. We give up on them and cordiality. We were very nice to them, at the beginning anyway, and where did that get us?"

"Remember that until recently the mortality rate for women in childbirth was quite high. Until this century, it was actually rare for a child to be raised by its natural mother."

"Yeah, yeah, yeah," we said. "So women died pretty often in child-birth, and somebody else had to remind somebody else's kid to use their napkin, and that somebody else was generally the next wife."

"You're missing it, you know, if you don't look at the fairy tales and read Bettelheim."

"We read everything, Margaret. It gets us nowhere."

"So the children live with the wicked stepmother who makes them pick up their clothes and eat dirt, and they wish for their natural mother who is as dead as a fish on a rock and clearly unavailable. Children can't handle this, the unavailability part, the abandonment part, so they idealize the natural mother, make the stepmother the fall guy."

"We are sick of being the goats. We are not goats. We resign from goatness."

"Goatness?"

"You know kids hate to be told how to behave," Margaret said. "Everybody does. It's just tough luck for them, and you've got to think about the future when they're responsible, productive adults with empathy for all of society and respect for the arts. They'll thank you for all this one day."

"We can't wait that long. We're not waiting that long. We resign from waiting."

"I want to kill her just one time. I want to get her. I want to do it this afternoon."

"Let's do it. Let's wipe out the whole tribe, and let's get the mothers, too."

"Waiter, another round, and more ink. We need more ink, much more ink. And we need more parchment."

The problem with Margaret's reading of the stepdaughter subject was that it lacked immediacy, contemporary grounding. None of our stepdaughters is an orphan, for example. We're not the maternal fill-ins. We're the targets. Their own mothers are alive, across town or closer, in continuing and exasperating influence, and probably getting their nails wrapped on the child support money even as we speak. They've taught their daughters from the breast—although every one of them was bottle-fed, you can just tell—how to keep their hair light forever and how to tap, regularly and with unfailing success, deep into their fathers' guilt and wallets.

"I still think that's wrong about the blond part," Laurel says. "And as someone who went to graduate school on a Clairol Professional Women's Scholarship, Ellen, you might back off some there. And, you just might remember who wrote you that recommendation."

Laurel is thirty-nine. She is a groomer and good at it. Like Grace, I've known her forever, but she's still a puzzle to me. She's smart, great-looking, a banking executive, one of the few people I know and trust in business, and she's got good taste, particularly in suits. But, for all the money she makes, I could never do what she does, which is to get up weekdays at 5:30 and hot roll her hair. Then she irons.

"Laurel, why do you do it? I'm afraid that dye stuff's going to rot your brains, if it doesn't blind you first."

"I still feel like a towhead, Ellen."

There were other problems with Margaret's notion, and one of those problems was Margaret. She has no children, hers or others. What did she know?

"Well, I've known you, Ellen, for ten years at least, and I know you're going to crack if you keep this up. I think you might consider resigning as Tenny's stepmother. Introduce yourself simply as Kenneth's wife. Let it all go. It will anyway."

"We will resign. We will resign in a flat minute. It won't do any good, nothing we do about them is any good, but we will resign. We are resigned to resigning."

"The real problem for me," Grace says, "is not knowing where to stand or what to say. Everything's always wrong, never comfortable. LouAnne comes to visit five or six times a year and Thanksgivings. The minute she walks in, I start feeling like a stranger in my own house. I get gawky, inarticulate. I trip over things. I leave the stove on preheat, if I turn it on at all. LouAnne watches and clucks, and then lets her birds shit all over my house. She does call her dad every week or so. I answer, she's polite, but so cold, and I never know what to say to her, so I just pass the phone on to him. She's an alien with green blood. I don't need to worry with the kind of dailiness you have, Ellen, although I did tell her last time I'd prefer she didn't bring her birds. You'd have thought I'd slapped her face off, but she didn't say anything. She just sulked, sat way off, and made her father draw her out. She wants to buy a condo in San Antonio. Jack said he couldn't help her—we're really broke right now—and then she started talking about

the breakfast nook in the condo, the pecan tree outside, how it reminded her of the one in the old house on Gramercy, all the fun they
had over eggs. Jack just fell in on himself, started crying, and called
the bank. I said, Jack, if it was so much goddamned fun, how come
you left? And he said, you can't understand, she's my baby. Then he
drank half a bottle of scotch and passed out on the sofa."

"Stephanie's just beautiful," Laurel says. "I mean, she is fabulous:
great skin, amazing legs, graceful, wonderful sense of style. I can't
believe she's just sixteen, so confident. She's smart, too, but the way
she treats her friends makes me sick. She jerks everyone around, and
they all take it, keep calling back. Why do they do that? Last Saturday
night the doorbell rings. It's this really nice kid Greg. He's nuts about
her. She's made a date with him for this dance, then got a better offer
and told Greg to pick her up at our house. She was at her mother's,
Greg called over there from our kitchen phone, and Stephanie told
him off, said she couldn't spend her time waiting around for a toad
who couldn't keep an address straight. I about died. I knew she was
going to that dance with this other guy, one of these hotshot Memo-
rial types with a red Vette. They were going to Brennan's afterwards
on our American Express card. Greg bought Stephanie's story, at least
I think so. I wanted to make sure he knew what really happened, but
Colin told me to butt out. I said, Greg, I'm so sorry, and he said, Mrs.
Mansfield, do you like gardenia corsages? So, I kissed him. I had
to—he'd rented a tuxedo and everything—and Colin gave me shit all
weekend for leading him on."

"You kissed him? You kissed him a real kiss."

"Yeah."

"Wow."

I love these women. We have been through three divorces, three
new marriages (if you wince at legalities), any number of career moves,
abortions, affairs, tax audits, cancer scares and cancer itself, political
campaigns, fantastic arguments, and a fair amount of gin until we
switched to Dubonnet. When my parents die, I will hear by telephone. Grace will cancel everything and go with me to Arizona, and
Laurel will drive us to the airport and feed my cats if I have any.

Grace's father died her first semester at Emory. She adored him and
doesn't talk about him much. His birthday was in August, and late
summer's still hard for her twenty years later.

Laurel was ugly. I've seen the pictures: real thick cat eyeglasses, muddy skin, ratty hair. She didn't date until graduate school and took ballroom dancing lessons by herself when she was thirty-five. There weren't any corsages in her life until recently.

My own father was never at home, and my grandfathers died early. I figure I lost bad on male dote. Tenny got a pony when she was three. Its name was Noel. She doesn't like it, and it's dead now.

"Noel is dead? What happened?"

"He bit Tenny, and Raylene shot him. She said she'd have choked it dead around the neck if she hadn't had her gun, and any decent mother would have done the same."

"Raylene's a pony murderer, Ellen? She packs heat?"

"Yes, and she's the mother of a blond."

So, we hate them because they are blond, and because they are beautiful, and because they are getting what they want right now and not having to pay for it yet. They work the system better than we ever will. They are not like us at all, like we were, like we are, like we're going to be. We do not understand them, they are aliens to us, and they are our family. We will attend their weddings as the Others, sit to the side, and underdress.

"What about stepsons?" I ask in the parking lot. I don't have any of those. They have a number of those between them.

"Totally different story," Grace says. "Randall reads the paper and talks about it. He brings me presents, funny coffees, scarves. When he leaves, I change the sheets and don't look too close."

"What about kids? You know, real ones?" Laurel says.

I have Zack. They don't and won't have any of their own.

"All the difference," I tell them, but I don't go into it because we've had a couple of drinks, actually quite a few drinks, and then a lot of coffee. Sometimes when I talk about Zack, they get a little sad-looking. I think their regrets about their own choices come up, and it takes a while to recover from this loop.

None of us has time for recovery today: It's nearly 3:00. Grace and Laurel need to get back to their offices and check their messages. I am currently largely unemployed. An answering machine and a list of errands wait for me.

"So, we hate them, right? And one of these days they'll pay. And we'll watch, and they will either die or finally get some character."

Three women—two in closed-toe Ferragamo pumps probably paid for—slap a high five until next week at 1:00.

Grace leans toward me to brush a piece of food off my cheek.

"Lipstick," she whispers.

Then she kisses me and heads for her car. Laurel and I wave. We never kiss.

I've got two and a half hours until I have to get Zack. It's a lifetime. I go to Target on South Main, buy diapers (maybe The Last Box), laundry soap, hair spray and shampoo for Tenny. I think she's way too young for hair spray, but if we don't buy it, she just brings it from her mother's in her book bag. It is a pump bottle, but it leaks. Sticky stuff gets all over her homework, and her teachers call. They never call Raylene.

Then I jump by the bank, the grocery, the post office, the art supply store, then home. I am a very efficient person when I have to be, and I love coming home to a silent and fairly picked up house with provisions, a gallon of milk, new graphite. I feel ready for anything, prepared, which is a good attitude because it's a Tenny weekend.

The buzz from the Dubonnet is off, and Tenny's baby picture on the mantel glares at me. I'm beginning to feel guilty about all that hate talk at lunch, although it was a lot of fun and true, although not complete.

I need to go get Zack, and Kenneth and Tenny will be here in twenty minutes. But I go over to the mantel, buff the silver with my sleeve, and look at the photograph.

Jesus, she was fat. She couldn't be more than a few days old. Who would've thought she'd become such a beauty?

I look close and see for the first time a hand in the picture, in the shadow, low in the frame and cropped at the wrist.

It is Raylene's hand. Raylene's hand is on my mantel. Is she reaching for Tenny or drawing back from her? Is she pushing her? Kenneth must be taking the picture, and Tenny's not grinning at all, but is about to roll off the bed and fall on her nose.

25

The Fall

|t *was an accident.*

Tenny was sick. She was sick with some virus, and she was in her bed at our house for five days. The school called Kenneth at work early Thursday morning, and he brought her home around ten o'clock with a fever of 102.

"Were you sick this morning, Tenny? Did you have fever when you woke up at your mother's?"

I wanted to know. I didn't understand how a kid could get this sick between 8:00 when school begins, and 9:30 when the nurse called Kenneth.

"Mom wouldn't let me stay home," Tenny told us. "She hates me."

Kenneth stayed home with Tenny the rest of Thursday and also Friday. He brought her soup and crackers on a tray, read her stories, took her temperature, and held her hair off her face while she vomited. I went to the grocery twice a day for supplies: juice, chicken broth, sugar-free Popsicles, kid aspirin. I took Zack to school and picked him up. Tenny's fever kept breaking and then coming back. I put clean sheets on her bed two, three times a day, and presoaked the smelly ones in extra Clorox for the full cycle.

The weekend came. We tried to keep Zack away from her for a while, but then figured he'd already been exposed. We read them both stories, and Zack napped on the rug in her room, inside her Ms. Piggy sleeping bag. We rented some kid movies, watched them, all of us in our pajamas and robes and slipper socks. We stayed in the house, and we tried to stay quiet. On Saturday night, Tenny's fever broke and stayed broke. On Sunday, she looked like she'd never been sick in her life.

When the phone rang about five o'clock Sunday afternoon, I was helping Tenny get her stuff together—school books, uniforms, an-other new umbrella—and Kenneth had gone to get gas for the car. Tenny is due at her mother's at six o'clock on our Sundays, and they never have tuna fish. Tenny told me.

It was Raylene on the phone. She was calling long distance from somewhere, and her plane was delayed, canceled, never scheduled to fly in the first place.

"Could you keep Tenny tonight? Just this once? This is an emer-gency, Ellen."

No, bitch, I wanted to tell her. We'll just drop her at your house and let her sleep on the front porch like we did the last time.

"Of course, we'll keep her," I told Raylene. "But why don't you tell Tenny about it yourself?" and I handed the phone to Baby Girl.

Tenny's face lit up at the sound of her mother's voice. She loves this woman, and I just don't get it. Wasn't she the one, Tenny, who promised you a trip to New York City, San Francisco, anywhere? Didn't those travel plans change at the very last minute? Don't they always? Hadn't I already slipped you a five-dollar bill to blow on your trip—"buy something for yourself, Tenny, but something you see that you love"—before I realized your father would do the same thing on the way to your mother's house in the car Sunday night? And didn't you wind up spending that weekend with your grandmother in Conroe anyway? Wasn't that the weekend your grandmother got sick, and we had to drive up and get you because no one could find your mother? She hadn't even left a phone number for emergencies.

Tenny is cooing to Raylene, going on and on about all her vomit. I'm heading for the next room. I don't mind graphic detail, but the

white sugar stuff turns my stomach. But her mother must have inter-
rupted her because Tenny stopped talking in mid-sentence, started
listening intently.

Tenny's face changed. The light went right out of it. She took in
her mother's bad news, and then she started screaming like someone
was pulling her legs off. Then she threw the phone at me.

I've got good hands. I caught the receiver before it blinded me. I
heard Raylene's voice yelling, "Get over it, Tenny Lou, and don't be
such a jerk. It's not my fault; it's the fucking airline's. Now I'll see you
tomorrow afternoon. Good-bye."

Tenny heard nothing of this. She was screaming.

"Get over it, Tenny," I said.

"SHUT UP," she screamed, and my hand reached out to slap her
face. I stopped just in time. I have never hit her; I have wanted to a
hundred times. I grabbed her shoulder and shook her hard. I've done
this one thousand times, and I ought to stop it. It doesn't have any
effect anyway. Tenny screams until she's finished, until her own noise
bores her. Then she threatens to call Child Welfare and report me for
child abuse.

"What is the matter with you, Tenny? I can't stand this noise. It's
inappropriate, and you're scaring Zack."

"She's with HIM, Ellen. She loves HIM more than she loves me."

This HIM is the best news I've heard in years. Raylene needs a
HIM, a new HIM; we all need Raylene to have a new HIM. This is
Great News. I am thrilled to hear about a HIM. I've thought about
fixing her up for years.

"Don't you know anybody?" I asked everyone.

"Are you Nuts, Ellen?"

Tenny is not pleased about HIM.

"I hate HIM," she spits at me, and then she lets go with another
scream that shakes the windows in their putty. Zack, who is used to all
of this, toddles over to her and sits down cross-legged on the floor to
watch until the end. I've got Tenny in the rocking chair. I am rocking, but my heart is not in it.

"You've got to cut this shit out, Tenny. You're nearly in the fifth
grade. Your mother loves you, Tenny. You know that. But she needs
her own life, honey. She's an adult. She's not *just* your mother. She'll

be back tomorrow, and you'll see her. Your mother loves you, Tenny. She just missed her plane. That happens. Your mother loves you, Tenny. You're too old for this shit."

"Do you think I am *stupid*, Ellen?" Tenny says and sits straight up in my lap. Her voice is suddenly steady as granite, as clear as glass. There's no gasping for breath here. She's not even trembling.

"You don't think she's really *missed* a plane, do you? She just wants to be with HIM. She hates ME. They're not even out of town."

I am stunned. I hadn't thought about it this way, and it is possible, I guess. Somebody's lying, I can't tell which, and there's nothing I can do to find out. I don't call Raylene. I don't talk to her. I don't like her.

"It doesn't matter which one's lying," Kenneth says. "Let's get Tenny to bed early. Maybe she can go to school tomorrow."

I didn't think Maybe was an option. She'd been free of fever for twenty-four hours, and I'd already ironed her uniform, which is generally Kenneth's job. Monday morning, it's back: 101 degrees. Her eyes look like a rabbit's. She is translucent against the Big Bird sheets which are not nearly as bright as they once were.

We've done nothing else for four days but take care of Tenny. Kenneth needs to go to work, and so do I. Nobody answers at Raylene's. It's her day off, they tell us at Foley's.

"Can you keep her, Ellen?" Kenneth asks me. "I'll stay home again if you can't, but I've got this regional meeting coming up Wednesday, and I haven't even started preparing for it, and I'm supposed to be in Clear Lake this afternoon."

I work at home during the day. I also work at home during the night. I work all the time is what I do. I'm trying to paint and not have to get a day job. It won't last forever—I'm almost out of money—but right now I'm here, in the house, working. I've got no day-boss, I don't have to account to anybody, and my wages don't get docked if the kids are sick too much.

I do it. I keep her. She'll probably sleep all morning anyway. We'll put the little Zenith in her room, if that doesn't work out. We've got a crate of chicken broth so going to the grocery again isn't necessary. I can work in the studio and check on her every now and then. She's nearly ten years old; she doesn't need constant supervision. She's not vomiting now. She's just got this fever. I do it. I keep her.

"I'll try to come home for lunch," Kenneth says.

"Forget lunch," I tell him. "You just be here this afternoon when Raylene comes to get her."

It was an accident. She fell.

Tenny slept all morning. I checked on her four or five times. She was hot, but sleeping. I took her hand, rubbed it until her eyes fluttered open.

"Are you dead, Tenny?"

"I'm hot, Ellen."

I gave her aspirin, juice. I took the tray downstairs, came back up, and she was asleep again. I pulled her thumb out of her mouth and headed for the studio.

Kenneth called twice. She was still sleeping. I worked, and I lost track of the time.

"Aren't you even going to feed me?" Tenny said, and I jumped, nearly dropped my brush and did turn over a coffee can of pale blue wash I'd just mixed up.

She was in the doorway in her nightgown, barefoot, her hair a mass of tangles. It was almost one o'clock. I'd been working, and she was sleeping the last time I looked, around eleven.

"You look like you're feeling better, Tenny," I said, stamping up the spilled paint with paper towels and newspapers. "But how did you get those cobwebs in your hair? You haven't been crawling around under the bed, have you? Now what do you want to eat for lunch?"

"Trout almondine," she said. "Let's go out."

Her fever's gone, her color's back, and she's starving to death. I make her lunch, more chicken broth and some pasta. She hates it.

"I hate soup. Actually, I hate *your* soup, Ellen," she says.

"This is not *my* soup, Tenny. This is canned soup, and you're alive because of it."

She wants to call her mother. I let her. She gets no answer, which is a disappointment for both of us.

"Look, Tenny. I want you back in bed. You can watch television in your room, and you can read if you want. I've got to get back to work."

"There's not a thing wrong with me," she says, revving up for a fit.

"Cut it out, Tenny. I don't need any of your shit today. You've been sick for five days. You get back in that bed and don't fan around. I don't want to hear a peep out of you."

These phrases just come out of my mouth. I don't think Tenny could ever peep. It's simply not possible for her. This kid's whispers make the house tremble. She'll be loud on her deathbed.

She protests all the way to her room—I have to carry her part way—but she goes. She settles into her bed, complaining bitterly about the way the sheets smell. I tell her she can change them herself this time. I bring her a set, and she kicks them across the room. I bring the television in. I turn it on. I tell her I'll kill her if she even budges out of that bed.

"What if I have to go to the bathroom? You want me to just pee in the corner?"

"That's exactly what I want you to do," I tell her and close the door. I stand there a minute in the hall. I hear her get out of bed. I hear her walk across the room. I see the knob turn.

"BOO," I say, and she screams. I got her good.

"You're giving me a heart attack," she yells, falling back on her bed and clutching her chest.

"That's not all I'm going to give you if you don't stay in that bed," I tell her and close the door again. I can't believe the things that come out of my mouth.

It was an accident. She fell. I didn't push her exactly.

I'm working in the studio. It's on the second floor, too, as far from Tenny's room as possible. Even so, I can still hear her television blaring. It's a game show. She loves those things, and I tell her that her teeth are going to rot if she keeps watching crap, but she doesn't listen. I don't like the noise, but I don't want to interact anymore with her for a while. I get up and close my door, but I can still hear her TV.

I work. I'm working pretty well. I like paper, but there's nothing like canvas. It's a big painting. It's had certainty from the beginning, and if it's still got it at the finish, I'm going to submit it to the Houston Area Competition.

I work steady for about an hour. I hear Tenny get up and go to the bathroom. I hear the toilet flush, I hear her go back to her room. I work some more, then stop to see what I've done. I'm sitting across the room from the painting, smoking one of the five cigarettes I allow myself a day—unless it's a bad day, when I simply quit counting and let my lungs go to hell—when I hear Tenny's door again. I hear her pad down the hall, stop just outside my closed door, then turn and go up the stairs to Kenneth's music room in the attic.

"Does she think I'm stupid?" I ask my painting.

"Yes, she does," my painting says. "She thinks you're an imbecile. She doesn't take you seriously. She doesn't believe you'll do what you say. She grants you absolutely no authority in or over her life. She hates you, Ellen. You better kill her."

I wait a minute. I smoke another cigarette. I hear Tenny walking around upstairs. There is no rug, the wooden floors squeak, and she's got a heavy step for a small person. Kenneth's room is off limits to the kids, and I don't even go up there without an invitation. I don't think it's been vacuumed since we moved into the house, but I'm not keeping up with the housekeeping like I used to.

I get up. I go into the hall, and I creep up the stairs to the attic. The double windows are open at either end. The wind is stirring the dust. Tenny is playing at one of her performances, and she doesn't see me.

Actually, she is not a child who plays. I've never seen her play with a doll, and she must have a hundred total, most of them those ugly, overpriced Cabbage Patch things she gets from her mother and her mother's family. Other toys interest her for no more than the time it takes to rip open the present. She doesn't play by herself at all. To do anything, she's got to have somebody there with her—some little friend, one of us—although she insists on controlling the game, turns mean if it doesn't go the way she wants it. She can't entertain herself. She can't play.

I thought maybe this was just how kids were—what did I know?—until I watched Zack sit in his playpen for hours and turn book pages for his stuffed animals. He makes his play phone ring and talks to Grandma. Then he passes the phone around to his bears and talks for them, too. Tenny never did anything like this, but the one thing she does like to do is to perform. She plays superstar—torch singer, gymnast, dancer—but I always thought she required an actual audience to do it.

I feel like I've caught her masturbating. She is dancing on the window seat, which is her stage, and she is revving up for a big finish—she's doing her spin thing—which will make her invisible audience shriek with pleasure and beg for more. She is tap dancing—she is a terrible dancer, by the way—and her face is getting flushed, and she's been sick for four and a half days, and I told her not to get out of bed.

"WHAT IN THE HELL DO YOU THINK YOU'RE DOING, TENNY?" I bellowed from the top of the stairs. I sprang like a cat into the room, and I hoped I scared the wits out of her.

I did. She screamed, a real scream. She lost her balance, and she fell back. The double windows were open. There weren't even any screens on them, no grates, no cross bars. She fell, she fell back against the windows, and then through them. She fell out the attic windows, three stories up. I saw her fall. I saw her fall back through the windows and disappear. I saw her hair, I saw her white nightgown, I saw her bare feet. I saw her fall, one part at a time.

It was an accident. She fell. I didn't push her exactly. She fell out the windows. She was dancing; she'd been sick, and she wasn't doing what I told her to do. She fell out the window. I pushed her out with my voice.

I remember running to the window, looking out. She was already on the ground. She was lying on the ground in the ivy, in the kudzu: this little shape in a white batiste nightgown surrounded by green.

I must have called 911 from Kenneth's phone. I must have run downstairs. I must have grabbed the quilt off the couch on my way out to her. I remember none of this. What I do remember is putting my hand on her heart, feeling it beat, thanking God she was alive. She was on her back, she was unconscious, her breathing was shallow, and her head was bleeding from a gash on the back. I didn't move her. I covered her with the quilt, held my hand against the back of her head, and tried to tamp the blood. Her shoulder was bleeding, too. There was blood everywhere.

"You're going to be all right, Tenny. You are going to be all right," I told her.

She couldn't hear me. She was unconscious.

The ambulance came. The paramedics took over. Her arm was broken at the shoulder, but it was internal injuries that worried them. They lifted her onto a board, strapped her to it, carried her slowly through the ivy, through the front yard, into the ambulance. They strapped an oxygen mask to her face, gave her a shot of something, and called ahead to Texas Children's Emergency.

"Are you the mother?" they asked me.

"Yes," I said. "Is she going to die?"

"You want to get in here?"

I was standing in the street, watching them work on Tenny through the door of the ambulance. I couldn't move. My arms dangled like dead things at my sides.

"Jesus, come on," I said climbing in. "Let's get the fuck to the hospital."

Tenny's eyes fluttered.

"Keep talking to her," they told me.

They drove like hell. Tenny never moved.

At the hospital a dozen pairs of hands take Tenny out of the ambulance, away somewhere. I am right behind them. I sign my name to a dozen forms, and I watch everything they do to her. The bone is coming through the skin of her shoulder, and blood is pouring out of the back of her head like water out of a faucet. They cut her hair away to get to the head wound. Pieces of Tenny's hair fall to the floor in matted bloody tufts. White shoes don't even bother to step around them.

"Keep talking to her," they tell me. "Hey, what's your blood type? She's going to need some."

I hold her good hand. I stroke her arm.

"Come on, Tenny. Wake up, we're going to Astroworld. Come on, Tenny, wake up. Your mother's coming to take you to the moon. Come on, Tenny . . ."

"We thought you said you were the mother."

"I am. Don't you fuckers stop for a minute."

"Are you the legal custodial parent?" and they actually pause in their work, take their hands off her.

"Yes, goddammit, and don't you dare stop helping her."

They want to do an EKG. They want to do a brain scan. They want to know medical history, all about a tumor she had when she was two. I give permission for everything. I know this kid, but I don't have enough details on the tumor. I don't know if she's ever had scarlet fever. I'm pretty sure her shots are current, but I can't swear to it.

"How come she's not waking up?"

"We don't know," they tell me and roll her off to X-ray. "You better find the father. Your blood's not a match, Ellen."

I find a pay phone, but I don't have any money. I didn't bring my purse. I didn't bring anything. A nurse who looks like Ruthie lends me three quarters.

I call Kenneth's office. He's not there, but they'll beep him, they'll call the police, get an APB out to find him somewhere on the Gulf Freeway and bring him to the medical center.

I know Raylene's not at work. I pray she's not at home, and then I pray she is. I dial—I had to look the number up—and the phone rings. I count: one, two, three, four.

"Hello," she answers in the middle of the fifth.

"Raylene? It's Ellen," I say to her. "Are you there by yourself?"

"What's it to you, bitch?"

"This is important, Raylene. Are you there by yourself?"

"Yes, I am. So what? Why are you bothering me? What do you want?"

"I want you to find your purse, Raylene, and then I want you to look outside. There's a yellow cab there. The driver is a tall black man in a cowboy hat. He's got two gold teeth in the front. He's about seventy, and his name is Willis. Go get in that cab, Raylene."

"What's happened? What's going on?"

"There has been an accident, Raylene. Tenny has been hurt, and it's serious. I need you to come to the hospital immediately, and Raylene, there are a lot of reasons to hurry."

I hear her drop the phone. I hear her feet running. I hear her front door open and slam shut. Then I don't hear anything, but I keep holding onto the receiver. It's the only thing that's holding me up.

Tenny is still unconscious. Her arm and shoulder are taped up, and she's not bleeding on the outside anymore. They're bringing her back from X-ray on a gurney through Emergency. Then they're taking her upstairs to Intensive Care where they'll wire her up to monitors, try and figure out what's going on, why she won't wake up.

I'm waiting for her in Emergency. Somebody's already swept up the floor, her hair is gone. They still want me to talk to her, but I'm flat out.

"What do the X-rays show? Is there brain damage? What is it? Why doesn't she wake up?"

"We don't know yet. We don't know anything," the aides tell me. "The doctors are looking at the pictures now. Keep talking, Ellen. It doesn't matter what you say. Just keep talking."

I try humming a little "Waltzing Matilda" to her, and I remind Tenny how much she always liked that song. Then out of nowhere it occurs to me that the song we should have been singing to her all these years was "The Tennessee Waltz," and why none of us had ever realized this. It could have made a considerable difference. I ask Tenny whether she thinks it might still, but it doesn't really matter what I say to her. It doesn't matter what I sing. Tenny just lies there on the gurney. She doesn't move at all. I never saw her so still, and I have to reach out every minute or so to feel her heart, make sure it's still beating.

We are waiting for the elevator. I am talking to Tenny, and I am talking about Tenny. We are taking her upstairs, these two aides and me. Others are waiting for us. They will meet us on the fourth floor. I don't know anything about how she really is yet. I'm going to call Ralph the minute she's settled upstairs and get some pressure going here. I don't know whether or not she's going to live.

The elevator announces itself. The door slides open, and people pour out all around us. The two aides are gliding Tenny's gurney into the elevator, one of those long skinny ones. I'm standing at the door, holding it open with my back. I'm telling the aides to watch it, don't jostle her. I'm directing the other people waiting to go upstairs for some benign visit to the other elevators around the corner.

"We've got a real sick kid here. You can go to that other bank of elevators, or you can wait on this one to come back. But I swear I'll kill you if you even think about getting on this one now."

I'm about to jump on myself when something—some ice cold air on my neck—makes me glance around behind me to the ambulance entry doors just sliding open.

It is Raylene. She's coming through fast, and Willis is right behind her, carrying her purse. She looks like shit. She's in a ratty bathrobe, no mascara, no shoes, and she's running.

"Raylene," I yell at her, "she's here."

"Where's my baby? Where's my baby girl?" she says to me, anybody, everybody.

"Right here," I tell her and shove her into the elevator.

"Oh, Jesus," she says and reaches for her daughter.

I stand back, let the elevator doors close. I touch them with my hands, lean into them and whisper, "I'm sorry," but nobody hears me. The elevator's already gone, lifting Tenny to the fourth floor.

. . .

Raylene's blood was the wrong match, too. Tenny has Kenneth's blood. The police found him on the road between Clear Lake City and Dickenson, and brought him in under sirens at ninety miles an hour.

"Isn't she all right?" Kenneth asks me.

I'm sitting on a bench outside this little glass room where they have her on the fourth floor. Raylene's with her. She's talking to her now, and Tenny's hooked up to monitors. She's still out.

"She was dancing, Kenneth. She fell in the ivy. Raylene doesn't have any shoes with her. Nobody knows shit. Ralph's coming."

They take Kenneth into Tenny's glass box. They lay him down, start taking his blood and feeding it into his daughter.

"How come we had to wait on Kenneth for the blood?" I wanted to know. "Don't you have this stuff frozen somewhere?"

"Big pile-up last weekend," the nurses told me. "Ten cars piled up on a semi. We used up all our reserve, plus most people these days prefer giving to their own."

I watch through the window. Kenneth is on one side of Tenny, and Raylene is on the other. It is The Holy Family, and the grandparents are on their way in from Lake Conroe.

"She did lose a lot of blood," Ralph tells me. "She's in deep shock. They think she fainted before she hit the ground, and they don't see any damage to the brain. They'll do the scans again if she doesn't respond soon. There ought to be some response by now. The best thing you can do is talk to her, be with her. What are you doing out here, Ellen?"

"They're in there. They're talking to her. They're her parents. This social worker was by and wants to talk to me about the accident. I said I'd come down and see her. They need to fill out some report."

"Get in there, Ellen. You're her parent, too. You've got a voice, haven't you?" Ralph says and holds the door to Tenny's room for me. Then he gives me the barest push.

I stand at the foot of her bed. Raylene glares at me, Kenneth smiles, and Tenny just lies there. She's not even sucking her thumb. She's not even moving.

I have a voice in this child's life. What is that voice? Where does it come from? Where is it now?

I take a deep breath. It comes.

"GODDAMN IT, TENNY, GET THAT THUMB OUT OF YOUR MOUTH."

Raylene is ready to leap on my throat, Kenneth is shocked to speechlessness, but Tenny's eyes flutter. The monitors dance. Aides, nurses, medical students, doctors, everyone in white, converge on the spot from all directions. They're watching the monitors, they're taking her pulse, they're rubbing her fat little feet.

Tenny's eyes open. She blinks, she focuses, she narrows her eyes. She is looking right at me. I wave.

"Fuck you, Ellen," she says in a high, scratchy voice. Then she puts her thumb in her mouth, closes her eyes, and goes on back to sleep.

I walk around in the parking lot of the Texas Medical Center for about twenty minutes until I remember I didn't bring my car. I am carrying my grandmother's pink and green quilt. It is stiff with Tenny's blood.

I'm walking home—it's only ten blocks—when a yellow cab pulls up alongside me. It's Willis.

"I've been looking for you, lady girl. How's that one?"

"She's all right, everyone thinks. I don't know. Jesus, Willis, I must owe you a fortune."

"You do that. You want to walk or ride? It's getting late."

"God, what time is it? I forgot all about Zack."

It was just after seven. It stays light in Houston until nine, nine-thirty in May. I got into Willis's cab, and we roared off to Zack's school. We got there just as Catherine was locking the front door, Zack on her hip. She was furious.

"I waited and waited," she said. "I almost called Child Welfare. You owe us eighty-seven dollars in late-minute fees, Ellen."

"There was an accident . . ." I began to explain.

"I last one, Ma," Zack said, and he held his arms out to me.

"I'm sorry, baby," and I took him, picked him up, held him. He hugged me tight around the neck. He smelled like a little goat.

"I sure am glad to see you, Zack-o."

It's not that I forget about him—I've never had to pay late minutes, I always get him before six, generally even earlier—but except for the Failure To Thrive business when he was just months old, Zack is no trouble. He's with us all the time—no flip-flopping in and out the front door—and he's quiet, independent, content usually. Tenny is our squeaky wheel, and I worry Zack feels neglected.

"You've got enough to worry about, don't you?" Willis said. "This is a fine child you've got here. I've got a few like this. Doesn't he look like a hot dude in my hat?"

We pull up to the house. The front door is standing wide open, and every light in the place is on.

Willis calls the police from his radio. They come quick—it's the same pair who came for the dope search—and after they've pulled their weapons and walked through the house, they wave us in from the front door with their guns.

I left the door open. They had lots of time, and they took everything with a plug. They took the Zeniths, and the radios, and the irons. They took the telephones and answering machine, and what they didn't take, they smashed.

"No more soup," Zack says in the dining room.

Pieces of my tureens are everywhere, every glass and plate has been pulled out and thrown to pieces on the floor. Paintings are slashed, pillows are ripped open, feathers are everywhere. Furniture is overturned, my rugs have been ripped up with knives, boot heels; books are scattered. I find pieces of my rag monkeys—arms, legs, tails—everywhere.

"Lady girl, you got any booze?"

"Huh?"

"You need a drink, lady girl, and you need a drink now."

"I don't know, Willis. I'm a little worried about my drinking lately."

"You worry about that later. Drink this cold gin down and put this day away."

We all have a drink—me, the cops, Willis. I'm holding Zack—there's broken glass and pottery everywhere—and for once he's not struggling to get down and run. He stays close, and Willis just gives him his cowboy hat.

I'm trying to figure out what to do, where we should go for the night—the phones are gone, I can't call anybody; I'm sure they found my purse, got my credit cards—when the doorbell rings. This strikes us all as hilarious. We've killed a good third of the Bombay, and the door's still standing wide open. That doorbell means nothing, and it never did.

Hilarity doesn't last. It's another set of cops and a social worker from Child Welfare. They want to ask me questions about an attempted murder charge.

At the Warwick Hotel, Kenneth sleeps dreamless in the middle of a king-sized bed. He's pale, and he looks like he's lost a lot more than two pints of blood. He stayed with Raylene and Tenny at the hospital until about 9:30, then came home and found my note on the door.

"Believe me: Don't even try your key. Come to Room 1123 at the Warwick. I'm sorry, Kenneth."

He found us and practically passed out drinking orange juice and beef bouillon. Now he sleeps. Zack tosses in a rented crib, but doesn't wake up. I can't sleep. I've tried.

I was dreaming. I was dreaming this dream. I was in labor again, on my back, splayed, my bare feet cold in cold metal stirrups.

"How did this happen, Kenneth? We never have sex anymore."

"It won't be long now," Sam said from the other side of the stirrups. "Let's push-push-push, Ellen."

I am screaming, I do not believe him, and I'm about to sit right up and tell him through the window that is my legs, when I notice my feet. They are no longer bare. I have on shoes. I have on a pair of red shoes but they do not match.

One is cadmium red light, soft leather, beautiful, a good fit, a pleasure to wear. The other is hot, red hot, like steel ready to melt. It's burning me, and I can smell my own flesh cooking. My foot dances in the red hot shoe. I cannot dance it off.

"Here they come, finally," Sam says, and I give birth to twins, a girl, then a boy.

"Hello, Mom," Kenneth says, and someone hands me two babies wrapped in pancakes.

"I think they're actually crêpes," I hear someone who is me say, and I look at my children.

She is pink and green, this girl. She is screaming, hungry I think, but she will not take any milk from me. The breast that is hers, the left, is full, nearly exploding with what I've got and with what I think she needs. She screams. She won't take any. I didn't know anyone could scream that loud, and milk pours out of me and down my shirt, a waste.

I look at the other, the boy. He is no color at all. He is all light. He glows in my arms. His sister's screams do not seem to bother him, and I worry there is something wrong with his hearing.

"Are you all right?" I say.

He smiles at me, he has teeth already, and then he sits up, only two minutes old, and begins to cut his own meat.

"Jesus, I really am Nuts," I conclude to the hotel room. No one disagrees. They are all sleeping.

I take Kenneth's car keys, and I talk Housekeeping into lending me a thermos. I drive to Texas Children's, and I sneak past the nurse's station to Tenny's room. She's not there. She's gone, but Raylene is there. Raylene is asleep in the bed in Tenny's glass box. Tenny is gone.

She's dead, I think. Tenny is dead, and no one called us. Or they tried to call us, but they couldn't get us because the phone's gone now. They tried to call us to tell us that Tenny was dead, but no one answered, and when they sent a messenger, no one was home.

I'm beginning to panic—What am I going to do now? Who should I call? How am I going to tell Kenneth his daughter is dead?—but then I see her. I see her through the glass box, on the other side of the glass box.

Tenny is alive. She is sitting on the counter at the nurse's station on the other side of the glass box. She is surrounded by nurses and aides and medical students. They are all laughing. Tenny is also laughing. She is barefoot, and she is sitting up on the counter, surrounded by hundreds of people in white. They are all laughing. They are all laughing together. It is 2:30 in the morning, and Tenny is alive and laughing.

Now: Raylene is asleep, Kenneth is asleep, and Zack is asleep. Tenny is alive and having a party for herself, and I am standing here with her blood on my shoes, holding a fucking thermos of hot chocolate.

I don't turn around. I just back up. I back right back into the elevator and press Lobby. I get out, and I'm looking for a trash can to

dump the thermos when I see Zack's face. Out of nowhere, I'm thinking about Zack and his face, about Zack's sister's face, about Zack and
his sister and their faces.

"Aw, shit," I say out loud in the lobby of Texas Children's Hospital.

"May I help you?"

It is a woman about 105 years old who is sitting at the reception and
information desk.

"Take this," I said.

"Why?"

"I can't handle it anymore."

"Is it for a patient?"

"Yes."

"Is it medicine?"

"Yes."

"What' the name? Take this receipt. Can you get to your car? Do
you want me to call Security for you? They can walk you to your car
if you're afraid."

"She'll need it first thing tomorrow morning."

"I understand. I'm a professional: You can trust me. This isn't a
bomb, is it?"

"No, it isn't a bomb."

"So, sleep well and don't worry about anything. Everything's going
to be all right."

"What do you know?"

"I know you. I know all about you. You had a lot to work out, but
now you're on the right road. You've started, Ellen, a little late, but
not too late. You're going to be fine, and no one's going to die for a
long time. Sometimes, Ellen, a cigar is just a cigar."

"Who are you?"

"I'm your grandmother, Ellen, and you really ought to get some rest,
sweetie."

Part Four

A Flash of Love,
Where We Dismiss
Freud and Other Things
Ridiculous

26

Sunday Brunch

Tenny has gone irrational, and Kenneth has asked her to leave. I get to hold the door. She screams even louder, but she won't budge. Kenneth has to pick her up—she goes to dead weight, all sixty-seven pounds of her not counting her party shoes——and carry her out to the front porch. She is screaming her brains out. She is going to ruin her dress. She is twelve years old, and we are all too old for this.

"You can scream as loud as you want, Tenny," Kenneth tells her. "But you may not do it in the house."

"I hate you. I HATE YOU."

"You have five minutes to get yourself in charge," Kenneth says in an even voice, untouched by reactivity. "If after five minutes, starting from right now, you are still out of charge, you will have to stay here with Emily and Zack. You will not be able to go to Courtney's birthday party, and you will have to stay in your room. Do you understand, Tenny?"

"Everyone's going to see you in your underwear, Ellen. You're embarrassing me, and I *hate* you. I Hate BOTH OF YOU."

"We know," we say and close the door, although it doesn't have much effect. We can still hear her raving, and I am not in my underwear. I've got on a robe and a full slip. I've got on socks.

Tenny is having an attack. I think she ought to be whipped, and I'd be happy to do it. I can't stand it when she yells like this.

"Kenneth, I don't think we ought to let her go to Courtney's at all."

"She's Nuts, Ellen, but I don't think we ought to let it affect our lives. I'd tired of giving in and being a responsible parent. Let's give her the five minutes."

If we give in—which is to say, if we take this hysteria attack seriously—our Sunday is shot. Tenny was looking forward to this stupid birthday party, until she found out we were going to Laurel and Colin's brunch. She likes doing the leaving, but she hates being left. The fact that she wasn't invited doesn't mean a thing to her.

But, if we do what we ought to do—if we cancel Courtney's party on her and make her stay home with the sitter—we won't be able to relax or have any fun. When we discipline Tenny, when we ground her after one of her outbursts, when we do the right, responsible, and adult thing, when we demonstrate clearly to her the consequences of her behavior, when we tell her she can't go, too bad, she brought it on herself—Tenny goes murderous.

After screaming her brains out, she sulks and turns mean. She picks on Zack, pinches him when she thinks we're not looking, kicks over his Lego things. When he hits her back, Tenny screams, "I didn't do anything," and then flies into a blinding white rage all over again when she gets sent to her room.

When Tenny's not picking on her little brother, she's breaking things "by accident." Nothing is ever Tenny's fault. She fuels herself on accusation, always unjust in her opinion, and I once watched her from the hall shove an eighty-pound antique mirror off the wall with her foot.

That mirror had been a part of Tenny's room forever. We all miss it. Kenneth bought it for her at a junk store when he was first separated from Raylene. It was big, very old, with thick glass, Victorian. It had an ornate frame painted a cheap pink, and we were always going to get around to refinishing it. Kenneth hung the mirror over her dressing table, which was sometimes a desk, and she spilled junk all over both of them. The dressing table was actually a sculpture crate I'd gotten from the museum, but I knew she liked them, both the crate and the mirror.

I'd sent Tenny to her room for belting Zack in the mouth. Normally, they get along fine, although normal isn't an operating word in our house normally. After a while—after I had cooled down and she should have been—I went upstairs to check on her, and I saw her lying on the end of her bed and shoving at the mirror with her bare foot. Before I could say anything, it fell, crashed into hundreds of long jagged pieces, any one of which could have pierced Tenny's heart if fate had had it in mind. I had to wade in there in Kenneth's old cowboy boots and carry her out. It scared us both, and Tenny was too upset to get the vacuum.

"It just fell," she said. "I didn't touch it. It was a Goddamned Accident, Ellen."

I wanted to slap her, but yelled instead. It took forever to get all the splinters up, and Tenny never said she was sorry.

It's tough being firm. You punish Tenny, you pay. You have to watch her every minute. I can't ask a seventeen-year-old to handle Tenny when she's like this. If we leave, I'll worry that Tenny will somehow set the house on fire with her own breath. I'll worry Zack will get really hurt, and it will leave scars. I'll worry Emily will get her fill after twenty minutes and run out of our house screaming for her own mind, and leave them both playing with the hot water heater.

To do the right thing—parentally speaking—we'll have to stay home, too, not go to the brunch. I've got a new dress. Kenneth and I were both looking forward to it.

So, what we'll do is this: We'll stay home and be grumpy. We'll fight all afternoon. I'll mope about never being able to have an adult life with any texture, but Kenneth won't discuss the subject with me in depth. He'll escape. He'll be outside cleaning out his glove box, washing both cars, taking the garbage cans around early. I'll start raving about the condition of Tenny's room, make her clean the tub, and then make her do it right. By three o'clock for sure, I'll be a screaming bitch, yelling at Kenneth about anything that comes up, and Everything will. I'll threaten to spank Zack for nothing, and I will make Tenny iron. It will be Full Hell until six o'clock, when Kenneth will drive Tenny and her book bag to Raylene's. And then, around 10:30, Raylene will call our machine and want to know how we can be so cruel to her baby girl, how we'll be hearing from her lawyer. Her voice will sound slurred on the tape; she's started to drink heavily recently, and we are all more than a little concerned.

I raise a hand to Kenneth. "Five minutes," I tell him, and he slaps me a high one.

We agree to say "screw it" for once to Tenny's character development. We're not doing so well on that job anyway, and when I think about it with some distance, I can see where Tenny is trying to set us up again. The worse Sunday afternoons with us go for Tenny, the better Sunday evenings go with Raylene. I like squirming out of her byzantine plans, however unconscious they may be. I think I'm getting smarter at this parenting stuff, and I like being in agreement with Kenneth. I also like it that this time Kenneth is going to keep track of the five-minute clock.

I go on upstairs to finish dressing, get my new dress out, and Zack comes with me. He is five now and has always liked unwrapping anybody's presents; he wants to pull the tissue out of my new sleeves, and I let him. I feel positively light-headed at our irresponsibility, but of course, that could be just the weather. It is in the low seventies, a beautiful Sunday morning in early October. Texas is never better—you can't even remember how sulky you were in mid-August—and if this kid outside would just quit screaming, it could turn out to be a fine day all around.

"Three minutes," I hear Kenneth announce through the mail slot in the front door. Tenny still screams.

"What do we do if she doesn't stop, Kenneth?"

"She's winding down, Ellen. She only had yogurt for breakfast this morning."

Tenny wants to go to Courtney's birthday party at the Hard Rock Cafe. She wants to go badly, which surprises us because we thought she hated Courtney.

"She's my very best friend, Ellen, and it's going to be so cool. Everyone's wearing their Guess."

I hate Guess, those French denim jeans with the ankle zippers. They run well over fifty bucks, and they're made in New Jersey, and they don't hold up in the wash. We won't buy her any, but Raylene does. Tenny's got four pair; she's going to wear the pinks.

I also hate the Hard Rock Cafe and how sick it is that anybody would pay twelve bucks to eat a greasy hamburger under an auto-graphed Chuck Berry poster. These kids don't even know who Chuck Berry is, and they'll never hear him either. The place plays Madonna on the box, and they know their audience likes it loud. The Hard Rock Cafe is all the rage with preteens now.

And, I also hate Courtney, whatever her last name is. She spent the night once last fall, and Tenny woke us up in the middle of the night crying.

"Courtney says I'm going to start bleeding soon and I'll never stop till I don't have any more."

Tenny was really upset. I had to talk to her for a long time about growing up. She had half-facts. The news of menstruation is a moth-er's job, I don't know why I had to do it, but my job description has never been very clear.

"Your mother hasn't talked to you about any of this?"

"Oh, sure," Tenny tells me at 3:30 in the morning. "You think I should go on the pill now, Ellen?"

Courtney had to go home in the middle of the night, and none of us was sorry to see her go. I hate her, a vicious little girl, so I was pretty surprised to see Tenny's enthusiasm about the party invitation.

"I thought we hated her, Tenny."

"I don't hate her, Ellen. I've never hated her. She's my very best friend. I want to get her silver earrings."

"We did the earring thing already, Tenny. We're not doing that again. We don't have the money to buy silver earrings for someone we hate."

It was earrings that got Tenny into real trouble. Over the summer Tenny and all her friends and near-friends had had their ears pierced.

"The only women I ever saw with pierced ears," my father said when I did mine on the sly at fifteen, "were whores and I-talians, Ellen."

I'd forgotten he'd said that until Tenny got hers punched, and I intend to ask my father the next time he drops in how many whores and Italians he actually knew in Oklahoma.

We took Tenny to get her ears pierced at Foley's one steamy July afternoon. It was for her birthday, and Raylene was mad because she wanted to arrange it herself—"it's a mother's job to do things like that, you asshole; how dare you mutilate my daughter without my permission"—but Tenny said her mother kept promising and promising and promising, and wouldn't we take her?

We took her. It was a mistake. Tenny was not brave, and we really should have left it to her mother and her employees' discount.

Saturday afternoon Tenny and Kenneth bought earrings for Courtney at James Avery's. They cost twenty-three dollars, silver ballet shoes.

"She's my *best* friend," Tenny told her father, and he paid.

"You're a gup, Kenneth. Why did you do that?"

"I'm just tired of talking to her," he said, and I understood fully.

Tenny wrapped Courtney's present Saturday night, got up early Sunday, and decided to wear a dress to the party instead of her pink Guess jeans. The party begins at noon, but she's ready at 8:15, completely dressed, and driving us crazy. She couldn't handle the waiting, she couldn't sit still enough to watch TV, and when she found out Kenneth and I were going to Laurel's for brunch, she lost her mind. It was just after eleven, and the earrings were the problem. She wasn't taking them.

"They're ugly," Tenny said. "She'll hate them."

"They're fine," we told her, "and we don't care if Courtney hates them."

"Take me quick to get something else."

"Forget it, Tenny," Kenneth said, and that's when she fell in on herself, started screaming, and Kenneth put her on the porch. She hates us.

It's been a solid four minutes. I look great in my dress, it is a great dress, but I'm beginning to worry. The windows are still shaking with the noise, and the neighbors can't help but hear the racket. I know they're peeping out their front blinds to see what's going on, and if perhaps the police should be called. Of course, they'll see right away it's only Tenny, and then they'll go back to fixing their Sunday pot roasts and side dish specialties.

Suddenly, it stops. It is pure bliss, peace on earth, a blessed relief: Tenny has quit screaming her brains out. I peep out our upstairs blinds to make sure she's alive, if she's got any brains left. She's got them. She's still out there on the porch, now kicking at the asphidistra. Kenneth gives her an extra two minutes for kicking plants, and then invites her in.

"I'm sorry, Daddy," she says, "but those earrings are trash, and Courtney's going to embarrass me. She'll say I'm cheap."

"I don't want to talk about it anymore," Kenneth says. "Are you ready?"

"You're not taking me in that truck, are you? I'm not getting in that truck, Dad."

They go. They go in the truck. Zack and I wave from the porch while they back out, and I really wish Kenneth would get a new muffler. Then I come back inside and spot it. Tenny has left Courtney's present on the top of the TV.

"Damn that kid," I say to Zack.

He nods, and I run out and catch Kenneth just as he's about to turn at the corner. They don't run over me, and I pass the present through the window to Tenny.

"Don't forget what Freud said," I tell her.

"Who's Floyd?" she says.

I came inside and said right out loud to Zack, "You know, honey, I don't think I am ever going to learn anything."

"That's all right, Mom. Want to do Legos?"

I sat on the floor in my new dress, and I did Legos with the hero of my life. Emily rang the bell. She was right on time. She came in, sat on the floor, and did Legos with us.

I heard Kenneth's old truck turn onto our street, and I got up to find my shoes. I am ready to go, I've got my purse, and we're not going to be so very late this time. Then Kenneth comes in the door, his mouth set tight, and Tenny is right behind him. She is wailing.

"I HATE HER, I HATE HER, I HATE HER, I HATE HER."

It was a joke, a ruse, a nasty, mean trick. There is no party at the Hard Rock Cafe. It is not even Courtney's birthday, which is always in April we now remember. The little bitch invited Tenny to a birthday party that wasn't a birthday or a party. She invited Tenny to be mean, and she was. It is horrible what children do to one another. It is terrible to witness. It makes us murderous.

"Tenny, I'm so sorry. That Courtney is a horrible little girl. Dad's going to call her mother right now, and Tenny, we're never going to speak to her again. She's never going to come to this house again because we hate her, right? Come on, honey. Try not to cry so hard. You're going to bust a lung. It's going to be all right, and you can keep those damn earrings for yourself."

Tenny lies down on the couch and yields to throbbing despair. She cries hard for a long time, and she hears her father scream at Courtney's mother on the phone. This makes us all feel better—Kenneth never screams—and in a while, her cries go to whimpers, then sobs, then just some sniffling.

"Want to do Legos, Ta-Ta?"

"Kenneth, I'm going to call Laurel. We can't go now. Tenny's a wreck."

"Look, Ellen."

Tenny has recovered. She has recovered completely, in just short of five minutes. She is on the floor in her good party dress with Emily and Zack, and they are building a space station with all four thousand Legos. The front of her dress is almost dry, and her face isn't even spotty anymore. It's all over, Courtney's ruse nearly forgotten, erased.

"Ellen, let's get the hell out of here before something else happens."

We go. Tenny, Zack, and Emily wave us away from the porch and then go back to their constructions.

"Are you Nuts, Kenneth? You're not thinking of driving a truck to the brunch, are you? Can't we take your car? You know mine's in the shop."

"First, I'm out of gas, Ellen, and second, I think I might kill you if you don't get in this truck right now."

Laurel and Colin have brunches. They have people in their house all the time. They have open houses during the holidays, and late afternoon barbecues around their pool in the summer. They have cocktail parties before the symphony, and midnight suppers after theater openings. They have formal dinner parties for twelve at least twice a month, and very often they invite whole groups of people to spend the weekend with them at their country house in the hill country, near Austin. On Wednesdays, their housekeeper, Milagro, does nothing else but hand starch, then iron, their table linens, which are all ecru, which is the color of their whole lives.

Laurel and Colin have parties all the time, big ones, little ones, but brunches are their favorite. They are famous for their brunches. They have brunches all the time. They have hundreds of brunches all the time, expensive brunches, catered brunches, brunches with waiters in white coats offering mimosas all around on antique silver trays. The food is terrific, although the company is largely lousy, and they rarely invite us.

"I never wanted to go to your goddamn house and eat eggs anyway, Laurel."

"Ellen, I would never do anything to hurt you or your feelings. You've got to believe this: It's not me, it's Colin. He thinks we shouldn't have the same people over every time. He wants to rotate groups. He thinks different people would mix better. He wants to mix people, Ellen."

Kenneth and I have no social life at all. We do not mix. We do not mix well. We work hard, we take care of our kids, we nap a little, and then it's dawn again. I have lunch with old friends, but I do that less and less now. My life is so very different from any of their's, even the ones who are still working for art.

We have lost current commonality, contemporary references, daily context. I paint and I teach a little. The circle of my world is very small now and rather quiet (except for Tenny days), while theirs are huge and full of problems, noisy all the time, the universe as defined by the *Wall Street Journal*. They buy pantyhose by the dozen, get runs right away, and then buy another dozen. They own and wear expensive suits and shoes, everyday they strap on watches that are about much more than time, and they are now all getting mobile phones for their purses, which they've recently started calling handbags.

After all these years, we are all getting older. My work is difficult to talk about—it is not about telling, it is about seeing—and I don't care much about their work anyway, and probably never did. Mostly, we trade on the years already invested and wonder how we ever became friends in the first place.

"Ellen, pick up the phone right now. This is an emergency, I'm nuts, and I need your help."

The problem with knowing somebody for nearly twenty years is: You've got to pay attention to a plea like this. You can't say no. You can't ever say no. You can't say no to "I'm nuts, I need your help," no matter how strained your last lunch was, no matter how many times you've been cut off their guest list. You've got to pick up the phone.

"Do you have any idea what time it is, Laurel? The coffee hasn't even dripped."

"Please, Ellen. I need your help."

"You're not in Mexico, are you, Laurel?"

It is a Sunday morning, barely seven o'clock. Laurel and Colin are having one of their brunches, and Laurel believes her marriage is going to blow up the minute Colin gets back from the golf course. She thinks I can prevent this.

"Can you come over here right now? I just unwrapped the new couch, and it's horrible. Colin will kill me, Ellen. It looks like it ought to be in a trailer. It's a terrible mistake. Please, Ellen, come help me shove this piece of crap into the garage."

"Now?"

"He'll be back from the golf course any minute, and the caterers are due. Please, Ellen."

"Okay, okay, okay. I'm on my way, Laurel."

"Ellen?"

"What?"

"Could you bring your tools?"

Laurel ordered a new couch she didn't need, and they swore they could deliver it by Saturday night. They finally brought it about midnight, it was covered in brown paper, and Laurel had them shove it into the sitting room and didn't tip any hands. The next morning she tore the paper off and lost her mind.

"It was supposed to be cognac. You know, brown?"

"Goddammit, Laurel, couldn't you get the caterers to help move it? It's a Tenny weekend. Have you got any idea what that means?"

"Have you ever known a caterer who could keep his mouth shut, Ellen? They've worked for Colin's family for years. They're on retainer, and they'll stooge. Please, Ellen, help me shove."

The couch is too big for even both of us to move. We have to take it apart with rachets, and we shove it piece by tacky piece into the garage. We get pretty sweaty, but we do it, and Laurel thinks her marriage might make it through Christmas.

"So you guys come on over later, okay? I've really been missing you, Ellen. We could visit. Tell Kenneth we're having a band."

"You're having a band?"

"It's just a combo, a trio. It's just three musicians and a synthesizer. They'll set up out by the pool. Oh God, what if it rains? I should get a cabana, a tent, one of those things they put over graves. Promise you'll come, Ellen. I really do miss seeing you. I'm never going to be able to thank you for what you've done for me."

"No, Laurel, you are never going to be able to thank me enough for all of this horseshit."

The caterers drive up right then, and Colin is right behind them with his clubs.

"How's it going, Laurel? What are you doing here, Ellen?"

"Everything's perfect, Colin," Laurel says. "Ellen was just returning some magazines."

"I'm not going to get any cappuccino, am I, Laurel?"

Kenneth wants to go to Laurel's brunch. I can't believe it.

"Why? It will be awful. Listen, I'll do eggs benedict right now, and we can get gout on our own time."

"I miss getting out in the world sometimes, too, Ellen. It might be fun. Tenny's got her party, and we could ask Emily to watch Zack for a few hours. We haven't done anything like this in a long time, Ellen. It might be fun."

Fun. Kenneth wants fun. Kenneth is missing fun. I don't even know what fun is anymore. All we do is work hard and then work real hard. I try to imagine Fun. It's been too long. I can't imagine Fun. I don't know Fun. I don't know Fun anymore. I am no Fun. I don't even know how to recognize Fun anymore.

"Who are you anyway?"

"I am the man what loves you, Red."

This is a Zack construction. We think it is hilarious, and we hold off correcting his grammar because we like the way he says it. Zack is our only Fun, and that is a lot to ask of a five-year-old boy.

"We can't go, Kenneth. I really don't have anything to wear. It's not a sweatpants sort of thing, you know?"

"You've got a great dress to wear, Ellen. We bought it yesterday for your birthday after the earring fiasco."

It is a Great Dress. It is a black rayon shirtwaist with white dots and a full skirt. It was made in the thirties and comes with a fat red belt. I love it. It is a cartoon of a dress, it is a joke of a dress, it is a dress made for Minnie Mouse.

"Tenny thought so, too. She said it was just odd enough for your birthday, Ellen, and she thinks we ought to get you a hat with ears."

Kenneth and I take the truck to Laurel and Colin's brunch. They could hear us coming blocks before they even saw us. Kenneth passes the keys to the parking valet, this kid who is maybe seventeen.

He holds the truck keys in his hand and stares at them. Then he stares at us.

"Are you kidding?" he says.

"It's a classic," I say.

"Damn, I know that. I mean, are you going to let me actually drive it?"

We're going to let him try and drive it. You have to double clutch to get out of first. He gets in, starts it up, and roars off. The truck wheezes and backfires, and I don't think there's a window on North Boulevard now that isn't cracked.

Colin opens the door for us before we ring the bell. Actually, we weren't even on the porch yet.

"I heard you coming. Nice of you two to dress up."

It is a beautiful day in early October in Texas. There is the barest nip in the air, the sky is deep blue and loaded with clouds. Texas has the best clouds of anywhere on this planet; you just ask anybody visual.

I walk all around Laurel and Colin's huge downstairs and look at my paintings. They own three of my best and a suite of the working drawings, and I have been missing them. I am looking around people and waiters in white coats at my paintings, and my paintings look pretty good.

Float is a damned masterpiece—it breathes on the wall—and *The*

Fall still makes my heart stop, but I don't think I ever would have hung it in a dining room. There is something, however, really wrong with the big diptych *Damage*. It's *The Wreck* panel: It's not working, not a good corner in it, and I might have to burn it.

I am backing around the room, looking at my stuff from twenty feet—*The Working Drawings* still sing for me—and I back right into a waiter with a full tray who drops a gallon of mimosas on Elliot's shoes.

"Nice to see you, too, Ellen. How are those brats of yours?"

I have a couple of drinks with Laurel on her washer/dryer, but she's Nuts, and it's not a real exchange. She's the hostess here—I knew we wouldn't have much of a visit—so I go back into the living room and walk around some more. I look at my paintings around the conversations of strangers. Everyone in this room is crazy for Bush.

"You got something against literacy, young lady?"

I don't know why we're here. I'm edging my way around the room, looking for Kenneth so we can escape, when some guy in heavy British tweeds grabs me by the arm.

"I'd like that elbow back, if you don't mind."

"I understand you're the artist here."

"Yep, they actually let me in the front door this time. Can you believe it?"

"Now, are you famous? Have I ever heard of you?"

"Yes, I am famously famous. You have heard of me every day since you were born."

"The thing I really want to know is, how come you artists don't wear anything but black. Every artist I've ever met has had on black: black pants, black shirts, black ties, black shoes, black hats. What is this black thing anyway?"

"Isn't it obvious?"

"No."

"We're in mourning."

"What?"

"We are in deep grief. We are in deep grief all the time. We are in deep and ponderous grief, and we cannot talk about it well or fully. Listen, you'll have to excuse me. I've had too many mimosas and not enough sleep in my whole life."

"But wait. Sometimes they do wear blue, right? Those denim shirts? Those jeans? What about those artists?"

"They're just kidding themselves. They're in denial, pretty sad and pretty total. Listen, I have to go now. Is that the roast burning?"

"Just one more question. Please?"

"That is *my* elbow, buster."

"Listen, I want to know: How long does it take to make one of these things? Exactly how long did you spend on this one, for example? An hour? Two hours? What do you do with the rest of your time?"

He is pointing to *The Fall*. He is pointing to *The Fall* with his cigar, and he is dropping ash all over Laurel and Colin's new Saltillo tile floor.

"Which one?"

"That one."

"That one? The red oxide one?"

"Is that like rustoleum? Yeah, that one. That one right there. How long did it take you to knock that one out?"

"That one. That one took my whole life. It took my whole life to make that painting, mister."

A woman in shawls and pre-Colombian jewelry comes out of nowhere.

"You're an idiot, Nick," she says to the tweed guy. "Was he being thick again? He is so thick, Ellen. He is Thick Nick."

"No problem. I know the type. They thrive on thickness. They gorge on thickness, and they don't matter to anybody."

"I've wanted to meet you for such a long time, Ellen. I was delighted when Laurel told me you were actually here. Your work is incredible. Are you represented?"

"Huh?"

"I'm a dealer. I've got private galleries in L.A. and Aspen, and I'm opening one here in Houston. I'd really like to talk to you about your work. I think I could sell quite a lot of it for you, if you're interested. Here's my card."

It is a business card, but it is no ordinary business card. It is European scale. It is nearly square, pure white, and weighs about five pounds. I turn it over and over in my hands. There is one word printed on the card. The word is Providence.

"Providence?"

"Yes."

"Your name is Providence?"

"Yes, but my friends call me Lisa."

Man, oh man, oh man. I've got to find Kenneth and get out of here. I am talking to Providence—she is wearing yellow cashmere and red kid gloves—and Laurel is walking all over her downstairs bare ass naked in a turquoise and silver Indian necklace that Colin has just presented to her in front of his partners.

I find Kenneth where I knew he would be. He is just outside the dining room on the veranda, and he is not talking to anybody. He is leaning against the doorjamb and watching the band; his left knee is twitching. Kenneth knows two of the three musicians from the old days, and they are playing "The Girl From Ipanema." They have on harlequin suits, red and black diamonds, and no one but Kenneth is watching or listening to them. I can't imagine why he is.

"We've got to get out of here, Kenneth."

"Did you see Joan? She's here, without Bradley, and she's getting married."

"Who's she marrying?"

"Bradley."

"They're second cousins, Kenneth."

"Actually, they are first cousins, Ellen. Joan told me."

"They are cousins by marriage."

"No, they're not. They are really first cousins. It's That Southern Thing, Ellen."

"We've got to get out of here, Kenneth."

Kenneth wants to go, too, but he wants to wait until the band breaks. I can't believe we are standing here watching brunch musicians playing a Sergio Mendez medley.

"You miss it, don't you, Kenneth?"

"I never should have sold the drums, Ellen. I could be doing this."

"Imbeciles could be doing this, Kenneth. I think you ought to get some drums and start playing again, but I don't ever want to see you playing brunch music under a funeral canopy. You're better than that, Kenneth."

"They're playing, Ellen. I'm not. Colin's probably going to pay them."

"Listen, can you see John Lennon playing a brunch? Jimi Hendrix? Elvis?"

"No."

"See?"

"They're all dead, Ellen."

We stand outside Laurel and Colin's brunch. We lean against the doorjamb, and we watch the band. We clap. No one else claps. It is pathetic, and they keep playing and playing and playing.

"I can't stand this, Kenneth. I'm going to call and check on the kids."

"I already did that, Ellen. I called twice. They're alive."

"And Emily?"

"Pushing the last mile. Listen, Ellen, we've got to talk about something. I'm thinking of giving up Tenny."

"What? What are you talking about?"

"I talked to Raylene about it this morning when she came by."

"Raylene came by?"

"You were at Laurel's. She brought Tenny another party dress."

"She didn't come inside, did she, Kenneth?"

"No, I met her at the curb, but we talked, and then I talked to Joan a minute ago. Things just aren't working out, Ellen."

"What are you talking about?"

"Tenny's twelve years old, Ellen, and this back and forth is getting old. Raylene is getting her luggage on wheels for Christmas."

"And she wants you to pay for it?"

"Yes, she does, but the thing is, Tenny's not getting any better, Ellen. I think she's getting worse. I can't put up with her attacks anymore. They happen every day, two and three times a day. They cost us too much, Ellen. We don't have any peace, and I'm worried about Zack. He's getting older, too. How are you going to feel when he starts shoving over the dining room chairs, Ellen?"

"Zack's fine, Kenneth, and you can't give up on Tenny. We can't do that. Raylene would kill her."

"Something's got to change, Ellen. How would you feel about having her full time?"

The whole idea makes my heart stop. Tenny, undiluted. Tenny, in my life every minute. Tenny in puberty in my life without any alternate-day relief.

"*Jesus*, Kenneth."

"I don't know how I feel about her anymore. I maintain her. We maintain her, we manage her, we manage around her. All I feel for her is worry."

"*Jesus*, Kenneth."

Suddenly, out of nowhere, a child appears. It is a girl child, a blond girl child, maybe three years old. She is running. She is running fast. She runs out of the house and right past us. We feel the heat of her when she runs by. She is running, and she is screaming. She is running right toward Laurel and Colin's pool. She is going to run right into Laurel and Colin's pool and drown.

I move, I leap. I have long legs, and I leap twelve, then twenty feet. I reach her, I catch her, I tackle her. We skid together on the cool deck, and we stop just four inches short of the water.

"MOMMY," she screams.

Her mother is instantly there. She is one of the musicians, this Tina, this red and black harlequin who plays the synthesizer. She picks up her daughter, holds her to her, pats her back. The child screams anyway, and from someplace else, upstairs, we hear another child screaming. It is a baby, it is a baby crying. It is upstairs in Laurel and Colin's guest room. It is screaming.

"We couldn't get a sitter," Tina says. "They've been upstairs for hours, sleeping under the coats. They are good children, my children, but we have gone a little long."

The brunch guests are all staring at us. They are all on the veranda. They are all silent and all staring, except Colin who is screaming at Laurel.

"What were you doing letting those fuckers bring their kids? I told you to book professionals."

"Think of it this way, Colin. At least they didn't smother under the furs and sue your goddamned ass."

Man, oh man, oh man. This is why I stay at home. My dress is ripped, my knees are bloodied, and I can't find Kenneth. I have got to find him, and we have got to get out of here. The sky's turned dark, and it's going to rain.

I walk all over Laurel and Colin's house looking for Kenneth. I look downstairs, I look upstairs, I look in the laundry room. Their place is a mess. People have stomped cigarettes out on the floor and left the butts. They've put sweaty glasses down on the Steinway without nap-

kins, and it's going to have to be refinished. Looking upstairs, I walk
in on a federal judge and one of the harlequins smoking dope in Laurel
and Colin's bathroom.

"Want a hit?"

"Have you seen Kenneth?"

"Who's Kenneth? We don't know any Kenneth."

I can't find him, and I'm going to have to walk home alone in the
rain. It hasn't really started, but it's dark. The malibu lights have come
on all around Laurel and Colin's pool, although the musicians have
started another set—they never know when to quit; don't these people
have anything else to do?—and Laurel is dancing with the little girl
who didn't drown.

"Come with me," I say to Laurel. "You need to get out of here. This
brunch is over, and so is your marriage."

"I can handle it a while longer, Ellen."

"How?"

"I don't know. I just can."

Maybe she can, but I can't. I walk out the front door. I leave it
standing wide open—they don't have any animals—and then I see
Kenneth. He is across the street at this little park. The storm is
coming up fast. The mercury vapor lamps at the park have come on,
the sky is nearly black, and Kenneth is walking around in this park
with a baby. He is walking all around, and he is singing to a tiny baby
wrapped in white flannel.

A lightning bolt blasts out of the sky and right through my heart.
It is a flash of love. I feel it, I take it, I welcome it, and that is a
shocking surprise. I feel myself fall. I feel myself fall one part at a time,
my head, my heart, my bloody knees. I fall. I fall in love with Kenneth
Joseph Goodson all over again.

Kenneth sees me, smiles, comes toward me with the baby, who is no
longer crying. The baby is sleeping.

"Don't you have enough sense to get out of the rain, Kenneth?"

Then I kiss him, a real kiss, a kiss like I haven't had time to give
him in years and years and years.

"Let's go home, Kenneth."

"Let's don't go just yet, Ellen," he says and passes the baby to Tina
who is standing right behind me. It is practically newborn, just four
weeks old. It still has that sweet, sweet smell.

"I'm not going back in there, Kenneth."

"I don't want to do that either. I thought we might get the truck and drive through WhatABurger for some coffee. Then we could go neck."

I hate drinking boiled coffee out of Styrofoam cups, and Kenneth has known this for fifteen years.

"Come on, Ellen. I stole two of Colin's cups."

"Marry me, Kenneth."

"Okay," he says.

We go, we go right then. There is nothing to think about. There is nothing I would rather do but go, and there is nobody I would rather go with.

We go. We leave all of them with their mouths open, and we go. We don't care what anybody thinks about us, and we never did: It's the one advantage of being born odd and finally accepting it when you're thirty-five or so. Thunder claps, and then another, and it starts to rain. The first raindrops on the windshield are as big as silver dollars and twice as lucky.

27 ....

Towels, Throwing Them In
and Otherwise

There are some things you just can't make up. The Christmas after Laurel and Colin's brunch, Kenneth got his divorce. It was a trick, it was Joan's idea, and it worked. It was actually New Year's, and I didn't think it would work, but it did.

Raylene had Tenny that year for the beginning of the holidays; we were supposed to get her for the last half. Switch day was the twenty-sixth—the twenty-sixth of December is the universal Switch Day; it is right up there with Sunday Night Tuna Fish—except Raylene kept calling and saying couldn't Tenny stay another day, and another day, and another day. All these cousins of Raylene's were in town. She has a huge family, they were coming in from everywhere, and Raylene wanted them all to see Baby Girl who was nearly thirteen.

Kenneth said yes, yes, yes, and then he said no. It was a surprise to everyone, but it wasn't hard once he got it out. He says "no" quite often now. Christmas with Tenny was always horrible anyway. They used to switch on the actual day, and nobody got anything hot to eat. We just waited and waited and waited for Tenny, and when she got there, we were sorry we had. We don't do that anymore. Now we say "no."

Kenneth told Raylene that Tenny had to be at our house by five o'clock that night, or else he was taking legal action. At the moment, it was just more tactics, and you must understand that legal action is an oxymoron anyway.

Kenneth did call Bradley and Joan, and when Raylene didn't show up with Tenny by the deadline, he called them again. They hatched this stupid plan. I didn't think it would work, but it did.

Kenneth told Raylene that he wouldn't accept Tenny unless she signed the divorce papers. Of course, he had to be willing to back that up, but he said that he was, and it worked.

The next day was New Year's Eve. Raylene had plans, and we were the baby-sitters. All of a sudden, we weren't the baby-sitters. There wasn't another baby-sitter available in the whole state, so Raylene— not one to let anything get in the way of her life, social and other-wise—went by Bradley and Joan's and signed the paper napkin agreement. She sent Tenny to our house in a cab, and that time I didn't mind paying the fare.

Some things you just can't make up. I know it's unbelievable, but most of what really happens in any domestic life nobody would believe anyway. It really happened just like that. Kenneth went down the next Monday and got a divorce in three minutes. It was right at ten years since he'd moved out and called me up for coffee.

If you think it got any better after that, you'd be wrong and stupid. Not a thing changed, and it may have even gotten worse. Actually, it did get a lot worse. Raylene passed quite seamlessly from her self-appointed role as Abandoned Mother of Infant Child to Single Mother Raising a Child Alone and Unsupported. She filed an action against Kenneth the first month after the divorce, and until Tenny is eigh-teen, Kenneth has to deposit the child support money with County Welfare by the tenth of the month or go to jail.

The whole issue of child support in the first place made me nuts since Raylene hadn't paid for anything but haircuts for Tenny since I've known her. She hasn't paid a library fine, a school fee, a doctor's bill. We bought every birthday present Tenny ever needed for her crummy little friends, every winter coat, every pair of shoes, and I am still pissed off about the towels. I used to have these great towels, thick, expensive, Egyptian cotton towels. They cost a fortune, and I let Tenny use them because I think you ought to use beautiful things.

She started taking them for swim team, and what came back were these little rags from Penney's.

"Raylene, I need those towels."

"I don't know what you're talking about, bitch," and she hung up on me.

Kenneth said, "Fuck the towels, Ellen," and I tried, but couldn't. I bought five hundred dollars' worth of new ones and sent Raylene an invoice. It's still outstanding, and that's been years now.

Our Zack is nearly ten years old. He is going to be taller than all of us and has always been twice as smart. He is still the hero of our lives and wants to be a scientist, and an artist, and a musician, and a Texas Ranger. I tell him he can be whatever he wants to be, except a marine, and he says, "Jesus, Mom, I don't mean Texas Ranger like a soldier. I mean, Texas Ranger like a baseball player." I love this boy.

I am painting and still teaching some. The money's better from both. Providence works hard, and mid-month I get a check for six bucks. She sold five paintings I love and killed myself to make to some collector in Sun Valley, Idaho; she's letting them pay out over time, and we should be done with the bookkeeping by the turn of the century.

We did move. Nobody felt the same about the Binz house after the burglary, although we did get a good chunk of money from the insurance company for the damage. I sold most of my antiques, a bit more primitive than they once were, and I also sold the Hussman. I didn't want it anymore; I saw Raylene's head in that thing every time I walked by, and I was glad to deposit a check for $7,500 for it.

"You could've told me they were investments, Ellen," my father said and he was impressed for once.

We live near Rice University now, a three-bedroom duplex with a balcony we thought we'd use but never do. We've only been out there three times, that long weekend some of Tenny's friends decided to throw sacks of dog shit at the house. I use the garage apartment for my studio, and we don't save any money on the new rent, but the plumbing is better, and on alternate Tuesdays Mr. Johnson and his friend Mr. Johnson rake up the leaves and put them at the curb at the landlord's expense.

And we did get married. We didn't think we were the sort, but we were. We decided to do it in a rush of feeling one May night over barbecue and got married in the backyard in June. It was ridiculous—a June wedding, for Christ's sake, our son seating everybody in aluminum lawn chairs—but we all cried anyway and then went out for Mexican food.

I still think any relationship could blow up in fifteen minutes anytime, anywhere, but so far I'd have to say I've been near happy. We're a regular Ozzie and Harriet, and just before Thanksgiving last year Kenneth and I stayed up until two o'clock in the morning cutting sandwiches into turkey shapes for Zack's party at school and discussing obsessive behaviors. We made ourselves sick laughing at ourselves, and that Thanksgiving party was the best that school has ever seen.

Colin dropped dead two weeks after that brunch; his guts exploded, and he died choking on the pea gravel in the driveway before he could get to the porch. Laurel is still in the house, and she's living now with a twenty-four-year-old track star. She doesn't have brunches anymore; she doesn't even answer the phone.

Grace is fine, still fixing things that can be fixed. I see her every month or so. Ruthie went to Hawaii on vacation and never came back. I don't see Alice anymore; she's always in Europe now, and I never hear from Judith or Joe. Every once in a while Ben brings me a sack of Roma tomatoes; I trade him for fresh basil. My parents live in Florida now but are thinking about the Carolinas. I don't see many people. I work, and Kenneth is playing again with a whole group of bald people. They're doing some recording now; Kenneth is writing some songs, but he's still working days. He wants cedar shoe trees for Christmas, and sometimes I don't know why I didn't leave him in that elevator.

My life is full enough and, except for Tenny, everything is all right right now.

We lost Tenny. She's gone. She lives with her mother now. We never see her.

When she was fourteen, Tenny had the legal right to choose which parent she wanted to live with. Raylene told Tenny that when she was only six, and Tenny reminded us of that every day for eight years. The day she was fourteen, she did it. We never see her. She's seventeen now.

We missed her. Kenneth still does, I know, and it's particularly bad on Zack. He—pretty fully—always liked her, would forgive her anything, and there was a lot to forgive.

I don't miss her, or I don't miss her much. I walked around for a couple of years feeling as if I were wearing one shoe. Then she'd come over to dinner, and I'd remember how bad it could be. We never see her anymore. We see her two or three times a year, if that. She never calls. I don't miss her noise. She is a sad child. Always was sad.

I think about her though. I still seem to see her everywhere. My eye lands on nearly every blond child I see. I turn them around to check and make sure, but it is never her.

I see a Tenny in the grocery store. She is three years old, but it is not her. I see one at Galleria, she is ten years old and pouting—it is not her. I see her at five turning cartwheels, at seven on the way to ballet, except she never went to ballet. I see her everywhere, but it is not her. I see her older, what I think she'll be like at twenty, thirty, fifty. I see her everywhere. I see pieces of her. I see pieces of her in my rearview mirror.

It is a car behind me, a woman driving, a little bitty kid sitting in the passenger seat. We are all stopped for a red light. The kid is so small she can't see over the window, and the woman driving is looking down and talking to her. I see them. I see her. Their sunroof is open, it is a beautiful day, and I can just see the top of the child's head. I can see her hair. It is not Tenny, but it is Tenny's hair. It is bright as light, fine as silk, smelling of leaves, and matted with gum. I see that hair of Tenny's everywhere.